Luci... ...life-
long... ...food
researcher for a national magazine. She happens to be the

e Hart was educated in England and France. A
lover of cookery, she has previously worked as a
She happens to b
result of a real-life Riviera romance – her parents met there
while at school. She lives in south London with her
husband and son.

WHICHKIND(?)

Lucie Hart

A Valentine's Kiss

EBURY
PRESS

Published in 2011 by Ebury Press, an imprint of Ebury Publishing
A Random House Group Company

The Random House Group Limited Reg. No. 954009

Addresses for companies within the Random House Group can be found at
www.randomhouse.co.uk

A CIP catalogue record for this book is available from the British Library

The Random House Group Limited supports The Forest Stewardship Council
(FSC), the leading international forest certification organisation. All our titles that
are printed on Greenpeace approved FSC certified paper carry the FSC logo. Our
paper procurement policy can be found at www.rbooks.co.uk/environment

Mixed Sources
Product group from well-managed
forests and other controlled sources
www.fsc.org Cert no. TT-COC-2139
© 1996 Forest Stewardship Council
FSC

Typeset in Adobe Caslon by Palimpsest Book Production Limited,
Falkirk, Stirlingshire

Printed in the UK by CPI Cox & Wyman, Reading RG1 8EX

ISBN 9780091937935

To Robert and Hector

Let him kiss me with the kisses of his mouth:
For thy love is better than wine.

The Song of Solomon

1

January

Never, ever again, Imogen thought as she stared at the road, her hands clenched on the wheel and her face set, would she pick up a hitchhiker. Especially a French one. She glanced across at the young man slouching moodily in the passenger seat. He, without a doubt, was the most infuriating person she had ever met. First, he had got into her car with barely a word of thanks when she was doing him a favour. And then, quite suddenly, he had become utterly embarrassing and inappropriate.

It must have been the fault of the Riviera weather, which was so unseasonally clement for early January. There was something about seeing palm trees against a sky of cobalt blue that turned you into a different person. Having started her journey two days ago on a bitterly cold London day, and wearing her usual uniform of practical clothing – combat trousers, trainers, her favourite fleece made slightly bobbly by too many machine washes and waterproof hooded coat – the closer she came to the south of France, the less she needed to wear, and she had rolled her combats up to her knees and taken off her fleece, revealing a baggy T-shirt underneath.

Somehow during the process, she – usually the picture

of discretion and prudence – had also let go of some of her British reserve. Even Monty, she thought, glancing at her black Scottie terrier lying on the back seat, whose habitual expression was one of solemn disapproval, was drunk with sunshine, and seemed almost to be smiling. He had not even let out a disgruntled woof when his mistress had stopped the car and picked up this guy, Dimitri. Both dog and young woman were acting out of character today.

Imogen and Monty had been driving through one of the many charming small towns along the Côte d'Azur, somewhere between St Tropez and Menton, when she had noticed a young man, a sailor's duffel bag slung over his shoulder, standing outside a deserted coach station. He stuck his thumb out and she stepped on the brake.

Why not? Imogen had thought, feeling pleasantly rebellious. This was exactly the sort of thing she would never have done in London, not in a million years. It just wouldn't have occurred to her. At home, she always liked to keep things as safe and familiar as possible, so that the idea of letting a complete stranger into her car would have made her pretty tremulous. But here in France, she felt somehow released from her own rules of behaviour. There was no one around to dictate or disapprove. She was on her own, and free to do as she pleased, so why not stretch her boundaries a little? Feeling quite dizzy with daring, she leaned across the passenger seat to talk to the hitchhiker. '*Où* . . . er . . . *vous allez?*' she asked stumblingly, adding, 'Where are you headed?'

'Saint-Jean-les-Cassis,' he had replied.

'*Oh oui, d'accord!* Me too!' she had said, pointing at herself enthusiastically and feeling very, very foreign and a bit silly. 'I can give you a lift. Hop in.'

He had climbed in next to her, muttering something that sounded like '*Merci*'. And had then sat in silence for quite a while, looking sullenly out of the window. All she took in initially was that he was tall and angular, and dressed in very scruffy jeans and a black T-shirt. He wore sunglasses, which he did not remove on getting into her car.

'Er . . . *Je m'appelle Imogen*,' Imogen said after ten minutes of driving in silence. '*Et vous?*'

'Dimitri,' he said.

'Are you here on holiday?' she asked in English.

'*Non.*'

OK, great conversationalist, Imogen thought, her laid-back good humour generated by the Riviera sunshine dissipating in the face of this stranger's taciturn behaviour, *don't strain yourself on my account. I'm only the blooming driver.*

As they continued on their way, she concentrated on keeping to the right-hand side of the road. There wasn't much traffic, which made it harder not to glide automatically to the left. She was also conscious of her passenger fidgeting; he appeared to be looking for something in his pockets. Then a match was struck and he lit a cigarette. Just like that, without even bothering to ask for her permission! Imogen clenched her teeth. It was her car, and she did mind.

'I'm really sorry,' she piped up, 'but I would prefer it if you didn't smoke.'

Now she sounded like a cabbie. It was ridiculous. Behaving like a free spirit while in France was turning out to be harder than she'd thought. Dimitri made an exaggerated pantomime of leaning out of his open window to blow smoke away from his driver, then put the cigarette out with a sigh.

'OK, OK. Typical English,' he said under his breath.

At this, Imogen pursed her lips. Unperturbed, Dimitri took off his shades to look at her directly. He had grey eyes and his prominent cheekbones, longish curly dark hair and stubbly beard somehow gave him the air of a musketeer.

'It is completely typical that you're against smoking,' he went on insolently in impeccable if heavily accented English, 'because the English are puritans. They're against fun and having a good time. Everybody knows that.'

'I don't know where you got that from, but it's just a silly cliché,' Imogen said, as patiently as possible. It was so important to keep your manners at all times, especially in a foreign country. 'It's not true at all.'

'Sometimes a cliché is true. You are puritans and that's why English food is so bad.'

'Oh, really?' Imogen said, laughing a little. It was especially annoying that his English was far better than her schoolgirl French.

'Yes. I've tried it. It's heavy, greasy and not very good.'

This hit a nerve in a big way. But before Imogen had a chance to explain just why she was heading to Saint-Jean-les-Cassis, her passenger changed the subject.

'I really like your air,' he said.

Now that was a little cryptic. Imogen wondered briefly

what sort of air she had. Capable, she hoped, or quietly confident, in keeping with the fact that she was on her way to start a new job. The job in question was amazing, and she was really looking forward to starting a new life in this beautiful place. Of course, it was her first time away from home and she couldn't help but feel rather apprehensive about new faces and new surroundings. It was just possible that she looked worried, and even a little harassed, because, come to think of it, that was certainly how she felt a lot of the time when at home in London, being bossed around by her family. So did she, in fact, look the very opposite of confident? Imogen frowned uncertainly.

Then the Frenchman reached out a hand and brushed a stray lock of hair from her face.

'Oh!' Imogen said, nodding briskly to conceal a slight sense of shock, for she hadn't grown up among particularly tactile people. She was a little disconcerted that Dimitri was paying attention to her hair, as usually it served as a useful curtain to hide behind.

'I see,' she added, to show that she had, in fact, understood him. The French always had trouble with aitches, she knew.

'What is that colour?' Dimitri demanded, frowning. 'Brown?'

'Well, it's dark chestnut, I think,' Imogen said, a trifle defensively, 'with a little bit of auburn here and there.' She did not mention that in her family her hair colour had always been known simply as English Mouse.

He nodded, absorbing this, then gestured towards her face, pointing, 'Also I like these.'

'Oh, my freckles! Yes, I have a lot of them.'

'You have them everywhere?' he asked conversationally.

Imogen drew back, staring at him. He returned her gaze with complete self-possession, managing all the while to suggest that he knew exactly what she looked like with no clothes on. She blushed. Just her luck to pick up a hitch-hiker who turned out to be a sex maniac. She had been in too much of a hurry to step outside her comfort zone, that was all. *Next time, think it through*, she told herself firmly. *Don't walk before you can crawl.*

'Are we arriving soon?' he asked, looking away with a smile.

'I think so,' she said coldly. In a few moments she would drop him off and that would be it, thank goodness.

'Maybe,' he said, as though he'd been reading her mind, 'when we arrive in Saint-Jean, we can meet for a drink. You give me your mobile number?'

'No, thank you. I don't give my number to people I don't know,' Imogen said stiffly. The arrogance! It was true what they said about French men. You really had to put them in their place.

'Oh? Then how do you make friends?'

'I have plenty of friends, thank you,' Imogen replied. Not strictly true, since she didn't actually know anyone in France yet, but he wasn't to know that. Spotting with relief the sign for Saint-Jean-les-Cassis, she indicated to turn right. After driving past a couple of modest-looking seaside cafés, they emerged onto what looked like the main high street, a vision in pink and white where fashion shops alternated with ice-cream parlours. At the top of this strip was a square shaded with pine trees, in which a group of men were busy (if that was the right word) playing boules. Imogen parked under a tree and waited silently for Dimitri to leave.

'Thank you for the ride. It was very interesting,' Dimitri said, his hand on the door handle.

Imogen nodded, not looking at him.

'*Salut!*' he said, letting himself out. '*Et . . . Bonne Année!*'

'Yes, goodbye – and Happy New Year to you too,' Imogen muttered. She watched him make his way across the square, his duffel bag slung over his shoulder. There was even something arrogant about the way he walked, as though he knew that her eyes were on him. He turned into a side street and disappeared from view. Good. No need to give him another thought.

She turned to check on Monty, who was snoozing on the back seat, and got out of the car to have a look around. It was early evening.

There was a café on the square, where a few people sat chatting and sipping aperitifs. Beyond, she could see the glittering expanse of the Mediterranean stretching under a now opaline- and lilac-coloured sky. A girl drove past noisily, bareheaded, on a red scooter; then the sound of chirping crickets rose again in the air, scented with pine and salt.

Imogen felt a wave of exhilaration wash over her, and almost pinched herself to check that she was, in fact, really and truly there. Inside the car, Monty suddenly roused himself and barked querulously. She let him out and poured water from a plastic bottle into his bowl.

Now to locate the modest hotel where she was booked in for the night. Tomorrow she would start work and her new life would begin. Imogen smiled. She had landed. The greyness of north London, her job at the nursery, her family and their many demands, her daily chores – all had receded far, far out of sight.

2

The previous summer

Six months earlier, as she was lying in the bath one Saturday morning, an exasperated cry had jolted her out of her reverie.

'Imo! Are you getting out?'

It was Hildegard's voice, the well-modulated, confident voice of an actress, coming from the 'dorm' across the landing. A set of two rooms which had once (in Edwardian times) been designed as the nursery wing, it now housed all five Peach children, with the boys in one room and the girls in the other – inconveniently, the girls had to cross the boys' room whenever they wanted to leave. Imogen sat up guiltily. Without waiting for her sister to call again, she bounded out of the bath, dried herself quickly, threw on her robe and hurried next door.

Going in, she nearly walked into the open wardrobe door. Within, her sixteen-year-old brother, George, stood staring at the mirror, meticulously shaving an almost imperceptible moustache. Fourteen-year-old Thea stood at his elbow, her hair pulled back into a tiny chignon, a pair of ballet shoes tucked under one arm.

'Oi, watch where you're going,' George said crossly.

'Sorry,' Imogen squeaked, side-stepping them and making for the bedroom she shared with her two sisters.

'I don't know why you bother,' Thea said, sniffing disdainfully. 'You don't even need to shave.'

'I'm practising, stupid,' George said. 'For when I do.'

'And that stinky Dior stuff you're always splashing on!' Thea went on, wrinkling her nose. 'Yuck and double yuck!'

'Be quiet, child. Aaargh! Now I've cut myself!'

Thea smiled sweetly, turned on her heel and headed next door for her bed, above which hung a large poster of Darcey Bussell.

'*There* you are, Imo!' Hildegard said crossly, emerging like an avenging angel from behind the bookshelves that divided her part of the room from her sisters', with a slice of burned toast in one hand and a pink drawstring bag in the other. Thea came to stand behind her, striking an attitude on tiptoe with her arms stretched out.

'What *is* the matter with you this morning?' Hildegard demanded, with the stern authority that befitted the eldest of the Peach children. At twenty-four, Hildegard looked down on twenty-two-year-old Imogen, the middle daughter, as a mere helpless child who needed bossing around.

'Sorry, Hil,' Imogen said, standing on one foot and hurriedly pulling her underwear up her legs with one hand while modestly holding her robe closed with the other. 'I lost track of time. I just need to dry my hair and we can go.'

'Don't bother,' Hildegard said with a dramatic sigh. 'It's absolutely *fine*. *I*'ll take the monkeys to their classes.'

'Are you sure you don't mind?' Imogen asked worriedly. She'd got into her jeans and was now yanking her arms into the sleeves of a grey hoodie as she moved back into the boys' room. Catching sight of ten-year-old Gus, who stood dreamily in the middle of the room with his cardigan only half on, she helped him into the other half and handed him his violin case.

'Afterwards I'm going straight to the theatre, but I'll never make it in time for this morning's read-through,' Hildegard went on irritably. 'I thought I'd mentioned that we're starting on a new piece. Some of us have real commitments, you know. All you have to do today is walk your dog.'

'Yes, of course,' Imogen said. 'I'm really sorry. Tell Stephen it was all my fault.'

'*And* I had to do my hair myself because you weren't around,' Thea added, with a stern look.

'Where's Mum?' Gus asked over Thea's shoulder.

'Studio,' Hildegard replied, inspecting her toast then chucking it in the bin. 'I think she slept there, actually. You know she's working on something really big.'

Gus nodded, then started down the stairs, followed by a skipping Thea.

'Will you be around later, Imo?' Hildegard said on her way out. 'I still need you to take in that dress for me, remember.'

'Yes, of course,' Imogen said meekly. After a tiny pause, she added, 'I'll do it after I've been to see Di. She's really enjoying *Great Expectations*.'

Her voice remained quite even. After so many years of keeping up the pretence of regular reading sessions with her elderly neighbour, she had almost come to believe in them herself.

Hildegard nodded, her mind on other things. No one in Imogen's family ever bothered to remember her appointments. They simply assumed that she would be available whenever they needed her.

Once she'd dried her hair and George had nearly knocked her over to dash like a missile towards the stairs and his mosaic class, Imogen automatically tidied away her brothers' and sisters' possessions and made all the beds.

Afterwards she went downstairs into the kitchen, which was, as usual, devoid of any signs of food preparation. She stood for a moment looking out of the window into the garden, where Monty could be seen disporting himself in dignified manner with his favourite squeaky toy. Beyond him stood the large garden shed which housed her mother's studio. Inside, Elsa Peach would be sitting on the floor in her dungarees, her hair tucked into a turban, enthusiastically flicking paint at an enormous canvas. The sky was an ominous shade of grey and it was rather chilly. Proper summer weather was proving to be its usual elusive self. Imogen sighed and zipped up her hoodie.

Then, out of the corner of her eye, she caught sight of a bright object dancing wildly over the garden wall. It was Di, standing on a ladder and waving a red bandana – their agreed signal for an emergency. Imogen leaped to her feet and ran next door.

'Thank goodness you're here!' Di said, looking agitated as she opened the door. Over her usual uniform of slacks and a blouse with piecrust collar, she wore a large striped apron. Imogen followed her into the kitchen.

'I'm really worried this time,' Di said. 'Because, you see,

this was a special order from our local MP. She gave very precise instructions. And now it's all gone wrong. Oh, help. This will finish me.'

'Di, stop it,' Imogen replied sensibly. 'You know you're the best . . .' she went on, looking critically at what lay on the counter. 'He looks great – really he does. It's just that . . . the, um . . .'

'I know, I know!' Di wailed. 'The chest hair is *all wrong*, isn't it?'

'Yes,' Imogen admitted. 'Too spiky. Like a hedgehog, or a punk hairdo.'

'Dear-oh-dear. That won't do at all. Should we just pull it all out?'

'I think we'd better,' Imogen said decisively.

The chest hair *was* wrong. And this was a serious problem, because the hair in question belonged to Tom Jones, who stood, in all his marzipan glory, on top of a large birthday cake.

'You've done a great job, though,' Imogen said supportively. 'Wonderful knickers!'

These, fashioned out of frilly pink, red and blue icing, were artfully dotted all over the sponge-and-buttercream rock 'n' roll podium.

'And what's that?' Imogen asked, pointing at a spherical black object that lay at the singer's feet.

Di peered at it, then said, 'Why, that's a marzipan sex bomb, dear. It only needs a wick to finish it off.'

Imogen looked at her friend with affection. The cake-maker was, as ever, a reassuring sight, with her snow-white hair cut in a neat pudding-bowl style and her alert, shrewd face deeply tanned from decades of gardening. Shifting her gaze to the singer's now hairless chest, Imogen was suddenly struck by inspiration. 'I know! How about pushing some black icing through a garlic press?'

'You *are* brilliant! That's *just* the thing.'

Moments later, the Welsh Wizard was sporting a surprisingly lifelike mat of curly fur in the deep opening of his edible gold lamé shirt.

'Oh, phew,' Di said, pressing the back of her hand on her brow. 'Another disaster averted. Do sit down, dear. Tell me your news.'

Bewildered, Imogen replied, 'I haven't got any.'

'No,' Di said wryly, looking at her young friend. 'I didn't think so. But have I got some news for you.'

And then, without further ado, Imogen's neighbour dropped her Thrilling Bombshell.

3

Ten years ago, when Imogen was twelve, her mother had hung a metaphorical 'Closed' sign on the kitchen door, banning cooking from the household for ever.

When an intrepid person (usually new to the Peach circle) questioned her about it, which happened every so often, Elsa would draw herself to her full height, narrow her pale blue eyes, and declare that no intelligent woman should waste her time on drudgery. Then, twisting her blonde hair into an impromptu chignon and pinning it into place with a paintbrush, she would add that the endless chopping and stuffing of things was a tragic waste of one's time. One should be free – free to pursue Beauty, Creativity and Truth.

At this point she usually left the room, only to return almost immediately, her delicate jaw now quite set, her teeth bared, and ask no one in particular whether they could think of *anything* more vulgar than those grotesque food-porn adverts with their revoltingly husky voice-overs. Television was, of course, another obstacle in the path that led to Beauty, Creativity and Truth, and though there was one in the house the Peach children were strongly discouraged from watching it. Then, almost invariably, came the monologue's finale, as Elsa latched on to her *bête noire* – only ever referred to as 'that *horrendous* finger-licking woman'.

However discomfiting this (well-honed) performance turned out to be for the person who'd asked the original question, it had become a source of pride and mirth for the Peach children, who revelled in their mother's eccentric ways. George had even pinned a picture of the hapless Nigella Lawson (for the horrendous finger-licker was she) in his mother's studio, to be used as a stress-busting dartboard between painting sessions.

But there was another side to all this. Just before her mother had closed the kitchen for good, Imogen remembered walking in to find her mother sitting in the semi-darkness, lost in thought, breastfeeding a tiny Gus. Red-eyed, Elsa had looked up at her twelve-year-old daughter and declared, 'Remember one thing, darling. Better to be a great screw than a good cook.'

This hadn't made a lot of sense at the time, but over the years Imogen had come to understand her mother's statement better. For, soon after Gus's arrival, Elsa's husband had run off with another, much younger woman, who, it turned out, had little inclination for cooking. As a result, Elsa, who had been a competent cook, turned her back on it completely. There were too many memories of carefully prepared meals left uneaten when her husband, otherwise engaged, had failed to come home. Cooking had become for Elsa the emblem of her desertion. As for Nigella Lawson, she embodied a sort of hateful amalgam of earthy sexiness and irresistible food, exactly what Elsa herself felt she had failed to provide.

The Peach children saw their father every now and again, but Elsa never wanted to hear a word about their outings with him. She had written her husband out of her life, and rearranged it solely around herself, retreating to her studio and giving herself over to her Art. And though the coolly beautiful and now unencumbered Elsa had attracted a few keen admirers, none of them had, as far as her children knew, ever been allowed to get close to her.

Since the divorce, the kitchen had been turned into extra storage space for Elsa's paints, brushes and canvases, and as a result smelled permanently of turpentine. The fridge had been moved into the garage. The oven had not been switched on since her husband's departure.

Gradually, a new style of eating had evolved within the Peach household. Food supplies had more or less dried up. Elsa herself now relied almost exclusively on powdered milk, instant coffee, vegetable stock and the occasional sachet of vitamin C when she really wanted to push the boat out. There were no more family meals. Instead, each member squirrelled away bits and pieces of food for their own consumption. The children kept a toaster and kettle in their 'dorm' and lived essentially on cereal supplemented by school meals.

On the whole, the youngsters didn't mind. Their interests lay elsewhere. After drama school, Hildegard had co-founded a small independent theatre company with her boyfriend Stephen. Sixth-former George and his younger brother Gus played the cello and the violin respectively and were always in rehearsal for some school concert or other. Teenage Thea was a ballet fanatic, forever striking swan-like attitudes around the house. It was as if they had all switched off from food.

All, that is, except Imogen.

Her passion had begun in infancy. When holding tea parties for her teddy bears, she had always provided plentiful and varied imaginary foods: Victoria sponge cake, almond fingers, Bakewell tarts, coronation chicken sandwiches, Dundee cake, vanilla-scented trifle with raspberries . . .

As her brothers and sisters lost interest in those childish pleasures, she simply learned to play food-related games alone. She might share her family's skimpy meals of Cup-a-Soup, boil-in-the-bag rice and – if she was lucky – the odd orange segment, but her toys continued to enjoy an indulgent diet.

Later on, she took to digging the Sunday papers out of the recycling pile in order to cut out any recipes and paste them into a diary, which she kept hidden at the back of her wardrobe. At night, as she lay in bed on the edge of sleep, she'd float away into a world of her own. In her mind's eye she'd see a blackboard. On it, a hand would write in white chalk the alluring words 'Today's Specials'. Snuggling up more comfortably, Imogen would begin to create the perfect menu. Mussel and courgette quiche, perhaps. Tomato tart with tarragon and mascarpone. Or an onion tart, with cubes of pancetta folded into it. No, not onion, leek – so much more flavoursome. As she drifted off, gently lulled by the tantalising aromas of bruised herbs and ripe vine tomatoes, of mussels and white wine and caramelised bacon that her mind conjured up, her hands would move unconsciously on the sheet, briskly folding a cold pat of butter into a rectangle of pastry, turning it clockwise and folding again, turning and folding, turning and folding . . .

In this way two years of rationing went by.

Imogen was fourteen when a new neighbour – a lady called Di Blanding – moved into the vacant house next door. One day, George accidentally kicked his football over the garden fence. By then, Imogen's status as her siblings' helper, fetcher and carrier had become well established, and she was duly dispatched to retrieve her brother's ball. Di – a fifty-something, grey-haired and rather brisk lady who wore an apron and sounded almost exactly like the Queen – came to the door and allowed Imogen to throw it back into her own garden.

As they walked back through the hallway afterwards, Imogen stopped in her tracks and asked what that lovely smell coming from downstairs was. 'I'm baking,' Di said. 'Do you like banana tea loaf?'

'Um . . . actually, I don't know,' Imogen replied. 'We never eat cake at home.'

'I see,' Di said neutrally. 'Well, would you like to come and help me?' Walking down the stairs to the kitchen, she looked back at Imogen thoughtfully and added, 'I think perhaps we had better make some scones as well.'

Imogen still remembered the joy of seeing the fruit of their labours emerge from the Aga, a tray of golden little cakes studded with currants. She and Di had shared a delicious and plentiful tea in the warm, sweet-smelling kitchen, then Imogen had gambolled home with a plate of scones.

Their reception was disappointing. 'Oh, thanks,' George said, taking one absent-minded bite.

'I made them, you know,' Imogen said proudly, 'with the lady next door.'

'Uh-huh,' Hildegard said, barely looking up from her book.

Meanwhile George, having put the scone down and forgotten all about it, went upstairs to play. Then her mother walked in. Unsmiling, she shook her head at Imogen, asked, 'Don't you have any homework, darling?' and headed back to her studio.

The scones sat for several days, unwanted and unpraised, until they became quite dry. Then one morning Elsa said, 'Oh, *do* get rid of those, will you, darling?' and a chastised Imogen had duly thrown away the rest of her first baking experiment.

Many similar incidents – such as having her birthday celebrated by sticking a small candle perfunctorily into a piece of fruit – had eventually reached critical mass, turning Imogen into a rebel. Up to this point, food had been a mere element of make-believe, like talking animals or princesses and dragons. Now it was a badge of independence. Imogen went underground.

She found an invaluable ally in Di – a fellow food lover who made novelty cakes for a living. Imogen escaped to her neighbour's house as often as she could and spent many happy hours there cooking, baking – and eating.

Di was rather lonely, Imogen told her family quite untruthfully. Nor had Di and Imogen been reading, as she had reported, the novels of Jane Austen, Trollope, Thackeray and most of Dickens, with occasional forays into Balzac. They had instead worked their way happily through the works of Eliza Acton, Elizabeth David, Jane Grigson and many others. Recently, they'd had a brief but intense infatuation with Heston Blumenthal and had brilliant fun with molecular cooking, magicking gels and foams out of the unlikeliest raw materials.

Meanwhile, since her teens, Imogen had developed another clandestine literary passion, moving on from the fairytales of her childhood – 'Cinderella', 'Sleeping Beauty' and 'The Little Mermaid' in particular – to romantic novels, perhaps partly because she knew how much her disillusioned mother would disapprove of them. Her absolute favourite, the one she read time and time again, was Georgette Heyer's *Venetia*. There was something unimaginably exciting about the scene in which the heroine found herself suddenly kissed and swept off her feet by a dashing stranger. And then, little by little, Venetia fell in love with him, and Damerel – cynical rake that he was – with her. It was *lovely*, and Imogen kept her dog-eared copy of the novel in her wardrobe, next to her cookery scrapbooks. Of course, she knew that it was only fiction, but fiction that hinted at the wonderful possibility that love could be just as deliciously satisfying as a perfectly timed and melting chocolate soufflé.

In the midst of tidying, cleaning or mending for her siblings, she often found herself daydreaming about this world of imaginary romance. Then she would snap out of it, thinking of her father. Men were untrustworthy. They left you. It was probably best to remain as independent and closed off as possible; that was by far the safer option.

In spite of these reservations, Imogen did, stealthily but regularly, go back to her local library to borrow more and more romantic novels. Over time she had become quite friendly with one of the librarians, a bespectacled, mild-mannered girl called Jo who always alerted her to the arrival of new love stories, rather in the manner of a friendly butcher saving the choicest cuts for his best customers.

Until about a year ago, Elsa, whose mind was solely focused on her art, had shown little interest in Imogen's activities. Then she had suddenly remembered her middle daughter's existence and the question of What To Do About Imogen had become an irritating but persistent preoccupation. It was bad enough that, unlike her four other children, who looked just like herself – tall, fair and androgynous – the shorter, curvier, dark-eyed Imogen, with her head of wild brown curls, was a carbon copy of her delinquent father. But the real problem was Imogen's lack of natural ability in the arts. There had been drawing and piano lessons, pottery and embroidery classes, and even a crash course in weaving, but they had all been for nought. Imogen, in Elsa's eyes, wasn't even *trying* to learn!

At her wits' end, Elsa had frogmarched her problem child to Bear Necessities, a local Montessori nursery and, somewhat to her mother's surprise, Imogen had not only agreed to go on a training course, but somehow also secured a job there after getting her qualification.

Not the most perspicacious of mothers, Elsa had no

inkling of the real reason why Imogen had jumped at the chance of working at Bear Necessities – namely its large stainless-steel kitchen, where members of staff took turns to cook lunch for the children.

4

'My darling girl,' Di had asked on the day of the garlic-press chest hair incident, 'how old are you?'

'Um, twenty-two.'

Di ought to know. She was the one who'd baked the birthday cake – a 3-D replica of a grinning Monty, complete with tartan collar – which they had shared a few weeks before.

'Twenty-two years old! My dear! And are you happy? Are you having fun?'

Imogen considered this. 'It's all right,' she had said, pressing a bit more icing onto Tom's chest. 'I'm getting along quite well at the nursery. And I have a nice time when I'm here with you.'

'Yes, I know you do, dear,' Di said with a shade of impatience. She sat down at the pine kitchen table and beckoned to Imogen to do the same. 'But is that as exciting as it would be . . . for example . . . to go and work in an actual restaurant?'

Imogen paused and looked up. 'Well . . . perhaps not. No,' she finally admitted.

'No. And what if the restaurant in question were . . . by the sea? Somewhere like the south of France.'

Imogen started to laugh. 'That *would* be nice,' she said. *But then*, she added privately, *so would flying to the moon on the back of a mutant pig*.

'That's just what I thought you'd say,' Di went on comfortably. 'You can start work in January and they've agreed to have you for six months. I *know*,' she went on as Imogen's mouth fell open, 'that's not very long, but it is a start, isn't it? When would you like to travel?'

'What are you talking about?' Imogen bleated.

'Did I ever mention my younger sister, Daphne?'

Imogen's eyes moved to a framed photograph on the wall, which showed two little girls in sun hats, standing on a beach. The practical-looking, older one staring at the camera was Di, the dreamy, younger one looking out to sea was Daphne.

'Yes,' she said, remembering what Di had told her. 'I think you said she'd moved away to . . .'

'France, yes. She was always the more adventurous of us two. She has a pastry shop in some small town in the Midi. Talk about taking coals to Newcastle, but she seems to love it there. It's called Saint-Jean-de-something-or-other.'

There was a click of recognition inside Imogen's head. 'Not Saint-Jean-les-Cassis?'

'Precisely. I know exactly what you're thinking. That is indeed the place where the great Michel Boudin has his restaurant. Do you remember that feature we saw the other day in the *Observer Food Monthly*? What's his place called again?'

'Boustifaille,' Imogen said in a small, wondering voice. Cursed with the sort of selective memory that had made overall academic achievement difficult, she had never had any trouble retaining information relating to gastronomy.

'Well, that's where you're going. Daphne set it up. It turns out that she and Boudin are friends.'

Imogen's mind was reeling. The south of France. On her own. With the freedom to do what she loved. She would escape at last, like ... Cinderella! Her heart expanded, then contracted again as she thought of her mother's disapproval, of Hildegard's angry disbelief, of her own sense of responsibility to her younger siblings. She shook her head regretfully. This was a wonderful dream, but her family would never allow it to become a reality.

'Oh, Di, it sounds great, but ...' she sighed. 'I can't possibly go.'

'What absolute nonsense! Of course you're going! Which part don't you fancy? Living in the south of France? Cooking at a fantastic restaurant?'

By now Imogen was surfing atop a towering wave of panic. 'Yes, it's brilliant, but what about Monty?' she asked, clutching at the first thought that popped into her head.

'Don't be silly, dear. Monty will love the seaside,' Di replied briskly.

'But he'll need a passport and everything,' Imogen said, biting her nails. 'It'll take months to organise.'

'You *have* months, dear. It's only July. And I've already downloaded all the forms for you. Now, then. I think, you know, that the best thing would be for you to drive down. You can have my car,' Di smiled. 'I'm planning on buying a new one anyway, I rather fancy sending it to retire on the Continent. It's never been abroad – it's like me, a stick-in-the-mud! We'll need to sort out the insurance, but that should be a doddle. Now, let's see ... The restaurant will pay you a pittance, but Daphne said that the job comes with a room. You'll need a bit of money to keep you going, of course. I can help with that too.'

'Oh no, no, I can't—'

'Nonsense,' Di said firmly. 'There's only me, you know. No children of my own. If I want to use some of my savings to set you up on your trip, then that's what I shall do.'

Imogen threw her arms around her friend, who carried on composedly: 'Jolly good. Now for the tricky bit – your mother. Perhaps *I* should speak to her.'

'*Noooo!*' Imogen cried, aghast. 'Oh no, please don't!' She chewed her lower lip pensively for a minute, then added, 'What would you say, exactly?'

Di shook her head, repressing what she would really like to say to Elsa Peach. 'I will say that you are over eighteen and free to make your own decisions. It's a proper job. Surely she can't object to that.'

Imogen said sadly, 'She can and she will. There'll be a terrible row. Oh, Di, she'll be so disappointed in me. I can't face it.'

Di narrowed her eyes at her protégée. She was certain that Imogen resented her underdog status, and that she was, beneath that meek and accommodating exterior, a passionate young woman, capable of very strong emotions. Indeed, in some ways, this was written in Imogen's dark eyes, full mouth, and the way the blood often rushed to the surface of her pale, translucent skin. The girl certainly cooked with passion. And yet, perhaps as a result of her father's desertion, perhaps as a consequence of putting the needs of her family before her own, Imogen had pushed her feelings under the surface and gone into herself far too much. She needed setting free. In fact, Di thought that a blazing row with her mother would be rather marvellous, but Imogen wasn't ready for it. Getting the girl to stand up to Elsa was like trying to convince her that she was pretty – a losing battle.

'I should be the one to tell your mother,' Di said, patting Imogen's arm. 'After all, it was my idea, wasn't it?' She got to her feet and Imogen automatically did the same. 'Come along, dear,' Di went on, leading the way out of her house. 'Follow my lead and all will be well.' Once in the street, she paused and said, 'We're just going to have to be—' she made a neat slashing motion with her hand '—economical with the truth.'

In a trance of fear and excitement, Imogen allowed Di to take her to her mother's studio and stood at her friend's shoulder as she knocked at the door. Displeased by the interruption, Elsa was not particularly welcoming, but her silence allowed Di to get stuck in. Rocking a little on her heels, her hands thrust in the pockets of her navy slacks, the cake-maker explained with brisk confidence that her sister was looking for an au pair.

'Daphne lives in France, you know. And I think a change of scene would do Imogen a world of good,' Di said, taking a few steps forward the better to examine Elsa's abstract white-on-white work-in-progress, about which she made no comment. Imogen knew that her friend only really liked detailed, realistic pictures of dogs and horses. 'Besides,' Di went on crisply, 'a girl needs to be exposed to the right sort of culture in order to find her true artistic gift.'

Imogen met her friend's eye and repressed a smile. Di was talking about gastronomy, but Elsa would, of course, be thinking on altogether different lines.

'There are artistic connections, too,' Di said without missing a beat. 'That chap Picasso lived nearby.' Seeing a glimmer of interest begin to play on Elsa's face, she pressed her advantage. 'And then there's Matisse, of course . . .'

Di continued in this vein for a little while, without ever mentioning Boustifaille, Michel Boudin or kitchen work. Prudently, Imogen said nothing.

'Darling, that sounds like complete heaven,' Elsa said vaguely, smiling in her daughter's direction.

Thus she gave her blessing to the project and turned back to her canvas.

It was time to tackle her brothers and sisters, who were not as easily bowled over by Di's references to art. When a loud chorus of protest arose from Hildegard, Thea and George, who suddenly realised that it was in fact Imogen and not some supernatural agency who had been taking care of the practicalities of their lives all those years, Elsa steamrollered over their objections, metaphorically unlocking Imogen's cage and handing her the key to a new life.

5

By midnight on her second day in Saint-Jean-les-Cassis, dinner service had been and gone and Boustifaille was closed. Sitting on the edge of the pavement outside the restaurant, Imogen wept.

On hearing of the evening's debacle, an informed observer would have concluded that the gentle surroundings of Bear Necessities had done little to prepare Imogen for her new job. She had not been forewarned about the emotional temperature of a professional kitchen. Having only very limited access to television at home, she had watched the ebullient Gordon Ramsay at Di's, but had always thought of his macho posturing as performance, never believing that such antics would actually be tolerated in real life.

Nor had she received a particularly detailed briefing from Di's sister, Daphne, when she'd paid her a visit on the morning of her first day at work. In spite of a potent mixture of excitement and trepidation at the prospect of meeting Michel Boudin and starting work at Boustifaille as part of his team, she'd managed to snatch a few hours of sleep in her hotel room, and had pretty much succeeded in putting her encounter with the ill-mannered hitchhiker Dimitri out of her mind. The enticing window of Daphne Blanding's pastry shop, Le Puits d'Amour, displayed neat rows of plump coffee and chocolate *religieuses* (so-called because their shape resembles little nuns), vertiginous puff-pastry *millefeuilles* glazed with caramel, delicate raspberry charlottes enclosed in biscuity ramparts and scarlet wild-strawberry tartlets, and last but not least, the house speciality, glistening *puits d'amour*, or puff pastry 'love wells', filled with caramelised custard.

Imogen had had no difficulty in identifying Daphne behind the counter, for she was the image of her sister, although there were noticeable cosmetic differences – her carefully made-up face, chic ash-blonde bob and flatteringly cut plum-coloured dress spoke of long exposure to French habits, and of a distinctly Gallic idea of how glamorous and *soignée* a fifty-something woman could – and should – look. After more than ten years as an expat, Daphne had even begun to speak English with a slight French accent.

Having kissed Imogen on both cheeks and welcomed her to Saint-Jean-les-Cassis, Daphne gestured to a tray of flattish puff-pastry cakes, each topped with a gold paper crown.

'You've come on a good day, Imogen. We've just baked our first batch of *galettes des rois*!' Galettes, she explained, were traditionally eaten in French households to mark the Feast of the Epiphany. Each cake contained a small hidden charm, which was the whole point of eating the cake: the person who found it in their slice would be declared king or queen for the day – an honour symbolised by the wearing of a paper crown.

Daphne looked at Monty with keen interest and said

gaily, 'Now, young man, how would you like to go for a walk with me while your mistress goes to work?'

Monty remained solemn in the face of this proposal, although the word 'walk' had clearly made a favourable impression, especially after having spent so long in the car – his tail was wagging.

'Oh, thank you!' Imogen said gratefully. 'That's very good of you. I imagine they wouldn't be particularly thrilled to see me turn up at the restaurant with him in tow!'

'You will find that the French *adore* dogs,' Daphne said. 'I shouldn't be surprised if they gave him his own table and monogrammed napkin ring within the week. But it's very sensible of you to keep things nice and simple on your first day. Now, shall we go for a coffee? See you later, Sandrine!' Daphne called out to her friendly looking brunette assistant as she stepped out of the shop with Monty and Imogen.

As they settled themselves at a nearby terrace, Imogen looked around, wide-eyed. She felt as though her life, hitherto shot in drab black and white, had suddenly burst into vivid colour. She looked down the street, with its row of houses painted in Mediterranean shades of pink and ochre yellow, and gazed at the bay that stretched lazily beneath emerald-green hills. The tranquil sea, dotted with white sailboats, was a clear aquamarine, marbled here and there with patches of dark sapphire blue and phosphores-cent turquoise. The cerulean sky was vibrant and almost entirely clear of clouds. With so many different blues on display, it was easy, Imogen thought, to see why the Riviera had come to be called the Côte d'Azur – the Azure Coast.

She turned her attention to Daphne, noticing her pretty tan and contrasting it with her own Girl-from-Atlantis pallor, and asked, in the respectful tones of the gastronomy enthusiast, 'So . . . Di tells me that Monsieur Boudin is a good friend of yours. What's he like to work for?'

'Michel is a wonderful friend and an absolute sweetheart,' Daphne replied, beaming. 'I'm sure he'll bend over backwards to make you feel welcome. Besides, that kitchen of his really needs a girl in it, as I've pointed out to him many times.'

Imogen grinned, her heart beating faster. *She* was that much-needed girl! Oh, it was so exciting: she couldn't *wait* to show Monsieur Boudin what she could do! She began to wonder happily which station he had in mind for her. Meat, perhaps? Or vegetables? Sauces? Or even puddings? It didn't matter, really. She was a good all-rounder and any one of those would be wonderful.

'How sweet!' Daphne purred after running her hand along Monty's back. 'You're like a nail brush all the way through!' she said to the dog, before looking at Imogen and adding, 'Speaking of bristles, I'm told that Michel can be a little, er, explosive at times, but it never lasts.'

'It must be a very high-pressure job, running a place like Boustifaille,' Imogen said sympathetically.

'Well, he does take it all extremely seriously, of course – dear Michel! And lately, things haven't exactly been . . . but I mustn't gossip. You'll see for yourself. Now this,' Daphne said, reaching for something in her chic raffia shoulder bag, 'is the key to your room. It's next to the restaurant.'

'Thank you,' Imogen said, pocketing the key.

Daphne glanced at her watch. 'And now I think that you'd better be on your way, dear. Boustifaille is very easy to find,' she said, gesturing gracefully in the direction of the seafront. 'Walk down the street, turn right and you'll see it there – right on the harbour.'

Imogen stood up hurriedly, her heart thumping, and almost knocked over her chair. Daphne smiled at her with infectious insouciance. 'Don't worry about a thing, dear. I'm sure all will be well. I'll feed Monty and you can collect him when you're ready for bed. My flat is above the shop. I always stay up late. Have fun!'

When she walked into the restaurant five minutes later, Imogen was greeted by a sleek, dark-haired man in a black suit, who, taking in her own casual attire, asked if Madame had a reservation. Evidently he was used to a more smartly dressed class of clientele. 'Madame' glanced around the dining room with intense curiosity. She wasn't quite sure what she had expected – a general impression of smart white linen and gleaming glass with a hint of earthy Mediterranean exuberance, perhaps? This was, after all, the famous Boustifaille, whose chef had – some ten years ago now – put his own mark on regional cuisine – or *cuisine de terroir* as it was known in France – and made it fresh and exciting.

What she saw instead was walls that were, like the floor, carpeted in a disconcerting and rather oppressive shade of oxblood and hung all over with paintings of sad clowns. While reflecting privately that these might not be to everybody's taste, Imogen also became aware of how extremely quiet the room was. Only a few tables were occupied. But it was still early – barely half past twelve – and no doubt things would liven up later on.

'No, I don't,' she said, smiling back at the maître d'. 'But perhaps you can help me ...'

'I'll see what I can do, Madame,' the man said archly. 'May I take a name?'

'It's Imogen Peach. I'm the new kitchen assistant – the new *stagiaire*.'

The man gasped, then said in a very different tone, 'You don't belong here. Staff enter by the kitchen door.' He shook his head severely. '*Ah là là*, Monsieur Boudin will not be pleased. No, he will not. Already he was not in a good mood, so now ... Well, what are you waiting for? Quick, quick, hurry!'

After being bustled out of the dining room, a flustered Imogen walked through the kitchen door into a bright room full of sweaty men and Gallic shouting.

And then, her first experience of service: an interminable blur of white-hot embarrassment. She had begun by introducing herself to Michel Boudin, attempting, in her rusty schoolgirl French, to express her admiration for his restaurant's reputation and to thank him for a marvellous opportunity, but the chef – a large, tall hunk of a man who looked strikingly like Eric Cantona and exuded testosterone – had impatiently brushed aside all polite formalities.

'Ah yes, the new girl,' he said in heavily accented English, looking her up and down appraisingly. 'You peel the onions, yes?'

Vegetables it was, then. Imogen wondered excitedly what delectable dishes she was going to be cooking. Rustic Provençal cookery was famous for its inventive and aromatic ways with courgettes, aubergines, beans . . . Her mouth was watering in anticipation.

'Right,' she said, once she had put on the ill-fitting chef's whites someone had handed her. Tucking her hair under her white skullcap, she eyed a large sack of onions lying on a counter. 'Where's the sink?'

'What?'

'It's just,' Imogen explained politely, 'that I'd rather peel them under the tap so they don't sting my eyes.'

Monsieur Boudin planted himself in front of her, fixing her threateningly with a pair of glittering dark eyes. 'No, but what is this delirium? Hey, you!' he shouted, addressing a young man who stood close by, busily hacking away at chicken carcasses.

'Chef?'

'You understand this? The little assistant, she can't peel an onion because it stings the eyes. That makes sense to you?'

'No, Chef!' he replied, half-turning to face them. It was, Imogen realised with a hot wave of embarrassment, none other than Dimitri the lecherous hitchhiker. But before she could speak, Monsieur Boudin's voice made her jump again, 'What are you waiting for? You think this is a holiday camp? It's my kitchen, you understand that?'

'Yes, I understand, but . . . would you mind telling me a bit more about the dish?' Imogen asked stumblingly in French.

'What dish?' Boudin thundered. '*You* are *not* here to *cook*,' he said, devastatingly. 'You are not a cook, are you? You are here to help, to assist. So get on with it. *Allez!*'

Imogen stared at him, aghast. But that wasn't at all what Daphne had given her to understand! So she'd been hired as . . . as a dogsbody, nothing more. She opened her mouth to protest that she was, indeed, a cook, but Boudin shouted, 'Go peel the onions – over there – now!'

Shaken, Imogen started peeling the onions, and was soon weeping profuse tears. It didn't help that Monsieur Boudin stood cross-armed for a long while watching her every move. Eventually, he was called away to the other end of the kitchen and she was able to breathe more naturally. As she paused to wipe her face, she looked across at Dimitri. Their eyes met.

'So – it's you again,' he said, without much warmth.

Imogen gave him a strained smile. He might have been rude to her yesterday, but it was still a relief to see a familiar face in this brutal environment.

'Hi! How weird that you work here too!'

'It's not that weird,' he replied. 'I'm a chef. And you?'

'Actually, I've been cooking for donkey's years,' Imogen said, squaring her shoulders a little. 'For pleasure, and also at the nursery where I work in London. My spicy fish pie and Moroccan chicken have become a bit of an institution there! The children keep asking for them.'

'Oh!' Dimitri said, nodding with exaggerated deference. 'You make lunch for *little kids*. In *London*. Very impressive.'

There was a longish period of quiet and outwardly meek peeling, until Imogen had managed to subdue her annoyance enough to ask, in a reasonably friendly tone, 'So, what's the recipe?'

'What?' Dimitri said ungraciously.

'Can you talk me through the dish you're making so I have some idea of what's going on?'

'You've finished with the onions?'

'Yes!' Imogen said triumphantly.

'Then start on the carrots. They're right here.'

'But I was hoping to help you at the meat station,' Imogen said, startled by the young man's baleful glare. 'I'm quite good at deboning. Look—'

She reached across and Dimitri slapped her hand. '*Hé!* You do *not* touch my knives!' he said. 'They're not for a *gamine* like you.'

'Little assistant!' Monsieur Boudin bellowed from across the kitchen. 'Go peel the carrots! And after that you peel the potatoes!'

Dimitri looked at her with a sardonic smile. 'You heard that? Just get on with it. Don't worry about the recipe for *my* dish.'

Imogen glanced around her. All over the kitchen wonderful mouth-watering food was being cooked and she wasn't allowed to play any part in the *real* preparation. It was maddening.

With considerable effort, she managed to keep a hold on her temper and shook her head resolutely. She had no choice but to get through tonight and see what could be done tomorrow. Just then, another young chef sidled up to her and whispered, 'You think that because you're a good cook you should not be made to peel potatoes?'

They were all determined to pick on her! Imogen spun on her heel, ready to snap back, but was disarmed at the sight of the young man's open and friendly face. Blond-haired and blue-eyed, with a broad leonine nose and faintly ruddy countenance, he had the look of a happy-go-lucky Breton sailor. He smiled at her, introduced himself as Bastien, and returned to his station across from Dimitri's. As his question echoed in her mind, Imogen shook her head, blushing, because in truth that was exactly what she thought.

'It's your turn, that's all,' Bastien went on, turning his attention to the handling of small silver fish. 'You're the last one in. We've all had to peel potatoes – me, Dimitri, Monsieur Boudin, everybody. OK?'

' OK,' Imogen murmured.

'Good. I'm filleting sardines for the *mousseuse*,' Bastien continued, following the direction of her fascinated eyes. 'One of our starters.'

'Right.'

'Then I make the fillets into a purée, with asparagus and crème fraîche, and then with the mixture we make a sort of quenelle, you know, like a dumpling.'

'That sounds really yummy.'

'Yummy?'

'It means delicious.'

'*Gourmande, hein?*' Bastien said, winking at her. 'That's good. I'll give you a taste later.'

Much cheered by Bastien's kindness (he had called her a good cook; not that he knew her yet), Imogen had kept her head down, resolutely ignoring Dimitri, and managed to complete her peeling marathon.

After what had seemed to an exhausted Imogen like an impossibly short break, the kitchen had geared up again, this time for dinner. She had soldiered through this, keeping out of Monsieur Boudin's way and trying hard not to draw too much attention to herself.

When service began to wind down, she allowed herself to relax a little – a fatal mistake, as it turned out. As she stood washing her way mechanically through a ridiculously high pile of pots and pans, she sensed Monsieur Boudin's presence behind her. 'You finish this later, OK? Now you go empty the bucket.'

'Sorry?'

By then the great French chef was beginning to feel tired after service, so that anyone hoping for an exquisite display of courtly manners from him would have been disappointed: 'Go empty the bucket! *Go empty the bucket!* GO EMPTY THE BUCKET!' he shouted without pausing for breath.

Bastien came to her rescue again, discreetly pointing out a white plastic bucket sitting on a shelf, into which the chefs had been pouring the grease from their frying pans. A staggeringly rank smell emanated from it, and Imogen gagged as she drew near. Reaching up, she noticed a large frying pan sitting beside the sink. It still needed emptying.

Lucky that she'd spotted it, really. At least Boudin wouldn't be able to accuse her of cutting corners. Carefully, she lifted the heavy pan and proceeded to tip the grease into the bucket.

Like a thing possessed, the bucket slid off the shelf and somersaulted with surprising grace before ricocheting on the top of the counter with a terrifying crashing sound, spilling grease all over the stove on its way down and disgorging the rest of its contents on the floor – and also, as a final, grotesque flourish, on the trousers and steel-tipped shoes of Monsieur Boudin, who'd been standing at her elbow.

Imogen, who had shut her eyes tightly during this collapse, slowly opened them again. The kitchen had fallen completely silent. What would Monsieur Boudin do? she wondered. Have her hanged, drawn and filleted? No – too fiddly. Seize one of Dimitri's super-sharp knives and dispatch her with it? This was France after all, and if he called it a *crime passionnel*, no court in the land would convict him. Most probably he'd make her spend the night in the walk-in freezer. But first he would, of course, take the opportunity to shout at her *again*.

'I'm so sorry,' Imogen said in a strangled voice. 'I'll get a cloth.'

'That,' Monsieur Boudin said in a strangely calm voice as he looked down at the spillage, 'was special goose fat from our very best supplier. I was saving it for the *pommes de terre à la sarladaise* we're serving tomorrow at a lunch party in our private room.'

Imogen turned scarlet. So she had also ruined his special dish. Great. Brilliant. What a wonderful way to begin.

Without saying another word, her boss gave her a look of infinite scorn and walked away, his shoes squelching a little as he went.

6

Still sobbing, Imogen heard the door open and shut behind her. Somebody was locking up the restaurant for the night.

'*Eh bien alors!*' a male voice exclaimed sympathetically. 'Are you OK?'

Imogen looked up. Through the veil of her tears, she received a general impression of ebullient friendliness. It was Bastien, now clad in jeans and a navy polo-neck jersey.

'You mustn't get upset like this,' he said, helping her to her feet. 'Come on, I'll buy you a drink.'

Imogen rubbed her face, vainly trying to put the trauma of the day behind her. 'I have to collect my dog,' she managed to say in halting French. 'From Daphne Blanding's place.'

'Ah, the beautiful Madame Blanc-Dingue!' Bastien exclaimed as they walked towards Daphne's apartment. 'You know, at first people here weren't sure about having an Englishwoman run a French *pâtisserie*. It's a national tradition, you know? People are proud of it, and very possessive. But her cakes are so good and so elegant, and she is so charming. Everybody really likes her. And now she's been here so long that she's almost one of us. So she's your friend?'

'I only actually met her earlier today,' Imogen answered.

'It's really her sister who's my friend, but it was Daphne who arranged this job for me.'

As the door of her flat opened, letting Monty fly out like a cannonball to greet his mistress, Daphne smiled at Bastien, who grinned back and said, nodding in Imogen's direction, '*Bonsoir, Madame.* I didn't know the English mafia was taking over the restaurant.'

'Oh, but we are! Beware, beware!' Daphne answered, laughing. 'How was it, Imogen? How was Michel? Tell all!'

Imogen exchanged a glance with Bastien and then, swiftly composing her face into a mask of cheerful enthusiasm, the traumatised Boustifaille trainee said, 'It went well, thank you.' It wouldn't do to start complaining right away to her benefactress.

'She's on peeling duty,' Bastien added. 'Not what she expected.'

'Oh, I shouldn't worry about that!' Daphne exclaimed gaily. 'You'll soon wow Michel with your expertise.'

Imogen nodded, then said, sighing, 'I think I need a drink.'

'Quite right too,' Daphne said, looking from one to the other. 'You two go and make friends. Good night.'

Bastien shepherded her and Monty into La Sirène, the nearest bar-café, whose name was picked out in pink neon letters, and ordered two kirs, easy on the cassis. Monty began to sniff Bastien's trainers with cool, scientific interest.

'It's not as bad as you think,' Bastien said, helping himself to handfuls of pistachio nuts from the bowl that had been placed before them. 'You'll get used to it.'

'No, I won't.' Imogen said, putting her elbows on the

table and hiding her face in her hands. 'I can't go back after what happened.'

'You mean the bucket? Oh, come on, that was nothing.'

'But Boudin will think I'm an idiot, and he'll treat me like one.'

'So you see, nothing will have changed,' Bastien said, and he smiled when she laughed.

'I know what you mean,' Imogen said, taking a sip of her drink before adding primly, 'but all the same I think Monsieur Boudin is a fascist pig. I wish I could set Monty on him.'

Monty reared up to put his paws in her lap and gave a short enthusiastic bark. Bastien smiled. 'So,' he asked, finishing his drink, 'you have some formal training?'

'No, not exactly. I learned to cook with Daphne's sister, Di. She's my neighbour in London.'

'Ah, she has a restaurant?'

'No,' Imogen admitted. 'But she makes cakes for special occasions – birthdays, weddings, you know.'

Bastien bit his lip. His blue eyes were twinkling, 'So it was just you two nice ladies cooking together?'

'You're laughing at me. Just like Dimitri.'

'Well, maybe a little bit,' Bastien said with a grin. 'But it's because I like you. You are *sympathique*. And actually, you should try to understand Dimitri's point of view.'

'Oh,' Imogen said frostily. 'And what point of view is that?'

'Well, he's about the same age as me. We started training when we were fourteen.'

Imogen was silent, reflecting that when *she* was fourteen

she'd been at school all day, unaware that other people her age were training for work.

'Plus things are tough at the moment,' Bastien went on, his face serious. 'Because Boudin is . . . And the restaurant isn't . . .' He broke off and shook his head, then smiled at her. 'Monsieur Boudin is a brilliant chef,' he wound up, 'and so I'm sure that all will be well.'

Imogen nodded, mystified. She was willing to believe that Boudin was brilliant, but she had been struck by his explosive behaviour today, and not only when it had been directed at her. For example, when Dimitri presented him with an immaculate rack of lamb, Monsieur Boudin had glared and said coldly, '*Ah, la vache! Mais je rêve ou quoi? C'est quoi cette merde?*' – a question which Imogen learned later had nothing whatever to do with a cow – *vache* – mad or otherwise, but translated meant something like, 'Crikey! Am I dreaming? What on earth is this excrement?' Dimitri had stood silent and impassive, his eyes fixed on the middle distance.

'I tell you what it is,' Boudin had continued, towering over Imogen and appearing, terrifyingly, to want to include her in this exchange. 'And you, little assistant, you can learn something also. It–is–a–plate–of–crap. Yes?'

'Yes, Chef,' Dimitri said.

'And you, you're a bonehead. Yes or no?'

'Yes, Chef.'

Dimitri might not be her favourite person, but Imogen had to concede that in the circumstances his self-control was impressive. Perhaps that was why Monsieur Boudin had picked on him – because of the young chef's quietly arrogant core that no amount of insults appeared to shake.

Bastien pushed the bowl of nuts in her direction. 'Another kir?'

Imogen shook her head, smiled at him, and suddenly found herself overcome by a momentous yawn. Bastien yawned in turn and stretched. 'It's contagious,' he said, grinning at her.

After a short detour to collect Imogen's luggage from her hotel, they headed back together to the staff sleeping quarters, a narrow whitewashed house next door to the restaurant. As Bastien explained that quite a few of her Boustifaille colleagues, including himself, also lived there, Imogen thought to herself that the building hardly looked large enough to fit them all in. They walked into the small nondescript hallway and she was struck by a pervasive and throat-stripping smell of disinfectant. Her expectations sinking with every step, she and Monty followed Bastien to the top floor, where, as they got to the end of the corridor, her new friend said lightly, 'By the way, I hope you're not claustrophobic.'

As Imogen opened the door and eventually located the light switch, her heart plummeted. The room was a window-less cubbyhole. A naked light bulb illuminated a narrow bed and a wardrobe that looked barely wide enough for three items of clothing. The smell of disinfectant permeated everything. Monty let out an indignant volley of barking.

Bastien bent down to stroke the little dog. 'Not great, I know. But you can make it a little bit nicer. I have posters in my room, pictures of my family, you know.'

'And does your room have a great view like mine?' Imogen asked in a defeated little voice.

'Yes, of the car park. So don't be jealous. Also, you get used to the smell after a while. Good night.' And he departed down the corridor.

7

In the course of a dreadful night in her airless cell, Imogen was only saved from despair by the comforting presence of Monty on her bed. In the morning, she got up as early as possible and had a shower in the drab communal bathroom. She felt very depressed and couldn't wait to get outside.

After a walk in the shady pine grove, where she came across many other dogs and their owners – all systematically ignored by Monty, who snobbishly trotted on ahead with his head held high – she repaired to La Sirène for breakfast. Once settled with a fragrant coffee and a glossy, blond croissant before her, and gazing down the street towards the glittering seafront – a dark blue line beneath the pale and radiant sky – she began to feel a little better, and remembered why she had come to France. She checked her watch; there was time to get her bearings around Saint-Jean-les-Cassis before she had to report to work.

What struck her most forcefully about the town was that, in relation to its modest size, it was home to a considerable number of food shops. The French clearly considered food a number-one priority. Briefly, she thought of her local high street in London, with its uninspiring corner shops and garish kebab shops. Here, she could count at least five bakeries and *pâtisseries*, several butchers, three fishmongers and as many cheese shops on the two main streets. All appeared to be thriving despite the presence of a supermarket alongside them, and she also noticed a poster advertising a weekly open-air market that took place on the harbour.

In passing, she made a mental note of which bakery attracted the longest queue, for she was well aware that there existed, even in France, a distinct hierarchy between OK bread and roll-over-onto-your-back exquisite sourdough heaven. She also paused outside a cheese shop for a moment to observe its owner, an austere and rather professorial-looking man in a grey smock, and marvel at the way he directed an indecisive customer towards a perfectly ripe goat's cheese with the sort of relaxed authority that bespoke a true specialist.

All this made Imogen feel at home. Putting aside, for a moment, the stress levels attached to her high-octane workplace, she reflected that she was now in an environment where, for the first time in her life, she was just like everyone else. She too, like ordinary French people, believed that when it came to food one could never be too particular.

But in other respects, she thought ruefully, noticing over and over again the sleek confidence that emanated from the Frenchwomen she passed in the street, she was definitely out of her depth. It wasn't that these women were all beautiful or young, but they all had lovely clothes and moved well, swiftly, as though unencumbered by their bodies. Which was the exact opposite of how Imogen felt about her own.

Tentatively, she pulled the zip down on her fleece and began to take it off – it wasn't that cold. Then she quickly did it up again. The roomy garment went a long way to disguise her bust. This was how she'd always coped with her shape and, regardless of French attitudes, she wasn't about to change her ways.

She and Monty then went briefly to the beach. It was hardly thronged, this being, technically at least, winter, but a few mahogany-coloured bodies adorned with a rainbow of showy bikinis were on display nevertheless, and some brave souls were even swimming. Imogen liked to swim, but she had never been a sunbather – far too much physical exposure. She sat on the sand, resolutely keeping on her fleece, combat trousers and practical bucket hat and ignoring the curious glances thrown her way. Instead, she watched Monty's cautious exploration of the water's edge. 'I'm not sure about this moving frothy substance,' he appeared to say, turning back to look at her. Then, after a couple of enthusiastic but short-lived sprints after passing seagulls, he threw himself into an orgy of tunnel digging.

As they walked back along the seafront, where low-slung white apartment blocks built in the style of ocean liners stretched out their serried balconies, Imogen's eye was drawn to a house she hadn't noticed before – a cream-coloured, turreted villa that stood some way back from the street, partially obscured by an overgrown garden. It looked, to Imogen's eyes, not unlike Sleeping Beauty's castle. Intrigued, she peered through the railings. The villa's blue shutters were all closed. Monty began to tug on his leash.

Wondering idly who, if anyone, lived there, Imogen headed once more for the centre of town.

The time to report for duty at Boustifaille was drawing near, and she didn't feel particularly thrilled at the prospect of peeling spuds and washing up. How her mother and siblings would laugh if they could see her at work. But surely she wouldn't remain a drudge for ever? After the nursery, she longed to cook for discerning adults for a change and to put in practice the skills she had taught herself in Di's kitchen. Imogen bit her lip resolutely. She *would*, somehow, get Monsieur Boudin to recognise her talent.

Turning into a side street on her way to Boustifaille, she noticed a green shop sign announcing 'Mitch's Paperback Wonderland'. An English-language bookshop, by the look of it. Imogen's spirits lifted a little; a quick look at the cookery section would fortify her before her next encounter with her boss.

The inside of the bookshop was much larger than she had expected – she watched it spread out before her eyes like an Aladdin's cave. The curving, slanting walls appeared to be *made* of books, all stacked higgledy-piggledy under sloping rafters painted in shades of Provençal red or ochre yellow. Hundreds of pictures and photographs were pegged or propped among the bookshelves. Several library ladders allowed access to the higher reaches of the display, and there were also a great many mismatched armchairs. The owner of the Paperback Wonderland clearly did not discourage browsing.

But how on earth did anyone find anything in this warren? Instead of the usual categories – history, fiction, travel – there were a great number of whimsical labels, all written in an assertive, spiky hand which must be the owner's. 'Life is a bitch' read one, then 'What d'you mean, jellybean?', 'Think Pink', 'I told you I was ill', 'Pretend it's a rainy day in Prague', '*De trop*' and 'Don't even think about it'.

Bewildered, Imogen walked past a circular sofa upholstered in shabby scarlet velvet that stood in the middle of the room, and turned into another, tiny room, which was jam-packed with a wild array of books of all kinds with one thing in common: blue spines of different shades. Down three well-worn stone steps was another room, this time filled with black-spined books, large gilt-framed mirrors and a crystal chandelier – all far too big for the space, but resulting in a dazzling jewel-box effect.

Beyond that was a precipitous little staircase. A sign on the wall read: 'What part of "By Invitation Only" don't you understand, you knucklehead?' Intimidated, Imogen was turning back towards the black-book room when she heard the sound of voices.

'What do you mean you don't know if you have it?' a female British voice asked querulously.

'Just that,' a male American voice replied drily.

'But it's on bestsellers' lists all over the world!'

'So?' the man said, marching into the room where Imogen had instinctively retreated behind a sofa.

The man, whom Imogen tentatively identified as Mitch, owner of the Wonderland, was probably in his early seventies, tall and spare with close-cropped salt-and-pepper hair and a thin pencil moustache of the kind sported by Errol Flynn. He wore a dinner jacket over a gold lamé shirt and Bermuda shorts with knee-high dark socks and black brogues. Close on his heels came a stout lady in a lobster-pink trouser suit.

'Well, couldn't you at least have a look in your stock-room?' she said.

'Listen, lady,' Mitch said languidly, turning around to gaze at his irate customer, 'if you're really meant to read that book, then my advice to you is to stop looking for it. Just keep real still and let it find *you*.'

'What? What nonsense.'

'That,' he said, absent-mindedly smoothing his moustache, 'is just your opinion.'

'Oh, never mind,' the woman said. 'I knew I should have gone to the English bookshop in Cannes.'

'Maybe so.'

The disappointed lady flounced out. Mitch stood for a moment rearranging a pile of books on a table with his back to Imogen. After a moment, he said slowly, '*Some*body looks disapproving.'

Imogen reddened. 'Oh, no, not at all!'

'Right,' he said, turning to face her. 'You looking for anything in particular?'

'The cookery section,' Imogen mumbled. 'If you have one.'

'Ah,' he replied, stretching his arms behind his back. 'See, here at the Paperback Wonderland we believe in paths of desire, and so should you, if you have any sense.'

'Paths of desire?'

'Hell yeah,' Mitch confirmed.

'Is that why you have all those . . . unusual labels on your shelves?'

'Yeah. They're mind-shaking, y'know?'

'I see,' Imogen said, with what she hoped was intelligent scepticism.

'Never had your mind shaken before, huh?'

'No, I don't think s—'

'Can't say I'm surprised. You the new girl at Boustifaille?'

'Yes, but how do you—'

'Small town. Kind of easy to stay plugged in. So what's going on? They let you cook anything yet?'

'No, I—'

'That guy Boudin shout at you yet?'

'Yes. Quite a lot.'

'He's a perfectionist, that's his problem. I'm not like that, see. Just ploughing my own furrow. That's always been good enough for me.'

'But you're the only English-language bookshop in town,' Imogen interjected reasonably. 'Boustifaille is in competition with a lot of restaurants in the region.'

'Hmn,' Mitch said, making a face. 'Competition is for alpha males. They're welcome to it.'

'Well, I'm not an alpha male,' Imogen protested, 'but I'd still like to cook at Boustifaille.'

'Well, whaddayaknow . . .' He stood looking at her for a moment, not unkindly, then said, 'The food stuff is all in the main room.' He set off ahead of her, striding on long legs. 'See?' he said, pointing. 'Where it says "In the soup".'

8

A week had elapsed since Imogen's arrival in Saint-Jean-les-Cassis. Tonight, inside La Sirène, she sat in silence with Bastien and the rest of her Boustifaille colleagues, Monty at her feet. She was cautiously sipping a fizzy red drink called a Monaco – pomegranate syrup topped with shandy. Her first reaction when Bastien had ordered it for her had been annoyance, but then she had found that it was surprisingly thirst quenching. It was also quite amusing, she discovered, to imagine how scandalised her mother would be to see her drinking something that looked so vulgar.

She surveyed the evening scene around her. Even out of season, it was a far cry from her infrequent and timid outings to her local pub in Archway with Jo, her nice and sensible but rather dull librarian friend, and the occasional addition of her Bear Necessities colleagues Kate and Becky, who always got embarrassingly raucous when drunk. When out with this gang, Imogen had always felt out of place and rather bored; she was always the first to leave.

This, however, was a radically different experience. Yes, she did feel like a tourist and an outsider and she *really* wished, rather late in the day, that she'd paid more attention to French lessons at school. It was one thing to read her way calmly through a recipe with the help of a dictionary; quite another to decode what her colleagues were now saying in quick-fire French made even less intelligible by their sing-songy southern accents. She could only follow a tiny fraction of the conversation and certainly didn't feel confident enough to join in. But, despite her qualms and shortcomings, Imogen was quietly and unobtrusively enjoying herself.

La Sirène was packed with locals who all appeared to be having fun – and Imogen found the atmosphere contagious. The *patron*, a good-natured man called Bernard, was joking behind the bar with his team of waiters while the café's sound system pumped out upbeat French pop songs. Meanwhile a steady stream of gleaming sports cars cruised in front of the café before turning right towards the pine grove and, beyond it, the town's small casino. It was all rather glamorous and exotic.

Around Imogen's table sat most of the Boustifaille staff. Besides Bastien, her kitchen comrades now included friendly Régis, who looked like a shaven-headed and tattooed teddy bear, the short, stoatlike and intense Emmanuel (known as Manu), and Pierrot, who was tall, skinny, pony-tailed and not terribly communicative. Front-of-house was represented by waitress Larissa, a pretty, sassy local girl with long dark hair, and waiter Patrice, a shy bespectacled young man fresh from the Ecole Hôtelière de Lausanne, one of the most prestigious catering colleges in the world.

Monty had missed Imogen terribly at first when she went to work, but had now become accustomed to Daphne taking care of him while his mistress was away. As for

Imogen herself, she was learning the ropes. She was now familiar with the lengthy Gallic ritual of hand-shaking and kisses on the cheeks – *bises* – that were an obligatory prelude to every service. It had been tricky at first to remember whom to kiss and whose hand to shake, and Bastien's help had proved invaluable. A mortifying disaster had been avoided one evening when her friend had cleared his throat meaningfully just as she had been about to plant two kisses on Monsieur Boudin. It was enough of an honour to be allowed to shake her boss's hand; beyond that the great man was entirely out of bounds.

Another ritual was the way, every night after service, the staff piled into La Sirène to let off a little steam. There were exceptions to this rule: haughty maître d' Jean-Jacques and Sidonie, the elegant female sommelier, usually went home to their respective families. On those evenings out everyone was pleasant enough to Imogen, with the exception of Larissa, who seemed determined not to warm to her. Then again, Imogen thought, perhaps Larissa's bad temper had something to do with the atmosphere of the Boustifaille kitchen.

Tonight, for example, service had been especially tense. The atmosphere had not relaxed for a single minute. Imogen was beginning to understand a little more about what it meant to keep such a place going, not just as a purveyor of delicious food, but also as a successful business.

'It's quite a small restaurant, this,' Régis had told her as they shared a break in the courtyard. 'I've worked in much bigger places with four times the number of covers, and it was intense but they didn't have a reputation to maintain like Boustifaille. People are always waiting for you to fail. I think Chef is finding it hard at the moment.'

It was true, Imogen reflected, that Monsieur Boudin always looked exhausted and rather glum. Not once had she seen him smile. The rest of the staff also looked pre-occupied. Did this, she had later asked Bastien in hushed tones, have anything to do with the fact that the dining room was very rarely full?

'Well,' her friend had replied after a quick, anxious look in his boss's direction, 'bookings *have* been down for quite a while.'

'What do you think the problem is?'

'The economic climate, in part. People think twice about spending a lot of money on a meal. But mostly it's to do with . . .' Bastien had broken off and inclined his head to the side, indicating Monsieur Boudin himself.

Walking back from the larder, Manu, who'd overheard them, had paused to say in an undertone, 'I don't think he enjoys the challenge any more. He's not hungry for success in the way that you have to be to stay at the top.'

'I can't understand that,' Dimitri had said coldly, leaning in. 'Now if this were *my* restaurant . . .'

'But it's not yours, is it?' Imogen had interrupted, annoyed at his arrogance.

'No,' he'd replied, staring her down, 'but one thing's for sure: I'm looking around to see what's out there.'

'You're looking for another job?' Imogen had whispered, at once impressed and scandalised. 'Really? But you're doing so well here.'

'It depends on what you call doing well. Boudin doesn't

know what I'm worth.' And with this further display of arrogance, Dimitri had turned his back on her.

'Anyway,' Manu had resumed, looking at Bastien, 'it's really beginning to affect everyone's morale. Jean-Jacques has been with Boudin from the beginning, and he looks like he can't take much more. And look at Larissa. Bastien, you remember how funny she used to be? A real ray of sunshine. Now she hardly smiles any more.'

Bastien had nodded, his face set, and looked across at the new *stagiaire*.

'I'm sure it's just a blip.' Imogen had smiled encouragingly. 'Things will get better, you'll see.'

Manu had glanced at her dismissively, shrugged and walked back to his station.

Imogen sighed. All her colleagues, even the friendlier ones, still treated her like a negligible junior: a *gamine*, a slip of a girl who could have no notion of sophisticated French cuisine, especially since she was, after all, a foreigner. All this rankled, and crucially she was still doing *zero* cooking. It was insanely frustrating.

As was her habit, Imogen kept these feelings of dissatisfaction to herself, only opening up a little when on the phone to Di. 'It's wonderful to be here, of course,' she had told her friend, 'but I'm not getting anywhere. I'm not sure that Monsieur Boudin has any use for me at all.'

'Talent will out, dear,' Di had replied briskly. 'If you're capable of cooking professionally, then you will. And don't be too shy about it – tell them you can cook!'

A lot of it came down to confidence, Imogen realised. If only she were more like Hildegard or her mother, or even like Thea! Although – or perhaps because – she belonged to a family of confident exclaimers who naturally knew how to take centre stage, Imogen found it incredibly hard to assert herself. Di was right: she needed to unlock that part of herself, but how? Imogen wondered despairingly. It wasn't easy to change her ways after a lifetime of keeping a low profile.

'Well, dear, you're not at home now,' the cake-maker had said firmly, concluding their phone call. 'Remember that I'm happy to help take care of things here. This is your chance to speak up and spread your wings. Goodbye, dear. Oh, and please *don't*, whatever you do, bother about any silly requests from this end.'

And indeed, since her departure, Imogen had been deluged with text messages and emails from her siblings demanding to know where their red socks were or whether there were any plasters in the house or how to clean a marker-pen stain. Di had recently intervened and as a result the requests had slowed down to a trickle. Now all Imogen needed to do was to stop feeling guilty about not responding to their requests – something else requiring a sea change in her behaviour.

The sudden electronic din erupting from the café's vintage pinball machine – adorned with a glamorous picture of Batman, the caped crusader – made her look up from her drink. There was Dimitri, hogging the machine again and, typically, keeping himself to himself while his colleagues all sat together. He stood with his back to the others, slim-hipped in his black jeans and T-shirt, his hair slick with sweat from the heat of service. Imogen watched him jerk his body and slap the sides of the machine with palpable aggression to propel the pinging ball with the flippers, swearing under his breath, alone in a world of robotic utterances and red, blue and white flashing lights. And then, as she shifted in her seat, looking away with a bit of an effort, she wondered once again why she found the spectacle of these macho pinball antics so intensely, well, *irritating*.

There was only one person intrepid enough to attempt conversation with Dimitri at La Sirène: local DJ Cheyenne, who liked to drop by before his gigs in Saint-Jean and its environs. Cheyenne – whose real name was the more prosaic Stéphane – was in his mid-thirties, with shoulder-length dishwater-blond hair, crinkly blue eyes and a general air of sun-kissed, carefree *joie de vivre*. He usually wore oversized surfer-style gear – bright T-shirts and cut-off denims – with the latest trainers. His trademark was the spray of feathers he liked to stick in his bandana, Native American-style.

Cheyenne, Bastien had told Imogen on a previous occasion, was an inveterate ladies' man or *dragueur*: he tried it on with every pretty girl he met and (like a doctor, which was exactly how he would have put it himself) was *always* on duty. There was, Imogen had observed, something of a Jekyll-and-Hyde quality about him: when addressing a man, he was very much the superstar DJ, dispensing cool handshakes and talking expansively about gigs and remixes. When faced with a woman, however, he dropped his voice to a low, caressing purr while turning up his sunny charisma, which was not negligible, to its maximum. This systematic approach tended to yield fairly good results, the pay-off, as Bastien had concluded with reluctant admiration, for leaving no stone unturned.

Tonight, after a brief conference with Dimitri, Cheyenne came over to the table where the rest of the Boustifaille staff were gathered. Ignoring all the men to begin with, he said flirtatiously, 'Ah, Miss France. Et Miss Angleterre,' making lingering eye contact in turn with Larissa and Imogen before kissing them both on the cheeks. Imogen accepted this with reasonably good grace although she had never actually *spoken* to Cheyenne. But when in Rome . . . As his hair brushed her face, she heard the fizz of static electricity, not for the first time: the DJ's synthetic extensions could get a bit crackly.

'So listen, guys,' Cheyenne began, once seated. 'We're having a special night next week at the Koud'Soleil.' He pulled a sheaf of acid-coloured flyers out of his yellow messenger bag and started to hand them out. 'Yours truly will be on the decks. It is going to be *mental*! We are going to *raise the roof*!'

Imogen had walked past the Koud'Soleil – an exotic-themed establishment decked out in woven grass and bamboo – a few times but had never been inside. It didn't look like her kind of place. But since Cheyenne was sitting immediately opposite her, she dutifully studied the bright orange flyer: the dress code for the event was 'Tahiti Paradise'; ladies would, of course, get in free. Following DJ Cheyenne's '*super-hot, super-tropical*' set, there would also be a Tahiti-style floor show. Hmmm. It all sounded pretty scary to her. Suffice it to say that she and Monty would be safely tucked up in bed in their stinking cell long before any of this kicked off.

Looking up again, her eyes met those of Dimitri, who had rejoined the group and sat down next to Cheyenne. She held his unsmiling gaze for a minute, then looked away, flustered. To give herself something to do, she glanced again at her flyer and noticed that a tropical buffet was included in the evening's programme of delights.

'I didn't know the Koud'Soleil was also a restaurant,' she said, turning to Bastien.

'It isn't,' he replied. 'They get a caterer to do the food for these events.'

Catering, Imogen pondered, private catering. She frowned as an idea began to sketch itself in her mind, tentatively at first, and then with greater clarity. She wanted to cook, didn't she? And for the time being, she wasn't being given the opportunity to do so at Boustifaille. Granted, in between bouts of Claustrophobic Nights in Smelly Box and Getting Shouted At By Hulking French Boss, she wasn't left with that much free time, but perhaps something could be done all the same?

Well, she thought, sitting up straighter, why not? She would speak to Daphne about it and ask her advice. The *pâtissière* had a small but very decently equipped kitchen in her flat, perhaps she'd be prepared to let Imogen use it? She could advertise in local shops and offer to do small jobs – children's parties, that kind of thing – and see if anything came of it. It was worth a try. Anything would be better than nothing – and she was *itching* to cook. Again she met Dimitri's eyes and, her mind still on her plan, automatically smiled at him. He smiled back, and she was surprised to feel a small but definite thrill of excitement. *Oh, dear*, Imogen thought, confused. *What was that?*

9

Imogen was standing alone in the Boustifaille kitchen in the T-shirt and boxer shorts she usually wore only to sleep in, when suddenly Monsieur Boudin marched in with a live, honking goose on a lead. As she stared at him, dumb-struck, he placed the animal in her arms and snarled, 'So you think you can cook? Well, you show me what you are capable of! Make me the *crumble de foie gras à la bergamote* RIGHT NOW! Make it PERFECTLY! WITH YOUR BARE HANDS!'

What? The foie gras crumble? But . . . that's just impos-sible, a panicked Imogen thought as her eyes met those of the goose.

Meanwhile, in his impatience, her boss started running up and down the length of the counters, hammering them with his fists. This made an unbelievable racket, and while asking herself how on earth she was to caramelise the berg-amot jam to the exact required degree of *blondeur* with her bare hands, to say nothing of the horrific goose-liver conun-drum, Imogen hared after him, crying, 'Stop! Please stop!' and trying to make herself heard above the frightful din caused by the disturbed and anxious goose.

'Please, *please* stop that noise!' she whimpered for the hundredth time, and opened her eyes. There was Monty, licking her face and staring at her with concern – had she been shouting in her sleep? – and beyond him, the stuffy interior of her car, with every window rolled up.

Of course. Now she remembered. Tonight she had gone home, after the usual outing at La Sirène, feeling rather low. Her catering ad, posted over a week ago in the window of Daphne's shop and on the supermarket noticeboard, had been met by deafening silence. By contrast, her stay in the restaurant's barracks had been made even more of a trial by the proximity of a night-club that made the walls of her room thump in time to its techno tunes until the small hours of the morning. Tonight it had all seemed too much to bear and, as she and Monty once again surveyed their grim little abode, Imogen had shaken her head and immediately stepped out again.

Blinking sleepily at Monty in her car, she felt wonderful relief at first that the foie gras crumble challenge had been nothing but a nightmare. Then she realised that the banging hadn't stopped. It sounded like somebody knocking on the window. She scrambled up into a seated position and stared, bleary-eyed, into the street. Daphne Blanding stood there, flanked by the American man from the bookshop, Mitch. Imogen wound the window down and felt the welcome caress of fresh air on her face.

'Hi, Daphne,' she said sheepishly. 'Hello,' she added, addressing Mitch, who looked resplendent in a baby-blue cashmere jersey, pale pink linen trousers and Basque-style laced-up espadrilles.

'Imogen?' Daphne looked puzzled and worried. 'Are you all right?'

'I'm fine.'

'Would you mind stepping out, dear? I'm getting a crick in my neck with all this bending.'

Imogen unlocked the door and got out, followed by Monty, who stared at Mitch's espadrilles with delighted surprise before edging a little closer to inhale their exotic scent.

'Were you proposing to spend the night in your car?' Daphne asked, raising her elegantly plucked eyebrows.

'Well . . .' Imogen replied, shuffling a little. 'The truth is that I just couldn't face my room tonight. This is a quiet street, so I didn't think anyone would notice.'

'*I* noticed you,' Mitch said. 'I saw you sleeping in your car so I went to get she-who-must-be-obeyed.'

'Imogen, we can't have you sleeping in the street! Whatever next? You should have told me that there was a problem with your room.'

'I didn't want to whine about it,' Imogen said, embarrassed. 'It was so kind of you to get me this job, and . . .'

'Nonsense,' Daphne said, sounding exactly like her sister Di. 'There's whining about things, and there's simply being practical. In order to do your job, you need to be able to sleep properly.'

'That means not in a car, you little beatnik,' Mitch chipped in with mock-severity.

Imogen nodded penitently.

'Now, Imogen,' Daphne said, 'I can offer you my sofa bed, but I have to say that it couldn't possibly turn into a permanent arrangement.'

Imogen sighed. 'Of course.' Daphne's pretty flat was about the size of a pocket handkerchief.

'Say, you a poet?' Mitch asked suddenly.

'Er, no,' Imogen replied, confused. 'Just a cook.'

'I gotta ask,' he said, after smoothing his slim moustache thoughtfully. 'Ever wrote a novel or a play maybe? Or . . . a political pamphlet?'

Daphne smiled. 'Mitch has a room above the bookshop,' she explained. 'For a writer in residence.'

'It's a sanctuary for any writers who happen to be passing by. I don't charge for it. You'd be safe there. Unlike here. Sound good to you?'

Imogen stared at him. The possibility of escape from her noisy and smelly cell was extremely appealing. 'Er, yes, it does,' she admitted.

'But then you don't write, so I dunno. I've got to have a few rules,' Mitch resumed, folding his arms. Imogen yawned. She was very tired and it was all beginning to sound a little complicated.

'I know,' Daphne said briskly. 'Why don't you put her down as an aspiring cookery writer? You do write recipes down, don't you, dear?'

'Yes, sometimes, I—'

'Quite so. Mitch? Would that fit your exacting criteria?'

'I guess,' he said with a shrug.

'Then it's settled,' Daphne said, taking Imogen's arm. 'Thank you, Mitch, you're a treasure. Say thank you, Imogen.'

'Thank you very much,' Imogen echoed. 'It's very kind of you to take me in.'

Mitch ground his teeth with theatrical emphasis. 'That's OK.'

'No, really, I—'

'Drop it, will you? I'm not so good at touchy-feely stuff. Even after decades of therapy. Right – let's go get you settled in,' he said, addressing Imogen. Then he peered at Monty, smiled and added, 'And your little *dawg*, too.'

10

'An old married couple and their surprisingly hirsute son – that's us,' Mitch intoned without turning around, as Imogen and Monty joined him in the kitchen for breakfast after two weeks in residence. 'Mr and Mrs Smith – or do I mean S'Mitch?'

'Good morning,' Imogen said, smiling at his paisley-print dressing-gowned back.

'Ditto.'

As she opened the bread bin and placed a loaf of raisin bread into Mitch's waiting hand, he wordlessly reached above her head for the Rice Krispies she wanted. After an initial orgy, Imogen had discovered that, much as she loved croissants, she couldn't actually eat them every day of her life, so she had decided to switch to cereal, like most French people. She gave Monty a biscuit, automatically took one step back to allow Mitch access to the electric juicer, and while he pressed enough oranges for a mammoth jug (for himself) and an ordinary-sized glass (for her), she set the table and got two yoghurts out of the fridge. After which they sat down side by side and began to eat.

She and Monty were by now happily ensconced in the bookshop. Their room was large and airy, lined with books and furnished with a vintage roll-top desk, an opulent brass bed, bright kilim rugs thrown over the terracotta floor and,

Monty's favourite touch, a comfortable battered sofa. The window gave out over a cluster of orange trees that grew so close that Imogen only had to reach out to touch them. If she leaned out, she could catch a glimpse of the sea.

A lovely room of her own at last – that was more like it. Imogen felt like she'd been released from jail, sprung from her airless, smelly sleeping quarters in Boustifaille's barracks, and also, even more wonderfully, from memories of the 'dorm' she had shared for so many years at home, having to listen to her siblings' squabbles when she wasn't being ordered around and generally treated like an unpaid servant.

Upstairs at the Paperback Wonderland Imogen could relax, chat to Monty, dream up new recipes which she would then test out in Mitch's kitchen and simply be herself. She'd also started reading her way through the bookshop's typically quirky selection of cookery books, interspersing them with French translations of Georgette Heyer in the hope that this would help broaden her vocabulary. So far she had got through *Quadrille de l'Amour* (*Bath Tangle*) and *Adorable Sophie* (*The Grand Sophy*), greatly helped along by her familiarity with the stories. That was the lovely thing about romantic novels, Imogen thought. However well you knew that the happy ending was coming, it was always so much fun to see how you got there. Next on her *en français* list was her all-time favourite, *Venetia*.

As for Mitch, you really had to take him as you found him – he *was* given to spectacular tantrums and mood swings. Not for nothing did he refer to his own room, which was downstairs from hers, as his boudoir. The word, he explained, was derived from the French verb *bouder*, which means 'to sulk'. Since she and Monty had moved in, there had been a few 'oh-dear-dark-shades-worn-in-the-house-best-to-leave-well-alone' days, but that was all right, as Imogen had received many years of training in how to be unobtrusive.

On the other hand, Mitch was scrupulous about his young guest's privacy and though he showed appreciation, in his sardonic way, of her polite efforts to help around the house, there was absolutely no attempt on his part to turn her into a skivvy – a highly unusual experience in Imogen's book.

But what had clinched things for her had been Monty's reaction to the move. After much solemn sniffing, the little dog had made it clear that he felt at home here. And though they were both given to a certain spikiness, Monty and Mitch had really taken to one another. 'We give each other diva respect,' was how Mitch liked to put it. 'He's a diva. I'm a diva. We don't compete for centre stage.' Mitch had taken over the task of looking after Monty when Imogen was at work, which was every day except Wednesday, when the restaurant was closed.

Imogen had now got to know a little more about Mitch, who always held forth like an acerbic rattle at breakfast time. It was getting easier not only to follow his idiom – which had become somewhat exaggerated over the years, due to being cast as the token American in Saint-Jean – but also to take it in her stride. Deadpan statements such as 'Just tell Boudin to blow it out of his ass' (in response

to another one of her outpourings) no longer disconcerted
her.

Mitch originally came from a place called Noo Yawk
Ciddee – which Imogen realised pretty soon was synonym-
ous with New York – but had lived on the Riviera for so
long that he had almost come to feel like a native. 'First
time I came here,' he'd once reminisced, 'was with a dear
friend, when I was a very young man. He was much older
and knew *everybody*. I thought it was the most beautiful
place I'd ever seen.'

Mitch did not stoop to name-dropping – there was no
need. By then Imogen had had a chance to examine the
black-and-white photos hanging in the bookshop and had
spotted a gawky, rakish teenage Mitch in a stripy jersey
sitting on sailboats and restaurant terraces amid devastatingly glamorous company that might include Gary Cooper
and Picasso, for example, or Brigitte Bardot and Sophia
Loren.

'And then, you know, he – my friend – died.'

'Really?' Imogen had said, startled. 'That's terrible. I'm
sorry.'

Mitch had looked away and shaken his head briskly,
dismissing her words, then gone on, 'Shit happens, you
know. But I stayed on. I fancied myself as a beat poet in
those days and I started to buy books. My friend had also
left me his library, so before long I had quite a collection.
Then I bought the shop – only selling paperbacks at first,
and then branching out, but the name kinda stuck. Things
went great for a while. I settled down again with someone
and I guess I was what you'd call . . . happy. But then,

I dunno, I couldn't help myself and I just . . .' His face had darkened and he'd broken off, staring at the wall behind Imogen's head.

Since he'd discovered her love of Georgette Heyer, Mitch had been openly scathing of Imogen's taste in literature, and she had put this down to his own, far loftier leanings – he appeared to read almost nothing but obscure poetry and political biographies – but it now dawned on her that his wholesale rejection of romance might have something to do with his difficult personal history.

After his disclosure, Mitch's eyes had appeared to refocus on Imogen. He'd smiled and gone on with confidential emphasis, 'And *after that*, I discovered my frog-queen side.'

'What's a frog queen?' she had asked, intrigued.

'Well –' Mitch had said, smoothing his pencil moustache '– it's a man who enjoys the company of other men, especially if they're French . . . Smatturh?' he'd then asked, producing one of his distinctive New York sounds.

'Oh, nothing's the matter!' Imogen had been well aware of having blushed furiously, but had been unwilling to admit to Mitch that sex talk of any kind always made her feel slightly uncomfortable, perhaps because the whole thing remained, to her, something of a closed book.

Mitch had arched his eyebrows into circumflexes, and then, with a worrying instinct for picking the topic she most wanted to avoid, started quizzing her about her love life. There wasn't much to say: she had gone through school as The Invisible Girl, notching up an impressive series of unrequited crushes on inaccessibly glamorous boys. The very few relationships she'd actually had – the longest of

which had involved Benji, a slightly overweight and mono-
syllabic mature student who worked weekends at the local
delicatessen, and, more recently, Phil, a well-meaning but
terminally unexciting librarian she had met through her
friend Jo – had been characterised by distinct lack of enthusiasm on both parts. The sex had been lacklustre to say
the least. At least Benji and Phil enjoyed her cooking, but
that hadn't been enough to stop both liaisons from petering
out after a few months.

The truth was that cooking had always given her far
more satisfaction than men. At least with food you knew
where you were – it was comfortingly real. Romance was
fine in books, but when actually experienced it so often
turned out to be full of treacherous illusions – a fact that
had been amply demonstrated by her episode with Adrian.
And the less said about that, the better.

'I'm single at the moment,' she had said curtly in response
to Mitch's questions. 'That's it.'

Mitch had looked at her sympathetically. As a gay man
of a certain age who had lived through less liberal times
than these, he knew camouflage when he saw it. It was
plain to see that Imogen was a lovely girl with zero sexual
confidence, who was doing her damnedest to disappear
behind the most tragically unflattering clothes he had seen
in a long time. There was *something* about the girl, though,
something that wanted to be unleashed but didn't quite
know how. At least not yet. He recognised that, too.

This morning, however, while she ate her cereal, Imogen
became aware that Mitch was staring in her direction with
steely disapproval.

'What's wrong?'

'*Some*body could do with some grooming. And soon. You know what I mean?'

Imogen was mortified. So she'd never been particularly meticulous about shaving her legs – so what? And how could Mitch possibly have noticed through the table?

'Do you have X-ray vision like Superman?' she asked defensively.

'What? Oh, I don't mean you, you little knucklehead. I mean *him*.'

Imogen looked at Monty, who peered back at her through luxuriantly bushy eyebrows.

'There's this little salon called Bonjour les Toutous,' Mitch resumed, in between sips of coffee. 'I guess that would translate as "Hello Doggy", or something like that. Anyway, the owner is called Faustina. She's great – a pocket cutie. She's from Corsica, like Bonaparte, and boy, does it show! Go to her. She knows her dogs. She's *the* best.'

11

Though she was now on smiling-and-nodding terms with quite a few local dog-owners, Imogen still felt like the odd one out among them in one important way. Saint-Jean's dogs were taken out to be *paraded*, and she had yet to see a scruffy-looking animal. The dogs of Saint-Jean started the day trotting smartly alongside their lissom mistresses who jogged on the promenade before breakfast, when the sky was still pale over the silvery sea, and ended it as fully fledged members of the cocktail-hour crowd, bathed in the glow of neon lights and often sporting a rakish bandana that matched their owners' gleaming pastel-coloured Harley-Davidsons. Imogen, on the other hand, walked Monty purely in order to exercise him.

Well, perhaps it *was* time for Monty to have a Côte d'Azur makeover. As for his mistress, Imogen told herself firmly that she was fine just as she was. Which was not to say that she didn't keep noticing how insouciantly French girls carried themselves, many of them exuding a playful, confident femininity that she felt herself incapable of emulating.

As she pushed open the white door of Bonjour les Toutous, Imogen wondered briefly how on earth Faustina managed to prevent her four-footed customers from abandoning their treatments to follow the intoxicating lure of the butcher's shop next door. Customers would willingly queue outside Boucherie Ponceau for ages and, once inside, nod along to Madame Ponceau's spirited monologues about the state of the nation in order to secure some of her famous and delicious roast chicken.

But once inside Bonjour les Toutous, an air-conditioned capsule that smelled only of shampoo, all thoughts of chicken were forgotten. The interior was covered from floor to ceiling in white rubber, with two white cubicles equipped with grooming tables and hoses. In the midst of all this whiteness, the liquorice-coloured Monty looked like a punctuation mark on a blank page.

Soothing electronic trance music played in the background. Imogen looked around, impressed by this demonstration of confident monochrome chic. In her customary sludge-coloured combats and baggy T-shirt, she felt suddenly underdressed and out of place. Fleetingly, she wondered again how it would feel to be as well groomed and feminine as the girls of Saint-Jean, then dismissed the thought with a shrug. That sort of thing simply wasn't her style. Practicality came first.

A young woman a few years older than herself came out from behind a counter. To match the décor, she was clad in immaculate white (a coat, trousers and clogs that put Imogen in mind of a glamorous dentist – she instinctively scanned the room for a drill, but couldn't see one). She wore her black hair parted in the middle and pulled back into a severe-looking chignon. She had a heart-shaped face and large green-brown eyes over which dark eyebrows stretched assertively, a small pug nose and a full mouth made glossy by an uncompromising shade of red. All of these combined into a vision of forbidding Mediterranean beauty. Mitch had been right to describe Faustina as a 'pocket cutie' – she may have been tiny, but she carried herself with such chin-up confidence that Imogen knew that she was in the presence of innately regal charisma.

'*Bonjour*,' the salon's owner said, looking at Monty and ignoring Imogen. Not easily intimidated, Monty returned her stare, sniffed, then barked challengingly.

'*Bonjour*,' Imogen replied nervously. After which, lacking the precise vocabulary required, she indicated Monty and made snipping motions with the fingers of both hands. God, French was hard.

'But of course. And maybe *Montee* needs a bath too?'

'Yes, please,' Imogen said automatically before blinking with surprise and asking, 'But how do you know his name?'

'This is a small town.' Faustina said with a tiny smile. 'You know, most people here call you "the girl with the little black dog" or "the Tintin girl" because of Milou, Tintin's dog, you know?'

That must be Snowy's French name, Imogen thought.

'I too have seen you on the promenade,' Faustina went on. 'But it was Mitch who told me your names.'

'Oh.'

'Normally, I detest Americans,' Faustina said coolly, 'but Mitch is *sympa*. He makes me laugh. OK. You can go away and come back later, if you like. Or wait here, if you prefer.' She indicated a cluster of white leather beanbags next to which a pile of women's magazines sat on a clear perspex shelf. 'Help yourself from the kitchen. There's some herbal tea in the cupboard on the right.'

Imogen took one step towards the compact open-plan kitchen, then stopped, biting her lip. This was the point at which things usually turned ugly.

'I should warn you that Monty never enjoys being groomed. And he hates the bath part. Perhaps I should go in with you to help hold him down.'

Faustina pouted and narrowed her eyes. 'No, no, that's my job. Don't worry.' She bent down, fearlessly unbuckled Monty's collar, handing Imogen the lead, and started to walk towards the washing booth.

'*Tu viens, Montee?*' she asked in a relaxed sing-song, without even turning around.

Imogen raised her shoulders to her ears and closed her eyes, waiting for the usual explosion of canine outrage, but nothing came. After a minute or so, she opened her eyes again and watched, astonished, as Monty allowed Faustina to lift him up into the bath.

'Good boy, Monty,' Imogen murmured as she opened her copy of Escoffier's *Ma Cuisine* and began to study the recipe for a brilliantly complex chicken dish called *suprêmes de volailles Jeannette*.

She looked up anxiously from time to time, but was gratified to see that, while Faustina spoke to him in low, soothing tones (in what she later discovered was Corsican dialect), Monty meekly held out his head for the noose of the grooming arm, then allowed himself to be brushed, combed and trimmed. Meeting his mistress's eyes, he gave the odd joyous little yelp, as if to say, 'I *like* this one!'

An entranced Imogen had almost finished reading all about *nymphes à l'aurore* (a dish of frogs' legs served in a champagne jelly streaked with chervil and tarragon leaves that gave a poetic imitation of water weeds) when Faustina said, '*Voilà!*' and Monty – looking 'tailored' to within an inch of his life and quite the Côte d'Azur canine – trotted back into his mistress's arms.

Oh Monty, you do look the part! Imogen thought, before looking down at her scuffed trainers and adding to herself, *Unlike me.*

12

The ultra-sharp, freshly made-over Monty drew many approving glances along the promenade. *Welcome to the club*, other dog owners appeared to say as they greeted Imogen (though they still managed to convey implicitly polite reservations about her own appearance), while the dogs themselves expressed the same sentiment by means of effusive sniffing.

She and Monty were heading back into town when Imogen's mobile phone rang. It was an unknown number, and the voice that spoke was American, female and quite young.

'Pahdon me,' the person said in a lazy drawl. 'Am I speaking to Imogen Peach?'

'Yes.'

'Mah name is Bunny. Bunny Doucet.' Imogen narrowed her eyes slightly – she had never before heard anyone speak so *extremely slowly*, stretching out every syllable. 'I was thinking maybe of having a party at my house,' Bunny went on, 'and your advertisement caught my eye. I was wondering if you could see your way to helping me with the catering.'

'Of course!' Imogen said, her heart giving an enthusiastic leap. A client – hurrah! 'When is your party?'

'On Valentine's Day. In a couple of weeks.'

Imogen exhaled slowly. She must be careful not to bite off more than she could chew – and this sounded like a bigger commitment than a children's party. Then she thought of Daphne – Daphne would surely help.

'May I ask how much experience you've had of this kind of thing?' Bunny Doucet asked.

Hmmm. A slightly tricky question, because in truth Imogen had never catered such an event. But it was best to be upfront about it.

'Well,' she began hesitantly, 'I learned the ropes with a friend who makes special-occasion cakes and . . . I also used to cook children's lunches at a nursery in London—'

'London?' the American girl interrupted. 'Hey, wait a minute. Are you British?'

'Yes.'

'Oh, I love the British!' Bunny somehow managed to exclaim without changing her languid tempo. 'I love everything British! And I love your Queen – she is just darling, really gracious and classy.'

That seemed to do the trick. Imogen's national credentials having been established, Bunny Doucet gave Imogen her address and, as she listened to the American girl's directions, it slowly dawned on Imogen just where her prospective client lived. And that, she thought to herself, was pretty intriguing.

The next day, when Imogen and Monty presented themselves at the gate of the mysterious turreted villa on the seafront, the blue shutters had been opened. As Bunny came around the overgrown garden path to greet them, Imogen took in her wide-eyed, friendly face with its gap-toothed smile and her neat, glossy blonde bob held in place with a pink-and-green grosgrain ribbon. Pristine in her jeans and crisp stripy shirt, the American girl looked incredibly alert. *So the abandoned villa does, in fact, house a beauty*, Imogen thought, *but she certainly isn't sleeping.*

Bunny shook Imogen's hand and then, kneeling in front of Monty, said, 'Well, hello, sir!' Monty regarded her calmly, and then, unable to resist her sunny charm, placed his paw in her hand.

'What a *precious* little dog,' Bunny mused as they made their way towards the house. 'He must be the love of your life!'

'He certainly has been,' Imogen agreed with amused ruefulness, 'so far.'

Over a glass of sweet iced tea – Bunny seemed unaware that it was winter, however temperate, and that Imogen might have welcomed a slightly warmer drink – the American girl explained that she had come to Europe to find herself, away from the strictures of her family.

'I *love* my mama with all my heart, you know, and my daddy too,' she said, kicking off her navy-and-brown dock-side shoes and examining the almond-pink polish on her toes with obvious satisfaction. 'But they are very traditional and I'm a free spirit. I want to do something real unconventional.' She paused, playing with her string of pearls, then added, 'You know, Daddy had chosen somewhere much bigger, but I said *no*, Daddy, *this* one, because I thought it'd be real good for me to live in such a plain little house.'

An odd thing to say, Imogen thought privately, glancing back at the solidly bourgeois dwelling that stood behind them – Bunny had hardly elected to move into a shack.

'I've only just arrived, you know. The house was a bit bare – it needed a few pretty things. I've been antiquing in all kinds of darling little towns. Meanwhile I've been staying in that little hotel in the hills,' she said, gesturing upwards. This, Imogen knew, was the luxurious Hôtel de la Plage, where many Hollywood stars chose to stay during the Cannes film festival. It was renowned as a model of understated barefoot chic, but, again, was hardly a shack. Bunny's daddy must be a man of some considerable substance.

'I came here to live the simple life,' the American girl went on, her eyes shining. 'And, you know, I always say that the most important thing is to have plenty of flowers everywhere. They're so essential to gracious living.'

Imogen nodded politely, thinking to herself that Bunny might be hideously spoiled and shallow but that a customer was a customer. Aloud she said, 'So . . . What sort of thing did you have in mind exactly? A classic French buffet? Or something different and a bit more Mediterranean? Italian food, perhaps? Or Spanish? Or Moroccan? Or do you want a full-on Valentine's Day theme?'

She braced herself slightly, if Bunny insisted on heart-shaped foods only, it would mean somehow getting hold of a whole arsenal of tins and moulds. The American girl sat up in her garden chair and opened the pink plastic folder that she had brought out on the same tray as the drinks. It was crammed with lists, drawings and pages torn out of magazines.

'I see you've done a bit of planning,' Imogen said.

'Why, yes,' Bunny said earnestly. 'Mama always says there's no point in entertaining unless you put of bit of effort into it! Sooo,' she went on, turning a page, 'this here is my little old guest list. There'll be a whole army of Americans! And that's the brochure from the fancy dress shop. Oh, I *love* fancy dress, don't you? I find it real . . . transporting! I just know that it'll make my Valentine's Day party extra-extra-special. Just look at this, isn't it darling?' she said, opening a catalogue and holding it up. Imogen leaned forward and peered at pictures of panniered gowns, riding coats and breeches.

'Oh, you're having an eighteenth-century costume party?' she asked.

'Yes. It's so pretty and romantic!' Here Bunny digressed at length about a film called *Valmont* starring Colin Firth, which had clearly made a strong impression on her and was set in just the period she had in mind for her party. 'Where I come from in the south,' she went on lazily, 'we have a real soft spot for historical re-enactments. I've been to dances as Scarlett O'Hara I don't know how many times. But I wanted this to be different – *really* French. The French understand romance, don't they? And the thing is that *I* have French ancestry – our name used to be spelled d'-O-u-s-s-e-y. Don't you think that's wonderful?'

Really, this girl was unbelievably ditzy, Imogen thought.

Aloud she said, 'Absolutely,' adding briskly, 'Let's talk about the food,' in the hope that her hostess would get back to the point.

'Well, Imogen, I don't care one bit if it's not real *authentic* food from the eighteenth century,' Bunny said, looking at her seriously. 'All I want is oodles of pink, you know, for Valentine's. And also green. I *adore* pink and green as a colour scheme.'

Having managed, for a few minutes, to compel Bunny to discuss actual practicalities such as the number of guests and her budget, Imogen promised to let her have an estimate in the next couple of days and took her leave.

'Next time you come I'll show you my studio,' Bunny said as they shook hands at the gate. 'It's got the most darling view of the bay.'

'Are you an artist?'

Imogen could just imagine the sort of thing someone like Bunny would paint – most probably sentimental land-scapes, or pictures of 'darling'-looking animals.

'Why, yes!' Bunny said perkily. 'That's really why I'm here. My family *adore* the arts, but at the same time they don't think artists are quite nice, so I'm afraid I told them a fib, which I know is wrong, but otherwise I would never have been able to get away to Europe.' She leaned towards Imogen conspiratorially. 'My mama approves of genealogy, so I said I wanted to go and find out about our French ancestors.'

'How strange,' Imogen said pensively, and began explaining her own family predicament, especially in regard to her mother.

'Well, I declare! We're just like two peas in a pod!' Bunny cried, squeezing Imogen's hand.

Up to a point, Imogen thought soberly, but did not say it.

13

'Have a taste of this,' Bastien said very early next morning, as he handed Imogen a small piece of bread topped with fresh tapenade, a paste made from black olives.

'It's gorgeous,' she said, wolfing it down. 'Thanks.'

It was only half past five and she was grateful for nourishment. However, the atmosphere of the wholesale food market alone would have filled her with energy, generating as it did a sense of pulsating, feverish excitement. She had expressed an interest in Boustifaille's suppliers and Bastien had invited her to tag along and see for herself. She stood on the spot, entranced, feasting her eyes on enormous banks of fruit and vegetables and crate upon crate of glittering fish – huge silver sea bass, John Dory, exotic-looking orange-red scorpion fish – and deep blue lobsters.

'*Ça va?*' Bastien said, shaking hands with the fish merchant. '*Des écrevisses, s'il vous plaît.*' As the man carefully placed two boxes of live crayfish in his outstretched arms, Bastien added, for Imogen's benefit, 'This is for a beautiful starter shaped like a flower – purple beetroot petals surrounding a chunk of crayfish.'

Buoyed up by the intoxicating influence of her surroundings, Imogen found herself overcoming her shyness and launching into a – slightly halting at first, but increasingly lively – discussion with the fish merchant about the merits of Mediterranean oysters versus those from Brittany, Normandy or the Bassin d'Arcachon. This involved saying the word *huître* repeatedly – quite a challenge with its 'r' sound and tricky vowels. But she ploughed on all the same. Who cared if her pronunciation wasn't quite right? She felt in her element and – a heady feeling, this – like a proper chef talking to a supplier.

'This is for you,' the fish merchant said, briskly opening an oyster and handing it to her with a smile.

Thanking him, Imogen tipped the whole thing into her mouth and smiled – there on her tongue was the taste of the sea, pure and simple. It occurred to her suddenly that it was silly, really, not to have been swimming even once since her arrival. Surely she could find time to exercise.

Later, following Bastien into the sauna-like environment of the market greenhouses, she pulled off her fleece and tied it around her waist. *God, it was hot*, she thought, fanning herself discreetly and ineffectually with her shirt.

'This is it – the real thing,' Bastien enthused, turning around to face her and carefully placing in her outstretched hand something that looked like a large, soft tomato. 'An authentic *kaki* grown in the hills above Cannes.'

It was, Imogen saw, a sharon fruit.

'We use it at Boustifaille to make a vanilla-scented chutney we serve with duck *magret*. It also makes great tempura, you know, with prawns. Be careful, Imogen – don't squeeze too hard. It's really, really ripe. Why don't you just eat it?'

Biting into yielding flesh and wiping sweet-acrid juice

off her chin, Imogen reflected that although she'd always vaguely thought of Bastien as nice-looking, today he looked really, *really* attractive, perhaps because he wasn't smiling quite as much as usual and because it was clear that he was just as passionate about food as herself. Besides which, his eyes were a beautiful shade of blue and it was rather nice to have him, as now, standing very close to her in the warm greenhouse. *Yes, yes, but he is my colleague*, she told herself, taking a deep breath, *and it really isn't professional to dwell too much on his good looks. It would only end up interfering with our relationship at work.*

After completing their purchases, they went off to load the van together, surrounded by a crowd of other purposeful food pros. While Imogen stood with her back to Bastien, considering how many crates of vegetables she could conceivably lift at once, she suddenly heard him call out, '*Oh, putain!*'

Perhaps as a reaction to the greenhouses' tropical atmosphere, to say nothing of her own recent train of thought, Imogen found herself reacting with uncharacteristic hot-headedness. *Putain*, she knew, meant 'whore'. Was he actually addressing her? How *dare* he? And what on earth had she done? Really, Frenchmen were animals! Carried away by a scorching wave of anger, she swung round, tapped Bastien on the shoulder and, when he turned, slapped him resoundingly across the face.

He stared at her round-eyed for a minute, rubbing his cheek vigorously, then burst out laughing. 'Wow! What was that for?'

Imogen drew herself to her full height and crossed her

arms. 'I'm sorry but nobody talks to me like that. It's completely unacceptable.'

Bastien narrowed his eyes, mystified, then his face cleared. 'But I wasn't talking to you! I swore because I dropped the crayfish – look.'

There was an overturned box of crustaceans at his feet. 'Oh, sorry,' Imogen stammered. 'I thought—'

'It's only an expression, you know,' Bastien said kindly. 'Everybody says it when they're angry. I'm sorry if I shocked you.'

'Oh Bastien, your face!' Imogen said penitently, noticing the angry red mark left by her blow. She had never, ever hit anyone in her life. What had got into her? The unaccustomed heat? The enticing displays of food? The bustle of the market? Or something else, something that emanated from Bastien himself? 'Wait here, I'll get some ice from the fishmonger.'

As they sat side by side in the van, he allowed her to hold an improvised ice pack to his face, smiling at her with a certain amount of irony. She smiled back and accepted a swig from the bottle of water he offered her.

'It's going to be a nice day,' he said, wiping his mouth with the back of his hand. 'The sun's coming out.'

Imogen nodded, glancing sideways at his bare, tanned shoulder, and thinking that Bastien really was sweet-natured not to hold her ridiculous outburst against her. Still feeling rather warm after her visit to the greenhouses, she tucked a strand of damp hair behind her ear. Bastien watched her do this, then turned his attention to the small fruit he was carving open with a sharp knife. This had been the last thing on their shopping list – the passion fruit needed for Boustifaille's signature pudding – *millefeuille au fruit de la passion* – layers of paper-thin, crisp, sweet pastry and exquisitely foamy vanilla custard mixed with sharp, crunchy pulp.

Bastien scooped a bit out with his finger and chewed critically. 'They're perfect,' he declared. 'The flavour is incredible. You want a taste?'

'Yes, please,' Imogen said, reaching out.

'No, wait,' Bastien said, holding his hand up. 'Let me help you.'

Imogen watched him put a little more fruit in his mouth, and then, before she knew where she was, pull her to him and kiss her.

It had been such a long time since her last kiss – with that charming fraud Adrian – that although she could distinctly hear the sound of ringing alarm bells she did not push Bastien away. Instead she kissed him back and the first thought that came into her head was that the delectably tart passion fruit would indeed make a glorious pudding.

'I've wanted to do this from the first day I saw you,' Bastien said between kisses. 'Did you know?'

'No,' Imogen replied truthfully.

'So,' he smiled. '*Encore?*'

'Yes,' she murmured. '*Encore.*'

They kissed again, and she was aware of intensely mixed feelings. The electricity generated by her mistaken slap had obviously stirred her up in a funny kind of way. Bastien's skin smelled sweet and the feel of his caressing hand gliding on her collarbone got her own skin tingling deliciously.

But at the same time other thoughts rushed into her head, tutting disapprovingly and demanding that she stop this nonsense at once. What on earth are you doing getting involved with someone from work? one voice hissed indignantly. Do you want to ruin your chances of getting anywhere at the restaurant? You don't even *know* him, another one pointed out. OK, you may share a love of food, but do you have anything else in common? *Please* don't be an idiot and let yourself be lured by another pretty face, pleaded a third. Remember Adrian and what a teeth-grindingly awful let-down *that* turned out to be.

Mid-kiss, Imogen came to her senses. She placed both her hands flat on Bastien's chest and pushed hard. He pulled away and looked at her questioningly.

'Shouldn't we be getting back?' she said. 'They'll be wondering where we are.'

He looked at his watch, raised his eyebrows and started the engine, muttering '*Merde, merde, merde*,' as he did so. As they picked up speed, he put one arm around her shoulders and pulled her close to him. He didn't appear to want to talk, so Imogen, at once relieved and not excessively relaxed, sat silently in his embrace all the way home. Her face expressed nothing but extreme surprise at her own unprecedented behaviour.

14

'*Bonjour, Montee*,' Imogen heard someone say directly behind her as she stood in the dog food aisle of the supermarket. She turned around and stared at the strange girl who'd addressed her dog.

'Hello?' she said uncertainly, taking in a voluminous mane of black curls, a full face of make-up, an extremely skimpy outfit whose bright colours – orange, shocking-pink and gold – pinged and fizzed wildly in front of her eyes, the whole thing finished off with a pair of oversized turquoise-studded hoop earrings vaguely reminiscent of the ones sported by the Laughing Cow.

'Hi, Imogen,' said Faustina, the dog groomer, stepping aside to reveal a large Dobermann who peered inquisitively at Monty. 'This is my dog Cristiana. Were you looking for something for Montee?'

'Oh, just a few treats,' Imogen said, doing her best not to stare goggle-eyed. Faustina looked like a completely different person out of her chic minimalist uniform, and Imogen knew full well what her mother's verdict would be in the face of such vulgarity – the mock-Latin family short-hand *Commonus tartus*. 'Like maybe something with bone marrow,' she wound up in an undertone.

'These are good,' Faustina said, reaching up for a pouch and handing it to her. 'Cristiana loves them.'

'Thanks. So how are you?'

'Really well. I'm off to the tanning salon after this. And then I'm having a pedicure.'

Imogen nodded, privately thinking that Faustina really needed to get out a bit more. There was more to life than grooming.

'And how is your job at Boustifaille?' Faustina asked as they walked down the aisles together, slowly filling their baskets. 'Does it get a bit boring?'

'Why boring?' Imogen asked, with a disconcerting sense that the tables had suddenly turned.

'I think cooking is *so* boring. I just can't be bothered with it. I mean, we have to eat, of course, but there's so much more to life.' In answer to Imogen's quizzical look, Faustina considered for a moment before saying, while counting on her fingers. 'Dancing. And also shopping and holidays. And sex, of course,' she stated with a clinical candour that struck Imogen as distinctly French. 'I never get bored of *that*.'

Walking away from the supermarket after saying goodbye to Monty's dog groomer, Imogen was pensive. Of course there was more to life than food – and though she herself had never given much thought to the vital importance of dancing, shopping and holidays, she recognised that Faustina must have a point about sex. But only in theory. Because in Imogen's experience no sexual encounter had ever felt really, really right. At best, it had felt like quite strenuous exercise, leading . . . nowhere. Perhaps she just wasn't that interested in the sexual side of things. If she thought about it, the only pleasurable sensuous experiences she'd had were from contact with food.

Monty barked, pawing at her shopping bag. After posting a barrel-shaped, marrow-filled taste of heaven into his mouth, Imogen smiled affectionately at the solemn, bristly and bewhiskered creature who, as Bunny had pointed out, was the love of her life.

In the window of a newsagent, she noticed a picture of Brigitte Bardot on a magazine cover, next to a headline about animal rights. Perhaps she herself would end her days like the reclusive star, who lived nearby in St Tropez with a huge menagerie of dogs, cats and ponies because she found their company so much more rewarding than that of human beings.

Briefly she glanced at her own reflection and sighed. A figure in chunky ankle boots, knee-length khaki shorts and an oversized T-shirt, selected in an attempt to conceal her shape, looked back at her. She might share Bardot's love of animals, but she had rather less to offer in the sex kitten department.

'Little and large, no?' Faustina commented a few days later, as Monty trotted ahead along the seafront, followed at a respectful distance by Cristiana. Imogen nodded, laughing. The two dogs made an unlikely couple.

'But I think they will actually get on OK,' Faustina went on, 'when they know each other better.'

Imogen reflected that this statement also applied to herself and Faustina. Yes, just like their dogs, they did look like chalk and cheese, but Faustina, perhaps because she was so different from herself, was interesting. There was also something very likeable about the air of quiet, serene authority that emanated from her. They were, Imogen realised, on the verge of becoming friends.

The two girls had run into each other again early that morning outside Bonjour les Toutous, and Monty and Cristiana had immediately managed to get their leads tangled. In the course of conversation, Faustina asked whether she had left a boyfriend in London, and Imogen explained the ongoing and still unresolved Bastien situation.

Following their kissing episode in the van, they had gone out for a drink *à deux* at Bastien's suggestion. On this occasion they had both been rather tongue-tied. Imogen had spent her time chattering about the restaurant while inwardly wondering how to bring the conversation around to telling Bastien the truth – it had been sweet to kiss him because he *was* sweet, but that she wasn't sure she wanted to take things any further. Bastien had listened to her on the subject of food without interrupting, nor had he made any romantic suggestions. Then, as she got up to leave, interpreting his silence as a tacit recognition that the kiss in the van had been a one-off and a mistake, he had suddenly invited her to the local cinema on the following Wednesday, and Imogen had been unable to think of a plausible excuse not to go.

This next outing hadn't particularly eased things between them, and Bastien, possibly discouraged by Imogen's deliberately rigid and uninviting body language, had fidgeted throughout the film, only mustering the courage to take her hand as the end credits began to roll. As a date, it couldn't have been said to be a success, but the film itself had certainly given Imogen some illuminating insights into the French mindset when it came to affairs of the heart – and body.

The film Bastien had taken Imogen to see was a French comedy entitled *C'est compliqué, la vie!* (or, as Imogen translated in her head, *Life is complicated!*) and starring all kinds of photogenic Gallic actors she had never heard of. The film was lively enough, but Imogen had some trouble following the plot. This was mainly due to the absence of English subtitles. She also found the story's goings-on dizzying, for various reasons. The first was the sheer amount of on-screen sex or, more precisely, *cinq-à-sept* action (a French concept Mitch had had to explain to her after she came home that evening – the five-to-seven-p.m. slot being prime time for adulterous trysts) and good-humoured wife-swapping. Nor could she keep track of who was actually supposed to be with whom, especially as all the actresses were nubile, dark-haired, doe-eyed creatures who did a lot of running up and down Parisian streets in improbably high heels in order to get from one hotel room to the next. It was, frankly, almost impossible to tell them apart.

The whole thing struck Imogen as terrifically French, especially the post-coital philosophical musings. In one scene, for example, a man said sententiously to one of the dark-haired women (who might even be his own wife – Imogen wasn't sure) as they sat in bed sharing a cigarette, 'Of course we never really know anything about *love* – only about *ideas* of love.'

As she watched the breathless comedy of errors – a series of set pieces that involved slamming doors, mistaken identities and hurried exits through the fire escape – unfold and resolve itself into a satisfactory happy ending where every Jack was paired off with his Jill, at least until next time, Imogen thought that surely this sort of thing has almost no bearing on real life? Surely the road to true love doesn't have to be this convoluted? *Or if it does,* she concluded, *then I really don't stand a chance of ever finding the way.*

Then, when she and Bastien had exited the cinema, still holding hands, Imogen had gently extricated herself and tried to let him down as gently as she could, explaining that she needed time to 'think about things'.

'But the thing is I don't think I've cleared the air at all,' she told Faustina, winding up her tale. 'He tries to hide it but he's upset. I shouldn't have let him kiss me in the first place.'

Faustina nodded, looking straight ahead. 'Those things can be complicated. I'm also having a bit of difficulty at the moment with a man. My mother always says: "*Un basgiu par fórza un vale una scorza.*" In Corsican, this means that a kiss taken by force is not worth a piece of fruit peel.'

Bastien certainly hadn't kissed her by force, Imogen reflected, but she knew what Faustina's mother meant. Privately she blamed her slightly reckless behaviour on the atmosphere of the market: all that raw produce had turned her head. She had acted completely out of character, almost like some sort of food nymphomaniac. She shrugged and looked up at the radiant blue sky. It was also possible that the climate was having some sort of transforming influence on her. She felt less buttoned up here, both literally and emotionally. Perhaps this atmosphere of freedom was partly why so many Americans and British people flocked to the Riviera year in and year out.

Anyway, when it came to Bastien, it wasn't a good idea to get involved with a colleague, however attractive, she told herself, all the while trying to brush aside the image of the ever-irritating Dimitri, which for some reason kept intruding itself into her head.

Meanwhile, Imogen's personal drama was being enacted against a wider professional one – that of the kitchen at Boustifaille. At break time, on her way out to the courtyard, she would sometimes peer into the dining room through the porthole; not only was it often half-empty, many of the customers also seemed tense because they were being kept waiting for their food. One recurring feature of service, Imogen had noticed, was the number of mistakes made in the orders.

And the reason for this state of affairs appeared to be Monsieur Boudin himself and his oddly self-sabotaging behaviour. The chef would often waste precious time overseeing and criticising the preparation of a dish by someone as competent as Bastien while ignoring a crisis at the other end of the kitchen until it was too late to intervene. Or he would suddenly decide to change the whole presentation of a dish at the last minute, throwing the kitchen into a panic and delaying the order.

'What *is* his problem?' Imogen had asked Bastien in an undertone, after witnessing one such incident.

'I'm not really supposed to talk about it,' Bastien had begun, confidentially, 'but Monsieur Boudin's had a run of bad luck. First, about two years ago, his wife Honorine left him.'

'Oh dear. What happened?'

'Well . . .' Bastien sighed. 'At the time, nobody knew why she'd gone. And then, last year, Boudin had a terrible falling-out with his brother Marcel. They were partners in the business and Marcel managed the financial side very well, while Boudin was in charge of the creative side of things. Anyway, they'd always had rows but this time it got out of hand. We all heard them screaming at each other. And it turns out that Marcel and Honorine had been . . . you know . . . for quite a while.'

'That's terrible,' Imogen had said, horrified. It was worth remembering that the whole *cinq-à-sept* thing wasn't always fun for everyone involved. 'Poor Monsieur Boudin!'

'Marcel and Honorine left town together. It was a terrible blow to Boudin's pride. And since then, he has refused to admit that he's having trouble managing on his own, that he's in over his head. We're all quite worried about him, and about the future of the restaurant,' Bastien had wound up, looking into her eyes.

Imogen had held his gaze sympathetically for a moment,

and then, watching his face soften and sensing that he was about to ask her out again, she had looked away, feeling like a complete coward, and turned her attention back to preparing leeks.

15

In the course of subsequent walks with their dogs, Imogen began to get a more complete picture of Faustina. Her new friend was, Imogen discovered, an unusual combination of the practical and the romantic. She had grown up in a small village in Corsica, a beautiful, unspoiled island off the French Mediterranean coast. Imogen had once put her foot in it by calling Faustina French and been sharply corrected: Faustina was Corsican, and most definitely *not* French. Though Corsica was, in fact, part of France, Imogen had made the same sort of mistake as calling a Scottish person English. It was clear that Faustina's distinctive sensibility had been shaped by her background. For example, she believed in ghosts.

'The dead come back to visit,' she once declared. 'And you can tell when they're in the house because their tread is so much heavier than that of the living.'

Many times Faustina had sat in the kitchen at home, listening to those unmistakable footsteps overhead. 'Ah – that'll be your aunt Angelica come to have a look at her old room,' her mother would say, while calmly getting on with preparing supper.

Likewise, the dead enjoyed the odd visit from the living, and as a child, on All Saints' Day, Faustina had regularly shared a picnic of liver sausage and figs with her grandmother – a wizened lady who, like all older women in the village, always wore black from head to toe – as they sat companionably on the graves of departed family members and kept them updated with local gossip.

Imogen had also learned something about the peculiar sexual politics her new friend had absorbed while growing up on the island. On the one hand, a glittering head-to-toe femininity was expected of Corsican girls, but on the other, it must be accompanied by as hostile and chilly a manner as possible.

'Where I come from,' Faustina had explained crisply, 'if you smile at a boy in public, it's like saying that he's had his way with you on a hillside.'

'But that's just ridiculous!'

'Maybe, but that's how it is. So you get used to not smiling at men – to smiling as little as possible, in fact. It saves trouble.'

In that sense, and regardless of her sentimental attachment to her roots, Faustina's move to what she referred to as 'the Continent' had been tremendously liberating. The only trouble was, as Imogen soon discovered, she hadn't come alone.

Imogen first met Enzo after one of these early morning walks, when Faustina asked her to hold the fort in the salon while she ran upstairs to get changed in time for her first appointment of the day – a neurotic poodle.

Imogen let Monty and Cristiana out into Faustina's tiled courtyard, which was filled with large pots of mimosa and bougainvillea, and then noticed somebody standing outside the shop: a young man clad in a leather jacket, artfully distressed low-waisted blue jeans and biker boots, but, oddly, minus a poodle.

She walked over to let him in, and noticed with a small shock that he was without a shadow of a doubt the most beautiful man she had ever seen – tall, dark and blessed with the sort of chiselled features she associated with statues of Greek gods. Before she could compose herself, she found herself grinning at him like an idiot, then exhaling a feeble '*Ah . . . bonjour.*'

He did not smile back, but instead asked, '*Elle est là, Faustina?*' while fixing her with large, liquid black eyes. His upper lip, she noticed, was the shape of a perfect Cupid's bow; his lower lip was a plump, voluptuous cushion. Good God. As Imogen opened her mouth to gurgle something in French, she heard the sound of Faustina's white clogs clattering down the stairs.

'Ah, there you are!' Imogen said brightly, turning to face her friend.

Faustina stopped in her tracks, then drew herself up and said, 'Enzo,' in a flat, cold tone of voice.

'*Faustina – cume stai?*'

'*Va bè.*'

The pair stood glaring at each other in silence for a moment, and then, with a slight movement of her head, Faustina signalled to Enzo to follow her into the court-yard, closing the sliding glass door behind them. Imogen busied herself with making a cup of tea, but although she couldn't make out a single word she couldn't help noticing that some sort of passionate argument was under way. Enzo appeared to be asking something with great urgency, while Faustina did a lot of mutinous head-shaking and foot-stamping. Eventually, he hooked a finger around the gold chain she wore around her neck, scrutinised it and gave her a triumphant smile before opening the sliding door and striding out of the shop without a backward glance.

A minute later, Faustina came back in.

'Are you OK?' Imogen asked.

'Yes, of course. Men are just impossible!'

'Mmm. Yes, I suppose they are.' Imogen paused, then, unable to contain her curiosity, asked, 'Was that your boyfriend?'

'No. Well, in a way. Enzo and I are – used to be – childhood sweethearts. You know, we grew up in the same village and he always liked me, and he is—'

'Very, very good-looking!' Imogen blurted out.

'Yes, I suppose he is,' Faustina said impatiently. 'I'm so used to him that I don't really notice any more. No, the problem is that he wants to get married, and I do not.'

'Oh.' Imogen digested this. 'Why not? I mean, he's *so . . .*'

'Handsome, yes.' Faustina considered. 'He's always been a real macho, very dominating – you know, in bed,' she explained, with a fleeting smile of reminiscence.

Imogen nodded, unable to think of a sufficiently sophisticated rejoinder. Faustina might only be a few years older than herself, but in terms of sexual experience she was in an entirely different league and made Imogen feel like a wide-eyed goody-two-shoes.

'And that was fine,' her friend resumed as her smile

faded. 'But now he wants to run my life as well, and if we got married it would be the end of –' She gestured around her shop '– all this. He would want us to move back home – to the village. When he and I came here to work we were very young and I wanted that too, but not any more. We broke up a lot of times and then got back together again, but . . . He was happy just now, because he saw that I'm still wearing the little cross that he gave me. And I do love him, of course, just not in the way he wants me to.' She sighed and tucked her gold chain inside her white coat. 'He'll have to get used to it.'

Just then, the shop's door opened and in walked a lady carrying an elderly, apricot-coloured poodle.

'*Bonjour, Madame Verdier*,' Faustina sang out, reverting to her professional manner. '*Bonjour, Coco!*' she added brightly, addressing the dog.

'*Say*,' Mitch said, peering at Imogen with interest when she walked into the Paperback Wonderland with Monty, 'what happened to you?'

'Nothing,' Imogen said, surprised.

'You look different than usual . . . Oh, wait a minute, wait a minute,' he went on, his face clearing. 'One word, two syllables: *En-zo*. Am I right?'

Imogen burst out laughing. 'Yes, you are. I met him a moment ago. But how did you—'

Mitch snorted knowingly. 'You have that post-Enzo glow.'

'That post-Enzo *what*?'

'Oh, don't be embarrassed. Everybody feels that way.'

'He *is* quite lovely,' Imogen admitted.

'Are you kidding? He's a panty-dropper.'

'If you say so,' Imogen said, smiling, before making her way upstairs to her room. Something else was bubbling at the back of her mind. *Adrian.* The delightful shock of Enzo's good looks had taken her right back to the beginning of her greatest infatuation – in the rather smelly upstairs room of a north London pub where, a little over a year ago, she had gone to see *Hamlet* performed by Hildegard's theatre company.

From his first black-clad appearance, Imogen had found her eyes irresistibly drawn to the lithe fair-haired man who played the Danish prince. Not only did he have the loveliest face but also, she thought as she watched him slouch and prowl about the stage, the most compelling *presence*. He spoke the verse so clearly and beautifully that Imogen – not usually a fan of Shakespeare – thought she saw at last what all the fuss was about.

It had taken a certain amount of suspension of disbelief to forget the humble pub surroundings and imagine instead that this was the castle of Elsinore, but she had found herself immediately under Adrian's spell. She gazed at him avidly when he came on to deliver 'To be, or not to be' through doors marked 'This way to the Ladies'. She shivered as he spoke of 'the pangs of despised love'; the cruelty of his 'To a nunnery, go' made her start as though he'd been addressing her personally, and by the time he lay down at Ophelia's feet, snarling, 'That's a fair thought to lie between maids' legs', Imogen was in such a heightened state that she didn't know whether to run away or dash onto the stage and embrace him.

Hamlet, she found out from the programme notes, was a twenty-five-year-old named Adrian Spry. Oh, to be in love with someone like that – a brilliant, charismatic actor! By the time the play reached its conclusion and almost everyone on stage was dead, Imogen could barely stay in her seat – she was dying to meet him. And meet him she did, in the bar downstairs where he came in for a drink, still wearing his stage make-up.

'So . . .' he purred, scrutinising her from beneath kohl-rimmed eyelids. 'The gorgeous Hildegard has a little sister. I had no idea!'

Imogen didn't remember saying much to him that evening but her idol must have interpreted her body language correctly because – much to Hildegard's puzzled amusement – he lost no time in asking her out. There had been five near-identical dates: pre-theatre suppers during which Adrian talked at length about his career while an entranced Imogen listened, followed by disconcerting experimental fringe shows featuring his friends. Each time, he took her home afterwards and gave her a big stage-worthy kiss, crushing her in his arms. Surprised not to find herself as physically transported as she'd expected, Imogen consoled herself with the fact that Adrian was still undeni-ably in a different league from her past lovers. Benji had been an irredeemable groper and Phil an exhausting face-eater.

It was at the end of their fifth date that he asked her

back to his flat – the only possibility, since Imogen could hardly take him home to the 'dorm'. At last, she thought, delighted, at last they would really be together.

The night of passion that she had been dreaming of went as follows. Once in his bedroom, Adrian removed her clothes, then his own, and placed them, carefully folded, on the back of a chair. He then joined her in his bed and performed the sexual act for an approximate duration of three minutes – though perhaps four was closer to the mark. Afterwards, he had a shower and suggested she do the same. When a very subdued Imogen returned to the bedroom she found her prince sitting up in bed, now clad in flannel pyjamas and sporting a sleeping mask on his forehead. A slim red velvet cushion lay on his lap. Climbing into bed, Imogen eyed the cushion warily. What was it for?

'All set?' Adrian said, giving her an absent-minded, sleepy smile.

'Um, yes.'

Her dashing lover lay down on his side, pulled the sleeping mask into place and slipped the cushion between his knees.

'It's the only way I can sleep,' he explained, covering them both with the duvet. 'Night-night.'

The light went out. Imogen's eyes and mouth remained open in sheer astonishment. Then she felt him stir by her side. Her heart leaped. Now he was going to take her in his arms, hold her close, devour every part of her body!

'Imogen?'

'Yes!'

'Your breathing is really, really loud. Could you try to make a little less noise?'

Thus had ended Imogen's last sexual encounter.

16

One day, as the two girls were walking their dogs along the seafront, Faustina turned to Imogen and said seriously, 'You should come shopping with me, just for a short while. You work hard – you deserve to relax.'

Imogen frowned hesitantly. Shopping was one of Faustina's favourite activities, whereas she herself had never enjoyed it. *She's right, though*, Imogen thought, *I could do with a bit of relaxation*. She'd been entirely focused on her work, even using her free Wednesdays to teach herself how to cook a few of Boustifaille's dishes at home, which she had mastered to the point where she could make them unaided from start to finish.

However, her attempts to get Monsieur Boudin to let her demonstrate these fresh new skills had fallen on deaf ears. As Bastien stood nearby, looking on encouragingly – which was very sweet of him under the circumstances – she'd launched time after time into her painstakingly rehearsed little speech of self-promotion while realising that her boss, who stood with his arms folded and his eyes fixed on a point beyond her left shoulder, snorting from time to time, had his mind on other things. And sure enough, he'd automatically waved her back to her station. Yesterday, the same thing had happened again and Imogen, by now quite annoyed, had raised her voice – not something she did as a rule – to get his attention.

'Please, Chef!' she'd cried. 'Daphne Blanding thinks that you could do with a girl in your kitchen. Don't you think she has a point?'

Then, astonished at her own audacity, she'd instinctively taken a step back in case a furious Boudin decided to launch himself at her like a rocket.

'Daphne . . .' Monsieur Boudin repeated, and his eyes appeared, for the first time, to focus on Imogen properly. He smiled at her. He was really rather handsome, Imogen noted, when his face relaxed. But afterwards, reverting to his listless and drained expression, he'd shaken his head, saying, 'Not now, *petite*. It's not a good time.'

Staring at her friend through enormous heart-shaped sunglasses, Faustina went on earnestly, 'Or we could just go and sit on the beach for a while. You know, unless you start to sunbathe soon, you're going to end up with a brown face and a white body.'

Imogen shrugged, though she had in fact noticed the beginnings of this phenomenon. 'Oh, I don't mind that. And anyway, I'd much rather swim than sunbathe.'

Faustina wrinkled her small nose. 'The water is still a bit too cold for me, but you can go in if you think you'd enjoy it.'

'The problem is that I didn't pack a swimsuit when I left home.'

Faustina laughed incredulously, gesturing at the glittering sea. 'You come to a place like this without a swimsuit?

That's what we should go shopping for.'

Imogen thought for a moment, then nodded. This would be shopping with a practical purpose. She'd get herself a dark, plain one-piece. And maybe a tight swimming cap. Good sturdy goggles. Yes, that would do very well.

Turning tail, Faustina marched her towards a boutique on the promenade. Imogen looked up at the shop's name – Ultradonna. *Ultra-woman?* Oh, dear. That didn't sound like her kind of place. She glanced anxiously at the headless female torsos modelling barely there garments in the window. On the threshold, she shied like a horse.

'Look,' she said, 'I really, *really* don't want to go in here! It's . . .' What? What was it? Too French. Yes, that was it. It was far, far too French. 'Isn't there a normal sports shop?'

'A sports shop?' asked a puzzled Faustina. 'What for? I thought you wanted a swimsuit.'

'Yes, but—'

'All I ask is that you have a look around. This is the nicest shop in Saint-Jean, trust me.'

Trust you? Imogen thought. *Certainly not – you have the most terrible taste!* Out loud she said, 'Maybe I should go to Nice another time – they must have a big shopping centre with a sportswear place? This is a tiny shop, and buying a swimsuit is a bit . . . private.'

Faustina sighed, then said with a touch of asperity, 'OK. But when you see somebody drowning in the sea, you don't walk away thinking, "Ah yes, it's a private thing, I leave her alone." You dive in and pull her out.'

It took Imogen a moment to understand this unflattering

image – Faustina obviously didn't think much of her dress sense. This was a nightmare, but all she needed to do was keep her head down, show no interest, and Faustina would soon find out that she was a lost cause. The owner came out to greet them.

'*Salut, ma belle!*' she said, kissing Faustina on both cheeks. '*Salut, Mylène!*'

Intensely tanned, with long hair dyed bright red and a fox-like countenance, Mylène wore a skin-tight pink velour tracksuit. She smiled at Imogen, gestured for her to come in and, wasting no time, said, 'You are a 90 C, no?'

'I don't know my French size. I usually take a medium. Do you have anything like a one-piece, very simple? In black, and with—' she placed her hands on her throat '—good coverage?'

Mylène stopped in her tracks, a skimpy gold-lamé triangle bikini in her hands. She and Faustina exchanged a look.

'I knew it – you're not taking this seriously,' Faustina remonstrated, stamping her tiny foot.

'I am!'

'Then try this on. It's so pretty and it looks so beautiful with a tan.'

'I happen to prefer more practical things,' Imogen said carefully, not meeting anybody's eye. 'Because of my figure.'

Both Mylène and Faustina raised their eyebrows interrogatively.

'Which is not that great,' Imogen concluded under her breath.

'And who told you that?' Mylène demanded to know.

'My mother. She's always advised me to dress discreetly, not to look vulgar.'

Faustina burst out laughing. 'You mean because she thinks your figure is vulgar?'

'Yes,' Imogen said sadly. Her mother's exact words, coolly and repeatedly delivered, had been, '*Please*, darling, no cleavage – it's so dreadfully common' and 'It's *such* a shame your bottom sticks out like that, darling.'

Mylène was silent, and Faustina stopped laughing. 'Imogen, that's terrible,' she said.

'Of course it's not!' Imogen cried, feeling inexplicably upset. 'Why do you say that?'

Faustina pouted, narrowing her eyes. She only spoke again when Imogen had composed herself. 'OK. But do *you* like the way you dress?'

'Yes,' Imogen said decisively. 'I like to be comfortable.'

Faustina smiled. 'That's quite funny.'

'Why?'

'Because actually you never look very comfortable.'

Before Imogen had time to deny this, Mylène said meditatively, 'I wonder if it's a question of underwear. Do you wear the right kind of bra?' She reached across and pulled on Imogen's T-shirt so she could have a good look at her bra strap.

'What are you doing?' Imogen exclaimed indignantly, just as Faustina shrieked, '*Oh my God!* What's that?'

'It's none of your business,' Imogen said crossly. 'But if you must know, it's a sports bra.'

'A sports what? You did some jogging this morning? Or you've joined the Saint-Jean fitness club?'

'No – I always wear sports bras! They're so much more practical.'

Faustina hid her face in her hands while Mylène's own face slowly set into a mask of incredulous horror.

Imogen went on regardless, her voice getting higher. 'I've never worn anything else. They're very reasonably priced. I buy them in packs of two, and—'

'Stop! Stop!' Faustina cried. 'I can't take any more!'

Embarrassed, Imogen fell silent.

'*Bon, alors,*' Mylène said gently, after returning the scraps of lamé to their place on the rail. 'Maybe we try a compromise. What about this one?'

She held up a green-and-white gingham bikini for Imogen's approval. Actually, Imogen had to admit to herself, it wasn't too bad. It even looked like it might conceivably contain her anatomy.

'Yes – it's charming, that,' Faustina decreed. 'Very Bardot.'

'OK, I'll try it on,' Imogen said wearily. Anything to get Faustina off her case.

In the changing room, she quickly undressed, put on her very first bikini, and then and only then looked at herself in the full-length mirror – not something she ever did if it could be avoided. Her chest didn't look as disproportionately large as usual. That was good. It was a bit weird to see her thighs exposed, but not as traumatic as she had feared. She turned sideways: her stomach was flat and her waist looked quite small. How very odd.

'*Alors?*'

Mylène and Faustina popped their heads around the curtain to have a look. They both smiled.

'That's great – really *balnéaire*,' Mylène said, nodding approvingly.

'What's that?' Imogen asked worriedly.

'It means it's a good look for the seaside,' Faustina translated. 'Except . . .' she hesitated, frowning.

'Absolutely!' Mylène said. 'She needs a trip to the tanning salon.'

'I'll see if they can fit her in today,' Faustina said, reaching for her mobile phone.

'Stop!' Imogen said. 'No tanning salon!'

'But—' Faustina interjected.

'No, I mean it,' Imogen said through clenched teeth. Then she had another look at herself and her face relaxed. 'But I'll take the swimsuit.'

17

'See, what I make is these statements in 3-D,' Bunny Doucet said with a perky smile as she sat with Imogen on the Paperback Wonderland's red velvet sofa. 'They're real political.' After tasting a wide array of Imogen's canapés, the American girl had finished perusing the suggested menu for her Valentine's Day party by expressing her full approval and the conversation had now moved on to Bunny's main pastime – her art, which she was hoping to show in a local gallery.

Though her client remained cagey about disclosing precisely what kind of things she made, Imogen was beginning to revise her first impression – Bunny's artworks sounded not so much 'darling' as distinctly odd. The American had expressed a wistful admiration for 'the Shoreditch district of London town' where she had always dreamed of living cheek by jowl with the Chapman brothers and Tracey Emin. Imogen nodded along, but she was finding it hard to associate someone as outwardly prim and proper as Bunny with anything as messy as, for example, Tracey Emin's *Unmade Bed*.

'I'm working on a new series at the moment,' Bunny went on, 'but I'm only at the preparation stage, so mostly it's about handling chemicals.'

'What kind of chemicals?' Imogen asked, intrigued.

'Well, you know, that's my little old secret,' Bunny said, giggling. 'But I'll show you the pieces when they're finished, if you like.'

'That would be great,' Imogen replied, turning around as she heard Mitch's returning footsteps from the stock-room, where he had been closeted when Bunny turned up. It immediately became clear to Imogen, as she introduced them, that Mitch was in one of his difficult moods. Sure enough, he and Bunny did not get off to a great start.

'Excuse me, sir,' Bunny asked politely. 'I don't imagine you'd happen to have any art books in your wonderful store?'

'What do you mean – aahrt books?' Mitch replied, mimicking his customer's drawl and ignoring Imogen's pleading looks. Damn and blast him. If he was trying to lose her that first catering job he was going about it the right way. 'Where are you from, child?' he asked severely.

'Charleston, South Carolina,' Bunny said, beaming. 'And I guess what I mean is contemporary art with a bitty bit of *shock* value, you know?'

Mitch looked heavenward, muttering 'Fiddle-dee-dee, Miss Scarlett,' before heading for the black-spine book room where most of the art books lived.

'He's really nice,' Imogen said quickly, 'when you get to know him.'

'Oh, don't worry. I can handle him,' Bunny replied with aplomb, 'I've met Yankees before.'

When Mitch returned, he plonked a large and colourful tome on the counter and said, 'OK, y'all! Gilbert and George – they make some real *precious* work with their bodily secretions. That the sort of thing you want? Or maybe you wanna call your mammy for advice?'

Obviously, Imogen thought, he didn't take Bunny's professed edginess seriously.

The American girl flicked calmly through the book's illustrations, then said, looking up at Mitch, 'I sure hate to keep imposing on your kindness, sir, but do you have any of Robert Mapplethorpe's photography? Those *wonderful* genital close-ups – you know the ones?'

Imogen smiled a little.

'Yeah – I guess,' Mitch said, disconcertedly smoothing his pencil moustache. 'Anything else?'

'Well, yes,' Bunny said pertly. 'You know what would just tickle me completely pink? Something on Jeff Koons and those pornographic pieces he did with his wife?'

Mitch narrowed his eyes at her, and then turned on his heel to fetch the requested items.

'So,' Bunny said, looking at Imogen, who grinned back. 'Somebody gave me a flyer about a party tonight at this tiki bar – the one with a funny name.'

'The Koud'Soleil,' Imogen said helpfully. 'It means sunburn in French.'

'Oh, it sounds like so much fun. I want to go so badly but I don't have an escort.' Mitch returned, holding up some books for her approval, and when Bunny nodded sweetly, rang them through the till without comment. 'Of course I would ask *you*, sir – as a fellow *American*,' she went on, looking at him. 'But with you being so *busy* and all I wouldn't dream of taking up *any* more of your time.'

'Just try and keep me away from that party,' Mitch

snapped. 'My vintage Hawaiian shirt is crying out for an outing.' He held Bunny's steady gaze for a moment. 'Feisty, huh?' he said, unable to keep a note of approval out of his voice.

18

Turning up at the Koud'Soleil party with Bunny in tow rather than on his own arm didn't appear to have weakened Bastien's resolve, Imogen reflected while holding on to him for dear life during a particularly frantic bit of hip-to-hip dancing on the small, packed dance floor. Hanging from dimly visible bamboo walls – beneath blue neon letters that spelled the words 'Tahiti Paradise' – the carved wooden masks of Polynesian gods looked down on her with what she felt was understandable mockery. Monty, whom she had left watching television with Daphne in her flat, was the lucky one. Unlike Imogen, his dignity was wholly intact.

Meanwhile, she wondered, what was she doing exactly? It had seemed easier, when asked, to dance with Bastien than not – after all, there was far too much noise to be able to talk to him. And what could she possibly have said? Same again? That she wasn't sure about taking things any further? That wasn't what he wanted to hear.

Now the joint was, to quote Mitch, well and truly jumping, and the stiff mai-tai she had gulped down on arrival had done very little to steady her nerves. The lighting inside the Koud'Soleil was so subdued as to barely allow her to see much beyond her own nose – which was currently squashed against Bastien's neck. She disengaged her face as tactfully as possible and looked around, taking in the club's décor, which was tropical with a vengeance.

'Don't you love it?' Mitch had said to her on arrival. He'd made a point of ignoring Bunny for about a minute, before weakening and commenting favourably on the tropical wrap she had gamely fashioned out of a floral-print tablecloth. 'It's like some crazy Hollywood art director's been let loose, like . . .' Mitch struck an attitude, hand on hip, and began to point urgently in every direction. 'OK, people, I'm thinking *Fiji*, I'm thinking *awesome*. We want artificial *palms*, honey, and we want them sprayed *gold*! What's this? Cocktails served in *plain* coconut shells? What are we – *poor*? This isn't some minimalist Ian Schrager joint, you know. Can we *dress* the drinks a little? Give me a plastic lion, a maraschino cherry, a piece of pineapple and a red rosebud! Now, I want *torches*, I want a *fountain*, I want *carvings*! *Thank* you! Now we're talking. Aaaw, God – it still looks *naked*! Where's the *murals*? Where's the panorama of hula girls, people? Come on, come on, *come on*!'

After that, the party had begun in earnest. Bunny had been introduced to the Boustifaille gang, and was now dancing with Régis – a great mover, as it turned out. Imogen was mildly irritated to see that Dimitri, usually so aloof, was joining in for once and dancing with Faustina – a Koud'Soleil regular whose white dress glowed a shade of ultraviolet blue under the strobe lighting. And there was lovelorn Enzo standing at the bar, looking sullen and devastatingly attractive.

On the stage, Cheyenne could be seen in silhouette

punching the air in time with the music – the cunningly crafted medley of Afro disco, bossanova beats and funk promised on the flyer. Larissa, whose long dark hair was crowned with flowers, Hawaiian-style, stood near him.

Suddenly the music stopped; everyone was encouraged to clear the dance floor and take a seat in one of the surrounding bamboo-clad booths. Bastien ordered more cocktails, and Imogen, who was thirsty, drank hers quite fast.

Then, to the sound of syncopated Polynesian music, nine female dancers clad in coconut bras and short grass skirts split to the hip gyrated their way into the room, beaming at their audience from beneath headdresses made of stiff green leaves. Everyone began to clap, even Imogen joined in eventually. Bastien got up, signalling that he would be returning shortly. A moment later, another couple materialised in the booth: an unsmiling Larissa accompanied by Cheyenne, who looked both exhausted and hyper-agitated after his set.

'*Hé*, are you OK?' he asked, leaning over to squeeze Imogen's arm. 'You enjoying the floor show?' he said, gesturing at the performing dancers.

Imogen frowned at him, trying to put her lack of enthusiasm into words. 'Well, it's a little . . . sexist, don't you think?'

'Oh yeah, that whole tropical vibe is super-sexy,' Cheyenne agreed, mishearing. 'Look at Larissa – doesn't she look unbelievable in her sarong?'

'It's just fancy dress,' Larissa said, giving Imogen a cold stare. 'Are you against fancy dress in England?'

'Of course not,' Imogen muttered. Clearly there was no

point in trying to get through to these people. 'But their costumes . . .' She grimaced a little.

'*Hou-là!*' Cheyenne burst out laughing and held up his hands for protection. 'You are *féministe*? Help, I'm scared!'

'No – I don't know.' Imogen said, becoming annoyed. She remembered Dimitri's remarks about the puritanism of the English. Had he been right? Was she just being a prude?

'This is getting a bit deep for me,' Larissa said stiffly, getting up. 'I came here to have some fun. I'll see you later.'

'I'll see you out there, baby,' Cheyenne said, following her with his eyes, before giving Imogen a good-natured smile. 'You know what your problem is?'

'No,' Imogen replied crossly, staring him down. 'What is my problem?'

'You always look so *serious*. You need to have more fun. Did you like my set?'

In truth, Imogen had been too preoccupied with the difficult conversation she needed to have again with Bastien to take much notice of the music.

'Basically I'm still a freak for funk, you know,' Cheyenne went on without waiting for her answer. 'It's a shame I didn't bring my glow sticks.' He stared into her eyes and smiled flirtatiously. 'I'm famous for them. They're my trademark.'

Imogen nodded uncertainly, before turning away to watch the dancers who were now stepping from side to side in formation. The song ended and the troupe of girls exited, still smiling like a line-up of Stepford wives. A popular disco tune began to play, tempting everyone back to the dance floor. Bastien returned at last.

'Sorry,' he said, taking her hand. 'I ran into Larissa.'

As Bastien prepared to slide into the booth on Imogen's other side, Cheyenne jumped out and pulled them both to their feet. 'No, don't sit down, you'll bring down the energy. Come on, let's dance!' And he grabbed Imogen and tugged her into the crowd, leaving Bastien behind. Imogen looked back and waved, then tried, without much success, to keep up with the DJ's complicated moves. To begin with, he'd strutted robotically across the dance floor one way then the other, before moon-walking back and forth. Now he stood waving his arms, hands and fingers in fluid motion.

'Look at that!' he commented enthusiastically. 'It's like a *wave* travelling through my body. You try it. Be loose!'

Imogen did not feel at all loose. While Cheyenne danced around her in circles, popping his chest in and out, she stomped desperately on the spot. She looked over at Bastien, hoping for rescue, but Larissa had returned, and he was now deep in conversation with her. The music selection had become very mainstream – easy-going wedding-disco hits that had everyone on the dance floor waving their arms in the air. Imogen spotted Mitch nearby, jiving with Bunny like an old-school pro.

'Come on, Imogen,' Cheyenne cried gleefully. 'You want to become, like, engulfed by the pulse!'

Just beyond her dance partner stood Dimitri, giving her an ironic thumbs-up and mouthing the words to some silly French song about sea, sex and sun. In spite of herself, Imogen began to laugh. Taking advantage of another one of Cheyenne's complex routines, Dimitri beckoned, indicating that he had something to say.

'What?' Imogen half-shouted in his ear.

'You want to come to the beach with me?'

Imogen stared at him. 'When? Tomorrow?'

'No, now.'

Sitting on the beach in the middle of the night. At this time of year. And alone with him. What a ridiculous suggestion! She would, of course, say no.

'Or maybe,' Dimitri said with that infuriating smile of his, 'you want to stay – to be *engulfed by the pulse*?'

'No – I could do with a bit of fresh air,' Imogen said, heading for the exit. She *did* feel light-headed after drinking those unaccustomed cocktails. Perhaps as a result of this, it seemed tremendously important to show Dimitri that she wasn't a little goose.

19

'I think sex is overrated,' Imogen announced the next day in Mitch's sunlit kitchen. Earlier, she and Faustina had run into Bunny on their way back from their early morning dog walk, and Imogen had invited everybody back for coffee.

Monty did not react to this proclamation, continuing to snooze in his basket instead. Bunny giggled. Faustina rolled her eyes and blew a long plume of smoke out of the corner of her mouth. Mitch said, 'Hmn' absently. He was busy decanting two pots of Petit Suisse onto his plate and delicately peeling off their paper wrapping. Imogen knew better than to disturb him during this heart-in-mouth operation. She waited respectfully while the small cylinders of curd cheese took on the soft contours of a Christmas landscape under a snowstorm of caster sugar.

'Oh, mama,' Mitch gasped, after taking his first mouthful. 'This stuff is the *top*.' He looked at Imogen. 'So you got some action last night, huh?'

'Not really,' Imogen replied, wincing and trying not to think too much about the salt she had tasted on Dimitri's body. 'I'm just making an observation.' In the ensuing, expectant silence, she drew herself up, then said, 'Just because you feel a bit attracted to someone you shouldn't necessarily sleep with them. And, by the way, I *know* you all think that's silly.'

'*I* don't think that's silly at all,' Bunny protested. 'It's always better to wait for the right person.'

'Like Prince Charming, you mean?' Faustina said with a cool, mocking smile. 'Life isn't a fairy tale.' She put out her cigarette on the side of her saucer.

'I'm not sure I agree,' Bunny said calmly, after taking a sip of her tea. 'There's nothing wrong with a happy ending.'

Mitch snorted. 'Ain't no such thing, babe, ain't no such thing.'

Faustina nodded, siding with Mitch against the newcomer. Imogen was silent during this exchange. When she and Dimitri had got to the beach last night, not having spoken at all on the way, she had found herself – possibly under the influence of alcohol or because it was dark or because she was determined to make a point – behaving quite out of character, even more so than with Bastien at the market.

Without consulting him, she had stripped completely and walked straight into the sea, biting her lip when the cold water made her catch her breath. She might as well let Dimitri see that she was made of reasonably stern stuff. Besides, she told herself resolutely, it was far better to be naked than to wear a silly costume like those dancing girls. Dimitri had followed suit, swimming close, but not too close and, oddly enough in view of their antagonistic relationship, those brief moments spent in the glittering water under the stars had felt peaceful and rather magical. Afterwards, he had handed her his shirt so that she could dry herself. Her bracing swim had left her feeling good – powerful and invigorated, but not particularly clear-headed

– so that, once dressed, she had followed him to his room without thinking too closely about what she was doing. It was only later, as Dimitri handed her a cup of coffee and sat back in his chair, eyeing her without smiling, that she had once again begun to feel self-conscious. Then he had said casually, 'I really wanted you just now, in the sea.'

She had blushed, looking down at the table. This was the first time a man had spoken to her this directly.

'But you're with Bastien, so . . .'

'I'm not *with* Bastien.'

'No?'

'No.'

He had hooked his foot around the leg of her chair and pulled her closer. Enclosing her legs between his, he had then leaned towards her until their lips were almost, but not quite, touching.

'So . . .' he had murmured, fixing his eyes on hers, 'if I kissed you now, what would you do?'

Imogen's eyes flipped open, and she looked at her companions across the breakfast table.

Mitch was staring at her. 'Come on – who was it?'

'Dimitri, actually.'

Faustina smiled triumphantly and Mitch, making an exasperated 'Tch' sound, fished in his trouser pocket for a ten-euro note, which he handed to her.

'Which one's Dimitri?' Bunny asked, adding, once he'd been described to her, 'Oh, I know – real cute. And do you like him, Imogen?'

'I don't know.'

She *had* enjoyed the sensation of his hands running up and down her bare back and sliding once in a while beneath the belt of her jeans – that was true. But it was also true that throughout the couple of hours she had spent with him on his bed, kissing with some intensity, she had experienced that familiar feeling of detachment, of floating above her own body, watching the proceedings without really being a part of them.

Faustina gave a small feline shrug and lit another cigarette. 'I went through a phase when I was younger where if any guy showed interest in me I ended up in his bed. It gave me a lot of sexual experience.'

Imogen watched Bunny's face stiffen slightly on hearing this matter-of-fact statement.

'But you, Imogen, you're sensitive,' Faustina said, smiling at her protectively. 'And so it's not something I would recommend to you.'

'Oh, *I* would,' Mitch sighed wistfully. 'I used to be such a slut – that was my golden age. I say get as much action as you can while you're young and hot.'

'But that's just awful!' Bunny exclaimed, eyes wide with shock. 'You have to love the man and be treated properly.'

'Geez,' Mitch said, dropping his spoon, 'did you timetravel here all the way from the 1950s? That would explain the starch in your dress and the way your hair doesn't move.'

Bunny favoured him with a tolerant steel-magnolia smile and, addressing herself to Imogen, said, 'I was brought up to believe that it's real important to respect yourself, or else—'

'Nobody's going to respect you, yaddayaddayadda. *What* a lot of BS,' interjected Mitch. 'Believe me, *I* know. The moment you open yourself to somebody else emotionally, it's just one big mess. Much better to be a great big horny slut and keep it all simple and clean.'

Mitch sounded so upset suddenly that Bunny and Imogen stared at him in surprise. Faustina put a hand on his arm, but he snatched it away. 'And you, don't you *dare* say a word about Gene,' he snarled. 'Nobody talks about Gene but me. You got that?'

'OK,' Faustina said placatingly. 'But you know, Mitch, other people have been in love before and then split up. It's not so extraordinary.'

'Who is Jean?' Bunny asked delicately. 'Was she your wife?'

Faustina snorted with laughter. 'No. Gene is short for Eugene. OK?'

Bunny turned pink with embarrassment. 'I'm sorry. I didn't know.'

'*Aaaanyways* . . . it was all a long time ago. I'm so *over* the whole thing,' Mitch said unconvincingly.

'What I don't understand,' Faustina said calmly, picking up the pieces of the coffee cup Mitch had knocked off the table, 'is why you don't look for him? You know that he's probably still based in the region.'

Ignoring her, Mitch began to clear away the rest of the breakfast things.

'Let's get back to the first item on the agenda,' he said, once he had returned to the table. 'Imogen's night of hot loving. You kids get up to any fooling around?'

'A bit,' Imogen admitted grudgingly.

They had, in fact, got as far as the crucial point where Dimitri, kneeling over her with his fingers hooked into the loops of her undone jeans, had paused and said, *'Alors? Oui ou non?'*

When she just stared at him in confusion, tempted to say yes but unsure of how she really felt, he had taken his hands off her, leaned back on his heels and said coldly, 'I want you to say it. In fact, I want you to *beg* me for it.'

'What?'

'I think I deserve the satisfaction,' he went on, reaching over to graze her breasts with the back of his hand. 'After all your silly little girlie dramas.'

Imogen had sat up at that. *'What* girlie dramas? I've always *ignored* you!'

He burst out laughing. 'Oh, of course, sorry! You were *ignoring* me! That's why you pretended to go off with Bastien?'

'I wasn't *pretending*!' she cried furiously, getting up and refastening her jeans. 'I . . . With Bastien, it's . . .' She finished getting dressed, her back to him. 'It's got *nothing* to do with you!'

In Mitch's kitchen, Imogen stood up, gathering her things before going to work and trying to keep her inner turmoil to herself. In the harsh light of day, she felt very uneasy about her behaviour. It really wasn't like her to behave in this way – fooling around with two different men like some sort of hussy! She would never have been so brazen in London. *But perhaps only because the situation had never arisen*, a small sardonic voice commented in her head. What was happening to her in this place? And could she ever look Bastien straight in the eye after this? He'd probably never speak to her again and she'd have lost the best friend she had in the Boustifaille kitchen. How could she have been so stupid?

'The thing is that I don't think I *like* Dimitri very much,' she said out loud. 'As a person.'

'What about Bastien?' Faustina interjected. 'Now, *he*'s a nice guy.'

'Who's the better cook?' Bunny asked.

'They're both talented,' Imogen replied after a moment's consideration. 'Bastien's more generous, but Dimitri's technique is superior.'

'No kidding,' Mitch said sardonically. 'Face it, you're just not really into Bastien.'

'And how would *you* know what I feel?' Imogen asked belligerently, without adding how frustrating she found it not to fancy the kind and sensitive Bastien more than the infuriating and objectionable Dimitri.

'Ha! You should have seen you and Bastien on the dance floor!' Mitch replied, snorting with laughter. 'Just like watching a cobra squeezing a goat.'

20

Imogen had walked into Boustifaille feeling tremulous for two reasons. There was the question of getting Monsieur Boudin to let her have some time off in order to start preparing for Bunny's party. And then, one glance at Bastien's sombre expression had confirmed her worst fears – Dimitri must have told him everything.

In fact, there Dimitri stood at his station, against a fittingly satanic background of whooshing flames, sautéing the meat for his *médaillons de porc à la provençale*. Pausing only to grab the bag of potatoes awaiting her ministrations, Imogen marched over to plant herself next to him. 'You complete and utter bastard!' she hissed.

Dimitri turned to look at her and affected surprise. 'Look who it is,' he said coldly. 'What's your problem now?'

Imogen glanced anxiously at Bastien, whose eyes remained resolutely fixed on his own ingredients.

'Dimitri, it wasn't your place to tell Bastien what happened. I can't believe that even you would do this! Bastien, I *was* going to tell you, I swear it,' she called across to him.

'Tell me what?' Bastien said, his face closed. 'That you prefer him to me?'

Grateful for the surrounding din that allowed this mortifying exchange to carry on unnoticed by the rest of the kitchen staff, Imogen tried desperately to marshal her thoughts. 'But it isn't like that! I don't prefer him to you!' *At least not if I try very hard to think about it rationally*, she told herself.

'It wasn't Dimitri. It was *me*. I told Bastien what you've been up to.'

Imogen turned around. Larissa stood right behind her in her formal waitress's uniform, her face white with anger. 'Somebody had to tell him what you're really like, just a dirty little—'

'Larissa, that's enough,' Bastien said firmly.

Imogen was indignant. 'That was pretty sneaky of you. And anyway, how did you know?'

'I followed you,' Larissa said triumphantly. 'I watched you on the beach and then I followed you to Dimitri's room, where you stayed a *very* long time.'

'Hello, all having a nice little chat?' a familiar voice bellowed in Imogen's ear, making everybody jump. 'Larissa, what are you doing? Oh, you're having a nice manicure, perhaps? You think this is a beauty salon?'

'No, Chef,' Larissa said, hurrying back to the pass and collecting the half-dozen plates that were waiting for her.

Monsieur Boudin watched her go, then slammed his huge hand on the counter. 'Where's the beetroot? Is it ready?'

'Yes, Chef!' Bastien said, after glancing at his timer.

'Chef?' Imogen said tentatively. 'Can I talk to you about something? Daphne and I are going to be catering for a private party in a few days' time, and I wondered if—'

'All right.' Boudin sighed wearily. 'She mentioned this

to me. Listen to me, little assistant,' he went on, fastening his paw on her shoulder. 'I want you to stop coming in for lunch service.'

Imogen stared at him, dumbstruck.

'Because,' Monsieur Boudin went on, his eyes fixed on the wall beyond her, 'at lunchtime it is quiet at the moment, and so we don't really need you. That way you get plenty of time to prepare your party food, OK?'

Imogen nodded a few times, wondering frantically whether this was actually a roundabout way of sacking her.

'But,' her boss resumed, 'you continue to come in in the evening.'

Imogen's heart began to thump. *This* was the moment. *This* was her chance. She made eye contact with her boss. 'Chef, I really want to help with the cooking. Please may I?'

Boudin sighed, then said, 'I don't know.'

'I could use some help with the crayfish, Chef,' Bastien said suddenly.

Imogen looked at him, torn between gratitude and guilt. It was incredibly generous of him to help her out like this after the way she'd treated him. Tentatively, she smiled at him. He looked away.

'OK, then,' Boudin relented. 'Just this one time. Leave the potatoes for the moment and help Bastien. You take the roasted beetroot and you slice it very, *very* thin, you understand?' he said, staring at her with terrifying intensity, demonstrating by holding his thumb and forefinger a hairline apart. Then his face took on a dreamy look, 'Because you are making the exquisite petals for the crayfish flower.

Allez, petite, you show me what you can do,' he said, propelling her towards the oven where the roasted beet-root was waiting.

As she started handling the vegetables, wincing and shaking her fingers in between attempts to slide off their hot skins, Bastien threw her the odd sharp glance, but did not speak to her. Most of the time he kept his gaze fixed on Dimitri, who was plating up his own dish and smiling to himself.

'Hey, if you have something to say,' Bastien said, in a low, dangerous tone, 'why don't you say it?'

Without looking up, Dimitri mouthed something barely audible. It sounded worryingly like, 'Your little English girlfriend couldn't keep her hands off me, mate.'

'What?'

Dimitri looked him squarely in the eyes. 'She really wanted it. Is she like that with you?'

'For God's sake, shut up, Dimitri,' Imogen called wearily over her shoulder. 'Bastien – don't listen to him.' But on looking up, she saw that Bastien was no longer at his station. He had pounced on Dimitri and the two were busy rolling on the floor and punching each other in the face with great enthusiasm. Horrified, she ran around the counter and tried vainly to separate them.

'Boys!' she cried with tears in her eyes. 'Please don't fight!'

Monsieur Boudin crossed the kitchen in a couple of strides, like an ogre in seven-league boots. He unceremoni-ously picked his two sous-chefs up by the scruff of the neck and plonked them back at their respective stations.

'*Get – to – work!* And you too, with the beetroot.' He paused to select one of Bastien's vegetable knives. 'Use this. And be careful – it's sharp.'

'It's OK,' Imogen said, trying hard to pull herself together. 'I'm used to professional-standard knives.'

She picked up the heavy-handled knife and looked around the kitchen. After a few curious glances in their direction, all the others had gone back to their tasks. Dimitri and Bastien, both dishevelled and red-faced after their scuffle, also seemed to have regained their focus. She too must behave like a professional. She took a deep breath and set about slicing the beetroot as thinly and regularly as possible. As soon as she had produced a substantial amount, Bastien collected it wordlessly and trimmed it into petal shapes. Imogen kept on slicing. The mechanical activity gradually began to soothe her nerves.

She was attacking what was almost her last beetroot when she noticed a pool of lighter crimson juice on the chopping board. This was in fact, she realised with a dawning sense of unreality, not juice but blood – her own. Helplessly, she turned towards Bastien, whose eyes widened at the sight of her spurting finger.

'I think,' Imogen murmured, 'I'm going to faint.' And she collapsed into his arms.

Worse was to come.

Having been revived by Monsieur Boudin's highly effective but none-too-gentle method of throwing icy water in her face, Imogen watched Bastien's efforts to stem the blood while vaguely registering her colleagues' comments:

'Wow – it looks like it's cut to the bone,' someone said.

'Yeah, that's going to take some stitching.'

'*Mais non, mais non!* It's only a scratch, this.'

'She needs to go to hospital.'

'*What?* Is this some sort of joke?'

'No, Chef!'

'I didn't know that this kitchen is now an ambulance service!' Boudin roared. 'Everybody – GO – BACK – TO – WORK!'

Amid the sound of stampede that followed, Imogen, who was leaning on the counter with her head in her arms, heard Boudin's voice in her ear, brisk and businesslike, as he got hold of her hand. '*Alors*, we put a tight bandage on it, like this, and then this finger-rubber thing on top, really tightly like that. *Très bien.*' Imogen breathed a sigh of relief and gratitude. Now he was going to send her home. Thank goodness.

'Listen, little *assistante*,' her boss explained, 'Bastien must get on with the sardine quenelles, so *you* are going to dress all the beetroot-and-crayfish plates.'

Imogen stared at him in disbelief, but Monsieur Boudin was not joking. Briefly, she wondered about her boss's mental health. Then she met Bastien's eyes, and when she saw him nod encouragingly, she straightened up and made herself take a deep breath. She'd been complaining about the lack of opportunities in the kitchen. Well, here was one! She would rise to it and show Boudin what she was capable of, *and* with a wounded hand!

But she had underestimated how shaken she actually felt, and the next twenty minutes took on the texture of the worst kind of nightmare – the kind where you want to scream but can't utter a sound, or where you try to run but find that your legs have turned to rubber. Hell was probably something like this: eternally fanning beetroot on a plate in a stylised off-centre composition, inserting the crayfish into prime position without staining it, balancing a spring of chervil on it, squirting away with the raspberry-vinegar dressing so that the whole thing looked like a naïve child's take on a Jackson Pollock action painting – then starting again from the top. Imogen felt like a harassed cartoon mouse.

The cartoon mouse ploughed on valiantly, churning out plate after plate, until her injured finger suddenly began to hurt again – with a huge exclamation mark. She looked down and was horrified to see that both plaster and rubber had vanished. Wrapping her hand in a dishcloth, she bent down and checked frantically under the whole length of her counter – nothing. No, it couldn't be! Because the only possible explanation was that the plaster and rubber had accidentally gone into . . .

At this precise moment, Larissa appeared at her side and snatched the last four plates she had prepared.

'Nooooooo! Wait, wait, wait!' Imogen cried.

Larissa looked bored. 'What?' she asked, pausing for a millisecond.

'Something really, really bad has happened,' Imogen whimpered, and explained.

'Maybe you should concentrate on your job instead of flirting with all the boys,' Larissa said coldly. 'I have to keep moving.'

Imogen abandoned her post and scuttled desperately after the other girl. 'Can you at least let me check the ones you're carrying?'

'No. I don't want you to disturb the food. You'd have to replate the whole thing.' Larissa turned to push the dining-room door open with her shoulder and gave Imogen a cool, pitying look. 'It's *your* problem.'

Imogen grabbed Larissa's arm. 'Look, you *have* to let me go in with you! It may not be too late!' She looked into the other girl's eyes. 'Larissa, *please*.'

Larissa held her gaze, smiled prettily and uttered a crystal-clear '*Non*' before disappearing through the door.

For a moment a horrified Imogen stood on the spot like a pillar of salt. Then, after checking that Monsieur Boudin was, mercifully, otherwise engaged, she made her way back to her counter.

'What is it?' Dimitri asked, after a quick look at her face. 'You're as white as your uniform.'

With some effort, Imogen focused on him. Oh, how he was going to *love* this. She managed to stretch her mouth into a bitter smile. 'I think,' she said flatly, 'that the crayfish-flower starter is going to have to be renamed the *fleur de plaster très chewy and indigestible*. And we'll need to amend the recipe a little.'

Dimitri quickly reached for her hand, checked her finger and swore under his breath.

'What can I do?' Imogen said, fighting back her tears.

Dimitri looked at her seriously. 'Nothing. You don't do anything. Take this,' he said, handing her a clean dishcloth, 'and try to look busy.'

He walked around to Bastien, whose hostile expression changed to disbelief as he listened to what Dimitri was whispering in his ear.

Feeling like a piece of livestock waiting in line at the abattoir, Imogen watched as a fresh crimson stain spread slowly on the dishcloth that covered her finger. Looking up again, she saw with dismay that Dimitri and Bastien had fetched Monsieur Boudin and that they were all walking back in her direction. It looked like they had decided to *tell*. Wonderful. Meanwhile the unfortunate recipient of the plaster had probably stopped gagging sufficiently by now to be able to make a call to his lawyer. Well, she thought numbly, that was the end of the Boustifaille experience. And what was she going to tell Daphne and Di?

'OK, *petite assistante*,' Monsieur Boudin said in a slightly gentler tone than usual. 'These two boys here, they tell me that you really need to go to the hospital. One of them can take you, check that you are OK, and then come back *very* quickly, or he is *fired*. Understand?'

'Yes, Chef! Thank you, Chef!'

The next question was to decide who of her two colleagues would drive the patient to hospital in the restaurant van, and who would hold the fort in the kitchen and deal with the plaster situation, as and when it arose.

'That's the problem we have in general regarding you,' Dimitri observed, looking at her with mock-solemnity. 'You must choose between us.'

Imogen sighed and shook her head. Her finger was pulsating painfully and her legs didn't feel too steady.

'You can see how exhausted she is, no?' Bastien said. 'You think maybe that decision can wait until tomorrow?'

Dimitri caught Imogen's eye and smiled. 'Or maybe,' he said in a confidential tone, 'you want to try both of us together?' He raised one eyebrow suggestively. 'Because that would solve the problem completely.'

There was an awkward pause, during which Imogen, her head swimming, reflected on how very unusual this situation was for her. She felt like Alice in the topsy-turvy Looking Glass world. Were things really so different in a warmer climate? Or had she, in fact, undergone some sort of strange transformation? In London, she had always managed to blend safely into the background, almost entirely unnoticed by men. Here, on the other hand, it was as though her camouflage had begun to crack, allowing these French boys to glimpse . . . what? Some sort of temptress beneath? No, surely that was ridiculous. Dimitri was only making fun of her, in his characteristically crass and tactless way.

'Oh, shut up,' Bastien said, exasperated.

'*I* don't mind if *you* don't,' Dimitri replied, smiling. 'Why don't we let the lady decide?'

'I *will* decide,' Imogen said. 'Bastien, will you take me to the hospital, please? And as for you,' she went on, glaring at Dimitri, 'you are disgusting and shameless.'

'At your service, *chérie.*'

But as she stepped out into the courtyard, Imogen had a scruple of conscience, because in fairness Dimitri had been surprisingly kind and helpful about her finger. She turned around and found him back at his station but still looking at her. She mouthed the words, 'Thank you.' He nodded, mouthed back, 'Girlie drama,' and returned to work.

After a silent drive, Imogen and Bastien sat side by side in the hospital waiting room without looking at each other. Imogen felt strongly tempted to take Bastien's hand in her own. She didn't like to see him looking sad. At the same time she worried that he might misunderstand her gesture. She opened her mouth several times, but couldn't quite work out what she wanted to say to him.

At length she tried. 'Bastien . . .'

'You don't have to say anything,' he replied gently. 'I understand the situation very well.'

'Really? I'm not sure *I* do.'

Bastien turned to look at her and shrugged. 'I shouldn't have lost my temper. I know Dimitri. He says all kinds of things but he doesn't mean them. He's proud and he doesn't like to lose face.'

'Mmm.' Imogen was weighing in her mind the possibility that Dimitri did, in his screwed-up way, really like her after all.

'You'll probably have a bit of a scar,' the nurse said later, snipping the thread of Imogen's stitches.

'I shan't forget this in a hurry,' Imogen murmured.

'All cooks have scars,' Bastien said, cheerfully displaying impressively weathered forearms. 'They're a sign of bravery under fire. You should be proud.'

'I'm not at all proud, actually,' Imogen said, looking at him.

He nodded, acknowledging the apology, and helped her to her feet. Later, as they pulled up outside the Paperback Wonderland, Imogen's rang: it was Dimitri, with news about the lost plaster. Larissa had just admitted that she had spotted and discarded the offending plate, adding acidly that she had enjoyed teaching '*l'Anglaise*' a bit of a lesson. Imogen thanked him, looked down at her bandaged finger and sighed. It was time for some damage limitation.

'Bastien, look—' she said, meeting his eye. 'I know I've behaved like an idiot. I'm very sorry I upset you. To tell you the truth, I have no idea what I'm doing. Everything's so different here – I feel like a fish out of water.'

He nodded. For a moment she thought he was going to lean in for another kiss and wondered whether she should, perhaps, go along with it. She *was* fond of him. He was a much nicer person than Dimitri. Why shouldn't she give him a chance? But in the event he left her without pressing his advantage and she went home even more confused about what she should do.

21

The next day, over lunch at La Sirène with Daphne, Imogen tried to make a little more sense of her situation. She and the *pâtissière* had finished making a last-minute checklist for Bunny's Valentine's Day party, and while her friend told a lengthy anecdote designed to illustrate that although Michel Boudin was a wonderful chef he had absolutely no feel for the art of pastry-making, Imogen reflected that she too, like Daphne, though perhaps not quite to the same extent, had changed since first breathing the air of Saint-Jean-les-Cassis.

There was something magical about this sunny and temperate winter, about the openness of the horizon and the presence of the sea. And so, when not on duty in the tense atmosphere of Boustifaille, Imogen had found herself – like Monty, who abandoned himself to napping in the sun at every given opportunity – gradually relaxing in a way that she had never experienced in London.

She had taken to the beach, for one thing. Having been relieved of her lunchtime duties at Boustifaille, tagging along with Faustina to play Frisbee with Monty was now part of her morning routine. As a result, she was getting quite used to standing around in a bikini without feeling particularly self-conscious.

All kinds of other things now felt perfectly normal, like

eating and chatting with Daphne while at the very next table a man and a woman sat clasping each other passionately – they'd been kissing open-mouthed for the last ten minutes, which was pretty impressive. In the past Imogen would have felt embarrassed by such exhibitionism. Now she almost had to repress a tolerant smile and a philosophical Gallic-style shrug. But she also felt, deep down, a wistful pang of envy at the sight of other people in love, and lucky enough to have found each other.

'And then,' Daphne said, laughing, 'he came up with the notion of making macaroons filled with foie gras! Ah, dear Michel – how absurd he is!'

'It's not completely absurd,' Imogen said automatically, looking down at the pretty ballet shoes she had recently adopted as a replacement for her trainers. French girls, she had noticed, tended to wear trainers for training purposes only. And the ballet shoes made her feel so much lighter on her feet. 'Foie gras is quite sweet anyway.'

'Ah, well,' Daphne said indulgently. 'The young will, of course, enjoy experimenting. How does your poor finger feel now?'

Imogen frowned. Boudin had made it clear that, in view of the knife incident, she would be confined to her original skivvy's duties until (possibly much) further notice, but she was nevertheless gearing up to another attempt to impress her boss. The party, which Monsieur Boudin would be attending as a guest, would hopefully prove a useful showcase. 'It's all right,' she said. 'Still a bit sore.' She hesitated, and then, after perching her sunglasses on top of her head, went on, 'Daphne, can I ask you something?'

'Of course, dear.'

'The thing is, I'm a little confused.'

'What about?'

'Well . . . Before coming here, I'd never noticed men taking any particular interest in me: you know, chatting me up and so on. But now, suddenly—'

'It never rains but it pours?'

'Yes. I can't imagine why. Because, after all, I'm still me.'

'Yes – of course you are,' Daphne said, pushing her plate of salad away and lighting a cigarette. 'But the difference is – and believe me, I speak from personal experience – that you are yourself, but *here*. Do you see?'

'No.'

'What I mean is that, now, you are foreign, exotic, and therefore enormously interesting. At home you might have felt like a common or garden flower but here you're an orchid. You mustn't underestimate the appeal of the *petite Anglaise*, Imogen. It's considerable. There's the accent apart from anything else. And there's something else, too.'

'What's that?'

'Well, you may not realise it, dear – being wholly unaware of one's attractiveness is one of the fleeting privileges of youth – but there's a very particular quality about you. What is it?' Daphne said, gazing pensively at her protégée before blowing a curl of smoke into the air. '*Mystery*, I believe. You look like you're holding something back – something quite exciting.' Daphne's nose crinkled with amusement. 'I can certainly imagine how that would appeal to men.'

Imogen shook her head, bewildered. So Daphne believed

she had a *mysterious* quality? She, who peeled potatoes, took her dog for walks and enjoyed the company of her friends, was *mysterious*? She couldn't quite believe it, but liked the idea just the same.

'I think,' Daphne went on, 'that it might well be the effect of having kept your passion for food a secret for so long. Don't you agree? Yes – your appeal has something to do with an air of restraint, of being very much your own person. And also with having such dark eyes and a lovely figure which, by the way, dear, you need to show off a bit more in the way you dress. The French call it *se mettre en valeur* – it's terribly useful and important. It means making the best of what you've got. In my case – good legs. In yours . . . well, I'm sure you'll work it out.' Then, looking down at Imogen's feet, she added, 'Oh, well done, dear. These are a good way to start. Now work your way up.'

22

Two weeks had passed since Bunny had booked Imogen to cater her Valentine's Day party and in a few hours the celebration would begin. Standing in the American girl's garden with Monty by her side, Imogen reflected that Bunny had really done herself proud, putting as much planning and creative imagination into her Valentine's party as most people would dedicate to their wedding day. With every tree festooned with garlands of tiny white fairy lights, the garden looked utterly magical. Several long trestle tables covered with antique white linen had been laid out, awaiting the fruits of Imogen's labour: enough party food to feed a small army.

In the course of the last two weeks, Bunny's guest list, initially limited to her siblings and a few friends from America who were in the area, had grown exponentially. First of all, Imogen and Daphne had found themselves promoted from caterers to caterers *and* guests. And then Bunny had effortlessly trailed her way through Saint-Jean, making new friends and sending Imogen the text message: 'We're going to need more food' on a daily basis. She had even managed, with Daphne's help, to sweet-talk Monsieur Boudin into closing the restaurant '*pour raisons exceptionnelles*' in order to allow the Boustifaille staff to attend. Eventually, Bunny and Imogen had settled on the final number of guests to be fed, and at that point, feeling like a champagne cork at last allowed to pop, Imogen had gone to town, creating an extravagant feast.

Imogen checked the time: she was only hours away from the arrival of the first costumed guests. Daphne herself had just left to go home and get dressed. Frantic and happy, Imogen made her way back to Bunny's cool kitchen and set about putting the finishing touches to the food: vertiginous pyramids of luscious fruit, delicately layered salmon-and-sorrel terrines, veal-and-pork pies adorned with glistening Sauternes jelly, armies of shot glasses filled with chilled pale green vichyssoise or emerald-green herb salad studded with tiny bacon *lardons*. One particularly thrilling challenge she had set herself was to prove that it was possible, with a certain amount of architectural flair, to transform what was essentially a big mound of pink meat – thinly sliced duck *magret*, to be precise – into a thing of beauty.

Daphne's assistance, expertise and unflappable good humour had been invaluable, especially when it came to the centrepiece of their buffet: a gloriously rococo pistachio ice-cream cake adorned with pink meringue hearts, roses and swans – just the sort of thing that would have delighted Marie-Antoinette.

Imogen was sliding the last couple of glazed hams into the oven when she heard Bunny calling her from the other end of the house. After casting a sharp look around to check that all was in a fit state to await her return, and with Monty close on her heels, she made her way to the living room, still wearing her apron and calling out, 'Yes, what? I hope it's important!'

Walking into the room felt like stumbling by mistake on the set of a magazine shoot for an expensive brand of American sportswear. Bunny sat on one of three squashy sofas, surrounded by a group of unbelievably clean-limbed and well-groomed boys and girls who, like Bunny herself, had the air of having just arrived down to earth fully formed, and with not a hair out of place.

Imogen's hand instinctively rose to check that her own hair, which she had hastily pinned up when she started cooking, wasn't too messy, but – surprise, surprise – it was, hideously. She made a tentative attempt to remove her apron at least, then thought better of it. She wouldn't look particularly better groomed in the cut-off jeans and faded T-shirt she was wearing underneath it. She squared her shoulders: after all, there was nothing wrong with being a cook, was there?

At the sight of Bunny's English friend, everyone smiled and all the men stood up – a novel and furiously intimidating experience – so that Imogen found herself making some sort of nervous headmistressy 'at ease' signal, inviting them to sit down again.

'OK, everyone,' Bunny called out, having rescued her friend and made her sit down next to her. 'This here is Imogen, who's a wonderful chef. The four-footed gentleman is called Monty. And this,' she said, gesturing towards a pretty brunette whose wide blue eyes and wondering, gappy smile matched her own, 'is my sister Grace. Next to you,

Imogen, is my big brother Everett, and this is my baby brother Buddy, and my cousin Rose, and my baby cousin Mary-Kate, and . . .'

As Bunny continued with her introductions, moving on to her brothers' friends, Imogen allowed her mind to drift – Walker, Gage, Chuck, Conway, Heath . . . Oh, heavens. There wasn't a hope of retaining all those names. Nodding and smiling, and wishing very much that she hadn't left the kitchen, she received a general impression of impeccable side partings, crisp pink shirts and uniformly golden tans that bespoke glossy good health and an obvious love of the outdoors.

The thing about these people was that they all looked like movie stars – in the sense that their perfect appearance hinted at the off-screen presence of an army of make-up artists and dressers constantly engaged in powdering their shiny noses and straightening their clothes so that they fell perfectly off their frames. It was uncanny – unnerving, really.

'And this is Archer,' Bunny said eventually.

Dressed in black, Archer was standing over by the open French windows, gazing at the garden. He looked over his shoulder, mouthed the word 'Hey' and smiled distantly, before turning away again. Though tall, he was slighter than the others and Imogen noticed that he had a broken nose, the only slight defect in the sea of apparent physical perfection that filled the room.

'We're so looking forward to eating your wonderful food!' Bunny's sister Grace – a cool vision in white cashmere jersey and pleated skirt – called out. *Yes – food*, Imogen thought, *yes indeedy*. She was itching to get back to the kitchen: there was still a lot to do.

'Is it *traditional* French cuisine?' asked Bunny's cousin Mary-Kate with wide-eyed interest.

'Oh, I don't know,' Imogen said, flustered at being the centre of attention. 'I suppose it is French-influenced. But with a modern twist in the presentation, hopefully.'

'Well, so long as it's pink and green,' Bunny's older brother, dark-haired, blue-eyed Everett interjected, aiming a sardonic glance at his younger sister, 'Bun will like it.'

'It's *all* pink and green,' Imogen confirmed, smiling at him.

'I'm sure glad to hear that,' Everett said, warmly returning her smile. 'The thing about Bun, you see,' he said, turning back to Imogen, 'is that she's a visual type with hardly a taste bud to her name.'

'*Everett*,' Bunny said with mock severity.

'It's true, darling. You never notice what you eat.'

'It's because she's artistic,' Bunny's apple-cheeked younger brother Buddy said supportively. 'For a while she used to paint, and she was always dipping her brush in her iced tea.'

'Yes, and then drinking paint and not even noticing. That's just my point.'

The Doucet siblings all laughed at this, while Imogen noticed, out of the corner of her eye, that Archer had come over to join them and was now leaning against a sofa, close to where Grace was ensconced. He did not look at anyone in particular; nor did he join in the animated conversation some of Everett's other friends were conducting about the joys of sailing.

Soon after that, Imogen, mindful of sizzling hams that urgently required her presence, excused herself and escaped back to the haven of the kitchen.

23

A few hours later, her party about to begin, Bunny was now clad in full eighteenth-century costume – a glorious almond-pink muslin gown in the style of Marie-Antoinette and a very high champagne-blond wig. The latter had been sculpted, with much trepidation but to an impressive standard, by local hairdresser Madame Pignon (who for the last fifteen years had rarely been asked for anything more taxing than a blue rinse) around a toy frigate in full rig. It was a hairstyle that had been last sported by fashionable French ladies in the 1770s to celebrate a naval victory in the American War of Independence. Moreover, Bunny's face had been expertly powdered and rouged by Faustina in the style of the period. And yet she still looked exactly like herself: a perky, wide-eyed American girl rigorously intent on being the hostess with the mostest.

Imogen stood frowning in front of the mirror. She had taken a considerable leap out of her comfort zone. This was the first dress she had worn in years, having decided long ago that trousers were more practical. She had still tried to keep things plain: she wore no jewellery apart from a black velvet ribbon adorned with a pearl around her neck, and her cream silk frock was in the simplest style she had managed to find. Nevertheless the outfit transformed her figure in the most startling way. One part of her anatomy in particular, the one she had always taken such pains to camouflage, now featured as the star attraction.

Mitch came to stand next to her to examine his own reflection – he looked rather marvellous in a heavily embroidered gold riding coat. Glancing at her sideways, he declared, in a voice that still sounded entirely New York even after fifty years in France, '*Oooh-là-là – il y a du monde au balcon.*'

There's a big crowd on the balcony, Imogen translated in her head. *What on earth did that mean?*

'It's a French expression, my pretty,' he said, smoothing his moustache. 'It means you look *stacked.*'

'Oh no, no, but it's so *classy*,' Bunny hastened to add, seeing the rising panic in Imogen's eyes. 'And anyway, it's *historical*! You look like a British princess! Or a young queen!'

Faustina had advised against a wig and had put up Imogen's hair in a restrained style of the period, with two longish ringlets resting on the side of her neck. Nor had she overdone the make-up. In spite of her initial reservations, Imogen had to admit that she liked the end result, complete with a small black beauty spot pertly positioned near the corner of her mouth.

'Well, I think we're all ready,' Faustina purred, looking her usual flamboyant self in an incredibly low-cut scarlet frock. Then she glanced at Imogen, smiled and added, 'You especially – you look like you're about to go and do something incredibly naughty.'

An exceptionally balmy evening; large quantities of good food and drink; Cheyenne's astutely chosen playlist and, of course, the irresistible appeal of fancy dress – especially as the majority of the guests were wearing masks of every description, from plain black velvet to ornate gilt and silver Venetian-style hand-held affairs – all this ensured that Bunny's party ignited wonderfully, and kept on burning like wildfire through the night.

Imogen felt mildly cynical about the mystique of Valentine's Day. It was, after all, just a day like any other, and in her experience it had always failed to deliver anything terribly exciting on the romantic front.

But the other guests clearly felt otherwise. The occasion was so glamorous and other-wordly that it managed to infuse Valentine's Day with its truest and richest meaning – far, far beyond generic greeting cards and obligatory bunches of red roses. This was a night for love, a magical night when anything could happen – from love at first sight to the long-awaited consummation of an old flame. Any masked reveller was a potential lover, poised on the brink of a passionate affair.

As darkness fell, this heady atmosphere became so potent and infectious that in spite of her better judgement, Imogen, who had been wandering through the happy crowd feeling like a spectator, also began to feel a small thrill of anticipation.

She was strolling past Cheyenne's turntables, which he'd set up under a lit-up tree, when the DJ beckoned to her, excitedly calling out, 'Yoo-hoo, Little Mermaid! Over here!' She stopped in her tracks, bewildered – Little Mermaid? As in the fairy tale by Hans Christian Andersen? Why on earth was he calling her that? – then walked over to say hello. Looking tonight like a loved-up brigand in frilly white shirt and black breeches, his hair tied back with a black scarf in piratical style, he enfolded her in such an enthusiastic embrace that she almost lost her balance.

'What a great night, eh? Can you feel the energy? Hey, look at this,' he said, suddenly producing a large acid-green glow stick and poking it at her stomach. 'That looks so cool against your dress! *C'est psychédélique!* I can do the figure of eight, like, thousands of times when I'm in the zone. You dance with me later, OK? I want to show you some great moves.'

Imogen smiled, mentally rolling her eyes. Cheyenne hugged her again, adding, 'I'm handing over to one of the Americans in a minute.'

Imogen glanced across at the American boys, forming another picture of casual glamour as they all stood in a huddle beneath a tree. Bunny's brother Everett waved at her and she waved back.

'They want to do that 60s limbo thing, you know,' Cheyenne went on, 'where you dance under the pole? I bet you'd be great at that. I'll come and find you, OK?'

Old-fashioned gal Bunny loved old-fashioned party games. Limbo dancing was a pastime fondly remembered from her childhood in the south. The hostess had also, Imogen knew, set her heart on playing Blind Man's Buff, because she had heard somewhere that it was the sort of flirtatious game enjoyed by eighteenth-century aristocrats.

Looking up at Cheyenne, Imogen said 'OK' vaguely, not over-committing herself. In truth, she was perfectly happy on her own. Earlier in the evening, when Bunny's two brothers had asked her to dance, she had declined them both with a smile, and had slipped away at the earliest opportunity.

A little further on she stopped to speak to Daphne, who looked her usual serene queenly self in a golden-brown dress edged with black lace. Next to her, an imposing man dressed in black velvet and wearing a three-cornered hat was scrutinising the buffet. It was only when he turned around and removed his black mask that Imogen recognised Monsieur Boudin, looking quite different out of chef's whites and more darkly handsome, but just as intimidating as ever. He greeted her with a stiff nod. 'Daphne tells me that you made all of this food. Is it true?'

'Yes, Chef,' Imogen replied, glancing at her friend, who widened her eyes encouragingly.

'Hmm,' Boudin said, pinching a bite-size saltimbocca between thumb and forefinger and examining it closely. He sniffed it and nodded, before popping it into his mouth. His face deadly serious, he began to masticate. Daphne put a reassuring hand on Imogen's arm while they waited breathlessly for his verdict.

'It's quite good,' he said evenly. 'And also the presentation is clean and elegant. I like your duck *magret* skyscraper. Well done.'

'Thank you, Chef.'

'But it is only picnic food, this. Not restaurant food.'

'Well, of course it is, Michel,' Daphne said reasonably. 'Imogen's delivered what Bunny ordered.'

'Yes – I suppose so.'

'And I do believe that she would deliver what you ask for in your kitchen if you gave her a proper chance.'

'Oh, yes, Chef!' Imogen cried, unable to repress a small jump. 'I can do a test run for you on any dish you want.'

'OK, OK, *petite*,' Monsieur Boudin said, with a smile that softened his face considerably. 'Let me think about it. Now go and enjoy the party.'

'Thank you,' Imogen murmured, before walking off, her mind in a whirl. It was going to happen – her breakthrough at Boustifaille – and this time she would be properly prepared!

She looked to right and left, checking Bastien and Dimitri's whereabouts, and was relieved not to see them anywhere near. Since first stepping out into the fairy-lit garden, she had done her best to avoid them. Bastien, looking quite splendid in a scarlet army uniform, had sought her out early on to compliment her on the quality of the catering.

'I'm very impressed,' he'd said, looking seriously into her eyes. 'But not at all surprised. I knew you were good.'

'Thanks.' Imogen was touched. 'Daphne helped a lot. Are you having fun?'

'Not yet,' he'd replied, as his eyes came to rest on her mouth. Three Valentine's cards had come in the post for her this morning: the first one, jokey, dog-themed and written in Daphne's hand, purported to be from Monty; the second one, which read 'Be my funny Valentine, you little knucklehead', was, of course, from Mitch, and now Imogen felt she knew quite well who had sent the third – a straightforward declaration of tender regard containing a wistful allusion to passion fruit and signed with a mysterious X – Bastien, of course. He smiled at her and, just as she was beginning to wonder if he was about to Try Again, Imogen noticed Larissa's approach and took the opportunity to move on.

Dimitri, dressed as ever in black, was drunk, and infectiously so. As soon as he spotted her, he'd ambled over, grabbed her arm and said, 'Come here. I need to show you something interesting.'

'What?' she'd asked pertly, disengaging herself and trying vainly to sidestep him.

'Trust me – you'll like it,' he'd said, pulling her into his arms.

Imogen had tried to keep a straight face. 'OK, where is it? That interesting thing?'

Dimitri started to laugh. 'Not very far from where you're standing now. You could probably just reach out and touch it.'

Looking up at him, she was almost overcome with giggles and immediately felt annoyed with herself. This really wasn't the way to behave. The truth was, she thought, sobering up again, that the headlong preparation of the buffet had tired her out and left her feeling a little hysterical.

Dimitri placed a finger on her beauty mark. 'Nice touch,' he said, smiling. 'I thought maybe we could go over there, behind those bushes. Come on, you know you want to.'

'Don't flatter yourself,' she had said, recovering her equilibrium and walking away.

Meanwhile, this was Bunny's big night; she was

certainly the belle of the ball. She had been standing on a chair and making a charming little speech, thanking everyone for turning up and enthusing about life in Saint-Jean-les-Cassis, when the guest of honour made his picture-perfect appearance – claret breeches, rose-coloured coat, flower-embroidered white satin waistcoat and lace-frilled shirt – after a slight delay caused by a flat tyre on his moped.

'You know I've been researching the history of my family on the Internet,' Bunny had told Imogen breathlessly a few days before the party. 'Well, this morning I got an email from a French relative – a cousin who's exactly my age! He sounds so polite – real gentlemanly – and his name is—' she held her breath before drawling it lovingly '—Amaury d'Oussey. Isn't that lovely? He's some kind of local historian, I think, and he doesn't live very far away – you know . . . Montpellier? So I just invited him along. And he said he'd *love* to come!' Bunny beamed, her eyes shining. 'The first time I see him he'll be in costume. It'll be like looking at a family portrait!'

'Is he a distant cousin?'

'Oh, yes, *very*,' Bunny replied with a twinkle in her eye. 'So let's hope he's real dashing!'

'Real dashing' were not the first words that came to mind on beholding Amaury d'Oussey. More accurate descriptions might have included, in no particular order, 'bloodless', 'etiolated', 'a lot more forehead than chin' and (this one from Mitch, and rather too audibly) 'Oh geez – is it a man? Is it a woman? Is it a *giraffe*?'

But none of this mattered a jot to Bunny, who looked

like she might actually swoon with delight when Amaury introduced himself and kissed her hand with the stiff formality of an eighteenth-century courtier. '*Enchanté, chère cousine,*' he declared, amiably baring somewhat equine teeth.

'Oh, how darling,' Bunny's sister Grace murmured, entranced, before eagerly extending her own hand.

Leaping around in restrained fashion (so as not to capsize her coiffure) to one of Cheyenne's pumping techno tunes while holding on to her French relative, Bunny now looked very happy.

'Hi there,' Imogen said, spotting Faustina and tapping her on the shoulder.

Faustina jumped, then sighed with relief. 'Oh, it's you. I thought it was Enzo. I keep running into him – it's getting on my nerves. I knew I should have worn a mask. Anyway, I have to keep moving. I'll see you later.'

She walked off, looking harassed, and indeed it wasn't long before Enzo appeared, wearing a garnet-coloured riding coat, as though magnetically drawn to the trail of his beloved. Spotting Imogen, he stopped in his tracks. '*Salut,*' he said to her, accompanying this greeting with one of the devastating enigmatic looks she rather enjoyed receiving – so powerful were Enzo's attractions that even to a fairly detached observer like herself they always delivered some sort of charge to her solar plexus.

'*Salut,*' she grinned (another unavoidable effect of his presence). 'Are you enjoying the party?'

'Not really, no.' As Imogen nodded sympathetically, he looked intently into her eyes. 'It's like some terrible torture.'

'Oh, dear,' Imogen whispered. 'What's wrong?'

Enzo sighed. Imogen watched his long dark eyelashes come down like a theatre curtain, then rise again, while his lips parted just a little before settling into a moody, brooding sort of pout. The whole thing seemed to happen in slow motion. It was astonishing, really, that Faustina was capable of resisting this sort of display.

'I'm in love,' Enzo said, staring at her challengingly. 'You understand that?'

'Yes,' Imogen replied, trying to breathe naturally. 'I do.' Should she tell him where Faustina had gone?

'Do you know what it's like to be going mad with desire?'

'No,' Imogen admitted. 'Not really.'

'It's like a fever. It tears you up inside.'

'Gosh. That does sound quite—'

'One day you'll understand,' he said, bringing his face a little closer to hers. Then he turned on his heel and vanished.

Imogen blinked, rubbed vigorously at the goosebumps that had risen on her arms and turned towards the villa. She would go and check on Monty, last spotted asleep next to Cristiana in his basket on the floor of Bunny's bedroom. On her way in she almost collided with one of Bunny's friends – the one with the broken nose.

'Sorry,' she said. She couldn't for the moment remember his name.

'Oh, that's OK,' he replied. He stood there for a minute, looking as if he were about to say something else.

Beyond his shoulder appeared two masked revellers whom Imogen identified as Everett, holding a broom, and his younger brother Buddy. Everett grinned at her, waving the broom with inexplicable enthusiasm, while Buddy said excitedly, 'We're going to set things up! Come and join us later?'

Imogen, who had no idea what he was talking about, nodded politely before making her way into the kitchen, where she found Mitch sitting alone at the table with a generous tumbler of bourbon in his hand.

'You OK?' Mitch asked, looking up.

'Yes.'

'Hmn,' he said, giving her a piercing look. 'You wanna calm right down, babe. You'll bust something with all this freaking out and having the time of your life.'

Imogen smiled. She located a glass and a bottle of wine and came to sit opposite Mitch.

'Do you ever miss New York?' she asked.

'Nah – you out of your mind? What would I want to live there for? Don't you know how *rude* people are in New York?'

Imogen raised an eyebrow, looking at Mitch pointedly. He glared at her without blinking for a whole minute – something she had learned to read as a sign of affection. 'You can take the gal out of New York but you can't take New York out of the gal, right? All I know is, *this* is my home – nowhere else. I'm a sucker for the romance of the Riviera.' He smoothed his moustache and sighed.

'Yes, it *is* romantic here,' Imogen said pensively. She gazed at Mitch and considered whether to ask him about the discovery she had made that morning after breakfast. On opening the kitchen bin she had seen – unmistakable amid the coffee grounds and empty yoghurt pots – a red envelope addressed to Mitch and a card adorned with a large heart. It looked like they had both been torn in half. So, Mitch had been sent a Valentine, had read it and then discarded it. But why? Well, it really wasn't any of her business.

After a short pause, she asked instead, 'And what about . . . Gene?'

'What about him?' Mitch snapped back.

'What happened?' Imogen asked gently.

Covering his face, Mitch made a sound like a hissing kettle, then looked at Imogen through splayed fingers. 'Gene made everything . . . *complicated*.'

'He loved you,' Imogen offered.

'Yeah.'

'And you?'

'I behaved like the greatest shit in creation. I did everything I could to drive him away.'

'And it worked?'

'Oh yeah, baby – it worked. It took a while, though. But I broke him in the end. And then – kapow! – he was gone.'

There was a pause. Mitch looked out of the window into the garden.

'How long ago was this?' Imogen asked in a neutral tone.

'Twenty years, I guess.'

'And since then, you—'

'Well, the frog-queen thing, you know.'

'Ah, yes. Any good?'

'Nah, not really,' Mitch said, intent on pushing back his

cuticles with his thumbnail. 'And not lately, if you want to know.'

'Mitch, now *you're* the knucklehead. Faustina said Gene lived locally. Why don't you—'

The kettle hissed again, then, 'Nah. No point. He's moved on.'

'How do you know?'

Mitch snorted impatiently and poured Imogen more wine. 'Don't worry about me, kiddo. I'm an old man – though don't you dare spread it about that I said so or I'll kick your ass. But why don't you go party? How about one of those gorgeous American boys? They look so big and vital, even from here.'

'I don't know,' Imogen said slowly. She looked out of the window. For some mysterious reason, Bunny's brothers were now dismantling the broom while their sisters looked on approvingly. She turned back to Mitch. 'I don't particularly want that,' she said. 'I want—' She shook her head. Daphne's remarks about her air of mystery and its effect on men had been kindly meant, but Imogen didn't actually believe a word of them. 'The thing is,' she said earnestly, 'I've never known what it feels like to be . . . well, swept off my feet – you know, really caught up in something romantic and wild. And I'm beginning to think that nothing like that will *ever* happen to me. Men don't think about me that way.'

'Right.'

'No, really! They think I'm a . . . sure thing, because I'm a bit . . . I'm not very sure of myself.'

'Well, what I would advise is maybe putting away those

drippy romance novels you're so hooked on and getting down to some actual romancing. You thought about trying that? Besides, I gotta tell you – looking like you do now, you oughta be sure of yourself. You're a knockout.'

'Thank you.'

'Don't mention it. I can tell you don't really believe me.'

'Imogen? Hi!' Bunny's cousin Mary-Kate stood in the doorframe, holding her silver mask by its handle. She greeted the Yankee with cautious politeness, then added for Imogen's benefit, 'Bunny wants you in the garden.'

24

Moments later, Imogen stood in the heart of a large circle of revellers, blindfolded and also quite dizzy after being vigorously twirled around. She had never played Blind Man's Buff before and it hadn't been her intention to start tonight, but she had let Bunny bamboozle her and now she was 'It'.

Damn. Damn and blast. This really wasn't her idea of a good time. The other guests were taunting her, calling out her name, giggling, running circles around her and pinching her waist, almost knocking her off balance, while remaining tantalisingly out of reach. How was she *ever* going to set herself free?

She was too tired for this, she thought, flailing impatiently and to no avail. She would have been quite happy to play along for a minute or two, but this was too much. Now seriously annoyed, she pursed her lips resolutely, stood on the spot for a moment to get her balance, and then started to walk in a straight line with her arms outstretched. She would catch someone, anyone, and get herself *out*.

In the event, somebody caught *her* before she had the chance. She stiffened in surprise as she felt a man's hands gliding caressingly down her arms and covering her own hands, and almost immediately a soft, firm mouth closing over hers, an intoxicating taste of spice on his tongue and a wild rush of blood to her face, her throat, her arms and every one of her fingers, her legs and her belly.

Around them there had been initial whoops of delight, followed, as the kiss went on, by a disconcerted silence. Not that Imogen was listening.

This was a shock, a completely new experience. In her mind's eye she could see her body quite clearly. It was like one of those old-fashioned telephone switchboards. An army of invisible hands were plugging dozens of cords into their jacks, connecting hundreds of calls at once. Within her something shifted profoundly – for the first time in her life she felt entirely at one with her body. She sighed deeply. She breathed him in. She opened herself to the kiss – and it travelled through her like a voluptuous crack of thunder.

Somewhere, music started again. Imogen became vaguely aware of the circle breaking, of people chattering and going off to dance. Her hands were released and his mouth lifted from hers. She slowly opened her eyes under the blindfold and reached for him, but her hands encountered nothing but thin air. By the time she'd torn the blindfold off she stood alone on the trampled grass. He had vanished.

'I can't *believe* that none of you saw who it was!' Imogen cried, exasperated. 'Where the hell were you?'

First of all, she'd had to contend with a chorus of confused and contradictory replies from those few tipsy guests who were still present when she'd removed her blind-fold. They included Monsieur Morello the cheesemonger and his wife; Madame Pignon the hairdresser and her husband; Monsieur and Madame Ponceau from the butcher's; Bernard, the owner of La Sirène, and Mylène from Ultradonna, who was accompanied by her biker boyfriend.

They were all very keen to help. One of them swore that the man who had kissed her was tall and dark. Another said no, he was short and fair. Middle-aged, he was, definitely, someone else chipped in. No, no, really young, just a boy really. And you couldn't see his hair anyway because he was wearing a hat. He was dressed in white. Hang on a minute, no, it was definitely blue. No, no: scarlet. He was all in black – I remember it particularly. Yes, he seemed to know everybody at the party. No, he'd arrived on his own and stood alone on the edge, speaking to no one. Afterwards he'd gone into the house. No, he'd gone off in the direction of the music. No, no, wait: he'd left the party altogether.

Everyone agreed on one thing, however, the mystery guest had worn a mask to complement his fancy dress. Even Imogen could confirm this, for in the course of the kiss she had felt the brush of velvet. But it still amounted to the same thing: no one had seen his face.

None of this muddle made much of an impression on Imogen except the mention of scarlet and black, the colours that had been worn respectively by Bastien and Dimitri. *Of course*. The game would have presented them with the chance they had both been waiting for all evening. But which one had seized the opportunity to deliver that powerfully delectable kiss? Had it been Bastien's mouth on hers? If so, her own response must mean that she felt more deeply about him than she'd realised. But then again if it had been Dimitri's, there had to be more to him than met the eye. Both were intriguing notions, full of promise. Briefly, Imogen thought of Venetia, Georgette Heyer's heroine, whose quest for love also began with an unexpected kiss, though at least Damerel's identity was known to her from the start. Imogen flushed; it was all rather exciting.

She had hoped for more detailed eyewitness reports from her friends. But as it turned out, Mitch had remained in the kitchen to finish his drink (and, Imogen suspected, mooch about the loss of Gene) and had missed the entire episode. Faustina had spent that part of the night chain-smoking at the bottom of the garden, hiding from Enzo. That left Bunny, the organiser of the game, who when questioned admitted sheepishly that she, like the rest of her American visitors, had found herself irresistibly lured away to the joys of the limbo pole.

The aftershock of the kiss had made going back to work at Boustifaille something of an out-of-body experience. But Imogen was determined to capitalise on the impression her party food had made on Monsieur Boudin, and so, resolutely blanking out Bastien and Dimitri from her field of vision as she entered the kitchen, she made a beeline for the hulking shape of her boss and, before losing her nerve, offered her services as a roving *gâte-sauce*, a cook's junior sidekick, who is always in danger of 'spoiling the sauce'.

Monsieur Boudin turned towards her, looking preoccupied. 'OK, OK, if you want,' he muttered. 'You help Bastien and Dimitri with whatever they need.'

Slowly, Imogen exhaled. A green light – that was good. Now all she had to do was get on with it. Just get on with walking up to Dimitri and meeting his eye, for a start. And then looking across and meeting Bastien's eye. And not letting any of this interfere with her cooking. It was simple enough: on no account should she lose her focus, because then she would automatically travel back to the instant of the kiss, once again standing not quite close enough to *him* – whichever of the two he was – on the trampled grass, oblivious to anything that wasn't his mouth. And that really wasn't the way to go. She needed to behave like a professional and show Boudin what she was capable of. Smoothing her apron down with both hands, she approached her station.

'Hi, Imogen,' Bastien said. 'Did you enjoy last night?'

Cautiously, Imogen looked up. Enjoy *what*, exactly? He grinned at her, his face unreadable. If that was acting, it was very well done.

'I did, thanks,' she replied.

When he noticed her presence, Dimitri snorted.

'Bad hangover?' she asked, smiling to herself.

'The worst. Just keep out of my way.'

'Actually, Monsieur Boudin said I was to help you with anything you need.'

At this, Dimitri turned to look at her and smiled ambiguously. 'How compliant you are today! It makes a nice change from last night – you were as slippery as an eel then.'

Until you caught me and kissed me – is that what you mean? Imogen wondered, as she began to peel her way through a pile of carrots. As first Bastien then Dimitri began to ask her for help, things became more interesting, but also considerably more difficult. Swiftly pan-frying scallops and watching their delicate saffron-cream sauce come to just before boiling point; coating guineafowl supremes with a crust of dried fruit; layering paper-thin rounds of potato in a gratin dish, and in a perfectly symmetrical pattern. Thus ran her list of jobs, but where to start?

'*Coucou, petite assistante!* We are on the moon today?' Monsieur Boudin's voice made her eardrum spin in her head like a crazed sixpence.

'No, Chef, not at all.'

'It was a nice party last night, yes? We all enjoyed ourselves very much of course, but now real life, it starts again.'

'Yes, Chef.'

Real life . . . and the party . . . actually, Imogen reflected, perhaps it had been a mistake to block out the memory of the kiss. Closing her eyes, she now willed herself, with all her might, to recall it and the enormous rush of energy it had released within her. *Yes.*

The effect was immediate. Feeling profoundly fired up, she managed to string all her tasks together in some semblance of logical order, and though there were quite a few hiccups and moments of panic – having to discard a batch of over-cooked rubbery scallops and a battle with rebellious guineafowl that refused steadfastly to let the fruit mixture stick – Imogen felt she had pulled through with reasonable self-possession.

She worked her shift, and then, at the end of service, felt she had earned the right to ask one or two questions of her two kissing candidates. She approached Dimitri first. He heard her out, then said, smiling at her, 'OK – it was me. Of course it was me. Couldn't you tell?'

'Well, I don't know—' Imogen said uncertainly. The searing intimacy of the kiss had been nothing like those lustful skirmishes she had experienced with him before. And yet . . . '*Was* it you?' she asked, searching his face for clues. 'Really?'

He let his grey eyes rest on hers, then pointedly looked down the length of her body and said, 'You know there's only one way to find out for sure. Why don't you come back to my room tonight?'

When she didn't reply, he shrugged and turned back to his dish.

Bastien too was irritatingly evasive when she cornered him outside the walk-in freezer and asked him about the kiss. He listened to her tale, then said, with a twinkle in his eye, 'Well, I *was* there at the time.'

That was a little delicate. 'When you say you were *there*,' Imogen said tentatively, 'do you mean that you *saw* it happen or that you . . . *made* it happen?'

'Ah, so it is possible that it was me? Did it *feel* like me?'

Imogen pondered this, remembering the ringing purity of the kiss, its clarity. Really, whoever-he-was might as well have left his signature on the inside of her mouth. She could still taste him.

'N-no,' she said at length. 'Maybe not.'

Bastien leaned against the door of the freezer and his face took on a more serious expression. 'Tell me one thing: would you *like* it to be me?'

They looked each other straight in the eye. Seeing Imogen hesitate, Bastien's face darkened a little, but he still smiled at her gamely. 'Then let's say that it *wasn't* me. It's much simpler like this, no?'

But it wasn't simple, Imogen reflected. Not at all. What had begun as an unexpected romantic episode was turning into something quite different: a whodunit.

25

'It's *got* to be one or the other,' Imogen said a few days later, as she sat in Bunny's garden with Mitch and Faustina. 'But which one?'

'Both are real cute,' Bunny observed calmly. 'But which one do you prefer?'

'The one who kissed me, whichever one that is.'

'Music to my ears,' Mitch said approvingly. 'You're getting it, finally – no sentiment, just sex.'

Imogen shook her head. 'That's not what I mean.'

'Listen,' Faustina began carefully, unwilling to be the bearer of bad news. 'I'm wondering if *maybe* you're not making too much of that kiss.' Seeing that Imogen remained silent and did not appear overly perturbed, her Corsican friend straightened the fringed pom-poms of her white leather cowboy boots before going on. 'I mean . . . I know that for you it felt really special, but maybe for him, it was just one little kiss, you know?'

Imogen looked at her, digesting the idea.

'That would point to Dimitri, then,' Mitch said. 'He's got the right idea, that kid. He's only in it for the action. And it makes sense on account of his Batman fixation. That pinball machine in the café is like his wife. And he has a Batman poster in his room, right?'

Imogen nodded. When she had commented on the now

tattered film poster that was tacked above his bed he had told her how, years ago, he'd stolen it from outside a cinema as a drunken bet.

'Well, think about it. If he's into the whole secret identity thing, then of course he would love dressing up, putting on a mask, slinking off into the night, yaddayaddayadda. It's straight out of a Batman movie!'

'I don't know,' Imogen countered. 'He's always been quite happy to proposition me without a mask.'

'Well, maybe he thought he'd spice things up.'

'Actually, *my* money would be on Bastien,' Bunny said, smiling at Imogen. 'The sweet one. I think that if he hasn't admitted it yet it's because he's wondering what to do next to impress you.'

Imogen smiled back and then, while Bunny poured everyone more coffee, let her eyes wander around the peaceful garden, remembering how dramatic it had looked – mysterious, fairy-lit and filled with masked guests – on Valentine's night. She looked at the lawn, trying to pinpoint the exact spot where she had been kissed. Her heart beat a little faster.

It was quieter outside the villa than in. Bunny's home was still full of her friends and family, who, for the main part, were now getting ready to leave. Looking over her shoulder, Bunny glanced through the French windows and waved at her sister Grace, who waved back cheerily.

'Gracie's going home tonight,' Bunny said, turning back to her friends. 'And Everett's taking Buddy with him on a sort of grand tour. They're going to travel all over Italy and see *everything*! But first Everett wants to spend a few days with Archer and make sure he's OK. They've been friends since college, you know, and Archer's going through real difficult times right now. He needs a friend.'

'Difficult?' Faustina echoed. 'What kind of difficult?'

'Well . . . the *just-divorced* kind of difficult,' Bunny said, lowering her voice before stage-whispering the words: 'I think he's in the house with my brothers.'

'Just divorced?' Imogen said, her eyes still on the lawn, and thinking of her parents' own debacle. 'Oh dear.'

'Yes, poor Archer. Oh, it's been just terrible!' Bunny went on. 'He met this beautiful French girl, Constance, in Paris, just after landing a job at the Musée d'Art Moderne, and they had this whirlwind romance and got married real fast. Archer's family is part French, so it all felt like it was meant to be, you know. Everett was best man and he said that Paris wedding was *the* most romantic thing he'd *ever* seen. Afterwards they moved into this darling flat that had an actual view of the Eiffel Tower and for a while everything was dandy, but *then*—' Bunny sighed, spreading her hands in her lap. 'Well, I think Constance began to realise that she hadn't married money after all.'

'The frogs think all Americans are loaded,' Mitch said, smoothing his moustache. 'Dunno why. Maybe they don't see us as real people, more like weirdo fairy tale creatures.'

'Maybe so,' Bunny opined. 'Anyway, she had this notion that Archer came from money, and well, it's just not true. And so she left him, and not just that, she told him it was all his fault for leading her on and then turning out not to be super-rich! Isn't that the meanest thing you ever heard?'

'It does sound pretty low,' Imogen said, shocked.

'I guess she was no true lady, underneath it all,' Bunny concluded firmly. 'Anyway, there we are, and now Archer's broken-hearted and he says he's through with love.' Her eyes widened in dismay. 'Isn't that awful?'

'Nah,' Mitch said, rather sombrely. 'I say he's better off that way. Safer. And free.'

'You know,' Bunny drawled pensively, 'I'm not sure that's true. He's become withdrawn, and real bitter and cynical. Everett's worried about him. Anyway, we all hope that he can make a new life for himself here in the south. Maybe start afresh.'

'Well, *I've* made a new life for myself here,' Faustina said. 'And so has Mitch. I'm sure your friend will be OK. But,' she resumed crisply, 'getting back to your mystery kiss, Imogen, I think you need to be *systématique*. Don't pay any attention to what Bastien and Dimitri are saying. No – what you need to do is kiss them both again. Then you'll know for sure.'

Uneasily, Imogen pondered this radical suggestion. She wasn't sure about all this kissing-around business. It really wasn't her style, and she hadn't particularly enjoyed the complications of being semi-involved with both Bastien *and* Dimitri. Surely there must be another, less messy way of getting her mystery kisser to reveal himself? And yet . . . *Well*, she thought to herself, *in this case the kissing would be conducted purely in the spirit of scientific enquiry, wouldn't it? To get at the truth.* Besides which, she might be first-time lucky – and avoid having to kiss more than one man.

'It would be nice if you didn't have to pick just one,' Faustina said.

'Actually, Dimitri did suggest a threesome once,' Imogen said, shaking her head in disbelief.

'He *did*? And what did you say?'

'*No*, of course!'

'You turned it *down*?' Mitch thundered. 'What is *wrong* with you? You are *such* a knucklehead.'

'In my experience,' Faustina added, 'there's nothing wrong with trying something like that once in a while.'

Imogen was stunned. 'You're just a couple of perverts,' she said at length.

'But, Imogen, just think about it for a minute,' Faustina went on, unperturbed.

'*Yes*,' said Bunny, who appeared to have lapsed into a sort of trance.

Imogen threw a surprised glance in the direction of her American friend before turning back to Faustina and saying, 'Those things never work out.'

'They can if there's a clear understanding. First, both men should be entirely dedicated to your pleasure.'

Imogen stared at Faustina incredulously. 'But it's not *all* about pleasure. Somebody would be bound to get hurt! In fact, somebody already has!' She waved her scarred finger at her friends. 'Don't you think this is enough?'

'Maybe you should stop thinking about yourself so much, missy,' Mitch chipped in, his eyebrows arched to maximum capacity. 'There's no "I" in threesome.'

Bunny gave a small helpless snort. Faustina, who had not understood the joke, was still following her own train of thought. At length she said, 'And second, you must be very, very clear with them that it is *just* about the sex. And third, maybe it's best if you do it only *one* time.'

'But for as long as possible,' Bunny added, before covering her mouth and blushing.

'*Bunny!* Not you too!' Imogen protested. 'Whatever happened to respecting yourself and being in love and everything?'

'Well, I try real hard to live by that code,' Bunny replied, giggling. 'It's just that *sometimes* I wonder if it wouldn't be more fun, when it comes to boys, to shoot first and ask questions later.'

Her arms folded, Imogen watched her three friends burst into companionable raucous laughter. Then she jumped, seeing Bunny's brother Everett appear in the frame of the open French windows.

'Hey, little sis – there's a call for you. Somebody from the Galerie Provençale?'

'Oh, goody,' Bunny said, leaping to her feet and running into the house.

'I think,' Everett explained for the others' benefit, 'that Bun might just have got herself a space in which to show her work.' He dropped into his sister's deckchair. 'So. What's going on?'

'Nothing,' Imogen said, flustered by his questioning look. 'Nothing's going on.'

26

It was a Wednesday night, and Bastien and Imogen had been cooking together in Mitch's kitchen, something they'd been doing on and off on the day when Boustifaille was closed. Emboldened by a large glass of rosé wine and seeing an opportunity to carry out Faustina's daring suggestion, Imogen had just raised the possibility of another kiss – just to set things straight.

'You understand, don't you?' she said, attempting to make her request sound reasonable. 'I mean, you won't even tell me whether it *was* you at the party!'

Pausing in the midst of pouring delicious-smelling fish stew into a white china soup tureen, Bastien smiled at her, not without a hint of melancholy. 'The point is that I shouldn't *need* to tell you.'

As ever, when he'd been cooking something just for her, he looked at his sexiest, intense and brooding, and Imogen really wished he would accede to her wish, because if it turned out that it was he who had kissed her at the party, everything would fall beautifully into place and, hopefully, unfold into the sort of romantic experience she had always longed for. In silence, she brought to the table the thin, slanted croutons and garlic-scented *rouille* he'd prepared for their feast. She sat down and watched him ladle *bourride* into her bowl, then into his.

'No,' Bastien said at length, sitting down opposite her. 'I'm not going to do it.'

'Oh! Why not?'

They looked at each other. It was interesting, Imogen reflected, that Bastien's placid good looks should be so suggestive of a sunny, carefree personality. Nothing was further from the truth. He felt things deeply and was, it turned out, anything but carefree.

'Because I really like you. You know I do, Imogen.'

Imogen looked down, embarrassed. If forced to examine her feelings honestly, she would have to say that she was fond of Bastien, but probably nothing more. To give herself something to do, she tasted a little of his stew. It was ambrosial.

'If I'm going to kiss you again it has to be because you *want* me to,' he went on gravely. 'Not as some experiment.'

Imogen sighed penitently. He did have a point. She shouldn't trifle with him like this. And yet, and yet . . . What other way did she have of finding out if he was the one, since he was refusing to tell her of his own accord?

'You got the card I sent you for Valentine's Day?' asked Bastien.

'The one that mentioned passion fruit?' Imogen asked sheepishly. 'I thought it must be from you.'

'Yes. So you know how I feel, don't you? Now, if and when you decide that you have feelings for me,' he went on, 'and *only* then, I'll be very happy to kiss you as much as you like.'

Bastien certainly understood romance, Imogen thought, touched by his eloquence. She was sorely tempted to leap to her feet and kiss him right there and then, whether he wanted her to or not. Then she thought better of it. What was that Corsican saying of Faustina's? A kiss taken by force wasn't worth the candle? Something like that anyway. It was true. If she stole it from him, it was unlikely to reveal anything she wanted to know. Now was not the time. She had to wait.

A similar conversation with Dimitri had taken place in La Sirène, where Imogen had followed him to his usual spot – the pinball machine – and then stood irresolutely at his elbow, waiting for inspiration. He had glanced over his shoulder and said, 'You want a game?'

'Oh, no, I don't know how to play.'

Without really looking at her, he had pulled her into his arms so that she stood in front of him facing the machine.

'Put your fingers there, like this,' he said, positioning her hands under his and blowing her hair away from his face. 'And leave the driving to me.'

The game began and their bodies started to sway in unison. *Well, I really walked into this one*, Imogen thought, her face warm. She glanced over in the direction of the corner table where the other members of the Boustifaille gang were sitting. Larissa was glaring at her with icy disapproval, as usual, but Bastien had his back to her, which was fortunate. Monty ran around between the feet of the machine, entranced by its beepings and ringings.

Dimitri scored highly, as usual, and Imogen managed to disengage herself when he took one arm off her in order to punch the air in triumph. She turned to face him and, blushing and stammering, she explained her request. Dimitri watched her performance with every sign of enjoyment, then burst out laughing. 'This is great. You *have* decided to beg me after all!'

'I'm not *begging* you,' Imogen bristled, swiftly removing his other hand from her bottom and stepping aside. 'I'm *asking* you to do a small thing as a favour.'

'Say "please".'

'*Please*,' Imogen said through gritted teeth, mentally adding 'you bastard.' She did fancy him a bit, she admitted to herself. And there was the possibility that he did like her more than he let show. But he had to be the most exasperating man on earth.

'Hey, chief! Hey, Little Mermaid!'

It was Cheyenne. He kissed Imogen on both cheeks before giving Dimitri a lengthy, complicated handshake.

'Great party the other night *chez l'Américaine*! Really wild!'

Imogen nodded. Dimitri didn't move a muscle. He was looking at her.

'Little Mermaid, you let me down,' Cheyenne said, wagging a finger at Imogen. 'We never had that dance.'

'Oh no, we didn't, did we?' Imogen replied absent-mindedly. 'Sorry about that. Maybe next time.'

'It's cool, it's cool, don't worry because—' He took her hand and kissed it. '—I have *plans* for us. Oh yeah. Just leave it to Cheyenne.'

Startled, Imogen looked at him round-eyed. Plans? What plans?

Just then Dimitri snapped his fingers in front of her face to bring her attention back to him and said smilingly, 'If I do what you ask, what will you do for me?'

'What?'

'I *will* kiss you if you want,' he said, teasing out a lock of her hair and twisting it around his finger. 'But in exchange I want you to—' He leaned over and whispered a few words in her ear, then stepped back to watch her reaction.

Wordlessly, a furious Imogen kicked him hard in the shins and walked away, followed by an equally outraged Monty.

27

The next day, following a most uncharacteristic impulse, Imogen had decided to shop for some new underwear. Something within her had changed since the Valentine's kiss. It was as though her body had become more outspoken. After years of putting up with unexciting, sensible under-wear, it was clamouring to be given something pretty to wear. And so, walking past Ultradonna with Monty, she had found herself looking lingeringly at the window display before being greeted effusively by Mylène. After a lengthy – and surprisingly enjoyable – trying-on session, Imogen had left with three new bras and matching knickers in pastel shades of satin – ice blue, nude pink and pale green. She also threw her greying sports bra in the bin behind Ultradonna's counter, and was rewarded with a congratu-latory hug from Mylène.

Imogen's new purchases made her feel quite different, taller and straighter somehow, and also really suited the colour of her now pale golden skin, which, combined with her dark eyes and hair, made her look almost Mediterranean.

'You're going to need some new clothes to go with those,' Mylène had said sagely, walking Imogen to the door. 'That T-shirt has been through a few too many washes. And, you know,' she'd continued, placing her hands on her customer's shoulders and turning her around so that she could see herself in the nearest full-length mirror, 'you really don't need such baggy things. You're curvy – you should dress *près du corps*, like this, look,' she'd said, pulling at the excess fabric of Imogen's clothes. 'Now we can see your shape.' Mylène smiled. '*Une vraie pin-up, hein?* I want you to promise me that next time you visit you'll be wearing some well-cut denim and a *little* T-shirt – something cute and *sympa*, OK?'

'OK,' Imogen had said, smiling back. Her body, she felt, liked the suggestion of new clothes. 'Thank you very much.'

'*De rien, ma belle.*'

Now sitting at her desk in her room after the evening service, Imogen was checking emails and tidying her Inbox. There were a few of her siblings' usual silly domestic requests. After pressing Delete repeatedly and with considerable enjoyment, Imogen sent a message to her mother, in which she gave everyone her love and painted a carefully edited picture of her life in Saint-Jean as Daphne's fictitious au pair, adding as much local colour as possible to make up for her deception.

Afterwards, Imogen's thoughts turned to Di. She really wanted to tell her friend about the kiss and ask her advice. But how to describe her unusual 'sight-unseen' circumstances? Di would probably think she had sunstroke.

While she was wrestling with this a message suddenly appeared in her Inbox.

The subject was – in French – 'OPEN ME, IMOGEN'.

She stared at the words, then noted the sender's address: the-valentine's-kiss@mailenfrance.fr. Her heart stopped beating then changed its mind and went into overdrive. Holding her breath, she opened the message. It contained no text, only a picture.

It was a black-and-white photograph of a couple kissing as they walked down the street, seemingly without breaking their stride. The man's arm was wrapped around the girl's shoulders, while her arm hung down by her side, with the palm half-open and turned slightly upward, suggesting . . . what? That he had taken her by surprise? That she was returning his kiss unreservedly? Both. Both of those things. They were walking past a café terrace amid indifferent, busy passers-by. The city looked like it might be Paris.

Imogen smiled, her fingers trailing across her mouth. Then her eyes narrowed as she scanned the email once more for any overlooked text. But there wasn't any – just the image of a gesture that was at once impulsive and intimate. Yes, that was it. Exactly.

She got up to call Mitch to the computer.

'That's Robert Doisneau's *Kiss by the Hôtel de Ville*,' he said, after taking one look at the screen. 'You're right, it was taken in Paris in the early 1950s. That monumental façade in the background is the Paris Town Hall – l'Hôtel de Ville.'

'Yes, yes,' Imogen said. 'But what do you make of it?'

'He's got good taste. Personally, I love Doisneau – his work is so kinetic.' After glancing at her, he added, 'Oh, I get you.' He looked at her more sternly. 'Well, why don't you ask *him*?'

'Who's more likely to have sent it? Dimitri or Bastien?'

The corners of Mitch's mouth turned down doubtfully, then he said, 'Hard to say. It's an incredibly famous image, especially in France. You can buy posters and postcards of it all over the place. Either of them could have come across it.'

'What do you think I should say?'

Mitch's eyebrows arched expressively. 'It's your story, babe. The kid sends you this classy opening gambit – a real icon of romance. It's up to you to respond. I bet he's waiting at the other end, biting his nails and all. I'm going to bed. Let me know how it turns out, all right?'

He squeezed her shoulder and left the room. Alone again, Imogen clicked on Reply. She hesitated for a moment, then quickly typed, '*Qui es-tu?*' and clicked on Send Now.

To her surprise and delight, a reply came almost instantly. Mitch had been right. Her Boustifaille colleague had been waiting for her to respond – he was *there*. His message read – in French – '*Did you like it?*'

'It's lovely,' Imogen typed back, also in French, adding with élan, 'Doisneau is very kinetic.' That would at least show him that she wasn't completely clueless.

'*I couldn't agree more, but I meant the kiss.*'

Imogen inhaled sharply. 'Yes, that too,' she typed with trembling fingers.

'*Would you like to do it again?*'

'Why did you vanish like that?'

'*I don't know. But it doesn't mean that I wouldn't love to kiss you again.*'

'Who are you?'

A brief pause, then, '*I can't answer that just yet.*'

'I really think I should know who I'm going to meet.'

'*I'm not so sure. It was a Valentine's kiss, wasn't it? Isn't Valentine's Day about secret admirers?*'

He was right, of course. She had a Valentine, a secret admirer who wished to remain anonymous for a bit longer.

'I think I have a pretty good idea who you are, anyway,' she typed, smiling.

She closed her eyes, trying hard to imagine who this was – Bastien or Dimitri? They were both quite capable of teasing her like this.

'*Clever girl. It wouldn't surprise me at all. How about that kiss?*'

'I'm not sure what you mean. You want to kiss me, but you won't tell me your name?'

'*That's right.*'

Imogen frowned, then replied, 'But if we were to kiss again, surely I'd see your face and then the game would be up.'

'*That isn't quite what I had in mind – you've kissed me once before without seeing my face.*'

'Yes.'

'*And you liked it.*'

Actually, I *loved* it, Imogen thought as the blood rushed to her face. I don't think I've ever enjoyed anything half as much. Not even the first time I tasted lobster, and that's saying something.

'*You see?*' he wrote, having correctly interpreted her silence.

See? Imogen wondered. See what exactly? She narrowed her eyes at the screen, then typed, 'Not sure I'm following you correctly, but are you proposing another round of . . .' Desperately, she scrabbled for the French name of Blind Man's Buff. Oh, yes, that was it. '*Colin-maillard?*'

'*I'll think of something just as nice. Good night, Imogen.*'

And there the conversation had ended, leaving Imogen in a highly agitated and not at all unpleasant state. At last – at last she found herself in a truly romantic situation, communicating with an admirer whose identity remained teasingly mysterious, and last but not least, conducting the whole thing in French. Oh, this was far, far better than dreaming over the historical adventures of Sophy or Venetia. Now she, Imogen, was the heroine – her own story was happening – right here and now. And she had not the first idea of where it was going. Yes, she thought, as a thrill of excitement coursed through her body, this whole thing was entirely outside her sphere of experience – and all the more intoxicating for that.

28

Imogen was taking a much-needed break in the Boustifaille courtyard. Monty lay in his basket at her feet, snoozing. Lately she had taken to bringing him to work with her once in a while 'to visit'. Daphne had been right when she'd said that the French loved dogs, and her colleagues, Monsieur Boudin included, had all taken the little terrier to their hearts as a sort of mascot. It had been a particularly demanding service tonight, Imogen thought, pushing her hair out of her face. She had never seen Monsieur Boudin quite this volatile before.

She looked thoughtfully at her boss through the kitchen window. He had made it clear that there would be no question of the staff being allowed to decamp to La Sirène at the end of service tonight. Planting himself at the centre of the kitchen, he had thundered, 'I have an announcement. Tomorrow, the new *Guide Gastronomique du Midi* is published. I want you all to know that I am not nervous, not nervous at all,' he went on, mopping his brow. 'I am *quite certain* that we will retain our Golden Spoon, but . . .'

Imogen's ears had pricked up: the Golden Spoons awarded by the *Guide Gastronomique du Midi* were as fiercely coveted as Michelin stars.

'But I think,' Monsieur Boudin resumed, suddenly

looking haggard, 'that it will bring good luck if we all have a little drink, to bring the team together and reassure everyone, yes? But maybe you have better things to do, *les enfants*? Better than to support Boustifaille by drinking with me?'

He had glared at them all, and then, seeing them shake their heads, had brightened up just a little.

When Imogen walked back into the kitchen, Monsieur Boudin gestured for her to follow the others, who had begun to congregate in the dining room. She swiftly removed her chef's whites before joining her colleagues, who, now in civvies, stood around rather stiffly, singly or in pairs, surrounded by the restaurant's gallery of sad clowns.

'So, everyone,' Monsieur Boudin declared, looking around the room, 'we have a drink together, and then I know that everything will be fine. And if it's not fine, *you are ALL fired!* Ha ha ha – only a little joke. Sidonie, can you bring out the 1983 cognac, please?'

'Certainly, Chef.'

After that, Monsieur Boudin slumped into a chair, downing shot after shot of cognac with a sort of desperate abandon. Jean-Jacques, the maître d', looked like he had been through all this before, and slipped behind the bar. After a moment's programming of the restaurant's sound system, they heard the opening bars of Mozart's *Requiem*.

'Not a very uplifting choice,' Imogen commented discreetly to Bastien, who stood next to her. She stole a glance at him. In a minute she would drop a teasing hint about black-and-white photography and the romance of Paris – and see what came of that.

'I know. But look at him. He likes it.'

Monsieur Boudin, who had removed his crumpled chef's hat to reveal a sweaty thatch of black hair underneath, was smiling and nodding along to the solemn strains of the music. He helped himself to another drink.

'Does this always happen when a new guide comes out?' Imogen whispered.

'Only in the last couple of years. He used to be completely insouciant about all this, but now it's really getting to him. You know, he doesn't have any home life any more.'

Imogen nodded, remembering the sad story of Monsieur Boudin's betrayal by his wife and brother.

'So now,' Bastien went on, 'this place means everything to him.'

'But is there really a risk of Boustifaille losing its Golden Spoon?'

'Be careful!' Bastien whispered back. 'He'll hear you!' He pulled her a little further away from Boudin, then added, 'Dimitri thinks so. But then he's always pessimistic. He's not the only one looking for another job, though. Pierrot and Manu are thinking about it too.'

Imogen was appalled. 'I had no idea it was that bad.' She glanced across the room at Dimitri, Pierrot and Manu, who stood together speaking in undertones, no doubt about their plans to jump ship. 'And you? Are you planning to leave?'

'No, not at all,' Bastien said, looking at her gravely. 'I believe in Boudin, you see. So of course I'm staying.

Larissa, Sidonie, Jean-Jacques and Patrice feel the same way.'

Everyone was now starting to talk in a less restrained manner, and people even began to move about, some of them pulling up chairs. Seeing this, Jean-Jacques turned the music down a little, allowing the noise of chatter to compete with it. Impulsively, Imogen walked over to Monsieur Boudin and perched on the table next to him. He looked up at her, his dark eyes edged with pink. '*Ah, petite assistante*,' he said tonelessly. There was something intensely sad about seeing such a force of nature subdued to that degree.

'*Tchin-tchin, Monsieur*,' Imogen said as gaily as she could, clinking glasses with her boss.

The ghost of a smile passed over Boudin's face. '*Tu es gentille, ma petite*,' he said. 'I've always thought that Daphne has perfect judgement. I'm happy that she sent you to Boustifaille.'

'Thank you,' Imogen said, smiling.

Boudin said, more brightly, 'She is a remarkable woman, Daphne. Quite, quite remarkable.'

'Yes, I like her very much.'

He seemed a little less downcast now and Imogen thought how extraordinary it was to be sitting there, having an almost normal conversation with the great Boudin, who was, as it turned out, not only a larger-than-life human tornado but also a sensitive middle-aged man, anxious about his achievements. And goodness, that cognac was strong. She felt quite light-headed. Not light-headed enough, however, not to heed an ominous sound coming from the kitchen: joyous, excited barking. *Monty!* She must have left the courtyard door unfastened, and naughty Monty, who knew very well that he was barred from the kitchen, was now searching it for forbidden treats.

Imogen looked around the room. Nobody else appeared to have noticed the noise. She smiled nervously at her boss and moved towards the kitchen door. Looking over her shoulder to check that everybody was chatting away, she walked through the swing doors and closed them carefully behind her.

'Monty!' she hissed in the most authoritative voice she could muster. The little dog had gone completely quiet. Where was he? Had he somehow got into the walk-in freezer? No, that door was too heavy. But it was just possible that he had managed to turn the knob on the door of the larder. He was very nimble with his paws and it wouldn't be the first time that he'd managed to open an interesting cupboard. Now Imogen was worried: several sweet-smelling Bayonne hams hung in the larder and she dreaded to think what would happen if Monty managed to leap high enough to take a bite. With beating heart, she checked the larder. No Monty. She crouched down to check under the counters. No Monty there, either. She was just about to go and look behind the ovens when, suddenly, all the lights went out. At the same time, she was aware of a movement to her right. Soon after that she heard a short bark.

'Monty! Come here, you naughty boy!'

There he was, licking her hand, and obviously very

pleased with himself. Somehow or other he must have managed to filch something tasty.

'You're a little glutton,' she whispered fondly, scratching his head.

Around them the darkness was absolute. With Monty at her heels, Imogen edged forward gingerly, feeling for a wall. Next door in the restaurant she could hear someone speculate about a *panne de secteur* – a power failure – which might take a long time to sort out. Meanwhile the best thing would be if she could somehow locate the courtyard door and expel her misbehaving dog before Monsieur Boudin got wind of anything. Suddenly, Monty let out a volley of delighted barks.

'Quiet, Monty!' Imogen implored. 'You'll get us found out!'

She took another step in what she thought might be the right direction, and then, quite unexpectedly, bumped into someone else – no doubt one of her colleagues.

'Oops, sorry,' she said, giggling nervously. 'It's me, Imogen. I came to get my dog. Who's this?'

'Imogen, it's me,' the person said in French, very low, while taking her hand in his. 'Don't be scared.'

Suddenly quite a bit scared, she removed her hand and took a couple of steps back, hastily bending down to pick up her dog. Monty was fiercely loyal, and would gladly attack anybody who threatened her. But he appeared entirely undisturbed by the man's presence. There was no hostile growling – just lots of happy panting.

'I'm going to call for help,' Imogen said, in as steady a voice as she could manage.

'There's no need,' she heard him say in an undertone. Then he laughed. 'I know this isn't Blind Man's Buff, but . . . is it OK?'

'You?' she asked incredulously. Her heart continued to beat quite fast, now for a very different reason. Gently, she put Monty down and asked, 'Where are you?'

'Over here,' he whispered, finding and taking both her hands this time. As she listened to his breathing and to her own heartbeat, she began again to feel light-headed – not unpleasantly so. The warmth of his touch, allied with an instinctive sense of his relaxed physical presence and even with a strong, irrational conviction that he was smiling, gradually made her relax as well.

He kissed her hands, one after the other, and then very gently pulled her into his arms where he held her in a light embrace. 'Do you want me to leave you alone?' he murmured in her ear. 'If you want me to go, I'll go right now.'

But Imogen did not ask him to leave. Instead she found herself instinctively laying her head on his shoulder. At that moment, though she didn't realise it until later, all thoughts of Bastien or Dimitri went clean out of her head. She was only aware of the feel of his shirt against her cheek, of the length of his body against hers, of the close proximity of his unseen face. 'This is crazy,' she said, smiling a little. 'I don't even know who you are.'

'You do. You do know me,' he murmured, before cupping her face in his hands and kissing her until she fell into such an all-enveloping, liquid and languorous haze that her knees almost gave way. When she instinctively reached up to touch his face, he grasped her hands and held them firmly behind her back. Another kiss – again she tasted that intoxicating hint of spice and felt her body come together, tuning in, connecting.

Next door, she could hear the sound of voices. Somebody was saying something about the fuse box, or missing fuses, or something. She wasn't particularly interested. What followed unfolded like one of those accelerated nature films that show flowers blossoming in seconds – and in full Technicolor.

After a certain amount of ravenous kissing had taken place, for how long she did not know, he lowered his head to press his mouth against her throat. As in a dream, and astonished at her own audacity, she heard the sound of her own voice instructing him to undo her shirt. As in a dream, he obeyed and lowered her bra before trailing an ardent path of small bites across her breasts. She gave herself over to this for as long as she could stand it without crying out and then, when the desire to do so became irresistible, turned around in his embrace and nestled against him. One of her hands had come free and she reached up to touch his neck, the back of his head, before he seized it again, slipping his fingers between hers caressingly. He wrapped his arms around her, and she closed her eyes.

'*C'est bon, j'ai trouvé des fusibles!*' she heard someone shout triumphantly next door. As her brain reluctantly relayed the information that replacement fuses had been found, he crushed her mouth with a kiss, and then, in the blink of an eye, took his hands off her and moved away. She'd barely had time to register that the courtyard door had opened and closed, signalling the stranger's exit, when the lights came back on.

Straightening her bra with one hand, she grabbed Monty's collar with the other and dashed towards the door. 'Stay!' she ordered. 'Stay out there until I come for you.' While hurriedly doing up her shirt, she looked around the courtyard – no one there. On coming back into the kitchen, she noticed that the window blind was down. She stared at it. It had been up during service, she was certain of it. *He* must have pulled it down to ensure maximum blackout.

But – she suddenly thought, as her consciousness again came into focus with a sharp click – who was *he*? Well, that was easy, she thought, it was *definitely* the person who had kissed her at Bunny's party. She bit her lip, before bursting into laughter at the absurdity of her situation. All right then – but who was *that*? Her puzzled mind turned to Bastien and Dimitri, trying her best to make her memories of what it had been like to kiss them fit with the experience she'd just had, then shaking her head doubtfully. No. This had been something quite different, as her own response testified.

She walked back into the kitchen, paused for a moment behind the swing doors to pull her hair up into a neat twist and stepped into the restaurant. Several of her colleagues turned around.

'There you are,' Bastien said, giving her a warm smile. 'We thought we'd lost you.' He hugged her and she returned the pressure absent-mindedly. 'Where were you when the lights went out?' he asked.

'Oh, I had to pop into the kitchen to check something,' she said as guilelessly as possible.

Dimitri was leaning against the wall right next to the kitchen doors, talking to Larissa. He came over and, locking eyes with her, said salaciously, 'God, you look good enough to eat. Your skin . . . If I didn't know any better, I'd say you'd just been . . .'

'Oh, shut up,' she said, hurriedly moving away to give herself time to think. Her heart was thumping. She shook her head, remembering her unbelievably brazen and reckless behaviour in the kitchen just now. What had got into her? She'd always thought of herself as a fairly cautious and sensible person. Ah, but Mitch, who'd lived here a long time, had talked about the potent and enduring romance of the Riviera, hadn't he? Perhaps that was what she could feel bubbling up inside her?

What to do now? Where to start? She was beginning to realise one thing. One noticeable effect of *those* kisses on her brain was to blot out all investigative abilities and indeed any desire to know anything. It had been the same at Bunny's party. It was a strange feeling – and oddly liberating.

But now the kissing has stopped, she told herself firmly, so try to *think*. Who is he likely to be? He had spoken French just now, she reasoned, and his emails had also been in French. So he must be French.

'Thank God for Pierrot!' Sidonie said then, offering

Imogen a little more cognac and interrupting her train of thought. 'He saved the day.'

Hearing his name, Pierrot came over to join them.

'Well . . . it was the torch we found behind the bar that saved the day really,' he said modestly. 'We could have waited all night for the power to be restored – that wasn't the problem. When I got to the fuse box and had a look it was obvious that some joker had pulled out all the fuses, as well as hiding the spares we keep on top of the box.'

For a minute nobody spoke, then Patrice said, laughing nervously, 'It must have been one of us. Who was it? Come on, own up!'

Bastien held up his hands and shook his head, 'Well, it wasn't me.'

'Or me,' Manu said, swiftly echoed by everybody else.

'It *was* a good idea, though,' Dimitri said, looking quizzically at Imogen, who was trying her hardest not to smile delightedly. Whoever-he-was had staged all this – just so that he could kiss her again. 'Things were getting tense,' Dimitri went on, 'Boudin was seriously drunk and he wouldn't have let anyone leave. The blackout broke the spell.'

'Absolutely,' Bastien said. 'We would never have got out before dawn and then I would have had to carry him home and put him to bed, just like last year.'

Every inch his old alarming self, Monsieur Boudin now marched across to join his staff. He draped one arm around Manu's shoulders, and the other around Larissa's. Both of them sagged slightly under his weight. 'OK, *les enfants*,' he boomed jovially. 'Now everything is back to normal, I'm going home. And then, tomorrow, we celebrate our Golden Spoon all together, yes?'

'Good luck, Chef!' Patrice piped up imprudently.

'*Luck!* Boudin doesn't need luck!' Monsieur Boudin laughed unconvincingly before stalking off.

29

Imogen stared again at the radically customised plastic ducks poised on their AstroTurf base. Hmmm. It was hard to know what to say. She turned away for respite and found herself facing an entire wall of glass cases. These contained detailed scenes involving chickens – not plastic this time, but the real thing, plucked, headless and embalmed by the artist – engaged in a variety of activities. This one, for example, was pushing a supermarket trolley filled with sticks of dynamite. That one sat behind the wheel of a toy car. Another was propped up on a sofa clad in a T-shirt and Y-fronts and watching television. Yet another stood in front of a mirror wearing a wedding dress.

'Well? What do you think?'

It was Bunny, looking her usual immaculate self in a crisp navy shirt-waister. Imogen found it astonishing that this ladylike creature could produce such unexpected work.

'Oh,' she said, desperately casting about for a more intelligent response than, 'It's the stuff of nightmares.' 'They're really very . . . challenging.'

'Really?' Bunny said, squeezing Imogen's hand gratefully. 'Thank you so much! Do you think people are enjoying themselves?'

Imogen looked around the gallery's pocket-sized exhibition space. It contained Faustina, Monty and Cristiana,

Mitch, and Amaury d'Ousset, who had come especially from Montpellier for the show. The guests stood next to the buffet, eating the crostini and mini *pissaladières* – Provençal onion tarts – prepared by Imogen, who, after some consideration, had decided not to take up any of Bunny's original suggestions – meat-themed cupcakes topped with 'ham' or 'mince' fashioned out of icing and even, as a centrepiece, a large 'road-kill' hedgehog cake – though they would, of course, have been in keeping with the tone of the exhibition.

'Bunny, no, that's just too grotesque,' she had told her friend.

'But I'm sure it'll all taste delicious. And it'll be a talking point!'

'Exactly,' Imogen had said firmly. 'I don't think the food should detract from your art.'

'Oh, I wish there were more people,' Bunny said now, her smooth brow creasing the tiniest bit. 'It would be more fun for everyone.'

She looked a little tired around the eyes, Imogen noticed, which wasn't surprising: she had been working non-stop for the past couple of days in order to finish every detail of her display cases.

'Well, it's only the opening,' Imogen said soothingly. 'Your show is on for a whole week.'

Bunny Doucet – 'Ceci n'est pas un poulet/This is Not a Chicken' read a sign propped up on the pavement outside the Galerie Provençale. Imogen glanced at Pascale, the gallery's *soignée* owner, who sat in a corner looking shell-shocked. The Galerie Provençale usually showed the work of local craftspeople: rustic stoneware, coloured glassware, pretty textiles, that sort of thing.

'Bunny, you know when you first came to see Pascale?'

'Yes?'

'Well, did you show her any pictures? Of your work? For example the plastic ducks with the, er . . .'

'The phallic heads?' Bunny said with a perky smile. 'Do you know, I don't think I did. We got chatting and we *clicked* right away!'

It was just possible, Imogen thought, that a mixture of sunny goodwill and enthusiasm, allied with Bunny's limited French and Pascale's almost non-existent English, had resulted in a tragic misunderstanding. Imogen wasn't entirely sure what poor Pascale had been led to expect. Presumably barnyard animals must have entered into it somehow. Perhaps she had visualised traditional silk screens of delicate pastel-coloured chickens and ducklings. And yet here the conservative gallery owner was now, staring in barely disguised horror at the glass case that housed the pole-dancing chicken, frozen in an impudent pose and sporting a spangled thong and thigh-high boots carefully fashioned by the artist.

'Well, anyway, Everett's coming later with Archer,' Bunny said a trifle nervously. '*They* know about art. And they've always been very complimentary about my work.'

'I didn't realise your brother was still on the Côte,' Imogen said absent-mindedly.

'Yes. Buddy's here too. They've both been staying with him in Menton.'

'Who?'

'Archer.'

'Ah, yes,' Imogen said. That was Everett's friend with the broken nose – the one who was getting over a particularly traumatic divorce. Then, hearing the words: '*Félicitations, chère cousine*,' she looked up to see Amaury d'Ousset kissing Bunny on the cheeks. 'Your work is simply de-*light*-ful.'

'Why, thank you, cousin,' Bunny drawled, lowering her eyelashes.

Noticing his understated cufflinks as he moved to greet her, Imogen reflected that Amaury did not need period costume to look like a period piece. Everything about his style suggested a healthy disregard for current fashions. Some of Bunny's American friends had seemed impossibly well groomed but Amaury took matters much further. Looking at him, it was possible to imagine an alternative reality in which such people as Elvis, say, or James Dean – to say nothing of the Sex Pistols – had never existed, and in which young men, as soon as they were out of short trousers, still wanted to look exactly like their fathers. Not only was Imogen certain that Amaury had worn short trousers for years as a boy, she also knew that should he ever wear anything so vulgar as a T-shirt – a highly improbable notion – it would probably say something like: 'Traditionalists Do It Better'.

The transatlantic cousins were chatting and seemed to be getting on very well. Amaury probably had enough family feeling to forgive Bunny her unconventional art.

The Galerie Provençale's doorbell tinkled melodiously. Seeing a scornful frown paint itself on Faustina's face while

Pascale's expression changed swiftly from dark depression to incredulous delight, Imogen knew instantly, without needing to look around, that Enzo had arrived. He glanced in Bunny's direction, then met Imogen's gaze and held it for a while with his usual smouldering, penetrating intensity.

'Will you excuse me?' Bunny said to Amaury. 'I'd better go and say hello to my guest.'

With practised politeness, Amaury immediately turned to Imogen and began to talk about the best restaurants in the area. Had she been to Le Chat Gourmand up in the hills? No? Oh, but she must. How about La Rascasse on the way to Saint-Paul-de-Vence? Really, no? As Imogen explained gently that she was at work most evenings (without pointing out that she was also broke), they were joined by Everett, followed by his friend Archer. Shaking hands with the Americans, Amaury declared that he couldn't imagine anything more 'de-light-ful' than a little group outing to one or other of those 'hostelries'.

'That sounds good,' Everett said, smiling warmly at Imogen. 'I'm always glad of opportunities to educate Bun – and Buddy, for that matter. He's hopeless. Will you come along too?' he added, turning to Archer.

'What?' Archer said, jolted out of his reverie. He'd been gazing at Bunny's chickens. 'Sure, why not?' he replied coolly, evincing little enthusiasm.

Imogen glanced at him sideways. She remembered him as distinctly aloof, and meeting him again now her first impression was confirmed. Of course, now that she knew more about his disastrous private life, Archer's chilly manner made more sense, though personally she thought it wouldn't kill him to make a bit more of an effort in social situations. He'd barely acknowledged her, for example, and Imogen reflected testily that having a broken heart was really no excuse for being downright rude.

'How about luncheon on a weekend?' Amaury went on. 'Leave things to me – I'll organise everything.'

'Thanks,' Everett said, looking pleased. 'I'll go and tell Bun that we've found a good way to celebrate her first solo show.'

While Amaury engaged Archer in conversation about other local galleries, Imogen wondered whether Everett's friend was another of those Americans who, like Bunny and her younger brother, and indeed like her own family, were inexplicably indifferent to food. How could anybody fail to be thrilled at the thought of eating at Le Chat Gourmand? The chef there was a twenty-something prodigy who was particularly famous for his delectable way with offal. As for La Rascasse, she'd been dreaming of tasting the mythical *menu dégustation*, which Mitch, who'd been there a couple of times, had described to her with typical deadpan enthusiasm as a 'polymorphously perverse eleven-course orgasm'. She felt nothing but pity for those unfortunates who remained unmoved by any of this. They didn't know what they were missing.

'So what do you think of the art?' she suddenly heard Archer say, though it took her a minute to realise that he was actually addressing her.

'I . . . think it's very interesting,' she said prudently.

'Really?' he asked, his face impassive. 'Interesting how?'

She looked at him suspiciously. He knew a lot about

art, Bunny had said. Well, Imogen had grown up precisely among such types, and she knew just how much they relished setting her up in order to laugh at her lack of artistic sense. Clearly, Archer was just the same.

'Just interesting, OK?' she replied spikily. 'I'm not sure why I need to justify my opinions all of a sudden.'

'Oh, but you don't,' he said, looking at her with a half-smile.

Imogen stared back, standing her ground and reflecting that she'd never had the gumption to assert herself in this way when teased by a member of her family. Well, she was learning fast, and when she went home there would be no question of allowing Hildegard or her mother to walk all over her the way they used to.

'I almost forgot!' Amaury exclaimed, and she gladly shifted her gaze to him. 'I was dismayed to read in the newspaper this morning that Boustifaille has lost its Golden Spoon. Your boss must be very upset.'

Imogen was stunned. 'No! That's terrible. I haven't spoken to anyone at the restaurant yet – my shift only starts in an hour.'

Come to think of it, she had been so distracted by the previous night's encounter in the dark that she hadn't even switched on her mobile. As she did so now, the screen flashed to tell her that seventeen text messages had been received. They had all come from Bastien and told the story of the Golden Spoon debacle in a series of telegraphic vignettes.

First thing this morning, Monsieur Boudin had lurched into the kitchen in an abominable mood, clutching a copy of the *Guide Gastronomique du Midi*. Though clearly very drunk, he had insisted on beginning food preparation, assisted willy-nilly by his terrified staff. After a while, he had fetched a bottle of his favourite cognac and, while guzzling it down, had torn the guide to pieces. Jean-Jacques and Patrice had been summoned, interrogated about cancelled bookings, and made to confess that there had already been a few. News spread quickly about such matters in these parts. Whereupon Monsieur Boudin had whisked three dozen eggs in a bowl, added the torn pages of the guide to the mixture and attempted to make it into an extra-large omelette. Then, after hurling the flaming frying pan at the wall, he had fired everybody before bursting into penitent tears and insisting on an embarrassing group hug. While this was going on, he had passed out, after which Pierrot and Manu had loaded him into the van, taken him home and put him to bed.

The staff had then argued over whether they should close the restaurant for the day. The noes, led by Bastien, had won by a margin. It wouldn't do to lose face so publicly. They had managed to scrape through lunch, but Jean-Jacques, Patrice and Larissa had had to field endless questions from customers about whether Boudin was in the kitchen today. Bastien wondered if Imogen would mind coming in early for the next shift. All hands were needed on deck.

Imogen made her excuses at the gallery, left Monty with Mitch and rushed over to the restaurant. As she stepped into the courtyard, her eyes flitted to the fuse box. Pierrot had shown her exactly where it was, inside a cubbyhole that was tucked down a flight of steps and immediately outside the kitchen door – with its glass window. It would have been perfectly possible, Imogen had reflected, for someone standing in the courtyard to see her walk into the lit kitchen in search of Monty. In fact, could it be that whoever-he-was had encouraged Monty into the kitchen precisely in the hope of luring her there? Yes, quite possibly. And then, provided he'd already ascertained where the fuse box was, all he needed to do was to disable it and then . . . slip inside and . . . She knew perfectly well what had happened next. Just not with whom. That was the snag.

30

'Um, Chef,' Imogen began, soon after arriving at Boustifaille the following evening, 'I wanted to say how sorry I am about . . . that thing in the guide.' She stopped, not quite daring to look at her boss directly. 'If there's anything more I can do to help,' she went on, 'just ask.'

'Thank you, *petite*.' Boudin shook his head, then said lugubriously, 'Tonight we have a critic coming.'

'Oh.'

'So it's not really the time to give you more responsibility, you understand?'

'I understand, Chef,' Imogen said meekly, before adding, 'but tomorrow?'

'Perhaps, yes,' Boudin said, looking pale and ill. 'Now get to work.'

The presence of Nadine Picore, the food critic from regional newspaper *Nice-Matin*, had galvanised the whole kitchen, and Imogen was gratified to see Bastien and Dimitri, respectively, in charge of the critic's starter and main course, intent on producing work of consummate artistry. If only Monsieur Boudin had let them get on with it, all might have been well. But instead, he kept interrupting them at crucial moments to bark out confusing instructions, so that, inevitably, Bastien's dumplings were overdone, forcing him to start again, while Dimitri's sauce

– a delicate emulsion – kept splitting. More time was then wasted as the chef berated them for their mistakes.

But it was the unfortunate Régis who bore the brunt of Boudin's ill humour while he desperately attempted to make Madame Picore's passion-fruit *millefeuille*. Mindful of Jean-Jacques's nervous reports about the critic's deeply unamused demeanour – for both her starter and her main course had been considerably delayed – Régis looked agitated as he spread small dollops of *feuillant* – the almondy dough used for the pastry layers – on a baking sheet with his fingertips. He had almost finished doing this when Boudin sidled up to him, 'You're handling it too much. Wash your hands and start again. And keep an eye on the first lot – don't let them burn.'

As Régis walked towards the oven with his prepared sheet, he found Monsieur Boudin blocking his path to look down at his work. 'What is this?'

'It's the *feuillant* for the—'

'I know *what* it is. Why are the discs full of holes?'

'But . . . there aren't any holes, Chef.'

'*I* say there *are*. Start again.'

'OK,' Régis murmured, breaking into a sweat.

'And use your nose, for God's sake. The rest of your discs are burning.'

'*Trois millefeuilles!*' Larissa called out loud and clear. '*Et deux millefeuilles!*'

'Yes, Larissa!' Régis called back, while tipping the carbonised discs of dough into the bin.

'And now get on with the *sabayon*, OK?' Imogen heard Boudin telling Régis. 'You're running out of time.'

'But . . . it's already made, Chef,' Régis interjected. 'It's in the fridge. We use it cold, remember? What I need to make now is the passion-fruit caramel.'

'Tut-tut-tut!' Monsieur Boudin said, glaring at him implacably. 'You are telling me what to do?'

'No, Chef.' After swiftly removing his dough discs from the oven and lifting them onto a cooling rack, Régis got on with whisking egg yolks and vanilla sugar in a bain-marie. 'Oh, God,' he whimpered, 'I don't think I can take much more of this. It's like he's trying to sabotage himself, the restaurant, everything.'

'Régis!' Larissa called out sharply from behind the pass. 'Where are those *millefeuilles*? The customers are getting impatient. And Madame Picore looks furious. I must have hers *now*!'

'Five minutes!' Régis called out, while watching Monsieur Boudin advance towards him.

'Make the caramel,' his boss snapped, looking over his shoulder. 'That *sabayon* isn't thick enough! Where is the froth? Start again. And *don't* let your caramel burn! Oh, look – it's burning! Start *again*.'

'Chef,' Jean-Jacques called respectfully from behind the pass.

'Yes, what is it?'

'It's too late. I'm afraid those tables have all asked for their bills.'

'And the lady from *Nice-Matin*?' Monsieur Boudin asked without turning around.

'I'm sorry, Chef,' Jean-Jacques said, his face white. 'She left.'

Régis gasped and covered his face with his hands. Crestfallen, Imogen looked at her boss.

'She left,' Monsieur Boudin repeated a few times. Then, as he turned away, Imogen caught a glimpse of the expression on his face. It looked, incredibly, like relief. She shook her head. No, it couldn't be – she must have imagined it.

31

'OK,' Faustina said briskly, flicking back her carefully styled mane of curls. 'Let's get started.'

Meanwhile Bunny stood in Bonjour les Toutous' waiting area, setting up a large easel pad and unwrapping a packet of brightly coloured marker pens.

'Oh, this is so good,' Mitch said, pressing the palms of his hands together. 'Just like *Cagney and Lacey*.'

'Imagine if you will,' Bunny said, beaming, 'that we're in foggy old London Town, in the last chapter of a story by that great English lady Agatha Christie. We're going to have ourselves a brainstorming session, just like Miss Marple would.'

'I'm not entirely sure that Miss Marple would have used the word "brainstorming",' Imogen murmured, smiling. She was curious to see what results, if any, her friends' initiative would achieve. Now that she was no longer sure about her original suspects – Bastien and Dimitri – she really needed a helping hand.

'So,' Faustina said, rapidly drawing a floor plan of Boustifaille. 'Restaurant. Kitchen. Courtyard. Imogen,' she continued, holding out a blue pen, 'come and show me where everybody was when—'

'When the murder was committed?' Imogen said ironically.

'Tch!' Mitch hissed in her ear. 'Be nice!'

'OK, OK, I'll do my best.' She drew a small blue cross. 'That's Jean-Jacques, the maître d'. It can't have been him, because I know he stayed with Larissa and Sidonie during the blackout. They stood at the bar, there. So that leaves . . . every other man who was there,' she said, returning the blue pen to Faustina.

'Hmm, let's go through the kitchen staff,' Faustina said, counting on her fingers. 'Pierrot?'

'Actually, no,' Imogen said, relieved. 'He was the one who fixed the fuses, so he's in the clear. He couldn't be in two places at once.'

'You see?' Bunny said encouragingly. 'It's not as confusing as you thought.'

'All right,' Faustina ignored the interruption. 'Next. Régis?'

'I don't think so. Too, er, cuddly. He's quite well padded, whereas I think I could feel a bit of, um . . .'

'Bone?' Mitch asked sardonically.

Imogen flushed scarlet, while the others broke into ruthless giggles. 'Well, yes, I suppose so,' she managed with a reasonable amount of dignity. 'Shoulder. Ribs. That kind of thing.'

'How about Manu?'

'Too short.'

'How tall is he?' Bunny said. 'Your . . . Valentine?'

'I'm not sure exactly, but definitely taller than me.'

Mitch frowned. 'That fresh-faced kid who's Jean-Jacques's lieutenant – Patrice. He's tall enough.'

This was true. Imogen closed her eyes, reviewing her

relationship with the sweet-natured and diffident Patrice, which was close to non-existent, for he lived mainly in his mentor Jean-Jacques's shadow.

'Patrice is incredibly shy,' she said.

'Exactly!' Faustina cried.

'Yeah. Wouldn't that be a good reason for anonymity?'

'He . . . the person who kissed me in the kitchen didn't feel . . . shy,' Imogen murmured, remembering the feel of his hands on her wrists and the tormenting, *extremely* well-judged way in which he had let his teeth drag on her bare skin.

'You mean he had –' Mitch paused, then lowered his voice to a bass baritone for added emphasis '– *sexual authority*. Is that right?'

Imogen smiled. 'Yes, you could call it that.'

'Could even have been Boudin, I guess,' Mitch went on thoughtfully. 'Now *he* has authority coming out of his ears.'

Imogen was stunned. '*No!* He was pickled in cognac, for one thing. I wouldn't have been able to taste anything else.'

'Hur-hur-hur. Relax, I was only kidding.'

'We're wasting time,' Faustina interjected, contemplating the jumble of blue crosses she had drawn in the wobbly rectangle that represented the restaurant. 'Concentrate.' She folded her arms. 'You know, that guy who kissed you could just have come in from the street into the Boustifaille court-yard. No?'

Imogen stared at her.

'Yes,' Faustina went on confidently. 'Actually, it could

have been *anybody* who was at Bunny's party. I don't know why you got so fixated on Bastien and Dimitri.'

Imogen swallowed. 'I suppose it's because they're the only two people I've been involved with in any way.'

Faustina snorted impatiently. 'Yes, but from what you've told me, this man's kiss felt very *different*. I mean, you are a cook, after all. You know about flavour, no?'

Imogen nodded.

'Well?' Faustina insisted. 'What was it like? Think!'

'Oh look, we *are* brainstorming!' Bunny announced delightedly.

'Let me see,' Imogen said, her eyes closed. 'He tasted sweet, but not *too* sweet – there was also something aromatic – bay, maybe? – and spicy – cinnamon, was it, or nutmeg? Oh, I don't really know.'

'No, no, that is very detailed, very good,' Faustina said, nodding approvingly and underlining the word 'nutmeg' on the pad.

'Maybe it was something he'd eaten at the party,' Bunny drawled musingly. 'Pistachio ice cream from the cake?'

Faustina scribbled 'ice cream', adding a question mark, an exclamation mark and then, after a moment's consideration, a second question mark.

'Wait a minute. Did his mouth taste the same both times?' Mitch asked.

'Yes, actually it did.'

'OK,' Faustina resumed, crossing out the words 'ice cream'. 'So now it's quite simple. You're just going to have to kiss a few more people than I thought at first.' She selected a red marker pen and drew a mouth. 'There.'

Imogen stared at her. 'What? You expect me to go around snogging all and sundry? Are you mad?'

'It could be worse,' Faustina said, cool ribaldry dancing in her eyes. 'We are only talking about *kissing*.'

'Well, if you want to kiss *all* my male guests,' Bunny said, grinning, 'I can give you a list. It'll take you quite a while. And some of them have gone back home, you know.'

'Aw, honey, we could build you a little kissing booth and make them queue around the block,' Mitch said. 'I'm sure *they* wouldn't mind. But you'd get lockjaw for sure.'

'Oh, God,' Imogen said, head in hands.

'Hur-hur-hur. Get over yourself, you knucklehead. Youth is wasted on kids. I wish I could swap places with you.'

'We need to narrow things down,' Bunny said more seriously as she got up and uncapped a bright green pen. 'So . . . Male guests, male guests, male guests.' Flipping her pink Filofax open at the relevant page, she began to reel out names. 'Monsieur Boudin, Bastien, Dimitri – all real unlikely, didn't you say, Imogen? OK. So we can cross out all the Boustifaille people. *Next* we have the American gang. So there was . . . Chuck,' she said, scribbling down the name. 'Remember Chuck, Imogen? He's real cute. And a scream too.'

'No,' Imogen said wearily. 'I don't remember Chuck. I know you introduced me to all your friends, but there were so many of you sitting there, and I was so frazzled with the cooking and everything, that I'm not sure I remember any of them, really.'

'Hmm, yeah. And then Walker, Conway, Archer, Heath,

Gage . . .' Bunny went on, scribbling with determination, 'and of course my darling brothers. OK, that's everyone.'

'I do remember talking to your brothers at the party,' Imogen said.

'Yes – they were both real taken with you. *Hey*, wait, wait, wait! What if it was one of them?' Bunny circled her brothers' names and drew a flurry of little hearts next to them. 'Then we could be sisters!'

'Isn't Buddy twelve or something like that?' Mitch asked severely.

'He's eighteen!' Bunny protested. 'Plenty old enough to marry! And Mitch, you needn't look at me like that. I know what you think of us southerners.'

'I didn't say a word.'

'You didn't have to.'

'Frankly, I don't think your little brother is mature enough for this thing,' Faustina said. 'Imogen, did it feel like kissing a teenager? With the pawing and the slobbering?'

'Nothing like that,' Imogen said soberly.

'Fine,' Bunny resumed, testily crossing out Buddy's name. 'But Everett, now . . . He's twenty-eight. That's mature enough.'

'But the person who kissed me spoke French,' Imogen interjected. 'So isn't he more likely to *be* French?'

'Well, you know, Everett speaks French real well.'

'All right, then,' Imogen said, allowing herself to consider Bunny's brother as a possibility. 'For the sake of argument, where was he at the time of, er . . . impact? Anywhere near me?'

Bunny flipped over to a new page on the pad and began

to draw an unrecognisable picture of her garden, randomly dotted with trees and cute animals. 'Well, he was over *there* at first, setting up the limbo with the other guys. Then he joined me for a while when we were twirling you around before launching you into the circle. And pretty soon after that . . . well, you looked like you'd be OK on your own, so Everett and I just tiptoed away to see how the limbo was going,' Bunny said sheepishly, drawing pink dots across the page to represent her own trajectory. 'Of course I couldn't join in because of my hairdo,' she continued, sketching a pole held up by two matchstick men. 'But I did chant – "How low can you go . . . How low can you go . . ."'

'You are bizarre, you Americans,' Faustina said calmly.

'So,' Imogen said patiently. 'Um, Bunny? Getting back to the kiss?'

The four friends then spent several fruitless minutes attempting to establish the exact time of the kiss – a difficult task since not one of them had been wearing a watch on the night out of respect for historical accuracy.

'Aw, this reconstruction stuff sucks,' Mitch protested. 'It always seems easy enough on TV shows.'

'Well, I think I played Blind Man's Buff for two minutes or so before he caught me and kissed me,' Imogen said imperturbably. 'Maybe a bit longer. Bunny, was Everett with you, say, two minutes into the limbo thing?'

Bunny nodded, drawing two more matchstick men. 'I think so . . . The other thing is that Cheyenne joined in,' she said, drawing a long-haired figure in the act of sliding under the pole, 'so Everett and maybe a couple of other guys stood in for him on the decks. He's mighty supple, by the way,' she added admiringly.

'Which other guys specifically?'

'I'm just not sure.' Two matchstick men materialised next to crudely drawn turntables. Bunny's forensic picture was beginning to look very busy and confusing. 'A lot of them were wearing masks, so, you know, now I think about it I can't quite swear to who was definitely there and who wasn't.'

'So,' Mitch summed up, 'your brother Everett and possibly two others walked off at some point to go and man the decks, which . . .'

'Would have allowed one of them to nip over to the other end of the garden and kiss me?' Imogen put in.

Faustina cleared her throat, then suddenly asked the American girl, 'Are you close to your brother?' Then she drew a crinolined figure in the middle of the garden, and put a large question mark next to it.

'Yes, real close.'

'So if he'd done it . . . wouldn't he have confided in you?' As Faustina's eyes held Bunny's, there was a hint of accusation in her voice. 'Now I'm going to ask you frankly: do you know more about this than you have already told us?'

'Everett's his own man, you know,' Bunny said, drawing herself up. 'He doesn't need my permission to fall in love.' She turned to Imogen. 'And he hasn't said anything to me, I promise. I wish he had!'

'I'm putting him down as a possibility,' Imogen said, picking up the blue pen and scribbling illegibly in a corner of the page.

'Although—' Bunny said, her face serious. 'Now I think about it, there *was* something a bit ungentlemanly about taking advantage of a lady in this way.'

Imogen said firmly, 'He did *not* take advantage of me.'

'All right, if you say so. But I still feel that running off like that afterwards – instead of showing his face, introducing himself and apologising for his behaviour – was a little . . . underhand.'

'Or shy,' Faustina offered, writing down the word in a tiny white space that was left in the top corner of Bunny's sketch.

'Or you could call it playful,' Mitch said. 'Or dramatic. Or just classic Valentine's Day behaviour, plain and simple.'

'Actually,' Imogen said suddenly, 'I have a feeling that he was just as disconcerted by the kiss as I was. By its effect on him, I mean. That's why he left.' Then, pleasantly surprised by this surge of clear-headed confidence, she stared at her friends and grinned.

The others looked at her in silence, then at one another. Mitch gave a long, low whistle.

'What about the other Americans?' Mitch asked.

Imogen shook her head. 'I didn't even speak to any of them, so . . .'

'Bunny,' Faustina interjected, 'which of them were still around at the time of the blackout?'

'Well . . . *these* guys,' Bunny said, crossing a few names off her list, 'went home real soon after the party, with my sister and my cousins. And *those* are the people who stayed, and that includes my brothers, but they all moved on, you know. Nobody stayed here in town.'

'I see,' Imogen said, losing interest. 'What about the rest of the guests?'

'OK, yes, that leaves us with the men from Saint-Jean. So there was Monsieur Ponceau, the butcher . . .'

On hearing the name, Monty barked enthusiastically.

'Yes, Monty – *chicken*!' Imogen whispered, before turning to Bunny. 'He came to the party with his wife. I mean . . . Do you really think he's a likely contender?'

'No, you're right. Let's face facts. I'm also crossing out my hairdresser's husband – he never left her side. Mylène's new boyfriend is off the list too – they couldn't keep their hands off each other.'

'Hey, what about that cousin of yours?' Mitch asked. 'The human giraffe?'

'Oh, Amaury?' Bunny smiled indulgently. 'Did you meet him, Imogen?'

'Not properly, no,' Imogen replied. 'Besides, he was there for you, Bunny – to meet you.'

'That he was, yes,' Bunny drawled with a satisfied cat-like smile, before turning to Imogen. 'We need to narrow things down a whole lot more. Try to think. I know it was dark in the kitchen when you kissed, but did you notice anything else about him? Like his voice? I know he didn't talk much, but . . .'

Imogen shook her head. 'He said very little, and his voice was so hushed anyway that I really wouldn't be able to recognise it.' She covered her face with her hands, then exclaimed triumphantly, 'Oh, wait – he had short hair! I touched the back of his neck and his hair felt quite closely cropped – like stroking a kitten.'

'At least,' Faustina said, 'we can strike *one* name off the list.'

'Who?'

'Cheyenne, of course. You would know if you had made contact with those extensions. You could probably have restored the power supply that way. By plugging him directly into the fuse box.'

'OK, so, to recap, we're looking for a fairly tall, short-haired guy,' Mitch summed up testily. 'Oh, and kind of taciturn. Great. Anybody willing to hazard a guess?'

Imogen now found herself looking uneasily at Faustina who, at that moment, was gazing in one of the salon's mirrors and tucking a red silk rose behind her ear. It made her look like a pocket-sized Carmen. A thought was forming in Imogen's head, one she didn't particularly wish to entertain. But there it was. A tall, short-haired person who didn't say all that much? In her mind's eye Enzo's gorgeous face flashed suddenly. Oh, but it couldn't be, could it? He'd never paid her the slightest attention.

Although . . . he had been at Bunny's party and they *had* spoken in the garden. Yes – and what had he said, exactly? *I'm in love. You understand that? It's like some terrible torture.* And then, *Do you know what it's like to be going mad with desire? It's like a fever. It tears you up inside.* And finally, *One day you'll understand.* All this while looking into her eyes. Damn. Damn and blast. What should she do? Faustina was her friend! And it was to her that Enzo really belonged – whatever she might say about their relationship being over. Say nothing, Imogen decided, that's what she should, and would, do. Push it out of her mind completely.

'Are you OK, Imogen?' Bunny asked with genuine concern. 'You look like you've seen a ghost.'

Imogen smiled at her distractedly. 'I'm fine. I'm just . . . thinking.'

Oh, but what if it *was* him? Well, what about it? Think about it soberly for a moment. So they had kissed a few times, and it had been . . . yes, yes, all right, the most deliciously erotic experience ever, but aside from *that*, he didn't sound exactly like Imogen's soulmate, did he? Faustina had said it all: he was domineering, controlling, a real macho. There couldn't be any future in *that*. And he wasn't available, anyway, not really. Most likely – if he *was* indeed the one – he had set his sights on Imogen temporarily, as a distraction from the woman he truly wanted, or even in an attempt to make Faustina jealous. But then again, *I'm in love. One day you'll understand.* It was to her, Imogen, that he had said those things.

'Shall we call it a night?' Mitch said, watching her. 'I think we've all had enough for now.'

'*Alors*, sleep well, all of you,' Faustina said, seeing her friends out with a serene little smile.

As they approached the bookstore, Imogen turned to Mitch. 'Just out of interest . . . how are things between Faustina and Enzo these days?'

'Dunno. I think she said that he'd calmed down a lot since the party.'

Oh dear.

Imogen sighed and rubbed her face with both hands. 'Really? She must be . . . relieved. *Is* she relieved?'

'It's hard to tell with her. She ain't no gusher. But I guess so,' Mitch said absent-mindedly, unlocking the door.

32

That very night, there was a new message from the-valentine's-kiss@mailenfrance.fr entitled, in French, 'FORGET ME NOT'. There wasn't much danger of that, surely. Imogen stared at it for a minute. Holding her breath, she clicked it open.

This time he had sent her a painting. Eighteenth century, by the look of it. It represented a couple standing near a half-open door, she on the inside of the room, he on the outside. Most of the light fell on the girl's dress – a lustrous cascade of artfully crushed cream satin. In one hand she held a shawl, which evidently she had been in the process of fetching from the room; her other wrist was held by the young man who had appeared quite unexpectedly at the door, pulling her to him – with such determination that her waist was bent into a diagonal – in order to kiss her cheek, very close to her mouth.

'Well, what do you know – a gorgeous Fragonard,' said Mitch, after being summoned. 'A good choice – witty. This is called *Le baiser volé*, by the way.'

'*The Stolen Kiss*?'

'Yeah. He's making a point, huh?' Mitch said, looking at her with affectionate severity. 'It's a real doozy of a painting,' he went on. 'If you look closely, you'll see that through the other door at the back – the one she most likely came through – there's a bunch of women praying in the next room. She's looking at bit *startled*, the poor little girl,' he went on, chuckling, 'but she's obviously having a much better time with him. You know, your kid is *good* – he's really growing on me.'

'Yes, it's very appropriate,' Imogen said, smiling. Then she thought of Enzo and her smile faded. 'And is it really, really famous?'

'Pretty famous,' Mitch said musingly. 'But I mean all you'd need to do is google "stolen kiss" or whatever, if that was what was on your mind, and it'd probably pop up.'

After Mitch's departure, Imogen typed a cautious reply in French, '*Merci.*'

Once again, he appeared to have been waiting for her, and his response came swiftly in the same language: *'I'm sorry I had to leave you so abruptly.'*

Enzo? Could it be? Imogen exhaled slowly, then replied: 'Please tell me who you are.'

'You tell me, Imogen – how much do you really want to know?'

That was pretty shrewd of him, she thought, startled. How could he possibly have guessed how powerfully the act of kissing him appeared to obliterate her ability to reason things out? Was it because he felt the same way?

'I *do* really want to know,' she typed back after a brief pause. 'But when I was with you, I forgot all about it. It's strange.'

'Not so strange as all that. We were busy. Would you like to do it again?'

Just as she was about to type an enthusiastic 'Yes yes

yes yes yes yes,' Imogen checked herself, staring at the screen. Wait. Think about it. What was she doing? Was this Enzo or someone else entirely? It was, she reasoned, no longer Valentine's Day, so that what she should do now, surely, was arrange to meet him face to face. Yes, that was it. While she dithered, another message came through. It contained a French word that she didn't recognise at first: *odorat*. Then she remembered that it was the name of one of the five senses. He'd written, *'By the way, I assume your sense of smell is pretty good – being a chef. Is it?'*

An odd change of tack, Imogen thought. 'Yes,' she typed back. 'Why?'

'It's a surprise. I'll be in touch, Imogen. Over and out.'

A surprise. How deliciously tantalising. Intrigued, Imogen made a deal with herself. She would allow him to play his next hand and wait for the surprise, and then insist on the revelation of his identity. Definitely, without fail.

33

Annie Picore's review in *Nice-Matin* made for depressing reading. Though the critic granted in passing that Boudin's kitchen still turned out good food, she mainly dwelt on the unreliability of the service and on the restaurant's tired décor. She also underlined, rather cruelly, Imogen thought, the loss of Boustifaille's Golden Spoon. Monsieur Boudin had quickly forbidden any mention or discussion of the article among the staff, but he also displayed a worrying apathy; there were no signs that he might be working out a strategy to restore Boustifaille's reputation.

Customers, on the other hand, were quick to react – bookings had fallen away to almost nothing. Tourists still came to Boustifaille out of curiosity, but there were some devastating cancellations from high-profile visitors. For the first time in years, the mayor of Nice chose to celebrate his birthday at La Rascasse. Hollywood movie stars, once a regular ornament of the dining room, now confined themselves exclusively to the restaurant of the Hôtel de la Plage, which, reassuringly, still sported two Golden Spoons.

Meanwhile, after a few days' agitated soul-searching, Imogen, resolved to settle the question of Enzo's involvement in the Valentine mystery, sought him out at his place of work, a menswear shop called Les Cowboys de Minuit that catered for the town's see-and-be-seen Saturday-night crowd. She had to know, one way or another, and was willing to throw herself at Faustina's mercy if it turned out that Enzo was, in fact, her own enigmatic Valentine.

Before her shift at Boustifaille, she walked past the shop a few times, glancing at the colourful window display of clothes set among plastic cacti and other Wild West props, and eventually mustered the courage to go inside. She almost had to hurl herself through the door, landing breathlessly on one foot, just shy of the counter. Behind it stood a disdainful and very tanned boy dressed entirely in box-fresh white clothes and wearing a turquoise bandana as a headscarf.

'*Bonsoir*,' he said without looking up from the celebrity magazine he was perusing.

'*Bonsoir. Enzo est là?*'

The boy stared at her impassively.

'I just need to ask him something,' she went on in nervous French. 'It's quite important.'

He shrugged, with a suggestion that many other women had made similar requests before, and said, 'He's in the storeroom,' indicating a door at the back. 'Just go through.'

In semi-darkness, Imogen made her way between shelves of brightly emblazoned T-shirts, not daring to call out Enzo's name. She went into the next aisle and stopped in her tracks: there he was, pulling a bright orange hoodie out of a stacked pile. God, he was beautiful. Hearing her approach, he turned to stare at her, looking for all the world like a startled fawn from a Disney movie.

'*Salut*,' Imogen said, smiling at him.

He smiled back – the first time she had seen him do so – came over and kissed her on both cheeks. Not an unpleasant experience, not by a long chalk. Goosebumps rose instantly on her skin, he did have the most amazing knack for eliciting a positive response.

'You're looking for something,' he stated rather than asked, locking eyes with her.

'Yes,' Imogen giggled before she could check herself. 'You, actually. Are you busy, or do you have a minute to talk?'

'We can talk, if you want.'

'Great. The thing is, Enzo,' she began hesitantly, 'I was wondering if you were around when we played that game at Bunny's party – you remember?'

'Yes, I remember very well, of course.'

They looked at one another.

'Right,' Imogen said at length. 'And so . . . did you play the game too?'

'Yes,' he replied, smiling at her. 'I played the game until the very end.'

'Oh, you did.' Imogen was beginning to feel rather dizzy. 'That's great. And then . . . the emails started?'

'Yes,' he said, looking surprised. 'I started to send the emails afterwards.'

Imogen took a deep, gasping breath, then managed to say, 'I loved your emails. They were wonderful. Mitch saw them, and he thought so too.'

'Really?' Enzo said, frowning gorgeously.

'Yes. Do you want to . . . tell me a bit more about . . . everything?'

'Frankly, I'm surprised,' Enzo said. 'I thought it was all supposed to be a big secret.'

Imogen nodded conspiratorially, remembering the elaborate lengths he had gone to in order to stage the blackout at Boustifaille. 'Oh, yes, of course! And secrets are great. But you know, when something this amazing happens to you, you need to talk to your friends. You understand, don't you?'

He stared at her, his beautiful eyebrows still slightly knitted. Gosh, was he actually going to tell her off? Faustina had always described him as a control freak. Now what? Should she just . . . lance the boil, as it were, and kiss him? That way she'd know for sure. *All right, then. Here we go.* Imogen cleared her throat, then murmured, 'Enzo, why don't you . . . come here?'

He narrowed his eyes at her. 'Why?'

'Oh, I think you know,' she replied, herself feeling rather uncertain. Enzo was incredibly good-looking, but now things had come to the actual crunch, Imogen found it quite impossible to behave in a suitably alluring manner. It was lack of practice, mostly, but also, perhaps, a fairly pronounced sense of guilt. As a result, she felt sick with nerves and wasn't particularly looking forward to the actual kiss. It was tricky, very tricky about Faustina, but in order to discover how she really felt about Enzo now that she had unmasked her Valentine, she had to bite the bullet. No two ways about it. She looked at him expectantly, but instead of pouncing, as she had anticipated, he crossed his arms and said, 'Are you coming on to me?'

'I suppose so,' she replied with as much confidence as

she could muster. Why not be direct? He *was* the one, after all. 'I mean, it would be great if you kissed me now. If you don't mind.'

'You're a funny kind of friend. Do all English girls behave like this?'

Disconcerted, Imogen pondered, then asked weakly, 'What do you mean?'

'I mean, your good friend confided in you and now you try to seduce me.'

'What? My friend? Who?'

Enzo stared at her. 'Now *I* don't know what you're talking about.'

'But . . . at the party, you played the game with *me*!' Imogen said, shaken. 'You sent *me* those emails!'

At this, Enzo nodded, then came over and patted her on the back in big-brotherly fashion. 'Ah, I understand the situation now. Don't worry. You're a nice girl. I'm sure that you'll find someone too.'

'I . . . what?'

'You see what your friend has with me and you want the same thing for yourself. It's very understandable.'

'So . . . you didn't kiss me at the party?'

'No.'

'You didn't send me picture emails of people kissing?'

'*No.*'

'And you didn't take the fuses out so you could kiss me in the dark at the restaurant?'

'No! But, my God, you have an incredible imagination – I congratulate you.'

Imogen stared at him, now quite annoyed. 'None of this

is imaginary, you idiot! I only made the mistake of thinking that *you* were behind it.'

Because you have short hair, primarily, she added to herself. Which did seem a bit flimsy, now that she thought about it. Briefly, she wondered what game he and Faustina had played at Bunny's party – well, it didn't matter.

'So . . .' she resumed, not wishing to leave any stone unturned. 'All that stuff you said to me at the party, about being madly in love . . . ?'

'It was about her, yes – my lady.'

'Of course,' Imogen shook her head, smiling. 'I should have known. You two are made for each other.'

'Thank you. I think so too,' he said, smiling back. 'I'm sorry about the misunderstanding.'

'Oh, that's fine.' *I'm sorry I tried to force myself on you. Cringe and cringe again.* 'Bye, Enzo.'

'Bye.' And he turned back to his boxes.

34

Returning from her break, Imogen walked into the Boustifaille courtyard and, as had become her habit, glanced towards the fuse box, thinking with a dreamy sort of urgency about more kissing, possibly in the dark – and wondering when it was likely to come her way again.

Nothing this exciting had ever happened to her before. Who was he? The tantalising question was playing on her mind. If not Enzo, then who could possibly be her Valentine? And what about the surprise she'd been promised?

All the same, she reasoned while still eminently aware that her heart was beating quite fast, she must somehow keep her mind on her work. She shook her head and turned her thoughts to the small catering job she had agreed to take on – a modest buffet for the tenth birthday of Monsieur and Madame Ponceau's daughter Nathalie, for which the colour pink would once more constitute the principal inspiration. It occurred to Imogen that Bunny's pink-icing 'meat-look' toppings would have been perfectly in keeping with the birthday girl's parents' occupation, but, she thought, smiling to herself, hardly the thing for a children's party. Best to go with a princess motif instead.

Tightening the strings of her apron, she headed for her workstation and spotted something the colour of pale Jersey cream lying on the counter. It turned out to be an envelope bearing, in scarlet ink, the letter 'I' – for Imogen?

'Is this for me?' she called out, holding it aloft. 'This note?'

Pierrot, who'd been in the larder, closed the door and walked across to her. 'Maybe one of those people left it behind,' he offered.

'What people?'

'Some people asked for a tour of the kitchen,' Dimitri chipped in.

'A big group of foreigners,' Régis added.

'When you were on your break, Imogen,' Bastien explained, joining them. 'Boudin would have said no, of course, but I think it's in our interests to be accommodating, what with all the gossip about our problems – so I said OK.'

'Who showed them around?' Imogen asked, opening the envelope.

'I did,' Larissa said. 'They just wanted to have a look around and they said hello to everybody. They were nice – very polite.'

Inside the envelope, Imogen found a sheet of notepaper folded in two, on which a message in French read, in elegant scarlet upper-case letters: '*DINNER WAS VERY GOOD BUT NOT AS GOOD AS KISSING YOU. I KNOW IT'S A LOT TO ASK BUT WHAT I WOULD LIKE ONE DAY IS FOR YOU TO FEED ME IN PRIVATE – VERY SLOWLY. AND LET ME LICK YOUR FINGERS AFTERWARDS. I'LL BE IN TOUCH.*' Blushing furiously, she folded it again hastily and put it in her breast pocket. He'd been here, in the kitchen, and at her very station, to plant this – her surprise. It was very lovely, though one thing puzzled her: what was the connection between this note and her sense of smell?

'Was the note for you?' Larissa asked curiously, giving her a sharp look.

'Yes,' Imogen said, by some miracle managing to keep her voice level.

'Who is it from?'

'Well, I'm not sure exactly. It's a sort of . . . private joke. Did any of those . . . customers ask to see me?'

'Of course not!' Larissa replied, frowning at this presumptuous question. 'They all wanted to meet Monsieur Boudin, but obviously we made sure he wasn't in the kitchen when they came in.'

'And where did you say they were from?'

'I don't know – they spoke English.'

'Oh,' Imogen said, improvising. 'English tourists? Maybe someone in the group knew me.'

'They weren't tourists,' Manu said. 'They were businessmen.'

'Expense account,' Bastien confirmed. 'They were Australian, from Sydney. You have Australian friends?'

Australian? Imogen was baffled.

'*Allez*, everyone!' she heard Bastien call out, with persuasive authority. 'Not long now before service. Start your *mise-en-place*!'

So she shrugged and, cutting the conversation short, got down to her food prepping.

At the end of her shift, as she walked into the Paperback Wonderland and headed, preoccupied, for the stairs, she heard Mitch call out, 'Hey, wait! Have you seen these?'

On the counter lay an enormous bunch of flowers wrapped in cellophane and tied with an extravagant red bow. Slowly, Imogen walked up to it and picked up the bouquet. Flowers! They had to be from *him*. Upon closer examination, it turned out to be a large arrangement of daisies and carnations in acid colours: orange, pink and yellow. The whole thing was very bright and blowsy, and, Imogen couldn't help thinking, really rather naff. She stared at it, registering slight disappointment that her mystery kisser had such bad taste in flowers, then at Mitch, who was proffering a small envelope between his thumb and forefinger. Her heart leaped: another note! And, she reflected, another surprise – this time sweet-smelling.

Things really were moving up a gear, Imogen thought to herself. And so surely the next thing would be his appearing before her in person. It was unbelievably exciting. She smiled at Mitch and proceeded to extract the card.

'So? Is it from him?' Mitch asked.

'I don't know.' No handwritten message in scarlet ink, this time – just anonymous computer-generated black print. Imogen held it up so that Mitch could read the words: 'FROM YOUR SECRET ADMIRER.'

Then Imogen buried her face in the bouquet – and found that the flowers had almost no scent. She looked at Mitch, nonplussed.

'The flowers came from a big florist in Cannes,' Imogen told Bunny the next morning – a Wednesday, her day off from Boustifaille – as they drove to Saint-Paul-de-Vence. 'The person who placed the order came into the shop and paid cash.' She shrugged. 'So there's no trace of his name.'

Bunny's eyes widened in delight while she changed gears.

'As for the note he left in the restaurant,' Imogen went on, kissing the bristly top of Monty's head as he sat in her lap, 'that wasn't signed either, but I *know* it was from him.'

'Really? How?'

'Well . . .' Imogen bit her lip, considering her answer. 'Because of . . . his tone.' Which was how? She closed her eyes to recapture it – intimate – caressing. Yes. She shivered deliciously.

'Oh, my gosh – he's *courting* you,' Bunny said reverently. 'Maybe not in the most traditional way, but he is.'

'Perhaps,' Imogen replied, looking pensively at the road and thinking, But in that case, where is he? Shouldn't he show his face? Declare himself?

On the back seat of the car, Amaury d'Oussey sat in discreet silence. Today's expedition, designed to appeal equally to Bunny and to Imogen – a stroll through the grounds of the Fondation Maeght to look at iconic twentieth-century art, followed by a leisurely lunch at a Michelin-starred restaurant in the company of Everett, Buddy and Archer – had been his idea.

'You know, I'm real confused about those Australian businessmen,' Bunny drawled. 'How do they fit in? Because I'm pretty sure there weren't any at my party.'

'I've been wondering about that. Maybe he gave the note to one of them to deliver to my station.'

'May I make a suggestion?' Amaury said, leaning forward politely. 'I imagine that he must have delivered it himself. That is certainly what I would have done. And I couldn't . . . I mean, he couldn't, have known exactly where you worked unless he'd been shown around.'

A little surprised to find him showing such interest in her baffling predicament, Imogen turned around to look at the Frenchman. 'So what do you think happened?' she asked, intrigued.

'I think,' Amaury said, smiling at her amiably, 'that he was having dinner at another table. Probably on his own. And sitting close enough to overhear the conversation about the kitchen tour.'

Imogen turned back to face the road. In her mind's eye, she could see a hand tracing the message in red ink. But whose hand? 'And do you think he wrote the note at Boustifaille?'

'No,' Amaury said without a moment's hesitation. 'He already had it with him. Men don't walk around with notepaper in their pockets. I think he intended to leave it with your maître d'. And then, when there was an opportunity to get a little closer to you, he . . . I mean, again, if it had been me, I would have attached myself to their party. It's easy to do if you're discreet and appear to know what you're doing.'

'Really?' Imogen asked, impressed. 'Just like that?'

'But yes, it's simple enough. I once did exactly that when visiting a *de-light-ful* palazzo in Florence. Some people were being taken on a tour of the private apartments and I went along with them. Nobody stopped me.'

'You didn't!' Bunny exclaimed, wide-eyed. 'Oh, Amaury, how naughty of you!'

'You're entirely right, of course, *ma chère cousine*. But you know, it was very amusing because when I was introduced to the *contessa* we realised that we were in fact distantly related, so it wasn't as much of an intrusion as I thought!' Amaury then broke into a short burst of braying laughter, to which Bunny added her own indulgent, silvery peals.

While they drove in silence for a moment, Imogen found herself dwelling uneasily on what Faustina had told her only the other day: namely that Bunny had perhaps been overly trusting in taking Amaury's word that he was, in fact, her relative. They had, after all, met on the Internet – not necessarily the most reliable of social networks.

'Bunny *is* very rich, isn't she?' Faustina had asked, suggestively. 'So . . . if he plays his cards right, he could make a very good marriage, no?'

Imogen didn't know what to make of Faustina's suspicions. Amaury seemed very nice, and perfectly plausible. Yet it was true that Bunny was trusting – it was her nature; she was a happy person who thought the best of everybody. Faustina had wanted to warn their American friend, but Imogen had asked her to keep her doubts to herself for now. After all, to the best of her knowledge nothing had happened between Bunny and her cousin. There was no need to upset anyone.

Then Imogen jumped a little as Bunny suddenly said, addressing her, 'I'm still wondering, you know, about . . .'

'What?' Imogen glanced at Amaury in the rear-view mirror.

'About Everett and whether . . . perhaps . . .'

Imogen breathed out, then smiled at her friend. This Everett scenario was pure wishful thinking on Bunny's part. Bunny's older brother was extremely presentable. And also charming – but, after all, he barely knew her. And yet, Imogen allowed herself to wonder, wasn't it *just* possible that he might have decided to kiss her at the party – just like that, following a romantic impulse?

And then, the Boustifaille blackout? That was harder to imagine, Imogen thought, blushing a little as she remembered the physical intensity of the encounter – Everett seemed so proper, almost a little prim, not the type to behave in such a reckless manner. But then again, Bunny herself was full of surprises, wasn't she? So why shouldn't gentlemanly Everett sometimes drop his reserve, especially under cover of darkness, and boldly display his . . . what had Mitch called it? Ah yes – 'sexual authority'. Imogen couldn't repress a small giggle at her own daring train of thought. 'It never rains but it pours,' Daphne had said. Well, it was certainly beginning to feel that way.

'Does Everett . . . ever talk about me?' she said out loud.

'Not really,' Bunny said, frowning a little. 'Once in a while he asks how you're doing. It's just that . . . whoever's romancing you is doing it in such an inventive and classy way. I'd be real proud if my brother were behind it all.'

'You could always ask him,' Amaury said, teasingly.

'Yes!' Bunny said, honking her horn ever so slightly for emphasis. 'Let's ask him if he sent you that big bunch of flowers!'

'Mmm yes . . . the flowers,' Imogen repeated hesitantly. 'I don't know . . .'

She let the sentence trail off, unfinished. Now decanted into the most capacious piece of Mitch's treasured collection of 1950s Vallauris pottery, the flowers sat on her desk in all their glorious naffness. And they had almost no scent. Imogen just didn't know what to make of them.

35

'Have you been through the labyrinth yet?' a voice asked behind Imogen as she stood with Monty, Bunny and Amaury gazing at mosaic fish 'swimming' at the bottom of a shallow pool just outside the museum.

They turned around. Behind them stood a shortish elderly gentleman clad in a gorgeously cut Prince of Wales check suit. He smiled at them from beneath a soft brown felt hat, rakishly tilted. 'I do hope I'm not intruding,' he said in a purring American voice. 'I heard you speaking English. And it is so nice to meet some fellow expatriates.'

'I, however, am a Frenchman,' Amaury said politely but firmly. 'But isn't this a *de-light-ful* place?'

'I like it very much,' the old man replied, smiling. 'I come here most days. I live in Vence, where I have a little shop.'

'This charming young woman – *ma petite cousine d'Amérique* – is an artist,' Amaury said, holding on lightly to Bunny's elbow. 'I thought she would enjoy seeing the Giacometti courtyard.'

Bunny nodded enthusiastically, beaming at her compatriot. 'I wish I could just *live* here! Imagine having breakfast out here every morning surrounded by all this classic art!'

Amaury smiled at his cousin. 'It would be even nicer to

have breakfast surrounded by your own works, my dear Bunny. They are so much more *of the moment.*'

Imogen sucked in her cheeks. Amaury was laying it on a bit thick. Could it be that Faustina was right, and that this was the behaviour of a fortune hunter?

'And you, Miss,' the American gentleman said courteously, removing his hat and turning to Imogen. 'Where are you from? And are you an artist also?'

'I'm from London,' Imogen said, noticing that although he had a slight stoop and snowy white hair, his whole person – and perhaps especially his mischievous blue eyes – gave off an air of irrepressible, Mephistophelean youthfulness. 'And I'm not an artist,' she went on, grinning. 'Just a cook. And a beginner at that.'

'Oh, but she *is* a wonderful artist!' Bunny said. 'You should have seen the cake she made for my Valentine's party. It was like sculpture.'

'Pure rococo,' Amaury confirmed.

'And she works at Boustifaille!'

'OK, Bunny,' Imogen said, embarrassed. 'Thank you.'

The American gentleman chuckled. 'Very fancy! You sound like a young lady worth befriending. Tell me, do you live here in town?'

They had all begun to make their way through the garden's beguiling labyrinth of low stone walls punctuated with sculptures, and while Imogen explained about Saint-Jean-les-Cassis, the restaurant and Mitch's hospitality, Amaury and Bunny wandered on ahead to take a closer look at an odd-looking statue: shiny red dummy's legs crossed at the ankles and surmounted by blue and yellow bits of piping and machinery. Monty padded around it, sniffing as disdainfully as any two-legged art critic.

'This,' her American escort explained, pausing before it, 'is by Joan Miró – you know, the Spaniard. Gorgeous, isn't it? It's called *Jeune Fille S'Évadant*.'

'Young woman . . . breaking out?' Imogen suggested as a translation.

'Yes, quite right,' her new American friend confirmed. 'Tell me, do you feel like that, being here?'

'Like I've broken out, you mean?' Imogen said, frowning.

'Well, yes. Or maybe you're still in the process of doing it? I've lived here a very long time,' he went on, placing his hat on his heart, 'but I still feel newly liberated, just through being here and not . . . there. Do you see?'

'Y-yes, I think I do.' Imogen said, thinking about the family life she had left behind in Archway. And there was more to it than that. She was beginning to feel liberated, which she was sure had something to do with the gentle climate that had also bestowed upon her a new physical confidence. She stood up straighter now. Wearing that frock at Bunny's party had proved to be something of a breakthrough. She was no longer embarrassed by her shape. Rather, she was beginning to think of herself, tentatively, as . . . well, feminine, and in a good way.

She and the American exchanged a smile, then he spoke again. 'I'm so glad that you've found a home from home at the . . . what did you say it was called?'

'Mitch's Paperback Wonderland.'

'Yes. That sounds just right for you.'

His manner was so winning that Imogen was suddenly

overcome by a powerful urge to tell this complete stranger all about her predicament – the kiss at Bunny's party, the encounter during the blackout, everything. She even wanted to tell him about her episode with Enzo, though she felt so painfully silly about it that she hadn't mentioned it to anyone – not Mitch, not Bunny, and *especially* not Faustina. She opened her mouth to speak, then shook her head slightly, thinking better of it. Why should he be interested?

He stood considering her for a moment, then said gently, while replacing his hat on his head. 'While you're in the region, I recommend that you visit the city of Menton. That's if you haven't already done so. No? Then go with those nice friends of yours to look at the *Salle des Mariages* in the town hall there – that's where they have wedding ceremonies, you know. It's a terrific place.'

'Thank you. I'd love to see it,' Imogen said politely.

'Yes, I really think you should go. It was decorated by a French artist called Jean Cocteau. There's a beautiful painting on the wall – of Orpheus and Eurydice. Do you know the Greek myth? Orpheus was a poet and his beloved wife Eurydice died. He was allowed to fetch her back from the Underworld on the condition that he wouldn't look at her. But he did, you know, he turned his head and looked over his shoulder once, and she vanished for ever. Lose faith for a second and your love's gone for good – that's all it takes.'

Imogen nodded, uncertain what to make of this sudden confidence. The American smiled at her, his blue eyes entirely knowing. 'I apologise for being so morbid. Of course, the young don't want to hear about death and loss. Tell me, my dear, are you in love?'

Imogen felt her face prickle. If she was, it was love of the strangest kind, she thought – an affair with the Invisible Man. She smiled, saying nothing.

'Oh, I see that you are. Then you are blessed. Go and see that room in Menton. You know, I once stood in it with someone *I* loved, a long time ago, and we said, "Let's pretend we're married."' He laughed suddenly, not altogether happily. 'I'm going to leave you to enjoy the rest of your visit with your friends,' he said, shaking Imogen's hand. 'Say goodbye to the others for me, will you?' And then he turned and walked away, soon disappearing behind the trees.

36

Having made their way out of the sculpture labyrinth, Imogen, Bunny and Amaury had gone to a sumptuous restaurant called Le Petit Merlu where, sitting on a shaded terrace nestled within the town's ramparts, three Americans awaited them – the Doucet brothers, looking cucumber-cool in almost, but not quite, identical über-preppy outfits consisting of seersucker jackets, shirts and trousers in pastel shades; Archer, on the other hand, wore dark jeans and a grey shirt.

'Don't you look precious,' Bunny said with a twinkle in her eye. 'May we join you or should we leave you to it? Gentlemen are most relaxed with their own kind, I always think.'

'It depends,' Amaury said, smiling. 'I'm French and I'm always glad to be in the company of women.'

Imogen glanced in his direction, amused but also wondering once again whether he wasn't a little too good to be true.

'Why, thank you, cousin,' Bunny murmured, rewarding him with a dazzling smile. 'Now let's see – Imogen, why don't you sit next to Everett? Archer, do you mind moving down one seat? Thanks, honey. Amaury, next to me? And Buddy, dearest, on my other side.'

'At times like these you sound just like Mama,' Buddy said with a mixture of admiration and teenage annoyance.

Taking in the stylish setting of the restaurant, Imogen was glad she'd decided to wear the simple but pretty sea-green scoop-necked dress she'd bought on a recent shopping trip with Bunny. It was tailored in such a way that it hugged her form while gliding on her body like water when she moved. She never found herself tugging on it to make it sit better, as had always been the case with her baggy oversized shirts.

She busied herself first of all with pouring water in a bowl for Monty, leaving her friends to order drinks. Resurfacing at the table, she stole a glance at Everett, who smiled and immediately engaged her in conversation about the attractions of Saint-Paul-de-Vence.

Imogen played along, while allowing part of her mind to toy with Bunny's theory. Was it possible . . . ? But no, Everett seemed far too . . . civilised, surely, to pounce on a girl and kiss her just because he felt like it – even with the excuse of Valentine's Day. Imogen shook her head, dismissing any subversive thoughts about Everett, and concentrated on what he was telling her. Bunny drawled a little, but her older brother, who'd been at it longer, was an arch-drawler, and from time to time Imogen wondered whether his mouth might not actually be full of warm marshmallow – if so, it would surely interfere with his lunch. He was, however, very good company, and by the time their food began to arrive they were chatting like old friends.

'Just between you and me,' he was saying as the waiter lifted a silver dome and Imogen got an intoxicating whiff of distilled sea-urchin, 'my feeling is that Bunny's artistic talent will never be appreciated at home. I think she should settle here, or maybe in London or Paris.'

Distracted by the voluptuous intensity of her sea-urchin soup, Imogen nodded and wondered privately whether she might one day teach herself to make something even vaguely approaching its perfection.

'Everett believes in me, Imogen,' Bunny said, beaming at her brother. 'It comes from having been to college on the East Coast and picking up a coterie of pretentious artistic friends.'

'Thank you, Bun,' Archer said soberly.

'Don't mention it, honey.'

Imogen glanced at Archer. His divorce had left him withdrawn, cynical and bitter – according to Bunny. And Imogen did have some sympathy for his predicament. It sounded like his ex-wife had treated him appallingly. But did he have to take it out on all other women, herself included? Once again he'd barely greeted her. Nor had he looked in her direction since she'd sat down. Well, she too would ignore him.

Everett sat forward. 'You know, young lady, a dash of pretentiousness helps mightily when it comes to your kind of art. So, yes, guilty as charged. And lay off my "coterie",' he went on, nodding in Archer's direction. 'They're good men and true.'

'I don't know, big brother,' Bunny said teasingly. 'It's a good thing Daddy's so busy, because what *would* he say if he could see you swanning around on the Riviera with all manner of oddballs? People from Manhattan who live on the wrong side of the Park and don't even have a trust fund! I mean, really!'

Archer, Imogen thought to herself, seemed entirely unperturbed by Bunny's teasing. Or perhaps he was thinking about something else. She noticed that he had clear hazel eyes, and that his broken nose actually gave his face a lot of character. There were also a few lines around his eyes. Compared to the eminently unruffled Everett, his friend looked like he'd lived a little.

Just then he turned to look at her directly and said, 'Is this the sort of thing you cook in your restaurant?'

'Well, it's certainly the standard we aim for,' she replied, feeling defensive of Boustifaille's reputation. She noticed with scandalised disbelief that he'd barely touched his risotto. Didn't he realise how much care and artistry had gone into it, and how delectable it must be? 'Why?' she asked sarcastically. 'Don't you like "this sort of thing"?'

'Oh, I do,' he replied, looking down at his plate. 'I'm just not very hungry today.'

In that case, Imogen thought with a surge of irritation, what are you doing having lunch in a place like this? So Archer was an artistic type – like her mother – so what? Why, oh why were such people so often disconnected from the simple pleasure that came from eating good food?

'All Daddy really cares about,' Everett was saying, 'is that I don't miss any meeting with *our* trustees – and I won't.'

Looking across the table, Imogen noticed Amaury enjoying his risotto. Their eyes met with perfect understanding.

'*Merveilleux*,' Amaury said.

'*Oui, exactement*,' Imogen replied.

Amaury's expansively Gallic use of adjectives was a very good match for his cousin's perky enthusiasm, Imogen reflected. And Bunny had also appeared delighted with the Frenchman's encyclopaedic knowledge of wine, much of which was rooted in long-standing friendships with producers. On the surface, they certainly seemed quite well suited. What if Faustina was wrong and Amaury was, in fact, the real deal? Then, money or no money, Bunny herself wouldn't be getting such a bad catch.

Like everyone else, Imogen had found Amaury's appearance disconcerting at first (no doubt her mother – the aesthete – would have dismissed him as 'a bit of a snorter, darling') but repeated exposure had changed her mind and now she merely thought of him as pleasantly ugly. And Bunny, pumped up with Francophilia and family feeling, possibly went even higher in her estimation of him. So . . . would it actually be best to alert Bunny to Faustina's suspicions – just in case? Troubled, Imogen tuned in again to the conversation going on around her.

'Archer! You got the job!' Bunny was exclaiming. 'Why, honey, how marvellous! So you're really going to stay on in Menton? You're not going back to Paris?'

Archer cleared his throat. 'Well, it rather depends.'

'On what?'

'On a lot of things, Bun.'

Menton . . . Imogen thought vaguely, as another silver dome was lifted, this time revealing a perfect morsel of sea bass poached in red wine. The old American gentleman they had met this morning had mentioned Menton, suggesting a visit to . . . what was it again? Ah, yes, the Wedding Room.

She tasted a velvety mouthful of fish, and then, as she and Amaury exchanged another smile, Menton went clean out of her mind. Whether or not Amaury was genuinely Bunny's cousin, one thing was certain. Here, she thought, looking at the Frenchman, was a kindred spirit – someone who was as serious as she was about great food.

'Archer, honey,' Bunny said softly, 'I don't believe I've thanked you properly for getting your art critic friend to review my show. It's made quite a difference to get a bit of publicity in something as edgy as *Artpress.*'

Intrigued, Imogen looked at Bunny. Was she fluttering her eyelashes? Archer, Imogen knew, had been Everett's college roommate, so he and Bunny must have known each other for years. And now Bunny was an artist, they also moved in similar circles professionally. Perhaps she was wrong about Bunny and Amaury, perhaps there was something going on there instead?

'You know,' Everett interjected, 'Archer is also in a position to introduce you to the museum's director. She's a very gracious lady, and she knows everybody on the Riviera.'

'That would be *lovely,*' Bunny purred.

Archer, who'd been playing with Monty, looked up and grinned at his friend's sister. 'Any time, Bun – you only have to ask.'

He did have a very nice smile, Imogen admitted reluctantly to herself. Besides which, she reflected as she watched him with her dog, it was certainly a point in his favour that Monty, the greatest snob in creation, appeared to like him.

'And because he was there all of last year, he knows

plenty of other people in Paris,' Everett went on. 'Curators, gallery owners . . . could be useful.'

Imogen suddenly heard her name spoken in a very soft voice. It was Buddy, shyly asking what she thought of the food. He listened politely to her enthusiastic and detailed response about the technical complexities involved in producing the perfect *jus*, *nage* and *oursinade*, then said with heartfelt melancholy that he was beginning to miss the food from home and would give anything right around now for some plain old Jim Dandy grits. Imogen smiled sympathetically and turned her attention back to Bunny.

'Pascale sold my pole-dancing chicken the other day. Isn't it wonderful?' she was saying.

'Who bought it?' Imogen asked, refraining from adding, *Some weirdo lunatic?*

'Cheyenne.'

'I didn't know he was interested in contemporary art,' Imogen said, adding in an undertone, 'But pole dancers, now . . .'

'He was mighty taken with it, Pascale said,' Bunny went on. 'But I'm real disappointed with Madame Ponceau, the butcher's wife. I invited her to see the show, because you might say she's another person who's interested in chickens, and I thought she might like a glass case or two to hang on the wall in her shop.'

Imogen nodded, keeping her face as neutral as possible. 'And what did she say?'

'She said *plenty* and very fast, so I couldn't follow it at all. But Pascale was listening and told me that apparently

Madame Ponceau thought my whole show was just one terrible waste of good chicken flesh.'

Meeting Buddy's eye, Imogen burst out laughing, soon followed by the rest of the table, with the exception of Bunny, who said primly, while reaching for her glass of wine, 'Well, I'm just happy about my review *and* about my sale. It's a start, isn't it?'

'Yes,' Imogen said, recovering herself. 'It's wonderful and I'm very impressed.' Conscious of not having joined in with the conversation very much, she decided to make up for it now, while they were waiting for their puddings. 'I've always wondered what attracted –' instinctively, she omitted the words *someone as unlikely as* '– you to this kind of art.'

'Why, she was always an odd little girl,' Everett said affectionately, 'who enjoyed pulling the wings off flies.'

Bunny gasped, her hand at her throat. 'Everett Wade Hampton Doucet! I am *astonished* at you! That is a barefaced lie and you know it! A dead fly looks *much* prettier with its wings on!'

'Well, what about those ants?' Buddy chipped in, smiling at his sister.

'That was a whole different thing, Buddy.'

'When Bunny was ten years old,' Everett said, addressing Imogen, 'we had an infestation of ants in the house, so she helped the maid to kill them all and then she used the dead ants to start a series of collage pieces.'

'Delightful!' Amaury said, looking at Bunny admiringly. 'You must have been a remarkable child.'

'Mama found the art in my room,' Bunny said. 'And she was *shocked*.'

'Well, yes. Her technique was still real crude in those days,' Everett said, grinning at Imogen. 'So I took the blame like a good brother, and said I'd done it. For a while after that, Bun made animal sculptures out of chicken wire and we hid them in my room. And then, from the age of thirteen, she took up quail hunting and she got real good at it, so that was the beginning of her bird art – you know, starting small at first. She got Ole Crazy Pete to show her how to embalm things, and now . . . here we are!'

Imogen decided that while she still found him unnervingly clean-cut (the side parting in his hair looked like it had been traced with a ruler), Everett was also quite funny. Now she was aware of a slow, hesitant undercurrent of excitement. Because, after all, what if . . . But no, it was just too unlikely. She looked away from Bunny's brother and encountered Amaury's friendly eyes across the table.

Feeling oddly flustered, she shifted her gaze back to Bunny's face and said brightly, 'Actually, I've also had someone like Ole Crazy Pete in my life. My neighbour Di – Daphne Blanding's sister. She taught me to cook without my mother ever finding out.'

'Oh, Imogen!' Bunny said, a mischievous smile playing on her lips. 'You do *love* secrets, don't you?'

Imogen shrugged this off and began to make small inroads into the plate of vanilla-scented ricotta and salted-caramel ice cream that had just been laid before her.

'How is it?' Everett asked, leaning a fraction closer to her.

'Divine, actually,' Imogen replied with feeling. 'I've always thought that *caramel au beurre salé* is what the sea would taste like in a perfect world.'

'May I trouble you for a little taste?'

'Of course,' she said, watching him as he helped himself and then conveyed his pleasure with a brief, expressive frown.

'Getting back to Imogen,' Bunny resumed, to her friend's dismay, 'and her love of secrets. You like to keep things private because of your cooking history. And so I believe that in your heart of hearts you don't really want to find out about . . . you-know-what.'

'About . . . what?' Archer asked, puncturing the top of his chocolate soufflé and shooting Imogen an interested look.

'About nothing,' Imogen said curtly. 'Bunny's just being silly.'

'You know, I don't think I'm being silly at all,' Bunny went on teasingly. 'Why don't you tell these gentlemen a bit about what's been going on in your life? We're all *family*, after all.'

With beating heart, Imogen looked into Everett's eyes, which were blue and – superficially at least – quite candid.

'I'm sure we're all burning with curiosity,' he said slowly.

Oh, what the hell, Imogen thought, flushing just a little. 'OK. You know that kiss at the party, well . . . I still don't know who it was.'

'That is an interesting situation,' Archer said, really meeting her eye for the very first time. 'You don't have any ideas at all?'

Imogen stared at him, and then, intimidated by the directness of his gaze, averted her eyes.

'Well, um . . .' she managed to say.

'We've considered a few people, and it's still a complete mystery,' Bunny said. 'But we know he's around because he's been back to kiss her again.'

'Really?' Everett exclaimed.

'In the dark!'

'*Really?*'

'And he's been sending her notes, and emails, and flowers . . .'

Everett turned to Imogen with a grin on his handsome face. 'It sounds like one heck of a chase. Are you enjoying it?'

'Yes,' she said, smiling back.

'Good.' He looked at her silently for a moment, then said, 'Would you like to try some of my roasted pears with gingerbread?'

'Yes, please,' she said gratefully, spearing a morsel of fruit with her fork.

'*Alors*, forgive me, my dear Imogen,' Amaury said with smooth urbanity, 'but I wonder if maybe you are also a little afraid of finding out who it is?'

'Oh, she is,' Bunny opined. 'Because what if he turns out to be as ugly as a mud fence? Like Everett, for instance.'

Caught with her mouth full of succulent pear, Imogen shook her head vehemently. After swallowing, she said firmly, 'I'm not afraid.'

'Well, I'm sure glad to hear that,' Everett said, before turning his attention to his pudding.

After lunch, the Doucet brothers drove Amaury back to Montpellier, dropping Archer at the railway station on their way, while Imogen, Monty and Bunny headed home to Saint-Jean-les-Cassis. Only once did Bunny break the companionable and slightly stunned post-prandial silence that reigned in the car by saying teasingly, 'All the same, it would be wonderful. Sisters-in-law!'

Imogen smiled and said nothing. Over lunch, she'd discovered that she really liked Everett, and now, feeling slightly tipsy, she allowed Bunny's idea to take root in her own mind just a little.

'Well, anyway,' Bunny went on, nodding to herself, 'I'm sure we'll find out some time soon. This mystery can't last for ever. I'm expecting a sign any day now.'

As Bunny pulled up smoothly outside the Paperback Wonderland, Imogen noticed a familiar figure, looking lean and tanned and wearing his customary bandana, who stood with his back against the shop's window. As soon as he saw them, Cheyenne switched off his iPod and surged forward to open the door for Bunny.

'Hey, *la belle Américaine!*' the DJ said, kissing her, then walking around to the other said of the car. 'Hey, Little Mermaid!'

'*Salut,*' Imogen replied as his lips brushed her face. Something about this felt different, but she couldn't put her finger on what exactly.

'I'm playing a set at the Koud'Soleil on Saturday. You wanna honour me with your presence, ladies?'

'Saturday – yes – why not?' Imogen replied slowly, while Bunny nodded, her eyes narrowed.

'You're looking at my shirt,' Cheyenne said with obvious satisfaction.

'Yes,' Imogen admitted.

'I know! Isn't it wild? I got it in London the last time I was there.' Cheyenne's T-shirt was printed with lurid green letters that read, simply: 'Doctor Love' and underneath that, in smaller letters: 'I'm not a gynaecologist but I'd be happy to take a look.'

There seemed very limited scope for comment, so Imogen and Bunny remained silent. Quite suddenly, Cheyenne took Imogen's hand, holding her gaze while he did so, and then he said, 'So, Little Mermaid . . . you got my flowers?'

37

'Feel free to *stop* laughing any time you like,' Imogen said crossly, looking around at her friends.

'Your *face*!' Bunny gasped, tears running down her cheeks. 'It was priceless!'

'Yes, you've already mentioned that. I'm sure it was very amusing.'

'So what else did he say?' Faustina asked, trying to maintain a serious expression.

'It wasn't so much what he said . . .' Imogen began.

'*It was his hair!*' Bunny screamed, before dissolving into another fit of hysterical giggles. 'He got rid of the extensions.'

That was what had felt different – the absence of electric fizz when he kissed her.

'I know it was my trademark but it was way too much maintenance!' Cheyenne had gushed. 'Seriously! I was beginning to feel like a woman!' Then, in answer to Bunny's pointed question, he had confirmed that the change to his hairstyle had occurred only a few days after her Valentine's party, while he was away on a regional mini-tour of various Côte d'Azur clubs.

'So his hair was nice and short in plenty of time to fool around with you in the Boustifaille blackout,' Mitch threw in.

'He's the right sort of height and size,' Faustina added.

'And cute enough, as a matter of fact,' Bunny said languidly. 'For an older guy.'

'Yes, yes, I know,' Imogen said shakily. 'But I still can't imagine it.'

'Hell no,' Mitch interjected, smoothing his moustache. 'I mean, he's just too goofy – right?'

'Yes. Those flowers are goofy enough – pure Cheyenne. But the emails?'

'You got a point.'

'And I'm sorry, but I can't imagine him kissing like that.'

'Actually I can tell you that Cheyenne is an extremely good kisser.'

They all stared at Faustina, who rewarded them with a serenely feline smile. 'It happened last summer, at a time when Enzo and I were separated and he went back to the village for a while. I went out dancing on my own and I ended up going home with Cheyenne.'

Mitch let out a high-pitched whistle, then said, *sotto voce*, 'You mean you've actually . . . been there? Planted your little flag and everything?'

'Yes. And he's a good lover – maybe . . . seven out of ten? I had to show him a few things, of course. But the kissing was very good. I remember that.'

Mitch turned back to Imogen, eyebrows arched to maximum capacity. 'Well, there you go. Great kisser, *seven* out of ten, only needs a little bit of direction in the sack . . . Honey, come on! What's not to like?'

Imogen shook her head. 'I'm sure he's very good at

having a good time, but . . . he isn't a serious romantic contender, is he?'

And yet he had sent her those flowers. It was enough to make her feel a bit unsettled.

'He could have sent you those emails – why not?' Faustina said coolly. 'Maybe he's got a secret side, with all kinds of deep feelings that he doesn't choose to share with the world.'

Imogen narrowed her eyes, trying hard to imagine that she had in fact been kissed by Cheyenne and kissed him back. Not strictly impossible . . . entirely possible, in fact. Still, it would take her a minute or two to adjust to this new theory. And it did rather dash her wistful enlisting of Everett as the prime suspect. She and Bunny exchanged a look, and Bunny shrugged.

'The dumbass womaniser act would make a great cover,' Mitch said, perceptively.

'You'll soon find out, anyhow,' Bunny said. 'When you go and hear his set on Saturday.'

Late that night, Imogen found an email from the-valentine's-kiss entitled, cryptically, 'OÙ ÇA?' It contained a photograph of a sprig of dewy jasmine. More flowers! Had this come from Cheyenne? She tried to visualise him sitting in front of his laptop. Was he still wearing his feathered bandana, she wondered, or did he take it off when relaxing at home? Imogen giggled. What was hardest to imagine was that she had found herself so physically responsive to somebody she had never taken very seriously. But it was also true that her experience in such matters was extremely limited. She was only a beginner, after all.

'What do you mean – where?' she typed, also in French, hoping that the sender would be there to respond. He was.

'*Work it out and you'll know where to go.*'

That sounded interesting.

'Will you be there?'

'*I can't promise that.*'

'Why not?'

'*It'll be worth the trip. You'll see.*'

'Give me a minute,' Imogen replied, typing 'south of France' and 'jasmine' into her search engine. Amid a flurry of ads for holiday rentals something came up about Chanel No 5 and fields of jasmine in Grasse. Grasse – she had noticed that name on the map before. Another search told her that Grasse was *la capitale mondiale des parfums* – the world's perfume capital – because of a useful microclimate that encouraged the cultivation of flowers, including, apparently, tons and tons of jasmine.

By now, with her imagination fully engaged, Imogen no longer really cared whether the person at the other end was Cheyenne, Everett or anyone else in particular. She merely wanted the conversation to go on, and to find out the meaning of the jasmine connection.

If she had stopped to analyse her feelings, she'd have said that the enquiry she and her friends were conducting and the delicious private world she shared with whoever-he-was remained entirely separate in her consciousness.

'Am I going to Grasse?' she typed.

Pretty soon, another picture email materialised – Fragonard's *The Stolen Kiss* again – entitled 'COME HOME ON WEDNESDAY'. So he knew that Wednesday was her day off. Imogen frowned for a minute, then typed, 'I assume you mean home here – not in London?'

'*I mean his home.*'

Another quick search revealed that Fragonard was a native of Grasse, and that the family house had been turned into a museum. She smiled and typed, 'What/who should I look for when I get there?'

'*Enjoy the paintings. Get there early. I'll be in touch.*'

The next morning, Imogen put on the closely fitted blush-pink jacket and dark blue Capri pants she had recently bought, and which Faustina said made her look two sizes smaller than when she wore her old clothes. Underneath she wore some delicate broderie anglaise underwear. The ritual of choosing lovely frivolous things to wear next to her skin had become important to her, as a mark of respect for herself and for her body. This, she was beginning to see, was one of the keys to the self-confidence displayed by French women. They loved their bodies, cherished them, and enjoyed spoiling them.

While driving to Grasse with Monty and playing a CD of flirty bossanova songs that provided the perfect soundtrack for the Mediterranean landscape she drove through, Imogen reflected that, combined with the stirring influence of the Valentine mystery, her new surroundings had triggered something of a metamorphosis: it was as though she was slowly turning into another Imogen, the southern version of herself.

She reached the Villa Musée Jean-Honoré Fragonard – a large and elegant house set amid tall palm trees – just as it was opening. As she and Monty walked in, a silver-haired man standing behind a counter in the hallway looked up sharply, took in the picture she and Monty formed together, nodded to himself almost imperceptibly, and then said amiably in French, 'Good morning. Would you like a guided tour?'

Imogen looked around. She was the first and as yet only visitor. 'Shouldn't we wait for more people to turn up?' she suggested.

'Don't worry,' the guide replied, smiling. 'Let's start – the others can always catch up. I take it you want to see *Les jeux de l'amour*?'

When she looked blank, he explained, 'The sequence of painted panels by Fragonard – that's what it's called: *The Games of Love.*'

'Oh, yes.'

Listening with one ear to what the guide was telling her – *Les jeux de l'amour* had been commissioned by Louis XV's mistress, the beautiful Madame du Barry – Imogen gazed intently at the four paintings: *La poursuite*, *Le rendez-vous*, *Le billet* and *L'amant couronné* – The Pursuit, The Meeting, The Love Letter and The Lover Crowned.

Briefly, she tore herself away from the enchantment of the paintings, which mingled in her mind with the memory of those kisses in the dark, and made herself think of Cheyenne. Could it be that Mitch and Faustina were right, and that Cheyenne had been hiding his real self, that of a shy romantic, behind his dumbass-womaniser act? As for his sending her to this place, well, Cheyenne *was* French, and a local to boot. It made sense that he should be aware of it.

She turned her attention back to the paintings, once again falling under their spell. Because the period was precisely the one Bunny had chosen for her party, it was disturbingly easy for Imogen to imagine herself in the place of the girl in a pale yellow dress who, in one of the panels, sat waiting in a state of extreme agitation, looking one way and thus not noticing that on the other side of an imposing statue of Cupid and Psyche stood her lover, poised on top of a ladder, about to jump down to join her on the terrace.

'And in the last one, she places a crown of flowers on his head,' the guide was saying in conclusion. 'He's won her heart. They are truly charming scenes, aren't they?'

'Yes, charming,' Imogen murmured. Her eyes had filled with tears and she looked up at the ceiling, hoping to stem the flow.

'You realise, of course, that these are only copies. The originals were purchased by an American collector a long time ago. They're now housed in the Frick Collection in New York. *Ah, là là*, these Americans!' The Frenchman sniffed delicately, then smiled at her. 'Don't get me wrong – I have nothing against Americans personally! *Au contraire!* Still, it is a great pity that the panels are no longer here, but what can we do?'

Imogen nodded politely. Her mind was whirling, and she was having difficulty concentrating on what her companion was saying. Slowly, she realised that, with the now familiar duality at play in her consciousness, while part of her mind focused on Cheyenne as a possible contender, another part was holding fast to the mystery of the invisible lover, reluctant to let it go. She was also, contradictorily, disappointed not to have found him – Cheyenne? Or someone else? – here, waiting for her. Of course he had said as much, but she now realised how badly she'd been hoping that he would turn up to surprise her.

'And now,' the guide said, 'I believe I am meant to give you this.' He held out an envelope labelled with her name. 'You are the right person?'

'Yes,' Imogen said, astonished and delighted. 'Who left this for me? What did he look like?' As she waited for a reply, she ripped the envelope open – it contained a map of the Old Town in Grasse with a route traced in scarlet ink and ending, like a pirate's treasure map, with a cross. Did this mark the spot where he would be waiting for her?

The guide smiled at her. 'I'm afraid I can't tell you.'

'Did he speak to someone else? One of your colleagues maybe?'

'No, I mean we were asked most insistently not to tell you anything. The person said it was part of a game you're playing – a kind of treasure hunt?'

Imogen stared at him, her heart beating wildly. 'Yes – a treasure hunt,' she repeated. She considered for a minute whether she might be able to extract more information from him, then changed her mind and asked, 'How do I get to the Old Town?'

38

Short of breath, Imogen wound her way as fast as her espadrilles would carry her through a rambling network of narrow streets, from courtyard to courtyard and square to square, trying hard not to get lost. An excited Monty, picking up on her state of mind, led the way forward. Once in a while she looked over her shoulder, hoping to catch sight of *him*, but she only ever saw groups of sightseers and the denizens of Grasse going about their business: a mother with small children, or an old man carrying shopping. Eventually they came to the square marked on the map with a cross, upon which stood a gushing fountain topped with an obelisk.

Imogen's heart bounded in anticipation: were they about to come face to face at last? But . . . there was no one in sight. Slowly, she made her way around the fountain, and then, just as she caught sight of an object balanced on a narrow stone ledge at the base of the monument, Monty gave a sudden, triumphant bark. It was a parcel wrapped in red paper, with a note attached to it, which read, in a handwriting she recognised: '*CLOSE YOUR EYES AND IMAGINE THAT I'M HERE WITH YOU.*'

She looked around and up, shielding her eyes from the sun. Where was he? In one of the pretty yellow houses around the square? Could it be that he actually lived here?

She checked every balcony – no one there. Or had he in fact been here all the time, walking not behind her but a few steps ahead, and planted the parcel at the last minute, perhaps even as he saw her turning the corner? Quite possibly. She bit her lower lip. It was maddening to think that he was so close and yet out of sight.

She pushed her hair out of her face, sat on the edge of the fountain and unwrapped the parcel. A small black box opened in her hands like a book, to reveal a bottle of golden scent hidden within. It was engraved with one word only – her own name. So here it was at last, she thought breathlessly, the surprise connected with her sense of smell! Imogen narrowed her eyes: did this mean that Cheyenne's flowers were, in fact, unconnected with the Valentine mystery? She turned the box around and discovered a discreet label for the Parfumerie Madeleine, which gave an address here in Grasse. She unfurled her map and sought out the street in question. Surely it was worth a quick enquiry?

'Ah yes, that is one of our bespoke compositions,' an impeccably made-up girl with jet-black hair confirmed when shown the bottle. She, like everyone and everything else in the Madeleine shop, smelled heavenly.

'Do you know who placed the order?' Imogen asked, though she was fairly sure what the answer would be.

The girl shrugged and gave her an impish smile. 'We are not allowed to disclose that information,' she intoned carefully, like a child reciting a lesson. 'It's a matter of confidentiality.'

'I see,' Imogen said, sighing, then smiling a little. Her admirer, whoever he was, was going to a lot of trouble to cover his tracks. 'Can you tell me anything at all? Did he – the person in question – choose this himself?'

'The way it works is that the customer comes into the lab for a conversation with one of our "noses". The customer provides as much information as possible, and then we help him come up with the perfect composition. What I *can* tell you,' she went on, glancing at her computer screen, then turning it around so that Imogen could see it too, 'is a bit about the list of components for "Imogen". You have jasmine, rose, orange blossom, sandalwood and cinnamon in your scent, among other things. It's a beautiful juice, very feminine. And now that I see you, what the customer said makes perfect sense.'

'What did he say?' Imogen asked, her face growing warmer.

'That I can't tell you. Confidentiality, remember?' The girl giggled. 'But we all thought it was *very* nice.'

39

The following evening, with service about to begin, Imogen stood at her station, reflecting that there was a lot to be said for being the object of a romantic courtship. Not only did it fill her with delicious excitement – it also did wonders for her confidence. So why not act on it?

She eyed her boss thoughtfully. A shadow of his former self, Boudin looked as if he could hardly stand. She squared her shoulders, then walked over to him and, before losing her nerve, offered to take on more cooking. As he turned to listen to her and she saw how grey his face looked, she almost felt that she was taking advantage of his distress. On the other hand, the Boustifaille show must go on and she knew how useful she could be, if given the chance.

'OK, *petite*, if you insist,' Boudin said wearily. 'You have a go at the foie gras crumble.'

Imogen nodded, then swallowed hard. The thing was that the foie gras crumble was precisely the dish Boudin had asked her to make – with her bare hands – in her honking-goose nightmare. Was this a bad omen? She shook her head, dismissing any superstitious nonsense. By the time she had reached her station, she was smiling to herself. It had occurred to her that it would actually be a lot of fun to wrongfoot Dimitri, whose dish this was. And what a triumph if she managed to pull it off!

'Chef wants me to take over your foie gras dish,' she told Dimitri in a neutral tone of voice, and without looking at him directly. 'OK?'

'Oh, great,' he replied ungraciously. 'That's all I need.'

'How much have you done? The apples?'

'Nope, sorry.' He shrugged, his face set. 'Over to you. Good luck.'

'Thanks *very much*,' Imogen said sweetly.

'Dimitri, four chicken *balottines*! And five crumbles!' called out Larissa, who had wandered in close to their station.

'The crumble is hers,' Dimitri said, nodding curtly in Imogen's direction. Then he walked off in the direction of the larder.

Imogen acknowledged the order – *her* order! Hurrah! Now to fetch the apples, which needed to be cooked in butter until delectably soft and golden. Back at her post, she was peeling her fruit as fast as she could when she remembered the crumble mix. Damn and blast! She'd completely forgotten about it. Just then Dimitri reached across her, without apologising as usual, to snatch a pan off a hook above her station. His arm brushed her breasts. He gave her a quick insolent smile and she made a face back at him. Then she hastily threw the crumble ingredients together and spread the mixture on a baking tray. Dimitri was very annoying. Perhaps, she thought, professional kitchens *did* work best as single-sex environments.

'Where's the sauce, you goose?' Dimitri suddenly shot at her.

Under her breath, Imogen swore vigorously in French, noting in passing that her foreign-language skills were really improving under pressure.

'You need to caramelise the bergamot jam,' Dimitri went on. 'Get on with it.'

'I know, I *know*.'

Imogen scanned her own and Dimitri's station.

'Where is the jam?' she asked. 'Did you put it away?'

'No,' he replied, working deftly on his *ballotines de volaille au beurre de lavande*. 'It's right here. Use your eyes.'

'It isn't,' Imogen said, nervously rifling behind containers and pans.

Dimitri looked up, exasperated. 'It *was* here a minute ago. Go get another jar from the larder.'

Imogen went into the larder and scanned the shelves carefully, noting with rising panic the complete absence of bergamot jam. She ran back to Dimitri.

'We must have run out,' she announced, *sotto voce*. 'Shall I make the caramel without it?'

Dimitri glared at her. 'The dish is called *à la bergamote*, Imogen. What do you think?' Quickly, he finished plating his *balottines* and gestured to Larissa, who had been waiting behind him, to take them through. 'Right,' he said to Imogen, wiping his hands, 'I'll have a look around for the jam. Get on with the rest.'

Having miraculously rescued her crumble mix from burning, Imogen pan-fried the apples, keeping a hopeful eye on the roving figure of Dimitri and his quest for the misplaced bergamot jam. Now for the foie gras – the crucial ingredient, which it was vital to handle with the utmost sureness of touch. She needed, Imogen told herself firmly, to slice it as regularly as possible and then pan-fry the pieces with great care. It was essential to keep them the right side of pink or they would be ruined. *Right. Fine. Stay focused.* Imogen looked in the fridge, nervously humming under her breath: 'Foie gras, foie gras, where are you?' But after a fruitless search, she had to admit to herself that the goose liver was nowhere to be seen. She clenched her teeth. This was getting ridiculous. What the hell was going on with her ingredients? Then a light bulb went on in her head. *Dimitri!* Of course! *He* was behind all this, trying to undermine her because he felt that she was becoming a threat to him in the kitchen. She turned on her heel and marched towards him, ready to have it out.

'What is the problem, *petite assistante*?' she suddenly heard at her elbow. Her anxious eyes met the implacable glare of Monsieur Boudin. 'Where are the crumbles? Larissa's been asking for them.'

'Sorry, Chef, but . . .' Before she could explain, she noticed Dimitri waving at her with frantic urgency and hurried to his side.

'It's all right, Chef!' he cried, adding, 'Imogen, get your arse into gear. Here's the jam. I found it among Pierrot's things. No idea how it got there. And the foie gras was in the spare fridge upstairs. Did you put it there?'

'Certainly not,' Imogen replied furiously, seizing the foie gras and slicing it as fast as she could. 'I *know* it was you, so stop pretending,' she hissed. 'This is really feeble, even by your standards.'

'I don't know what you're talking about,' Dimitri said,

shaking his head. 'Look, I've started your caramel for you, OK? Can you do the rest?'

'Er, thanks,' Imogen replied, puzzled.

Now in a mad rush, she finished the bergamot caramel with a dash of duck *jus*, blanketed her foie gras under its crumble and slid the dishes into the oven. At last she was able to dress her plates. Dimitri tasted her seasoning, then nodded curtly, indicating that all was well.

'You are very late,' Monsieur Boudin sighed as she approached the pass, her heart beating loudly. Silently, he examined her work. He waved it through. As Larissa picked up the plates, Imogen met her eyes, which, glittering and triumphant, were staring into her own. Then the penny dropped.

'*You?*' Imogen mouthed incredulously. 'You hid my ingredients?'

Larissa brought her face very close to hers, hissed, 'Prove it, *l'Anglaise*!' and then turned her back on her, whisking the crumbles off into the dining room.

So her enemy in the kitchen was Larissa, not Dimitri. Thinking back, Imogen realised that the waitress had always been hostile to her – telling Bastien about her episode with Dimitri, doing her best to frighten her into thinking that a plaster had found its way onto a customer's plate. But why, Imogen wondered sadly, did the other girl hate her so much?

40

'It's something to do with your animal instinct,' Faustina had decreed the next day, as they walked their dogs. 'Like them,' she went on, nodding in the direction of Monty and Cristiana. 'The most natural thing in the world. There's a strong physical attraction between you and this guy – it's not complicated.'

'There *is* a physical attraction,' Imogen had conceded, smiling.

'Exactly.'

Imogen looked pensively at her friend, saying nothing. Faustina seemed slightly different today, she noticed. Her hair was more natural, for one thing, tied back in a soft ponytail rather than teased into a mass of elaborately styled curls. And though she was wearing hot pants and heels – one of her default options – they were paired with a knotted shirt rather than a strapless glittery top. Faustina returned her look before asking, with characteristic abruptness. 'Are you telling me that you don't want to sleep with him?'

'Er . . . no . . . I . . .'

Faustina rolled her eyes. 'You do or you don't?'

'Want to sleep with him?' Imogen blushed. She still wasn't entirely accustomed to calling a spade a spade and facing up openly to . . . well, sex, in Faustina's uncomplicated way. 'Ye-es, I *do*, but—'

'Then do it,' Faustina said crisply, snapping her fingers. 'Next time you meet him, just say, "Come on, let's have sex immediately." I think it's the only way you're going to make progress with this thing.'

Imogen couldn't help laughing at this, then her face took on a more serious expression. 'I think I'm in love with him,' she blurted out, then looked wide-eyed at Faustina.

'Don't be ridiculous,' her friend said severely. 'You can't be in love with him. You don't even know who he is.'

'I know.' Imogen took a deep breath before trying to put her feelings into words. Words that someone who wasn't in her shoes might not be able to understand. 'The thing is . . . you know what you said about my animal instinct? Well, instinctively I feel like I know him, like I've always known him. I trust him,' she ended, simply.

Faustina stopped in her tracks. 'No, be reasonable for a minute! You know very well how it happens when you fall in love! There's a lot of staring into each other's eyes, and then you just can't stop looking at him – like you're trying to memorise every little detail, you know?'

'Mmm.' It had been like that with Adrian, certainly. And look how well that had turned out. Both her fondness for Bastien and her flirtation with Dimitri had begun with lingering looks and smiles, too, yet neither had delivered anything like the charge she had received from the brief moments of contact she'd had with her Invisible Man. With an effort, Imogen visualised Cheyenne's face, then Everett's, and then, somewhat to her own surprise, Amaury's. Because, come to think of it, there had been something . . . intriguing about his manner on the day of the Saint-Paul-de-Vence expedition – he had been very attentive to her. But of course there couldn't be anything in that, because Amaury was interested in Bunny, wasn't he?

'And also, sex can happen right away,' Faustina was saying forcefully. 'That's why it's so great – but love takes *time*. And even with love at first sight, there must be a first sight, no?'

'Well, blind people fall in love, don't they?' Imogen responded. 'And maybe there *was* a first sight. We still don't know who he is.'

'If you don't remember meeting him, then it wasn't love at first sight.'

'Why not?' Imogen countered. She felt quite sure of her ground suddenly. 'I'm beginning to think that you can meet someone and receive a very penetrating impression, even if it's not completely conscious. And then when he kissed me, that impression became . . . stamped on me. And on him, too. It was love at first taste!' She giggled. 'I know it sounds strange.'

Faustina looked at her, disconcerted. 'It sounds crazy, actually. You've completely lost touch with reality. I mean, you've only been with this guy twice.'

'I *know*. But the emails—'

'Oh, please.'

'The emails,' Imogen went on firmly, 'give me a sense of his voice, of his whole personality. And it's not just that. It's everything – sending me to Grasse like that . . . And being with him feels the same: it's exciting, but I also feel at home with him. He's not a stranger to me.'

'*Sex!*' Faustina cried with a desperate intensity that made quite a few fellow dog walkers turn around and Imogen burst out laughing. 'That's all it is! Nothing more!'

As she got into bed that night, Imogen scattered a few drops from the perfume bottle onto her pillow before lying down. The scent of flowers and spice began to rise and she closed her eyes, slowly moving her head from side to side.

Drowsily, she thought about *The Games of Love* – which *he* had wanted her to see. 'Are you in love, my dear?' that shrewd American had asked her in the labyrinth in Saint-Paul-de-Vence. Despite never having met her before, he had known – had been able to read it clearly on her face. Love . . . The texture of her life had become very strange. Georgette Heyer certainly hadn't prepared her for this. Her thoughts turned to what Mitch had said when she had recounted her trip – about the Grasse jasmine festival.

'It's loud, terrific – pure unapologetic Mediterranean camp. There's a parade – local girls in bikinis waving at you from these garish floats, all piled up with masses of flowers. There are fireworks, too. But my favourite part is this weird pagan ritual where everybody gets doused with jasmine-scented water. Usually the girls do it, though last year the mayor of Grasse got the fire brigade to perform it instead – *with their hoses*!' Mitch clasped his hands reverently. 'Whew. That was just the best party ever.'

Imogen had listened, smiling. In fact, she had never been particularly interested in perfume before. She had dabbed on an imperceptible amount from a tiny sample phial given to her by Hildegard as a stocking filler a couple of Christmases ago, but it was really a token gesture, because her sense of smell had been entirely channelled into her cooking.

But now ... she turned over, buried her face in her pillow and breathed in deeply. Oh, now she felt like she'd been introduced to some sort of drug. She had refrained from wearing the scent during service, obviously, but afterwards she had rushed home to put some in her hair, on her hands, between her breasts, only just managing to resist the urge to pour the entire contents of the bottle all over herself.

If Faustina was right and what Imogen felt wasn't love, then what was this powerful yearning to be in his arms again, to be kissed, to open her eyes and see him at last? It wasn't mere curiosity to solve the mystery of his identity, Imogen reasoned, nor was it just about sex. There was more to it than that: a strong sense, even after such a short and unusual courtship, that she was deeply connected and tied to him, that they belonged together.

That night she dreamed about the jasmine festival. She could hear music, the sounds of the crowd, the crackle of fireworks in the sky. The deluge of scented water soaked her from head to toe. His arms closed around her. 'I love you,' she murmured rapturously. She turned her head and found his mouth.

41

'Oh wow, you smell amazing,' Cheyenne said as he gave Imogen a warm hug and kissed the top of her head.

'Thank you,' she replied automatically, sitting down next to him in one of the Koud'Soleil bamboo-clad booths.

She had only managed to get to the club very late, long after the DJ had finished his set. Now a succession of irresistible disco anthems was being churned out to an appreciative Saturday-night crowd.

As her eyes adjusted to the club's liberal use of strobe lighting and she turned to face her date, Imogen felt that after the dreamy rapture of the Grasse episode, she had suddenly come back down to earth with a thud. Objectively speaking, the DJ was an appealing-enough individual. There he sat, wearing his customary good-natured and slightly spaced-out expression, and singing along very approximately to 'Boogie Wonderland'. But she still had considerable difficulty in reconciling this puppyish individual with the person she'd been searching for since Bunny's party. Coming out of her reverie, she noticed Cheyenne staring at her expectantly. He must have asked her something, and was now waiting for her answer.

'Sorry, what?'

'I said, "Welcome, Little Mermaid, to the universe of

Cheyenne."' Rapidly, he traced a few figures of eight in the air with his glow stick.

'Thanks,' Imogen said drily. 'By the way, why do you call me that?'

The DJ leaned back, smiling at her. 'When I first started seeing you around, here and at La Sirène, you were always so quiet. And I thought, she's like the girl in the fairy tale, you know?'

Imogen, who had loved 'The Little Mermaid' as a child and remembered it well, was still struggling to see the connection. 'In what way?' she asked patiently.

'The Little Mermaid, she wants legs instead of a fish tail, yeah?' Cheyenne said, screwing up his eyes. 'Because she's in love with this prince? So she goes to a witch and the witch gives her legs, but in exchange she cuts off her tongue. I mean, *wow*.' He shook his head in wonder, then resumed, smiling, 'That was why you reminded me of her, because you never said a word. And also you had big sad eyes, like her.'

'Big sad eyes?' Imogen said, embarrassed. 'Really?'

Cheyenne took her hand and gave it a friendly squeeze. '*Ah ouais, tu avais le blues.* But now, I think that the blues, it's gone away – whoosh!' he said, tracing an upward arabesque with his glow stick. 'Am I right?'

'Perhaps,' Imogen admitted, smiling a little.

'You still remind me of a mermaid, but now you look like you're having fun. It's good for you, this place. You've been kissed . . .'

Imogen jumped slightly.

' . . . by the sun,' Cheyenne wound up, before moving a

little closer. 'And I hope that it's perhaps a little bit because of me that you are happier?'

Imogen stared at him, dumbstruck. Was this the admission she had been waiting for? 'I don't know,' she said carefully. 'What do *you* think?'

'*Ah, voilà!*' Cheyenne said, gesturing expansively as the waitress brought a bottle of champagne to their table. He flashed a smile at the girl, who grinned back. Imogen waited nervously while he poured the wine, then clinked glasses with him.

'This is great, *hein*? You and me together at last.'

'Mmm. But I thought that you and Larissa . . .'

'Oh, no. Larissa's gorgeous, but she loves somebody else.'

'Does she?' Imogen asked, intrigued. 'Who?'

'I can't say,' Cheyenne replied, shaking his head. 'It's so sad. She's right under his nose and he hasn't even noticed her. Anyway, I tried my best to take her mind off it, but it didn't work! And so I'm all yours! Step into the limousine of your life, relax and enjoy the ride.'

'Yes,' Imogen said, really meaning *No*. 'About that. There are a few things I need to ask you.'

'Oh, sure. What do you want to know?'

Imogen made herself look at him squarely. Cheyenne winked back at her, fingers drumming along to the French pop song now playing – a jingly number calling out to everyone to come dancing under the tropical sunlight. Imogen stared briefly at the spray of feathers tucked into her companion's bandana. The dumbass-womaniser act was very much in evidence tonight. But – just to suspend disbelief for a second – what if it *was* nothing but an elaborate cover for his true self? What if 'Cheyenne' was a made-up character and nothing more? Come to think of it, that wasn't even his real name, was it?

'OK,' Imogen said firmly, putting her glass to one side. 'Listen, er, Stéphane.'

'Whoa, who's Stéphane? I don't know any Stéphane,' he said, his glow stick dancing vehemently. 'Nobody calls me that apart from my mother.'

'Right. Cheyenne, then.' Imogen cleared her throat. 'You know, at Bunny's birthday party—'

'*Ah, la belle Américaine!*' Cheyenne interjected enthusiastically. 'How is she doing?'

'She's fine. At her party, did you—'

'You know, that was when I began to think that you were a *really* cool chick. That dress you wore, it was really—'

'Thank you. But did you . . . erm . . . kiss me on that night?'

Cheyenne brought his face close to hers. *Well, here we go,* Imogen thought, swallowing with difficulty, *my hour has come.*

'You were loved up too?' he said, staring at her ecstatically. 'Wasn't it great? I think I kissed everybody that night!'

'Everybody? So, you mean . . . not me, specifically.'

'Specifically? I'm not sure, Little Mermaid. It's all a bit . . . woosh, you know?' he said, making a sweeping motion over his head with the glow stick.

'So you don't, for example, remember playing Blind Man's Buff?'

'No,' Cheyenne said, screwing up his eyes. 'But maybe I did? Did I?'

Imogen decided to change tack. 'What about . . . emails?' she asked, trying to get him to concentrate. 'Did you send me any that you remember?'

'Depends. Are you on the mailing list for the Cheyenne Newsletter? You know, to keep you up to date with everything that's going on in the universe of Cheyenne?'

Yet another evasion! Was he teasing her? Though, as a matter of fact, Imogen did remember receiving the said newsletters, and deleting every one without opening them. 'Yes, I am on your mailing list,' she replied, adding pointedly, 'though actually I'm not sure how I got there in the first place, because I don't remember ever giving you my email address.'

'Oh, that's easy,' Cheyenne said with a good-natured smile. 'When *la belle Américaine* emailed me about her party, I just copied the list of other recipients.'

'You did?'

Which meant, of course, that any other guest might have got hold of her address that way.

'Yeah. I didn't think anyone would mind.'

'Cheyenne,' Imogen said, taking the bull by the horns, 'the perfume I'm wearing tonight – was it a gift from you?'

When he began to nod – in time to the song now playing – Imogen's heart threatened to go on strike and stop beating. But almost immediately he frowned and shook his head, 'No, Little Mermaid.'

'I didn't think so,' Imogen replied, repressing a sigh of relief. 'Listen,' she went on, gradually edging away from him. 'I wanted to thank you for sending me those flowers. It was really sweet of you.'

'No problem.'

'But I'm not looking for a relationship at the moment. I'm sorry.'

'Oh, that's cool,' Cheyenne protested amiably. 'Cheyenne's universe is a pretty intense experience, you know? Maybe you're not ready yet.'

'Maybe not,' Imogen agreed, getting out of the booth. 'Thanks very much for the champagne. *Salut.*'

'*Salut.* But remember you are on my special, personal and exclusive guest list. So if you change your mind, you can always jump the queue. We could have a lot of fun – good times, you know.'

Right on cue, 'Good Times' began to play, once again drawing everyone to the dance floor. Cheyenne grinned, pointing to his head with both hands to signify that he possessed telepathic powers. Imogen smiled back before she plunged into the dancing crowd and headed towards the exit. Looking over her shoulder, she noticed the pretty waitress who had brought their drinks hovering near Cheyenne's table. As though sensing her presence, the DJ looked over at her and immediately engaged her in conversation. *Pas de souci*, no worries – as the dumbass womaniser himself might have put it.

42

'So it ain't Cheyenne, huh?' Mitch said, as he and Imogen sat on the sofa while Monty lounged between them intently watching a French cartoon about rabbits and moles. 'Can't say I'm overly shocked to hear that.'

'No – neither am I.'

'So . . . are you going out of your mind yet? I mean, don't you wish that you could just . . . I dunno, call him on the phone, like a person in a normal relationship?'

'Hmm.' Imogen smiled at her unusual predicament. 'Sometimes, I wonder if I'll ever get to know him in that ordinary way – you know, in the light of day. But even with things being as they are, it's all been so intense that I can't help feeling very close to him. Everything's been accelerated.'

'Uh-huh, yeah. That doesn't sound too shabby.'

'It's not. But that also means that it's not an everyday relationship where—'

'You take turns taking out the trash and stuff like that?'

'Exactly.'

'Huh.' Mitch stroked his moustache thoughtfully. 'But that's just the point, you know. It's *not* an everyday relationship, at least not yet. At the moment, it's a *trip*.'

'Mind-shaking?' Imogen murmured, smiling at him. 'Paths of desire?'

'Exactly!' Mitch said, glaring at her with heart-warming severity. 'It's *theatre*. And it's being staged especially for you, you little ninny – God knows why.'

'You think that's why he doesn't contact me more often? And also why he hasn't revealed himself yet?'

Mitch nodded. 'Well, the whole Valentine's Day conceit is a guessing game, isn't it? Maybe he's waiting for you to out him. Besides, I'm no mind-reader, but I think he's trying to keep it pure – not to fritter anything away in mundane chatter. That way when you do communicate you get the full force of the romance – like when you're kissing him. It's not really about getting a peck on the cheek. That make sense?'

'Yes.' Imogen sighed.

'What? You've had enough of the amazing stuff? You wanna move on to taking out the trash?'

'No – I love the amazing stuff,' she said, laughing. 'But maybe I'd also like a peck on the cheek now and then.'

Mitch looked away for a moment, then said coldly, 'Well, I might not be the best person to advise you on that. You know my track record, right?'

43

Monsieur Boudin had fallen into a prostrated funk and now spent most of his time sitting in a corner of the kitchen staring at the wall. His staff believed that he would snap out of it sooner or later, but in the meantime someone else was going to have to step up to the plate, as it were, and ensure that service ran smoothly. This was put to the vote, and Bastien was chosen by a large majority as his boss's temporary replacement.

'This is just for the next few days,' he told a sullen Dimitri, who had made no bones about the fact that he wanted the job for himself, while Imogen stood nearby getting her peeling duties out of the way. 'But of course it means that someone else needs to take over my station.'

'*What?*' Dimitri snapped. 'You think I don't have enough to do with my own work?'

'Actually,' Bastien said evenly, 'I was thinking of delegating to you, Imogen.' Then, as Dimitri's mouth opened in outrage, Bastien added quickly, 'Dimitri will keep an eye on what you're doing and will, of course, help you with anything you want to know. Right, Dimitri? I'm sure Imogen will think twice before troubling you with trivialities,' he stressed, smiling at her.

Imogen smiled back, resisting the urge to thumb her

nose at Dimitri, then blurted out, 'But I thought . . . when I messed up with the foie gras crumble . . .'

Bastien nodded. 'Ah, yes. Well, Larissa confessed to me what she'd done, messing about with your ingredients.'

Hearing the word 'confessed', Imogen wondered if 'bragged about' might possibly have been a better description of Larissa's admittance of guilt.

'So we can draw a line under that,' Bastien went on lightly. 'I've no doubt that you can handle that dish perfectly, along with all of mine. So if you accept, I'll need you to start working the lunch shift again because—' Bastien nodded in the direction of Monsieur Boudin, slumped in his chair '—of the situation. Will you help us out?'

'Yes, of course!'

'OK, then,' Bastien said, shaking hands with her, then giving Dimitri a playful yet fairly disabling punch in the stomach. A certain amount of rivalry continued to simmer between the two, not all of it professional. In spite of the 'friends-only' relationship they had developed, Bastien's wistful feelings for Imogen were still discernible at times, while Dimitri, on the other hand, lost no opportunity to tell her that one thing was for certain: she'd have no choice but to succumb to his charms in the end.

'Imogen,' Bastien went on, 'you know the drill – *mousseuse de sardines, fleur d'écrevisse, courgette niçoise à ma façon . . . Ça va aller, oui?*'

'*Oui. Merci, Chef!*'

'My pleasure,' Bastien said, before heading off to give Manu, Pierrot and Régis a pre-service pep talk.

Though Bastien had not mentioned it, Imogen knew

full well that she was expected to handle her old skivvy's duties as well as her new, more creative ones. But there was no time to worry about any of that. *Just get on with it*, she thought. All around her the kitchen was a frantically dancing blur of rushing bodies, shouted instructions and walls of flame rising around clanging pans. In the midst of this, she remembered, with a kind of visionary intensity, the mysterious bottle of golden scent sitting on her bedside table, and an exhilarating rush of energy travelled through her.

Good. Use it and get the dish done. *Get it done*. It was simple: just make sure every component comes out tasting perfectly of itself. If she'd stopped to visualise it, she would have described the workings of her mind during service in terms of the hallucinatory telephone-exchange feeling that had accompanied the first kiss at Bunny's party – imaginary hands flying at super-human speed ensuring that all connections were made simultaneously, hyper-efficiently, without a moment's hesitation or dead time.

Asparagus – check; sardine fillets – check; dumplings in – check, she thought, surveying her work in progress while scooping potato peelings into a waiting bucket positioned at her feet. Then purple beetroot began to bloom into abstract patterns while lightly fried courgette flowers, yellow petals tightly furled over their anchovy-scented filling, leaped out of their hot oil bath. Plate after plate came together, kaleidoscopic colours and shapes singing out with pitch-perfect intensity. Though she kept her ears pricked for Larissa and Bastien, who called out orders, Imogen otherwise blocked everything out until, after two hours, she heard, very close to her face, Dimitri's voice saying very distinctly, 'Fine, fine, *fine*. I know when to quit.'

'What?' she snapped, without looking up. Now that she had really got the hang of punctuating her blond courgette fritter with a graphic, elegant squirt of basil oil, she had no intention of messing up. She was, as Cheyenne might have said, in the zone.

Dimitri began to laugh. Since she had, for the time being, finished plating, Imogen looked at him.

'You know what this is like?' he asked, crossing his arms and smiling at her without a trace of antagonism.

'No. What is it like?' Imogen said drily, while tidying her station before the next lot of orders came in.

'Looking in a mirror.'

'What do you mean?'

'I've been standing here taunting you for ages, Imogen. I was really, really creative and tried a lot of different things. Comments about your technique, your presentation, even about your body. But you didn't rise to a single thing I said.'

'I'm sorry, but I didn't actually *hear* you,' Imogen replied, straightening up and gracing him with a sardonic smile.

Dimitri nodded and smiled back. Then he walked around the counter and gave her a quick hug. 'You're good,' he said, releasing her. 'Not as good as me, you understand, but pretty good. I'm proud of you.'

'Thanks. Does this mean we're friends?'

'You know very well that men and women can't be

friends,' Dimitri said firmly, 'but let's call it that if you like.'

'OK. So . . . can I borrow your knives?'

'Don't push it.'

44

Imogen sat on the golden sand, hugging her knees and looking out to sea. She had wanted to be alone with her thoughts for a while before reporting to Boustifaille, and had driven to a small rocky creek a little way out of town. It was far too early in the morning for hardcore sun-worshippers, and in any case the temperature, though deliciously mild for early spring, was unlikely to rise high enough for them. There were only a few tourists in town, though a few locals – the hearty kind who swam in January – would no doubt trickle in later. Imogen had also chosen this particular beach because the only means of access – a charming but steep path of irregular stairs carved into the rock – was guaranteed to put off anyone who was in search of instant gratification.

She'd been sitting there for a longish while, and had several times given in to a compulsive desire to turn around and look up at the road, in case *he* should miraculously be standing there. But all she had glimpsed so far was the odd passing car.

Something within her had changed, had intensified considerably, in the wake of her Grasse treasure hunt. The various sensory impressions which she had only glimpsed at Bunny's party – the way he tasted, his addictive smell (that of sweet warm skin in the sun), the feel of the planes of his face when they kissed, the tenderness of his touch – had crystallised during the blackout encounter and she could now summon them at will with absolute clarity. Instead of fading, the effects of physical contact with him had continued to pulsate through her – like a permanent undertow that was almost indistinguishable from her own heartbeat.

Contact by email, though still teasingly telegraphic and nowhere near reaching the 'who's taking out the trash' stage of everyday ordinariness, had nevertheless become more frequent and comparatively more direct – almost like getting the odd peck on the cheek.

'Thank you for your gift,' she had written, soon after her trip to Grasse.

'*Where do you wear it?*'

'Everywhere,' she had typed back, smiling. 'Anywhere you like.'

'*Imogen, I like all of you. By the way, you've stopped asking who I am. I'm curious to know why.*'

'How do you know I haven't worked it out?' she'd replied.

'*Bluffer.*'

'Maybe.'

Sitting on the beach, she allowed herself another glance at the road. Still nothing. It was silly to feel disappointed. Yet since the Grasse episode she'd had a near-constant sense – voluptuous, heady, and just the slightest bit unsettling – that he was somewhere, everywhere, always just out of sight. He was getting closer, she was certain of it. And soon, very soon, she would know everything.

Imogen found herself in a deliciously ambiguous state. Of course she wanted to *know*. And she could feel in the air, between the lines, the silent promise of a more complete, unrestrained embrace with him – this time in light rather than darkness. She longed for this. But at the same time she was in no real hurry for the story, with its languid atmosphere and unresolved mysteries, to come to a conclusion.

She stood up, digging her toes in the sand, and pulled her dress over her head. Time to go for a swim. She whistled for Monty, who trotted over with his head held high, seating himself by his mistress's belongings and guarding them fiercely. This was one of the tasks he enjoyed most.

The water felt cold at first, so she waded in slowly, letting the sea lick its way up her legs to the top of her thighs. She splashed her shoulders and crouched down all of a sudden, enjoying the harsh prickling of the water on her scalp as her head went under. Resurfacing, she screwed up her eyes and considered a wooden raft tethered a hundred yards or so from the beach. Perhaps she could swim there and back.

For a while, as she propelled herself towards the bobbing raft, she forgot everything save the feel of the water on her skin, her own weightlessness, and how pale her limbs looked in the greenish sea. After looking around to check that there were no other swimmers nearby she reached back experimentally, unhooked the top of her suit, tucked it securely into her knickers and carried on swimming. The sensation made her laugh; her floating breasts felt like two separate entities – unbelievably freeing after a lifetime of confinement. She turned on to her back and kicked vigorously. Not far to go now.

She climbed the slippery ladder onto the raft and sat down, tucking her legs underneath herself and smoothing her hair, now as dark and wet as seaweed, around the back of her neck and over one shoulder. For a while she watched the sea crash against the rocks. There was something soothing, hypnotic even, about the intensity of the impact, its repetition. It was getting warmer. The beach was still empty of people, though she could make out Monty's small black silhouette, looking resolute and dignified even from a distance.

She closed her eyes and licked the salt off her lips. How would it feel, she wondered, to be with *him* in broad daylight, just for a change? Slowly, she lay down and stretched out, spread-eagled. What would it be like, for example, to make love right here on this raft, directly under the sun, and while looking into his eyes?

It was insanely frustrating to know that he was somewhere out there, not far away but that she had no way of getting to him. Perhaps she should try summoning him, willing him to find his way to the beach and to swim out to her. She crossed her arms over her face and wished for him as hard as she could. Suddenly the raft bobbed a little higher. It was almost as if someone . . . She opened one eye to check: she was still alone.

She turned over onto her front, cradling her face between her arms and listening to the hammering of the waves. Pretend, just pretend for a minute that he *had* come to her.

What would he do? Lazily, she shook her head from side to side. That wasn't the question. The question was, what would *she* do? Kiss him with her eyes open, of course. Ah yes – and what could she picture on the screen of her imagination? A lovely blur, that's what.

She inhaled the smell of the raft – salt-saturated wood. Really she was better off with her eyes shut. The illusion would be more complete that way. Patiently, she focused inwards. Feeling along the cool insides of her arms with her lips, she tried to conjure up his flesh out of hers. After a few breaths, she was aware of something shifting and opening out – like a camera lens. Her body tensed up pleasurably. *Yes.* In her mind's eye he was there, right there with her on the raft. She could feel his mouth travelling slowly from the nape of her neck to the small of her back. Then the raft bobbed again as he lay down next to her. Reaching out, she caressed his chest, then moved to lay her head on his warm stomach, and he laughed. She turned over, raised herself on one elbow and traced his hipbone with her fingertips. She lowered her head and her tongue flicked at him for a split second, then for much, much longer. Now there was nothing else but this caress, the sound of his breathing, his fingers entangled in her hair. After a while she felt his hips move and she closed her eyes again just as he flooded her mouth – as irrepressible as the tide.

45

A little later, while she was busy painting sheets of filo pastry with olive oil and melted butter for her *croustillant d'agneau au thym en feuille de brik* (a Provençal take on a lamb samosa), a new dish that Bastien had agreed to add to the Boustifaille menu, Imogen's mind flashed back, on and off, to her vivid daydream on the raft, and every time this happened she smiled, shaking her head in amused disbelief.

For as long as she could remember, sex had been nothing but a source of embarrassment, disappointment and boredom. And now . . . well, now she was developing an interest in it, certainly. And this, she reflected, came from an unprecedented sense of physical freedom. With the onset of spring, she had been spending more time in the sea and wearing fewer clothes even when she was out of the water. Today especially, the air felt caressing on her skin, like the most delicious bath. But something else was at play within her – a sensuous feeling of having her senses awakened that came from . . . well . . . intense physical desire, and from basking in the knowledge that *he* was thinking about her too. Oh, she wanted to *see* him now. Very, very much.

Folding the translucent pastry over a perfectly calibrated mouth-sized amount of aromatic lamb filling, Imogen reflected that although it had only been a few days since her promotion, she had almost forgotten by now that Bastien's station hadn't always been her own. She was about to check the texture of the accompanying tomato sorbet – a luscious, fruity, palate-cleaving counterpoint to the richness of the meat – when a distraught Jean-Jacques sidled over to her counter.

After looking over his shoulder to check Boudin's whereabouts, he stage-whispered, 'You know that stain we noticed yesterday, on a wall of the restaurant? Well, it's got much worse. It appears to be some sort of leak from upstairs. I've called a plumber. But in the meantime, as if we didn't have enough trouble already, there's one end of the dining room we can't use. The carpet on the wall is completely ruined. It'll have to come off.'

Well, that was possibly a blessing in disguise, Imogen thought privately. She had never been a fan of the restaurant's décor, and Nadine Picore *had* been scathing about it in her review.

At the end of service, the specialist who'd been called in did indeed diagnose some sort of massive plumbing coronary and announced the need for a complete overhaul. The walls needed to be replastered. The restaurant would have to remain closed for the duration of the work.

The tricky news having been broken to Monsieur Boudin, the chef made his way into the dining room, followed, after a prudent interval, by his staff. Looking like a broad-shouldered polar bear in his white uniform, he stood in front of the far wall, which had been stripped of its oxblood carpet, and began to weep.

While Bastien rushed over to talk to him and Larissa

convinced him to accept a cup of coffee, Imogen had a look at the wall. The carpet had been glued rather shoddily directly onto the previous cladding, tiles in shades of green and blue gleamed here and there underneath.

'What are you doing, *petite*?'

Imogen jumped. Monsieur Boudin stood at her side, staring at her with pink-rimmed eyes.

'I was just curious about those tiles. The colours are pretty.'

'Yes, they are pretty. I used to love those tiles when I was a little boy.'

Monsieur Boudin removed his toque, screwed it up absent-mindedly in his hand, and then used it like a rag to wipe his blotchy face. 'You know, *petite*, this place is my home. I was almost born in the kitchen.' He smiled, looking over his shoulder. 'But of course in those days it was much smaller and it was over there, where the bar is now. But I'm boring you.'

'No, no, please go on.'

'It was my grandfather who first opened the restaurant,' Boudin continued, examining his scrunched-up toque with apparent surprise before stuffing it into the pocket of his apron. 'It was a lot simpler than Boustifaille – we served only *fruits de mer* and fish. It was wonderful. We lived upstairs then and I would come down here to play with my brother Marcel.'

At the mention of the treacherous brother who had stolen Boudin's wife, Imogen winced inwardly, but her boss continued unperturbed.

'And then I began to help in the kitchen. I was a very

arrogant boy. I thought I could do much better.' He snorted, sounding not unlike an angry rhinoceros. 'So when I took over, I changed the whole place. I introduced a modern menu. But I also covered up the tiles and got rid of the scruffy terrace where all the local fishermen used to sit,' he said, indicating the harbourside wall, 'because I wanted Boustifaille to be a *restaurant gastronomique* – a chic, elegant treasure box and not a vulgar café.'

A chic, elegant treasure box? Imogen thought incredulously, looking at the drearily carpeted walls, at the hideous clown paintings. Good grief. Monsieur Boudin might be a great chef but, really, he had the most awful instinct when it came to interiors. Well, nobody's perfect, she reflected. Out of the corner of her eye, she could see that the rest of the Boustifaille staff had gradually edged away, congregating near the bar and leaving her to it. Oh, very well, then. Impulsively, she said, 'I'm going to walk you home, Chef. OK?'

Boudin nodded. 'Thank you, *petite*. I feel very tired.'

As they exited into the street, Imogen, keeping an eye on her hulking companion's unsteady gait and making sure that he didn't wander into the road, said firmly, 'You're a great chef, Monsieur. You know, restaurant reviewers come and go. What counts is the food you make.'

Boudin nodded, then said mournfully, 'But maybe the reviewers are right. Maybe I have lost my touch. My restaurant, I loved it so much, but now it's become like a monster. It takes so much energy and *always* I have to come up with new ideas and new dishes.' He stopped beneath a flashing neon sign which made his exhausted face glow blue, then red, as he declared, 'I'm tired and depressed, Imogen. I'm fed up with the whole thing.'

'Maybe you need a break – a holiday.'

Monsieur Boudin shook his head. 'Oh, no. I do not enjoy holidays – they make me feel tired and depressed.'

'I see.' She bit her lip. 'What *would* you like, Monsieur?'

If it was a question of everybody pulling their socks up in the kitchen, something could probably be done. Monsieur Boudin gave a heart-rending sigh, then said, 'I want to be loved.'

'Mmm,' Imogen said noncommittally. That was a slightly bigger wish than she had bargained for. She couldn't for the moment remember whether he had any children. 'Do you . . . have a family?' she asked prudently.

'No. Only Boustifaille.'

'Well, you still have that.'

'I don't know what I have any more,' Boudin muttered. Imogen took a tentative step forward, and was relieved when he followed her. 'I'm lost, *petite*. No map, no compass – lost.'

'But you must have many friends,' Imogen said, persevering. 'I mean, you know everyone in Saint-Jean, and everyone knows you.'

They turned from the promenade into the main high street, whose food shops were closed for the night.

'Yes, that's true. But Boudin is also a man, you understand?' he said, turning to her, his face a mask of despair.

'Mmm,' Imogen said again, not entirely certain where this was going.

'And a man needs a woman in his life.'

In a flash of paranoid terror, Imogen remembered Mitch's quip about Boudin being a possible contender for the blackout episode. No – surely not? Oh, dear. What if he suddenly lunged at her? she wondered nervously. Should she duck? Or just run away?

'But she's so beautiful!' Monsieur Boudin suddenly shouted, clutching at his hair. 'She's like an apparition! And of course she doesn't love me! Nobody loves Boudin! *Nobody!*'

'Who? Who doesn't love you?' Imogen asked, relieved and genuinely interested.

Wordlessly and pathetically, Boudin looked up. Imogen followed the direction of his eyes. They were standing before Le Puits d'Amour, Daphne Blanding's pastry shop, and Boudin was gazing at the lit windows of the *pâtissière's* apartment.

'Oooooh . . .' Imogen said slowly, remembering what a plausible couple they had formed at Bunny's party, and the way his face had always softened whenever Daphne's name was mentioned.

'I should go home,' her boss said in a strangulated voice. 'It's late.'

After making sure that Monsieur Boudin was safely back inside his villa, Imogen retraced her steps and found herself once more outside Le Puits d'Amour. Daphne's lights were still on. Imogen glanced at her watch: midnight. Too late? Probably, but on the other hand . . . She rang the bell.

* * *

'That's quite an extraordinary story, Imogen.' Daphne sat on a chaise longue in her pink toile-de-Jouy dressing gown, languidly smoking a cigarette. 'Are you sure you didn't get the wrong end of the stick?'

'Quite sure. He once told me that you were a remarkable woman. And just now . . . an apparition.'

'An apparition? Me? Oh, dear Michel! He really is a child.' But she was smiling, Imogen noticed.

'May I ask if . . . you share his feelings?'

'I don't know, Imogen,' Daphne said coquettishly. 'This is rather sudden.'

'How long have you known each other?'

'Well, you know I moved here about twelve years ago. Michel took over his father's restaurant soon after we met.'

'*Twelve* years?' Imogen exclaimed. 'And he's never said anything?'

Daphne ran her fingers through her hair and said dreamily, 'Well . . . no. We were such good friends, you see. Though perhaps I did wonder sometimes. Then again Michel is such a *grand timide* – terribly shy, really. Those big powerful men often are, aren't they, underneath all the bluster? And, anyway, he was married.'

'Of course.' Briefly, Imogen wondered whether Monsieur Boudin's obsession with Daphne might have played a part in his wife's defection. 'What was *she* like?' she asked pointedly.

'Honorine? Well . . .' Daphne sat up and looked squarely at Imogen. 'Honorine was nice enough, but she was indifferent to Michel, and in love with his brother. Those things happen. It was obvious to everyone except Michel, who is the most adorably upstanding man I've ever known. And so, we had our friendship, and that was it.' She smiled, shaking her head. 'I had a few boyfriends over the years, you know. But it never seemed to work out somehow, and when things ended, I'm afraid I always leaned rather heavily on Michel for comfort. He was such a reassuring presence, Imogen, so wonderfully solid and wise. He listened to me.'

Imogen burst out laughing. 'For twelve years! Poor man. No wonder he's cracking.'

'Put like that, it does sound rather silly, doesn't it?' Daphne said, smiling. 'I suppose . . . I enjoyed being adored – yes, that was it. And without any of the ordinariness of a relationship, without all that dreary familiarity. Michel never saw me without my make-up.' Catching Imogen's look of incredulous surprise, she said wistfully, 'You're so young, Imogen. You don't need to worry about preserving your mystique. Later on it becomes far more important for a woman.' Daphne put her head to one side and smiled. 'I must say that you do seem incredibly happy, dear. Your face is shining.'

'I am,' Imogen confirmed. 'Very happy.'

'It's that mysterious boy, isn't it?' Daphne said, leaning forward to put out her cigarette. 'Mitch told me about his latest stunt – in Grasse. What style! A young man after my own heart. But how strange it must be,' she continued, pensively looking at Imogen, 'not to know quite who he is – when he already means so much to you.'

Imogen smiled at her. In her mind's eye she saw the crowned lover of Fragonard's painting. *He's won her heart*, the museum guide had said.

'Yes, it is strange,' she admitted. 'But also lovely.'

'But really, in your heart of hearts,' Daphne said, with a girlish grin that made her look about seventeen, 'you must have some idea. Who do you think it is? Do tell.'

'Well . . .' Imogen said, blushing helplessly. 'There's . . . Bunny's brother Everett, though really that's Bunny's own theory rather than mine.'

'That tall dark-haired boy? Oh, yes, I know – lovely manners. Those American southerners really understand gallantry.'

'And . . . also, perhaps, her cousin Amaury. But I really don't know . . . because I think he might be in love with Bunny herself.'

'Amaury d'Ousset?' Daphne said, twinkling a little. 'A *charming* young man – such nice eyes. And quite a catch too, you know, in his own way. And what about your kitchen pals, Bastien and Dimitri?'

'Well, at first I was convinced it must be one of them,' Imogen replied, 'and then I changed my mind, because . . . the kissing felt so different. But now . . .' she wound up, shrugging, 'I just don't know.'

'Well, you'll soon find out, dear. And then perhaps,' Daphne said more gravely, 'you might learn something from my own experience. Don't wait for twelve years. When you find him, hold on to him – whoever he is.'

Hours later, Imogen was jolted out of sleep by the sound of her mobile phone. It was Bastien, who sounded very upset.

'Boudin tried to kill himself,' he said, getting to the

point. 'He stuck his head in the oven. Thankfully, he appears to have changed his mind halfway through. He managed to crawl away and call me before passing out. It's a miracle he didn't blow himself up.'

46

On first returning home with Imogen and Bastien after a week in hospital, where the chef had been diagnosed with exhaustion, Michel Boudin had begun by apologising for behaving like a sentimental fool and then, waving away his employees' protestations, had declared in sepulchral tones that although he solemnly promised, from now on, to use his oven only for the purpose of cooking food, nothing had changed in terms of his own predicament. This was it – the end of days. All he wanted now was to be left alone to lie in the dark and brood, and waste away. No, he was *not* hungry. In fact, he never intended to eat or cook anything again. Nor would Boustifaille ever trade again. It might as well be razed to the ground. As for Boudin himself, he was *une épave*, a wreck, and should be left to sink to the bottom of the sea, there slowly to disintegrate into fish food – a fitting example of poetic justice.

He had then shuffled into his kitchen and found Daphne Blanding there, elegantly perched on the edge of the table and smoking a cigarette. 'Hello, Michel,' she'd said cheerfully. 'I'm moving in for a while. You don't mind, do you? Would you like some roast chicken? It's from Ponceau.'

From where they stood on the threshold, Imogen and

Bastien were unable to see Monsieur Boudin's expression, but his ears had moved a little – he was smiling.

In the aftermath of the hasty closing of Boustifaille, Imogen had offered Daphne her services, reasoning that it wouldn't do any harm to earn some money and consolidate her pastry-making skills while she waited for the restaurant to reopen and for work to resume – for, under Daphne's influence, Michel Boudin's earlier apocalyptic outlook had softened somewhat.

Imogen now stood filling row upon row of puff-pastry 'love wells' with vanilla-speckled *crème pâtissière* under the owner's watchful eye.

'Excellent,' Daphne said. 'You have a very steady hand. The next step is to caramelise the top with a red iron. Can you handle that?'

'Definitely. Bring it on!'

Daphne observed Imogen's confident technique with approval before turning her attention to puncturing golden orbs of choux pastry that were waiting to be turned into *religieuses*.

'How are things, by the way?' Imogen asked her friend, teasingly. 'Still keeping Monsieur Boudin company in his villa?'

'Yes,' the *pâtissière* responded crisply, while getting a container of chocolate custard out of the fridge, 'in a manner of speaking.' There was a pause, then, as she fitted a nozzle onto a piping bag, she said, 'We're planning to get married.'

'Daphne!' Imogen cried, rushing across to hug her. 'When?'

'In a month's time. In June.'

'Oh, you're crying. Don't! You'll get me started.'

'You must think it's ridiculous, us rushing into marriage like this,' Daphne said, dabbing at her eyes.

'I wouldn't call it rushing exactly,' Imogen said, laughing through her tears.

'Oh, Imogen, we're so *old*!'

'Oh, no – not at all! I'm really happy for you. Does Di know?'

'Not yet. We only decided this morning. Do you think she'd come to the wedding? She's never been much of a traveller.'

'I'm sure we can convince her – I'll help.'

'Yes, please. And that's not all, dear. I need your help with something else. Michel is much improved, but he's still refusing to have anything to do with the restaurant. I've had to take over the management of the repair work.'

Imogen nodded.

'Come along,' Daphne said, pulling her apron over her head. 'The builders will have gone home by now and we can have the place to ourselves.'

'I'm really not sure about this,' Michel Boudin said the next day, reluctantly allowing Imogen and Daphne to lead him into the Boustifaille dining room while he kept his eyes shut.

One thing's for sure, Imogen thought, *it'll be far worse when you open your eyes.* She really wasn't confident, in spite of Daphne's protestations, that he was the type of man who enjoyed surprises.

The place looked an absolute mess – a necessary evil, of course. In order to tackle the breakdown of the plumbing, the builders had had to slice through the restaurant's façade like a piece of cake and remove the whole of the front wall. A large tarpaulin hung in its place, offering temporary insulation from the outside. Meanwhile, dust sheets were draped over the inside walls. It was all rather depressing.

'Can I open my eyes now?'

'Yes, Michel,' Daphne said. 'But don't expect too much. It's still something of a . . . blank page.'

Boudin looked around the room and sighed despairingly, shaking his head. 'This is terrible,' he muttered.

'Now, Chef,' Imogen said, bravely slipping her arm through his – a gesture almost as scary as putting your head inside a lion's mouth, 'we have a surprise for you.'

'Yes?' Michel Boudin snarled, his whole being suddenly radiating menace.

Don't show any fear, Imogen told herself, removing her arm as naturally as she could and forcing herself to maintain eye contact. 'I don't know if you've given much thought to the future of the restaurant,' she began carefully. 'But we were wondering, Daphne and I, what sort of décor you had in mind.'

Michel Boudin was disconcerted. 'The décor? What does it matter? This is a restaurant. Or it was.'

'Humour us, Michel,' Daphne interjected gaily. 'Just for fun.'

Michel Boudin looked at his fiancée and his face softened noticeably.

'For example,' Imogen resumed, aware that she was treading on a minefield, 'did you want something like what you had before? You know . . . the dark carpet on the walls and all those, um . . . art works?'

'Oh, no, no. It would remind me of how depressed I felt in the old days of Boustifaille. And now I am *not* depressed. Because now,' he roared happily, 'I get *married*!'

'Yes, indeed,' Daphne said, embracing him. 'Michel dear, do you remember when we first met all those years ago?'

'Of course, *chérie*. Like it was yesterday.'

'Well, I don't think I saw the restaurant before opening night, but at some point it must have looked something like it does now – a work in progress.'

'That's true, Daphne. It looked just like this . . .' Michel Boudin said pensively, 'before I made that big mistake.'

'What mistake?' Imogen asked, crossing her fingers behind her back.

'You remember the green-and-blue tiles on the wall, *petite*? You noticed them.'

Imogen nodded.

'Well, I wish I hadn't hidden them away like that. It was silly.'

'Then make that wish,' Daphne said, giving Imogen a delighted conspiratorial smile. 'And let's see what happens.'

'Are you feeling OK, Daphne?' the chef said, staring at her with concern. 'You have been in the sun?'

'No, don't worry. Make your wish, darling. You don't have to say it out loud if you'd rather not.'

'Perhaps it would help if you closed your eyes again, Chef,' Imogen suggested. 'Just for a minute.'

Michel Boudin snorted impatiently, then did as he was told. As fast as she could, Imogen ran round the room, pulling down the dust sheets until every one of the tiled panels, now thoroughly cleaned, stood exposed. Dating from the early 1900s, they were a very attractive representation of the fauna that dwelled at the bottom of the Mediterranean. Boudin opened his eyes and silently took in the graceful shoals of fish and clusters of jewel-coloured crustaceans gleaming against their luminous aquamarine background. He nodded a few times, then smiled.

'Good surprise?' Daphne asked softly.

'Yes – very good surprise,' he said, kissing her hand.

'You know, it was Imogen who guessed that you'd like to see the tiles again. I do like them too, very much. It really feels like standing at the bottom of the sea. A perfect sea.'

'A perfect sea,' Michel Boudin repeated dreamily. 'And all the fruit of the sea – the oysters, the mussels, the prawns and the lobsters. And . . .'

'Yes?' Imogen prompted delicately, unwilling to break the spell.

'And a grilled fish, served very simply, with a piece of lemon. With maybe a little bit of spinach and some *pommes frites* on the side.'

'That's it exactly.'

'What, *petite*?'

'Your restaurant. Reviewers come and go, remember?'

Seeing him look at her keenly, she grinned. 'What counts is the food that you make.'

'Well . . . I don't know . . .' the chef said, gazing at the marine tiles.

'It wouldn't be about chasing the next Golden Spoon, or anything like that,' Imogen went on carefully, worried about setting him off again. 'But standards would have to be excellent. Perfect oysters – immaculate fish.'

'Of course . . .' he said, warming to the subject. 'Simple and perfect. From now on this place is going to be about the ocean – just that, but done with absolute beauty and simplicity – direct from the sea!'

'Direct from the sea,' Imogen repeated. 'And what about this bit here?' she asked, gesturing towards the fourth wall – the front of the restaurant.

Boudin shrugged. 'I don't know. I suppose the builders will rebuild it as before once the plumbing is fixed.'

'So customers will walk all the way around the side and come in through that little hallway, like they did before?'

'Yes, I suppose. I always wanted Boustifaille,' Monsieur Boudin recited rather mechanically, 'to be a secret and exclusive place where you shut yourself away to concentrate on just the food and nothing else.'

'Oh, but this place shouldn't be kept a secret, Chef. Everyone should see how beautiful it is, and also why it happens to be right here – and nowhere else.' Imogen grabbed the large piece of tarpaulin with both hands and pulled it back like a theatre curtain. Framed by scaffolding, a wall of glass stood revealed, and beyond it, the dazzling stage set of the harbour, with its fishing boats, the glittering bay and the open sky. The warm breeze from the sea blew into the room.

'I think that's *much* better,' she said, smiling at her boss, who smiled back. 'What do you think, Monsieur?'

47

Two days later, Michel Boudin called a 'family council' at Boustifaille to lay his plans before his staff. The latter dutifully assembled from far and wide; Jean-Jacques and Sidonie breaking off from holidays with their families, Larissa and Bastien taking time off from their temping jobs – respectively working behind the bar at La Sirène and turning out spicy creole-style cod fritters in the Koud'Soleil kitchen – and even Dimitri pulled himself away from the Italian restaurant in Nice to which he had migrated, and which happened to be interviewing for a senior position in the kitchen.

It soon became clear that Boudin was entirely back to his old self as a worried question from Régis prompted the reassuringly furious response, '*Of course* we're *not* going to close Boustifaille! You think Boudin is a *little girl?*'

All members of staff declared their intention to stay on at the new-style Boustifaille, which was due to reopen in the summer, in time for high season. All except Dimitri, that is, who explained that while it was fine for his boss to downscale, *he* happened to care about Golden Spoons and was determined to earn his own.

'But I understand that *perfectly*, my dear Dimitri!' Boudin said, still managing to subdue his ex-sous-chef with a horrifically bone-crushing handshake. 'And believe me,

I cannot *wait* to eat your Golden Spoon-standard food in your own restaurant.'

After that macho exchange, the atmosphere had relaxed and they had all toasted Boudin's engagement, with the chef enthusiastically sketching out a new menu for Chez Michel – the new incarnation of the restaurant – in between singing the praises of his future wife.

A wedding . . . Imogen thought dreamily as she sauntered along the seafront in the early morning with Monty, automatically returning the friendly greetings of dozens of other dog owners. A wedding . . . Doisneau's *Kiss by the Hôtel de Ville* immediately flashed into her mind. But why? The Paris Town Hall, that was it. That charming American she'd met in Saint-Paul-de-Vence had recommended a visit to the town hall in Menton to look at the Wedding Room. Well, why not today? She would get a couple of hours off at lunchtime in between sessions at the pastry shop – that would do very well for a little jaunt with Monty.

Later, as she stood gazing at Cocteau's portrait of Orpheus and Eurydice facing each other on their wedding day – rendered in Mediterranean shades of blue, white, yellow and orange and spreading out over the entire back wall – Imogen suddenly had a funny feeling that she was being watched. She looked sideways at the handful of other visitors, all engaged in examining the room and reading their guidebooks. None of them was looking at her.

She shook her head and turned her attention back to the painting. Orpheus, she noticed, wore a fisherman's hat and Eurydice a peasant girl's bonnet. Though they were the stuff of legend, it was rather nice to see them represented like an ordinary local couple. After all, this room was for everybody. She sat down on a red velvet chair, smoothing down her denim miniskirt, and wondered what it would be like to get married here, to walk down that aisle, treading on leopard-print carpet. Pretty exciting, probably. This madly flamboyant room was really not what you'd expect to find in an administrative building. She wondered briefly if Mitch had ever been here – it was just his kind of thing.

Then she noticed, looking at the wall on the left-hand side, two chilling sentences that had been cleverly worked into another fresco. They translated as: 'Orpheus when he looked back lost his wife and his songs. Men turned to brutes and beasts became cruel.' For the first time she asked herself why the artist had chosen this particular theme for such a happy place as a Wedding Room. *Lose faith for a second and your love's gone for good*, the Saint-Paul-de-Vence American had said to her in the labyrinth. *That's all it takes.* So that was the point of the Orpheus story – unwavering faith.

It also occurred to her that the myth of Orpheus resonated oddly with her own situation – romantic encounters in the dark with someone whose face she didn't know. Though of course that wasn't quite right, Imogen reminded herself. She *did* know his face, she must do – just not in the context of her private relationship with him. And soon, very soon, he would reveal his identity to her. There was that feeling again, making the back of her neck prickle! Slowly, Imogen sat up in her red velvet chair and turned

around. Was it her imagination or had a door, barely noticeable since it was almost concealed in the decorated wall of
the Wedding Room, just been closed, firmly and quietly?
As she was making her mind up to go and have a look,
she heard a cordial, '*Ah, tiens! Bonjour!*' and looked up to
see Amaury d'Ousset sitting down beside her.

'*Bonjour*,' she said, surprised. 'What are you doing here?'

'Oh, I have a luncheon appointment in town,' Amaury
replied. 'And as I was a little early, I thought I'd come in
here for a minute. I like this place.'

A business lunch, no doubt, Imogen thought, and likely
to be somewhere pretty smart. Amaury, she knew, was
involved in the preservation of buildings of historical
significance and often had meetings with architectural
historians and the like.

'More Michelin stars!' she exclaimed. 'You lucky thing.
I'm very jealous.'

Amaury smiled at her. He looked, she noticed, at once
preoccupied and happy.

'Actually, my mind isn't on *la cuisine* at the moment,' he
replied. 'Tell me, Imogen, have you ever had the feeling
that your life is about to be transformed completely? Like
. . . like a veil being torn and suddenly seeing a world of
colour, fire and music that you never knew existed? And
all you need to do is take one step forward and that world
can be yours?'

Imogen narrowed her eyes at him. What was he talking
about? Could it be that he was meeting Bunny for lunch?
Perhaps even for a first date? That would certainly explain
his air of having butterflies in his stomach. She wondered

about Faustina, who had expressed her intention of checking out Amaury's credentials. She must remember to ask her what she had discovered.

'I know the sort of thing you mean, yes,' she replied, smiling at him encouragingly.

'And you, my dear Imogen? Are you here to plan your wedding, perhaps?'

Imogen burst out laughing. '*My* wedding? Oh, no!'

'That's what this room is for, you know. I thought perhaps your mystery man had asked you to marry him.' He gave her a very winning smile and added, 'I am very much in favour of marriage.'

'Are you?' Imogen said, giggling. 'Well – no, he hasn't asked me yet. I like to think that I'll have discovered his identity before we move on to anything like that. I don't even know if he's the marrying kind!'

'Oh, who wouldn't want to marry you?' Amaury said gallantly.

Imogen flushed slightly at the compliment, while Bunny's cousin went on, 'Your man might turn out to be quite conventional, in fact. And when you know who he is, I think you'll find that he wants the things everybody wants when they're in love.'

'That does sound lovely,' Imogen agreed. 'But I hope he won't be *too* conventional.'

'No, of course not.'

They smiled at each other, and Imogen found herself moved to open up a little, trying to make sense of her feelings.

'You know, I remember seeing an old black-and-white

French film with my sister years ago,' she began, folding her hands in her lap. 'It was the story of Beauty and the Beast.'

'I know that film,' Amaury interjected. 'It's by Jean Cocteau, who also designed this very room.'

'Really? Gosh, that's almost like . . . destiny, isn't it?'

'Perhaps a little,' Amaury smiled. 'Go on.'

'OK,' Imogen said, also smiling. 'Do you remember how, at the end of the film, the girl falls in love with the Beast?'

Amaury nodded.

'And then,' Imogen went on, 'the curse is lifted and he turns into a prince. Then he takes her in his arms and tells her that they're going to fly through the air to his kingdom and . . .'

'And what?' Amaury asked gently.

'Well,' Imogen said, glancing at him before looking away, 'he says to her, "You won't be frightened?" and she replies, "Oh, but I *love* being frightened – *with you*."' She giggled. 'Well, that's how I feel – something like that, anyway. I know it sounds silly.'

'Not at all silly,' Amaury said, looking at her pensively. 'I like your idea of love. I think it's wise to keep a little bit of a *frisson* going – however conventional one is.'

There was a longish pause, during which Imogen felt herself becoming rather flustered by the very real possibility that Amaury was, in actual fact, the person she'd been looking for since Bunny's party. It occurred to her that her mystery man had always expressed himself, very eloquently, in French – and Amaury was as French as could be.

'A love story that begins, like yours, with a game of Blind Man's Buff can never be *too* conventional,' she heard him say. 'I like that game very much. You know it was my idea to play it at Bunny's party,' he went on, as Imogen turned to look at him, her heart beating quite fast. 'Before we met, Bunny emailed me, asking for some historical ideas to jazz up her party and I mentioned that this was the sort of game they would have played in *Les Liaisons Dangereuses*. I think that is just what she was looking for.'

While Imogen digested this revelation, Amaury took her hand in his and said, '*Enfin*, when he does ask you to marry him, and if you fancy having the ceremony here, do you know what you should do?'

Imogen shook her head and stared at him. Her heart was pounding. What was he going to say now?

Amaury opened his mouth, then glanced at his watch. '*Ah mon Dieu!*' he exclaimed, letting go of her hand. 'I must ask you to excuse me, Imogen. I don't want to keep my guest waiting.' Then he gave her a quick kiss on the cheek and hurried out.

'What I don't understand,' Imogen told Mitch that evening, as she helped him unpack a bookshop delivery, 'is that whole thing about Orpheus not being allowed to turn around. Isn't it a bit pointless to have your dead wife returned to you if you can't even look at her?'

Mitch sucked his breath in through his teeth, plonking a pile of books onto the counter. Though not wearing his dark glasses – the usual shorthand for 'keep out of my face or else' – he had seemed particularly withdrawn since her return, and she wasn't having much luck in drawing him out. So it came as a pleasant surprise to hear him speak, albeit in an oddly strained voice, 'The point is, you little knucklehead, that he shouldn't have looked at her *while* they were ascending back from the Underworld. That was where he goofed,' he said, glaring at her. 'Once back in the light it would have been fine to look at her as much as he wanted. But he did it too soon, and the gods punished him because it showed a lack of faith in them. Got it? Or am I going too fast for you?'

'No, no,' Imogen said evenly. 'I understand.'

'That's swell.'

Imogen looked at him thoughtfully. She had learned to recognise those tricky moments when he'd been thinking about Gene.

'Can you get me a soda?' Mitch said, straightening up after emptying the last box. Imogen nodded. Then as she headed for the kitchen, she heard him say, 'Eternal lovers, my ass. God, I feel old today.'

48

'Rise and shine,' Imogen heard as she sat up in bed like a zombie suddenly awakened into action and slammed her ringing mobile against her ear. It was Hildegard's unmistakably melodious voice, complete with its characteristic steely edge. 'I hope I'm not interrupting anything important.'

'No, no,' Imogen replied groggily. 'Hi, Hil!' She sat up and looked at the time. It was six o'clock; five in London. A tad early, then.

'I just wondered,' Hildegard went on, 'if you know where Mum is.'

'No,' Imogen replied, rubbing her eyes. 'Why? Have you lost her?'

'Very funny. She's been gone for two days, we think. But please don't worry about us. You just carry on having a wonderful time in the sun.'

'Thanks, I will,' Imogen said, enjoying the startled silence that followed at the other end of the line. 'Now, explain a bit more. I've no idea what you're talking about.'

As it turned out, the only other information Hildegard appeared to possess was that their mother 'had been acting oddly for weeks' and had left, taking her watercolours, her green silk coat, her Chinese parasol and all her jewellery with her.

'Acting oddly – what do you mean?'

'Sort of guilty. She's been looking at us with tearful eyes and shaking her head. Imo, listen: you have to come home as soon as possible.'

After Imogen had finished speaking to Hildergard, she had glanced at the clock again. Di, she knew, was an early bird and would be sitting at her kitchen table eating a digestive and listening to the shipping forecast on Radio 4.

'I wouldn't be at all surprised, you know, dear,' Di said, once apprised of Hildegard's call, 'to hear that your mother was with a man. And frankly, good for her. It's about time.'

Imogen's eyebrows rose. Elsa Peach had all but shunned the society of men since her divorce. Was it possible that she'd had a change of heart? There was a small sound of crunching biscuit from the other end of the line, then, 'She's looked radiant for weeks,' Di went on.

'Hil said she looked odd and guilty.'

'One does not exclude the other. And of course there was that note she left.'

'Oh? Hildegard didn't mention a note.'

'No, dear . . .' Di sighed wearily. 'You know your sister. It was quite naughty of her to ring you so early in the morning.'

'My hair is still standing on end.'

'Quite. She, on the other hand, has been having a wonderful time, you know – staying up all night, pacing up and down. Lovely drama. She's even rung your poor father to tell him all about it.'

'Really? How is Dad?'

'He's in Florida, dear. With his . . .'

'Wife?' Imogen offered.

'Yes . . . anyway – that young woman. I think Hildegard contrived to wake him up in the middle of the night as well. She claims to have got confused about the time difference.' Di laughed drily, adding, 'Serves him right.'

Imogen smiled. Her friend was not quick to forgive what she considered tasteless lapses in behaviour.

'I have tried to tell Hildegard how straightforward the situation is really. But she won't listen. And of course she really misses having you around . . .'

Pleasantly surprised, Imogen uttered a small 'aaah' sound.

'To fetch and carry for her,' Di concluded.

'I see. And what did Mum's note say?'

'It said: "Dear children, I'm going away for a week, to pursue beauty in a southern light. Love to all, Mummy."'

'She's coming back in *one week*?'

'Yes, dear. It's what you might call a storm in a teacup, isn't it? Don't even think about coming home, Imogen. You stay put. I've been helping Hildegard look after the younger ones. And I'll see you in a few weeks at Daphne's wedding! Good luck with the cake – let me know how it shapes up, won't you?'

'Hil? It's me again.'

'Yeah,' came the bored reply. 'So when are you getting back?'

'I'm afraid I can't come home.'

'*What?* How can you be so selfish?'

'I'm just too busy here.' Avoiding the topic of the

restaurant, Imogen went on, 'I've got to help Daphne with her wedding reception.'

'Well, I think she can probably manage that herself at her age,' Hildegard said testily. 'The point is, *I* need you back here. We've been left stranded.'

'For one week.'

Hildegard was momentarily silent, then said, 'That's neither here nor there. Thea's new leotards need adjusting and I haven't got the first idea how to go about it.'

'Well, find out. Google it or something.'

'What?'

'Hil, listen. Mum's gone on a bit of a holiday, that's all. I agree that she should have warned you, but it probably didn't occur to her. You know what she's like. She never helped much around the house anyway. And you've got Di taking everybody to school, collecting them at the end of the day and cooking them supper.'

One revolutionary aspect of Di's involvement in the Peach household had been to introduce home-cooked meals.

'Ye-es . . .'

'So you can go to work as usual.'

'I suppose so . . .'

'Have you missed any rehearsals?'

'*No*, but . . . There's *a lot* of housework to do. I mean, the place is *filthy*. *And* all our shoes need cleaning.'

At which point Imogen most uncharacteristically lost her temper and shouted, '*Hildegard, will you stop being such a bitch!*' at the top of her voice. There was an audible gasp of outrage at the other end of the line. After that, feeling as though a new and rather wonderful chapter of family life was opening in front of her, Imogen smoothly moved the conversation on to her sister's current project (*Avatar: the Musical!*), guessing correctly that Hildegard, who played the lead entirely covered in Smurf-like blue make-up, would be unable to resist the pleasure of talking about herself for a while.

49

A little later, at the end of their early morning walk, Monty led Imogen towards La Sirène at a fairly brisk clip. She scanned the terrace in search of her friends. Neither Faustina nor Bunny had arrived yet, though somebody else caught her eye. That old man, sitting alone at the far end reading a newspaper, looked familiar. Securing a table, she ordered an *orange pressée* and it was while watching Monty drink his water that the penny suddenly dropped. Another covert look confirmed that the man in question was the American she'd met in Saint-Paul-de-Vence with Amaury and Bunny. How strange.

While Imogen was debating whether to greet him or let him enjoy his newspaper in peace, Faustina turned up with Cristiana. Monty looked up from his bowl and the two dogs engaged in an enthusiastic sniffing session. Faustina had the air of having dressed in a hurry, in jeans and a blue shirt, with her hair hastily pinned up and – an absolute first, this – her face free of make-up.

'I've never seen you look so casual,' Imogen said, disconcerted. 'You look like you've only just got up.'

'You know,' Faustina said impassively, 'some people think I don't look so bad without make-up.'

'Faustina, you're beautiful. You really don't need any make-up. But you *like* wearing it, don't you?'

'Maybe it's just a habit,' Faustina said pensively. 'Did you know,' she went on, 'that there are men who don't actually like fake tan very much?'

'I've never given it much thought,' Imogen said, frowning, 'but I'm sure you're right.'

'Where I come from, it's so important to look glamorous at all times. Corsican men insist upon it. At least until you're married, and then . . . it changes.' Faustina shrugged, pulling a compact out of her bag and dusting her face with blusher. She looked at Imogen and smiled. 'Just a dash of colour – it looks healthier.'

Imogen smiled back.

Looking in her mirror, Faustina pouted and said, 'I'm beginning to think that I'm more old-fashioned than I'd imagined.'

'Old-fashioned?'

'Yes. Don't worry,' she said, with a sardonic glance at her friend, 'I still don't believe in fairy tales, but . . . I think I actually *like* things like kindness and chivalry.'

'Chivalry – really?' Imogen was amused. It sounded like Faustina had decided to put her boyfriend through his paces. 'And what does Enzo think about that?'

Faustina smiled, her eyes lowered. There was a short silence.

'Before Bunny gets here,' Imogen then said, changing the subject, 'I wanted to ask you how you're getting on with your enquiries about Amaury? I saw him the other day in Menton.'

Faustina looked up sharply. 'Really? Did you speak to him? Was he . . . alone?'

'Yes, but he was on his way to lunch. I'm pretty sure he was meeting Bunny.'

Faustina chewed her lower lip before saying coolly, 'Well, he does appear to be who he says he is. He lives in Montpellier under the right name. He's listed on the website of the architectural historians' association – I checked, and there's a picture of him too.'

'That's great, isn't it?' Imogen said, feeding Monty a biscuit. 'Because, I mean, I think Bunny really likes him.'

'Yes. Of course it's great.'

Casting her mind back to her encounter with Amaury, Imogen thought privately that she must, while under the romantic spell of the room, have imagined any suggestion that he might be her Valentine. Well, never mind. The important thing was that Bunny was, it seemed, in no danger of being duped. And then, just as she opened her mouth to mention the mystery of Elsa Peach's disappearance, she felt a hand on her shoulder as Bunny brushed past to let herself drop into an empty cane chair.

'Sorry I'm late,' she said breathlessly, giving Faustina a sidelong glance. 'There was something I needed to finish before I could leave the house.'

Bunny, Imogen knew, was currently engaged in making a series of marine-themed works and had been enthusiastically embalming fish and crustaceans. For a moment nobody spoke, and Imogen registered with surprise that the American girl's face was flushed, and that there was an odd sense of tension between her two friends.

'Bunny,' she said in an attempt to clear the air. 'Do you see the man in the hat, a few tables behind me?'

Bunny stared in silence for a minute, then smiled, 'Why, it's that nice Yankee gentleman from the museum!'

Faustina, who'd been wrestling with her recalcitrant lighter, looked languidly over her shoulder to see what the fuss was about. She turned back immediately, her eyes wide, and proceeded to stub out her unsmoked cigarette. 'Oh, God,' she whispered. 'This is incredible.'

'What?' Imogen asked, staring at her. 'Do you know him?'

'No, but I know someone who does.'

'Who's that?'

'Do you think they've finally arranged to meet? After all this time?'

'What are you talking about?' Bunny said vaguely, trying to get the waiter's attention.

'The man sitting over there,' Faustina said, looking from Imogen to Bunny, 'is *Gene*. I recognise him from photographs.'

'Gene! Really? Are you sure?'

'I'm completely sure. He hasn't changed very much.' Faustina pulled out her mobile phone. 'I'm calling Mitch.'

'Oh, yes!' Bunny agreed fervently. 'And then he can come running in slow motion. Just like in the movies!'

Halfway through dialling, Faustina suddenly stopped. 'Wait. Can you imagine how furious Mitch is going to be? He always says that he doesn't want to hear any more about it.'

'Mmm . . .' Imogen was thinking hard. 'Yes, that's what he *says*. But lately he's been talking quite a lot about ageing and life being short. I don't know.' She paused, as the separate conversations she'd had with Mitch and Gene about the Menton Wedding Room suddenly came together to make a vivid picture: '*I once stood in it with someone* I *loved, a long time ago,*' Gene had told her, '*and we said: "Let's pretend we're married."*' She rubbed her face, then looked up at her friends. 'I think we have to *shock* Mitch into action. You're right. Don't call him. I have a better idea.'

50

'Good morning, sir,' Bunny said with her most charming smile, addressing the unfurled copy of the *Herald Tribune* behind which Gene was concealed. The paper came rustling down and he returned her smile without a trace of surprise.

'Why, how nice,' he said, rising and removing his hat, which today was a suitably summery panama. He wore a beautifully creased linen suit the colour of palest butter. 'I *thought* I recognised you.' He shook Bunny's hand ceremoniously, and then, as Imogen stepped forward, stretched out his other hand to take hers. 'Here I am again, you see,' he said, looking at her with mischievous eyes.

'Yes, and here we are. I'm Imogen, by the way.'

'A beautiful name. Hello, Imogen. Small world, ain't it?'

'I think so too,' she said, squeezing his hand. 'Have you been to see him yet?'

Not for a second did Gene pretend not to know whom she meant. He only frowned and shook his head. 'Oh, no! There's absolutely no question of that. I only wanted to see the Paperback Wonderland again, you know, from the outside, that's all. I haven't been able to get it out of my head since that day we met and you told me that you lived there.' Silently, the two girls sat down on either side of him. 'This is my first time back, you know,' Gene went on, staring straight ahead, 'but I knew he was still here.

I've always needed to know where he was. So long as he was still in France I could kid myself that he hadn't really left *me*.'

'Actually, I think that's pretty accurate,' Imogen said. 'Whether Mitch realises it or not, if he's still here it's partly because of you.'

'But I can't believe you never tried to contact him,' Bunny said gently.

'I did at first, my dear girl, many times, and he always made it quite plain that he didn't want to see me. He returned my letters *unopened*. Did you ever hear of anything so quaint? I didn't know people really did that outside of overheated 1950s Hollywood melodramas, but *he* did. Of course, if you know Mitch it makes perfect sense – we used to watch those films together. We knew every line of dialogue by heart.'

'I'm sure he really misses that,' Imogen said pensively. 'Having someone who understands his references. He's tried to educate me, but I know he despairs sometimes. Like when I get Joan Crawford and Bette Davis mixed up – it drives him up the wall.'

'Poor Mitch,' Gene said tenderly. 'I'd given up writing to him,' he went on. 'In fact, I'd made no attempt at communication for years, but this Valentine's Day felt like something of an anniversary – it had been twenty years since our separation – and so, I sent him a card. And what do you know? He didn't return it. And since then, I've been wondering if maybe he'd had a change of heart. Hope springs eternal, you see.'

Remembering the discarded Valentine she had found in

the bin of Mitch's kitchen, Imogen wondered whether Gene's instinct might be right. Yes, Mitch had got rid of the card, but he *had* opened it and read it first, which had to mean something. She considered Gene and asked teasingly, 'But I thought you said you only wanted to have a look at the shop, and nothing else.'

'Am I really that transparent?' Gene asked, smiling at her. 'I'd be lying if I said that I didn't position myself here – behind my newspaper – in the hope of catching sight of him. Just like a teenager,' he said ruefully, running his fingers through his white hair. 'Silly, isn't it?'

'I don't think it's silly at all,' Bunny said, grinning. 'You should hear about Imogen's love life. Now *that* is *wildly* silly.'

'The wilder the better, my dear. Who's the boy?'

'Actually, I don't know,' Imogen said.

Gene stared at her, before bursting into genuinely delighted laughter.

'They've only ever met in the dark,' Bunny explained breathlessly. 'Don't you think that's wonderfully romantic? *And* quaint? Oh, I think it's just like performance art. That's what he is, Imogen – an artist, and you know I would never *ever* use that word lightly.'

Imogen shook her head, smiling. Checking out of the corner of her eye that Faustina had departed to ascertain Mitch's whereabouts, she turned to Gene and said, 'Speaking of art, I went to Menton the other day to see the Wedding Room you'd mentioned. And you were right – it's a very interesting place. I liked it. It made me think.'

As she and Gene smiled at each other, Bunny suddenly

exclaimed, 'Oh, the Wedding Room! I didn't realise you'd been there! Hey, did you happen to see . . .'

'Yes, yes, I ran into Amaury! And . . .' Imogen had been about to say 'how did you enjoy your lunch with him on that day?' when her mobile beeped and she held one hand up while she read Faustina's message – Mitch was in the shop. It was time to act.

'Gene,' she said resolutely, 'I'm going to ask you to do something really scary.'

'You are?'

'Yes!' Imogen said, picking up his hat and placing it on his head. She stood up and Bunny followed suit.

'*How* scary?' Gene asked, also getting to his feet.

'*Unbelievably* scary,' she said, holding his gaze.

'But you know, faint heart never won fair lady,' Bunny piped up.

'Exactly,' Imogen said, giggling. 'And anyway, you're not allowed to say no.'

'Oh, my dear girl,' he said, slipping his arm through hers. 'I've waited such a long time for someone to say that to me.'

Imogen went in to the Paperback Wonderland first, leaving the door propped open, while Bunny and Gene waited outside. When the tinkling of the bell didn't appear to summon Mitch, she assumed that he must have gone upstairs. Then she spotted him right across from her, standing at the very top of one of his library ladders, busily rearranging books on the top shelf of the far wall, right in the corner of the room. He was muttering to himself and did not turn around. The other ladder was positioned near the opposite corner. Tentatively, Imogen cleared her throat. There was no reaction from him. Fine. She tiptoed back to the door and beckoned for the other two to come in.

The trio then advanced crablike towards the empty ladder, stopping every time Mitch so much as moved, causing his ladder to creak. Imogen watched Mitch pull a book off the shelf. He started reading passages to himself, not quite out loud, occasionally sniggering. *Go for it*, she thought, pointing out the empty ladder to Gene and indicating that he should get climbing. Poor Gene, looking rather pale, shook his head pleadingly. Aware of the terrible attack of giggles that was brewing inside her, Imogen glared at him as forcefully as she could, while Bunny, who stood closer to her compatriot, prodded him gently in the lower back. Gene began his ascent very gradually, desperate not to make any noise, while Imogen and Bunny looked on. As soon as he got near the top, Imogen nodded and Bunny gave Gene's ladder a little push so that it was sent gliding across the length of the wall on an unavoidable collision course. Holding hands, not daring to look up, the two girls heard the ladders come together with a neat clacking sound.

There was a profound silence at first, followed by a heartbreaking sound of startled delight – then silence again, of a different quality. The book Mitch had been holding dropped to the floor, followed by Gene's fluttering hat. Bunny and Imogen tiptoed out of the shop, turning the sign in the door to 'Closed' as they went.

'What a beautiful colour, Imogen,' Gene said, clinking glasses with her and looking with approval at her full-skirted halter-neck dress. 'Tea-rose pink, I'd say, though I think the French call it *cuisse-de-nymphe* – like a nymph's thigh, you know. It makes your eyes look like dark pools of mystery,' he went on with only the merest hint of irony, 'and it makes your skin look a lovely shade of pale gold.'

'Thank you,' Imogen said, smiling. 'I like your white tuxedo. You make me feel like we're all on a liner in the middle of the ocean.'

Even in the dark, the lazy pulse of the sea was percep-tible outside the bay windows of the Hôtel de la Plage, where they had gone for a low-key celebration of Gene's return to Mitch's life.

'This is a terrific hotel,' Gene said, leaning back against the smart little blue sofa they were sharing. 'Really worth that somewhat hair-raising cliffside drive. F. Scott Fitzgerald used to come here with his beautiful crazy wife, you know. Americans abroad – what a crew!'

They were all pleasantly drunk by now. Imogen took one sip of her champagne cocktail and looked across at Bunny who stood close by, her blonde hair a fuzzy halo beneath the golden light, leaning against the bar with her eyes half-closed and languidly nursing a mint julep.

Next to her Mitch was drinking bourbon and soda and, when he thought nobody was looking, staring avidly at Gene.

The bar, with its curved high ceiling and narrowish galley shape punctuated by tall rounded pillars, was a vision of art deco splendour, saved from excessive solemnity by its cheerful Mediterranean shades of cobalt blue and terracotta red. Scanning the length of the room, Imogen couldn't for the moment locate Amaury, the last member of the party. No doubt he would soon return, if only to take possession of the freshly mixed old-fashioned – what else? – now awaiting him on the bar.

'You know, Gene, it's amazing how much Imogen's taste has changed in the time that I have known her,' said Faustina, who sat on his other side in a very elegant strapless black dress. It occurred to Imogen that the exact same thing could be said of her Corsican friend. By gradually paring down her style – under what mysterious influence? – and shedding her initial excess of frills and glitter, Faustina had metamorphosed into what she had always been underneath: a true beauty.

'She's really blossomed,' Faustina went on. '*And* she's given up those horrible sports bras.'

'You're unbelievable,' Imogen cried, instinctively crossing her arms on her chest. '*How* do you know that?'

'You have a very good line, now. Your breasts look quite insolent. And Mylène told me you've been back to Ultradonna a few times.'

'Yes, yes, all right. *Ça va comme ça?* Can we move on from the subject of my underwear?'

Of course, Faustina was right, Imogen reflected. She hadn't really bought that many new things since coming to live in Saint-Jean, but she had, crucially, discarded her former ones, shedding them for good like an old skin. Her body, having been allowed to play in the sun and surf as never before — to say nothing of playing in the dark with *him* during the Boustifaille blackout — had rewarded her with such a dramatic surge of confidence that she no longer felt the need for any sort of camouflage. In fact, she felt wonderful. For the first time in her life, she was in love, and soon, oh, very soon now, she would be able to tell him so face to face.

'Hey,' Bunny said, looking up and lazily waving the fingers of one hand in the direction of the door. '*Hey*. You know, *that*'s a wonderful colour too. That shade of green, over there. Chartreuse? It's *so* lovely. Come and see.'

Imogen got up, intrigued. 'Chartreuse? Where?'

'That lady there — you see?'

Imogen followed the direction of her friend's eyes. Through an archway on the other side of the lobby, part of the hotel's dining room — an enclosed, nude-coloured, leather-upholstered box that resembled the interior of an expensive handbag, with the dramatic addition of sparkling crystal pebbles cascading from the ceiling — was visible. At one of the nearest tables sat a couple. The man, who faced in the direction of the bar, was almost obscured by his blonde companion, whose green-clad back was turned away. Hanging from her chair on its silk cord was, Imogen noticed as the blood suddenly drained from her face, a tightly furled Chinese parasol the colour of very strong tea. Really it was just like Elsa Peach to walk around with something this unpractical – the weather had recently turned to rain, not unusually for this time of year – just because it was pretty.

'Oh, God,' Imogen said, appalled. 'It's my mother.'

Bunny's eyes widened. 'That lady is your *mother*?'

Helplessly, Imogen watched Elsa rise from her chair and, followed by her companion, head out of the restaurant, mercifully turning away from them towards the street. 'It's all right, they're leaving,' she said, heaving a deep sigh of relief. 'Well, at least now we know where she's got to. I'd better call Hildegard. And Di, to tell her that she was right about Mum being with a boyfriend.'

Faustina, who had joined them, stared up at her. 'Excuse me, Imogen, but she's your mother. Aren't you even going to say hello?'

'She's not here to see me.'

'Well, you don't know that for sure,' Gene protested.

'I do. You've no idea how self-centred she is. We've never been close. She's on holiday, and I'm here living my own life. It's fine! Bunny, stop looking at me like that – it's absolutely fine.'

'Who's the guy with her?' Mitch asked, sidling over.

'No idea. I've never seen him before.'

'Your mother has a new squeeze and you're not even curious to check him out?' Mitch said, with expressively arched eyebrows. 'What gives?'

'Well, you can check him out now,' Faustina said serenely, as Elsa, coolly elegant in her full-length silk, and her companion walked back into the bar, closely followed by Amaury, who had missed the entire episode. Bunny put one hand on his arm and whispered 'Imogen's mother' in his ear. Elsa had stopped just shy of their group and was so deep in conversation with her companion that she hadn't even cast a glance in her daughter's direction.

Mistaking Bunny's words for a cue to play the host, the Frenchman advanced towards the couple and said, 'Good evening, Madame,' while bowing over Elsa's hand with admirable formality. 'Monsieur,' he then added, turning to her escort and almost, but not quite, clicking his heels.

'Good evening,' Elsa replied, looking at him vaguely. 'Have we met?'

'No, Madame, we have not. Forgive me. My name is Amaury d'Ousset. Delighted to make your acquaintance.'

'Ye-es,' Elsa said vaguely, waiting for him to state his business.

'May I offer you a glass of champagne?'

'Are you the barman?' Elsa asked, frowning at him.

Amaury threw his head back and laughed long and hard at what he took to be a hilarious *bon mot*. Then, skilfully piloting Elsa with his hand beneath her elbow, he turned to the assembled party. Imogen had instinctively positioned herself at the back, gripping the edge of the bar with both hands.

Amaury introduced everyone, taking care to provide Elsa with a bit of context – thus characterising Bunny as 'an intrepid daughter of America who holds the key to eternal life through art', a ramrod-straight and faintly snarling

Mitch as 'an accomplished polymath worthy of Benjamin Franklin', Gene, who was an antiques dealer, as 'a connoisseur of the past's highways and byways', Faustina, whose hand he brought to his lips, as 'the nimble-fingered queen of canine topiary' – and ending, with terrible inevitability, with Imogen, who turned around when she heard him say, with radiant good humour, 'And then of course you know—'

'Imogen?' Elsa exclaimed. 'Is that you?'

'Hello, Mum.'

'Oh, but of course . . .' Elsa said, kissing the air next to her daughter's cheek. 'Is this where you're based, darling? In this little village?'

'Not right here. A nearby town.'

'Saint-Jean-les-Cassis,' Faustina said with a hint of asperity. 'That's where she lives. With us, her friends.'

'Saint-Jean-les-Cassis . . .' Elsa repeated. 'Yes, that does ring a bell, now that you mention it. Mmm . . . ye-es . . . How funny to run into you like this, darling.' She turned to the middle-aged man in a dark suit who, all this time, had been standing meekly at her elbow. 'Paul, dear, this is my daughter Imogen. Darling, this is Paul Sterling.'

'You're the brilliant enterprising actress,' Paul Sterling said, smiling warmly at Imogen. 'Hello.'

'Hello,' Imogen said, shaking his hand. 'No, I'm not the actress.'

'Ah. The talented ballerina, then?'

'No.'

'No, no, no, Paul darling! Don't be so dense.

Concentrate. Imogen is my middle daughter. You know – the one who . . .' She paused, before dropping her voice to a stage whisper, 'Did I not mention . . . Not at all? Oh, silly me!'

'Mum,' Imogen said in a clear, sardonic voice. 'You do know that I can hear every word you're saying? I mean, this isn't just happening in your head.'

Elsa glanced at her daughter with a puzzled frown, then turned back to Paul. 'Imogen is spending a bit of time in France, trying to work out what to do next, really, and she's met all these marvellous people. Oh, and . . .' She snapped her fingers. 'Darling, remind me . . . How is what's-her-name?'

'Di's sister Daphne,' Imogen said evenly.

'Yes. It's so kind of her to be looking after you.' Elsa's eyes lingered over her daughter for a moment, then she said, surprised, 'You're looking very nice, darling.'

'Thanks,' Imogen said. 'You look beautiful, Mum – as ever.'

'Paul is a friend from my life-drawing classes,' Elsa said brightly.

'I didn't know you'd gone back to that.'

'Well, you know, darling, there's only so much one can get out of complete abstraction. After a while, it all begins to feel a bit empty and . . . arctic.'

Remembering the vast canvases of her mother's protracted all-white period, Imogen nodded sympathetically.

'I felt I needed to reconnect with—' she broke off to smile at Paul and slip her hand in his '—the flesh.'

Well, here I've also made that connection, Imogen thought, smiling slightly.

'Oh, you know, speaking of flesh,' Bunny interjected with such sunny enthusiasm that Elsa was automatically drawn into her orbit, 'I would really love to talk to you about my work!'

'My cousin makes art. Out of poultry,' Amaury explained amiably.

'Do you really?' Elsa said, intrigued.

'Yes, I embalm them and then I dress them up.'

'It's *drag*, really, but for chickens,' Mitch said, leaning in.

'And by the way, I adore your coat,' Bunny said, fingering Elsa's sleeve. 'It's just *darling*. Tell me, are you doing any work while you're here?'

'I've been painting seascapes,' Elsa said, smiling at the American girl. 'But we're only here for a few more days – it's a short adventure.'

Watching Amaury hand her mother a glass of champagne, Imogen began to relax a little. Until, that is, poor Gene, still unaware of her particular situation, innocently said, 'You must be so proud of your daughter – a wonderful girl. *And* a wonderful chef!'

Imogen sighed, looking up at the ceiling which, she noticed for the first time, was painted with an intricate 1930s geometric frieze made up of ferociously sharp triangles, not unlike rows of teeth.

'A *what*?' Elsa asked icily. 'A wonderful what?'

'Chef!' Gene confirmed, beaming. 'Only this morning she made us a terrific "cooked breakfast" – it was *typically* British, wasn't it, Mitch?'

'Yep. It was a doozy.'

'I enjoyed it rather a lot,' Gene went on, with the sort of childlike enthusiasm which, under any other circumstances, would have gladdened Imogen's heart. 'It was worthy of the best . . . whatchamacallit . . . *greasy spoon* in Old London Town!' he ended triumphantly, throwing his arm around Imogen's shoulders.

Aaaaargh, Imogen thought, shutting her eyes while, all around her, the hitherto solid walls of the Hôtel de la Plage crumbled in deathly horror-film silence into a great big mass of noise and dust. The greasy-spoon reference was really spot-on – the icing on the cake. It was bound to go down particularly badly with Elsa, though of course there was always a slim hope that Imogen's mother had simply never come across a greasy spoon. Fingers crossed.

'*Imogen?* Darling? Cooked breakfasts? Greasy spoons? What the devil is that man talking about?

'Stand your ground, babe,' Imogen heard Mitch hissing in her ear like a cranky, oversized version of Jiminy Cricket. 'You're a big girl now.'

'Darling! Is he implying that you are . . . a *cook?* Well?'

Imogen stood swaying on the spot, feeling alternately very cold and very hot. In her mind's eye, she could see herself peeling mountains of potatoes and spilling goose fat on Michel Boudin's feet, wrestling with beetroot, putting the finishing touches to perfectly crisp courgette flowers, pulling a tray of puffed-up lamb-and-thyme *croustillants* out of the oven and, most recently, in Mitch's kitchen, giving Bastien a taste of the sea-urchin soup she had devised after her experience at Le Petit Merlu and watching him smile at her with his mouth full.

She looked her mother in the eye and said decisively, 'Yes! Yes – I am a cook.'

52

After a few days of rain, the weather had once more settled and the sky beyond the orange trees had turned from a muted porcelain shade of almost-white to vibrant summery blue. Soon Imogen's six-month adventure originally envisaged would come to an end. She sat up in bed in the gossamer-thin emerald-green silk slip she had recently bought from Ultradonna. Imogen had to make a decision: whether to go home or take up Monsieur Boudin's offer of a permanent job at Chez Michel.

A black paw tugged at her knee; Monty gave her a look that was the canine equivalent of clearing one's throat respectfully and at the same time meaningfully. She smiled and scratched his head. 'Yes, Monty – walkies!' Once dressed, she tiptoed down the stairs carefully, carrying her dog in her arms. Gene and Mitch were still asleep.

They were almost at the seafront when they walked past La Couronne d'Or – the bakery that opened earliest in the morning and always had famished post-clubbing Koud'Soleil regulars queuing outside – from which emanated the most heavenly smell. Imogen paused, thinking how nice it would be to surprise a friend with warm croissants for breakfast. It was still a little too early for Faustina, so she texted Bunny instead, and got a characteristically breathless reply. 'Yes, come over, am working on something. Everett here though and eats more croissants than anyone I know so bring plenty.'

After kissing Bunny, who, goggled up and gloved to the elbows, was busy in her studio with lobsters and formaldehyde, working towards an ambitious composition that was to be her housewarming gift for the launch of Chez Michel, Imogen followed Everett into the living room, where they sprawled companionably on one of the sofas, with Monty between them.

'I'm sure going to miss these,' Bunny's brother declared after polishing off a third croissant. 'You know, Buddy and I are going home soon. It's the end of our holiday.'

'Oh, that's a shame.'

'That it is,' he said, smiling at her. 'But look here, come and stay with us next summer. I'll take you fishing if you want.'

'Maybe I will,' Imogen said, touched by his friendliness. 'And what about Bunny, Everett? Is she thinking of going home at any point?'

'Well, you know, it's a funny thing,' Everett said, frowning. 'She *was*, but she seems to have changed her mind all of a sudden.'

'Really?'

'But then that's Bun for you. Just like a weathervane.' Everett paused, then added, 'I don't know, Imogen. Lately she's been exceptionally distracted. Even by her standards. Going missing for hours on end, not answering her phone.' He looked at her, frowning. 'You're her pal. Do you know anything about any of that?'

'I wonder,' Imogen said, smiling mischievously, 'whether she has perhaps fallen in love – with a local?'

'Oh.' Everett looked at her seriously. 'I suppose it's possible. Who?'

'Well, I was thinking about your French cousin. Amaury.'

Everett nodded thoughtfully. 'Maybe so. Though it's not like her to keep quiet about such things. She usually sings it from the tree tops.' He shook his head, then grinned at her. 'Anyway . . . how about you? You're staying on too, aren't you, for a bit?'

'I'm not sure. It sort of depends on work. And also on . . . other things.'

'Oh yes, of course – your romance in the dark,' Everett smiled at her lazily, stretching his arms above his head. 'How's that going?'

Imogen looked straight ahead and not at him. She had seen Everett several times since that lunch in Saint-Paul-de-Vence, and he had always been his usual friendly self but nothing more, so that, in spite of Bunny's frequent teasing, the possibility that he might be her mystery man had almost completely receded from her thoughts. And now he was going home.

'It's tricky,' she said eventually. To her surprise, her throat contracted slightly. 'You see, for a while I really enjoyed not knowing. It was fun. But now I . . . don't think I really can . . .' She made herself pause for a couple of breaths until her throat relaxed a fraction and the threat of tears receded. 'I can't carry on like this for much longer.'

Everett nodded. 'You're dying to know who he is, I guess.'

'I am,' she said, looking at him frankly. 'Suddenly, I'm *dying*,' she said, laughing a little at the melodramatic phrase. 'Because I think I love him,' she blurted out.

'You do, huh?' Everett reached across and squeezed her arm. 'I'm sure he feels the same way about you. And I'm sure he's *dying* to see you too. So buck up.'

Imogen began to laugh. 'I know. I'm being silly. It's just that . . . my mother's turned up, and she's furious with me about the cooking thing.'

'You know, Bunny's asked me to break the news to our parents about her artistic career when I get home. I've always looked out for her, so of course I said yes, but it's not a conversation I'm particularly looking forward to. I don't think she realises what it would mean to find herself without funds, and it might well come to that.'

'Gosh,' Imogen said, thinking that she at least had no such worries. 'Sometimes what's wanted is a clean break,' she went on, talking about Bunny but also thinking about herself. 'To tell you the truth, there are moments when I can't really imagine going home at all, ever.'

He looked at her in silence, then said slowly, 'And stay here permanently? That's one hell of a big step.'

'People do it, don't they? Mitch and Gene, and Daphne.'

'True. And you know, there's also . . .' he suddenly stopped, appearing to change his mind about what he had been about to say, and smiled at her. 'Excuse me a minute, will you? I just need to make a quick call while I remember.'

'Of course,' Imogen said mildly, thinking that Bunny's brother had, in all probability, become bored with the intractable subject of her private life – an understandable reaction. Left alone, she looked around the room, remembering how she had walked in here, on the day of Bunny's party, to find the sofas piled with terrifyingly self-possessed and glossy Americans who hadn't seemed quite human. Everett had been there too, of course, just as intimidating as the rest, though now that she had got to know him better she felt entirely comfortable around him. How things had changed.

Her eyes landed on a well-thumbed paperback lying on the coffee table and, out of idle curiosity, she picked it up. It was a travel guide to Rome, one of the destinations the Doucet brothers had visited during their European holiday.

She turned a few pages, glancing at photographs of churches and statues and vaguely thinking how much she too would like to go to Italy one day. There were a few regional specialities she wouldn't mind trying – spaghetti with squid ink in Venice, for example, or that dish of boiled lemons they made in Capri, which sounded so good . . .

She was leafing through the book when something flashed before her eyes, making her sit up abruptly. She shook her head. *No.* It couldn't be. It was probably some sort of optical illusion or a superficial resemblance. Registering her agitation, Monty barked. Very slowly, Imogen began to turn the pages again in the other direction, retracing her steps. Then she impatiently picked up the book by its spine and shook it: two postcards fell out. She lay them side by side on the coffee table and stared. Even through swimming eyes, she could see exactly what they were – reproductions of Fragonard's *Stolen Kiss* and Doisneau's *Kiss by the Hôtel de Ville*.

Everett came back into the room. 'Sorry about that,' he said cheerfully, before jumping over the back of the sofa to join her. It was only on landing again next to Monty that he saw what was on the table. With loudly beating heart, Imogen turned to look at him and watched with fascination as a very slight blush travelled like a wave over his handsome face.

'Ah. Look here, Imogen,' he began, biting his lip.

'Monty! Down!' she ordered, pointing at the floor, before lunging forwards and throwing her arms around Everett's neck. After a moment's hesitation, he laid his hands on her shoulders and squeezed them affectionately. 'Imogen, darling, listen to me.'

'Yes,' she said, her face pressed against his shoulder while a blissful confusion raged in her head. 'Yes, I'm listening.'

'I'm sorry but it's *not* what you think,' Everett said gently. Feeling as though he'd suddenly doused her with cold water, she pulled away. 'Here's the thing,' he went on carefully. 'I *know* about the emails you received, because Bunny mentioned them. But I didn't send them. As for how these postcards got into my guidebook . . . I can't explain it.'

'So it wasn't you?' Imogen's nose was itching with the onset of tears, but she was *not* going to cry.

'No. I'm sorry.'

'*Prove it.*'

'You know that's a logical impossibility,' Everett said reasonably, stroking her hair in an attempt to calm her down, for he had seen the mixture of embarrassment and fury in her eyes. 'You can't prove something that you *didn't* do.'

'I can think of a way. You're going to kiss me.'

'Aw, Imogen.'

'*Right now.*'

'Not a good idea, girlie.'

'I say it *is* a good idea. I want to know and be sure.'

'Won't do any good.'

'Oh, come on! Just do it, for God's sake,' Imogen cried, exasperated. 'Are you a man or a mouse?'

Everett laughed at that, pressing on his eyelids with finger and thumb, and then, softly drawling, 'Well, then, I guess I'm a man,' bent his face to hers and kissed her.

After a minute or so, Imogen was the first one to pull away.

'Wrong number?' Everett said.

'Yes,' she admitted. 'Everett, can I ask you not to tell—'

'Of course not. I wouldn't dream of it.'

'Thank you.' They smiled at each other, a trifle ruefully. 'So how do you explain . . .' she gestured towards the post-cards.

'I don't know. The guidebook has been lying around this house for weeks and weeks since we came back from our trip.'

'But the postcards weren't in it when you were using the guide?'

'No.'

'So somebody who came to this house must have slipped them in here for some strange reason.'

'Yes, or it could even have happened in transit. We didn't come straight back here after Italy, you know.'

'Oh, I'm just so mixed up,' Imogen wailed.

'You know,' Everett said, looking at her sympathetically, 'I think it's going to have to be a question of you being in the right spot at the right time with the right person. Then everything will fall into place, you'll see.'

53

Imogen sat at her computer that evening, holding the bottle of perfume in her hands and with the map of Grasse and the note left at Boustifaille spread out before her. She was staring intently at the pictures of *The Stolen Kiss* and *Kiss by the Hôtel de Ville* on her screen. Everett was right, she thought, about her needing to be in the right spot at the right time with the right person. She had been knocking on all the wrong doors, it seemed, and looking in all the wrong places. Now she wanted to know the truth.

Pushing her hair out of her face, she refocused on her screen and, for the hundredth time that night, clicked on Send and Receive. There was a disappointing electronic bouncing noise signifying nothing.

'Well,' she said out loud, 'it's been a lot of fun, but the comedy of errors has gone on long enough.'

Sensing her agitation, Monty sat close to her, silent and supportive. She kissed the top of his head and asked, 'Shall we have a go, Monty? What do you think?'

Monty barked and licked her hand.

'Well, OK, if you really think so,' Imogen said, typing in the-valentine's-kiss address. 'Because the thing is,' she went on, 'unless we make contact soon I think I might self-combust or something, and then where will you be?' After a minute's consideration, she entered the words

'ENFIN FACE A FACE?' ('FACE TO FACE AT LAST?') in the Subject box. She decided to keep her message short and to the point. *'I want to see you.'*

Then she made herself leave the room to take Monty out for a quick walk before bed. On returning, she went straight to the kitchen and made a cup of peppermint tea, adding a spoonful of honey to it and letting it dissolve. She unloaded the dishwasher, putting the clean things away as methodically as possible, then reloaded it carefully with the crockery that was stacked in the sink. She fed Monty a biscuit, then another one. She gazed out of the window into the night. She stood at the counter and sipped her herb tea with slow deliberation.

When she walked back into her bedroom, she could see, even from a distance, that her modest attempt at voodoo had been rewarded. A reply had come in. She flew to her desk and opened the message, which read, *'So, no more kissing in the dark?'*

Imogen smiled at this, then replied, 'Never say never, but . . .'

'But now you'd like to shed some light on the matter?'

'Yes.' Oh, *plenty* of light, she thought, her whole body tingling. 'I want to kiss you with my eyes open,' she murmured yearningly. 'I want to kiss you for hours. I want to . . .' She sighed and sat back in her chair, hugging herself tightly. Don't tell him any of this yet, she thought, reining herself in with an effort. Wait until you are together.

There was a short pause, then he replied, *'Imogen, I'm in love with you.'*

She stared incredulously at the screen. Almost immediately, another message came through.

'*You probably think this is a crazy thing to say at this stage, but it's how I feel.*'

With a tremendous sense of release she typed, 'I'm in love with you too,' then added, 'Where are you now? Can't we meet right away?'

'*I have a better idea. You wanted light. Will you come and have a picnic in the sun? I believe it's my turn to feed you.*'

'When and where?' Imogen typed, smiling.

'*Soon. I promise. Just give me time to find the perfect spot for us. Good night, Imogen.*'

54

Imogen did not have to wait long for her invitation. Now that she had made her feelings clear, it seemed that there were to be no more languid meanderings from her mysterious Valentine, but rather, a faster momentum and a plan of action. Another email came the following night, containing a map of a beautiful spot in the hills above Saint-Jean and pinpointing a specific meeting place. There was even a photograph of it: a sunny clearing in a pine grove in which rose a majestic umbrella pine, with a bright red-and-white Provençal scarf tied around its trunk. At the foot of the tree lay a picnic rug, a large basket and, on a plate, rather sweetly, a bone for Monty. Gazing at it raptly, Imogen thought she would remember this moment of perfect happiness for a very long time. The accompanying text was kept to the strict minimum: a date and a time for the meeting – tomorrow – ending with a question mark.

That was why email was superior to the phone, Imogen thought as she typed a cool, 'See you there.' The squeals of delight she had uttered on finding his message would remain a secret between her and Monty.

The next day, Bunny hugged Imogen, jumping up and down with excitement. 'At last! I'm so happy for you! You're going to find out who he is!'

Faustina was less enthusiastic. 'I think going off to meet a guy you don't even know in the middle of nowhere is a stupid thing to do,' she observed coldly. 'Don't you ever read the papers?'

'But it's real romantic to meet in the hills,' Bunny argued. 'Just like in *Wuthering Heights*.'

'*Romantique?* Pfff!' Faustina rolled her eyes dimissively. 'If you like, yes. I'm not saying that it hasn't been fun so far,' she went on, turning to Imogen. 'It's true that since this thing started you've looked like a completely different girl, and I'm happy for you. But I worry a little because this man has controlled everything that's happened between you. You can't deny that.'

'But that's the way it should be!' Bunny protested. 'The boy does the chasing!'

'All I'm saying is,' Faustina went on patiently, 'that you need to be careful. We *are* talking about a stranger.'

'That's crazy talk,' Bunny frowned. 'He's not a stranger. She's met him before.'

'I have!' Imogen added defensively.

'She probably knows him really well.'

'I probably do!' Imogen echoed.

'I bet we all do,' Bunny said stubbornly.

'Possibly,' Faustina replied. 'But the point is that we're not exactly sure who he is. And so I don't think you should go.'

'What?' Bunny cried.

'Rearrange it. Treat it like a normal blind date and meet somewhere busy, with lots of people around. La Sirène, the Koud'Soleil, the beach – take your pick. Or I can come with you, if you like. In fact, I think I should.'

'Faustina, I know you mean well,' Imogen said as evenly as she could, 'but I'm a big girl and I don't need a nanny.'

'Hear, hear,' Bunny said.

'I trust him,' Imogen added forcefully. 'And besides, I know *exactly* what I'm doing.'

But later, only a few minutes before her tryst, as she sat in her car on the edge of the nature reserve, it began to dawn on Imogen that she hadn't been quite honest either with her friends or with herself. She'd claimed to know exactly what she was doing, but it simply wasn't true.

Yes, she did feel coursing through her a raging excitement at the prospect of finally seeing *him*, but at the same time, she noted, glancing at her watch, for some reason she had been sitting here for over twenty minutes without making any move towards stepping out. She heard a soft whimpering sound and turned to meet Monty's pleading eyes.

She let him out and watched him put his nose to the ground, entranced by a new wealth of exotic smells. The hills stretched out in front of her eyes, carpeted with yellow-flowered gorse. After a minute, she took a deep breath and put one foot down on the ground.

She looked up at the sky, which was a pale shade of grey that seemed to promise rain. Not exactly the radiant summer weather she'd been expecting for her big day. Was this a portent, a sign that the picnic wasn't such a good idea after all?

She pulled her map out of the glove compartment and

forced herself to study it with some semblance of concentration. Then she gazed at the deep valley stretching out in front of her. In the far distance, the mountains looked like a painted film set, so vivid were their variegated shades of purple and blue. Closer by, just beyond the next hill, she could make out the beginnings of a sprawling pine grove. This was the appointed place. And the sooner she got to that clearing, the sooner they would be together. When she thought about that, her heart beat so fast she felt it might actually burst out of her chest.

Monty barked happily, put both forepaws on her knees and gave her an encouraging look. His message was clear: come for a walk with me on this exciting new planet! 'Yes, all right,' Imogen said, gathering her bag, mac and umbrella. She happened to glance in the rear-view mirror and stopped dead. She really wasn't sure that she recognised the dazed red-cheeked girl with shining eyes looking back at her. All of a sudden she thought she could hear her mother's voice saying in cold, crystal-clear tones, 'What is the matter with you? You're not yourself, Imogen.'

Shaking off this imaginary warning, she got out, slammed the door and whistled for Monty, who'd wandered off in the opposite direction from the grove. She put on her mac over her strappy summer dress and once again checked the time. She'd have to hurry up if she didn't want to be late. But the problem was that she was finding it difficult to control her breathing, to the point where the idea of walking any distance at all from the car was beginning to seem impossible, superhuman and even supernatural – like flying. She felt dizzy – completely and utterly *drunk*. She leaned on the car with both hands and closed her eyes. What was this? Elation? A panic attack? Or a bit of both?

Reluctantly, Imogen began to think that Faustina had a point. Perhaps it had been folly to agree to a meeting here, in the middle of nature – though not exactly for the reasons her friend had outlined. Because Imogen wasn't frightened of him. No: it was something else she feared, something within herself.

Oh, for God's sake stop being such a goose, she admonished herself. *Anyone would think you'd never been on a date before.* Yes, but . . . this wasn't just any date, was it? It was *the* date, the blazing moment of revelation that may also mark the beginning of . . . the rest of her life. Or – if things didn't work out – the most crushing disappointment she'd ever experienced. She shook her head impatiently while fastening Monty's lead to his tartan collar. *You're making far too much of this*, she told herself. *It's a picnic, not an exam, remember? Just go! He's there, waiting for you! Go to him!* By now her breathing had slowed a little and become more manageable, so she made herself walk down the hill and towards the pine grove, under a darkening sky.

Soon she found herself among the trees, crushing pine needles underfoot. Hang on, she suddenly thought, startled. Was that a noise behind her? The desire to look over her shoulder was overpowering. Just like Orpheus, she thought. She bit her lip and waited, listening hard, to see if he would call out her name. Not a sound. When she eventually turned around there was no one in sight.

It was now the appointed hour, and he must be waiting for her in the clearing.

A crazy pulse started in her stomach. Run! Run to him now! She knew what she wanted: to be kissed again, to feel herself enveloped in his arms and the caressing pressure of his face against hers, to embrace him closely, sliding her hands under his jacket to get at his warm body, at the solidity of his presence.

Yes, but what if . . . what if his identity, once revealed, turned out to be a shock, an unwelcome surprise? Ridiculous, childish fears began to press on her from all sides. She thought of Beauty and the Beast, and also of Georgette Heyer's Venetia, whose Damerel was an alarming figure at first – a terrible man who might do anything. Yes, all right, both stories ended wonderfully well, but they were only stories, where the heroines magically transformed blood-thirsty beasts into princes and depraved seducers into loving husbands, whereas she, Imogen, found herself in a real-life situation, one in which she wasn't entirely sure, at this very moment, how to handle herself.

She took a few more steps forward, then looked around for Monty. He was playing nearby, running rings around a tree while somehow managing to retain an air of solemn dignity. Her legs felt rather unsteady. She walked straight to the tree and held on to it for support, pressing her cheek against its scratchy bark. This was it; she must make a decision.

All of a sudden she felt very vulnerable. Her heart contracted painfully. She loved him. She was frightened of seeing him. Oh, it didn't make any sense.

They hadn't exchanged mobile phone numbers, she reflected, because there had been an unspoken agreement that they would both, of course, be there. So she had no way of reaching him, should she decide . . .

Monty barked, making his presence known at her feet, and as Imogen picked him up and hugged him, the little dog managed to convey at the same time both his undying affection for her and his bafflement at her unusually agitated state.

'Monty,' she said, kissing his bristly muzzle. 'I'm scared. I thought I was ready, but I'm not.'

Still holding on to Monty, she looked up, hearing a sudden pattering sound overhead, scattershot at first. Then, almost immediately, she saw relentless waves of rain slanting in the wind. Now it was coming down hard. She turned around and headed back to the car.

55

The uphill walk in the pouring rain was hard going and took a while, but Imogen saw it as a godsend: it helped her to pull herself together. The wind was so fierce that it turned her umbrella inside out before whisking it out of her hand and driving it out of reach, over the hills and far away. When at last they reached the car, she and Monty were both bedraggled. They sat side by side for a few moments without moving, while Imogen, still in a sort of trance, asked herself whether she actually still remembered how to drive.

She switched the heating on and searched the radio for a station that played soothing, familiar songs. She towelled Monty dry as best she could and fed him a few treats while she drank a whole bottle of water. After that she felt more like herself. She put her hands on the wheel, and then, gingerly, indicated and got the car off the grass and onto the road. As she picked up speed, she found to her relief that all was well – her body, along with at least some part of her brain, knew exactly what to do. Nevertheless, she drove home with extreme care, like a beginner.

By the time she got back to Saint-Jean-les-Cassis, the rain had slowed to a steady drizzle. As she drove along the seafront on her way into town, she glanced at the sea, aware of an irrational impulse rising within her. Though she had decided on a sensible course of action – going straight home to a hot bath – a wilder part of her self (that girl she had glimpsed in the mirror?) suggested that it would be a lot more fun to stop the car, strip off and run headlong into the sea to go swimming in the rain.

But instead she drove home. When she walked into the Paperback Wonderland with Monty in her arms, Mitch looked up from behind the counter, snorted appreciatively at her appearance, then said, 'You're back early.'

'I didn't go in the end,' Imogen admitted in a small voice. 'I lost my nerve. I know it's ridiculous, but please don't laugh at me.'

'I'm not laughing, babe,' Mitch replied, his eyes searching her face. 'You OK?'

'Not really, no.'

'You wanna talk about it?'

Imogen sighed. 'Well, I'd better get dry first. And email him to explain. Let me just run upstairs and do that.'

'Sure thing,' Mitch said, 'but actually there's someone in your room. Waiting for you.'

'Who?'

'I really can't say.' And, with his eyes on the delivery note he held in his hand, he headed for the stock room.

One thought and one thought only came into Imogen's head, with an accompanying wave of relief. It was *him*. She'd failed to turn up in the hills, so he'd decided to come to her instead. And now he was upstairs, waiting for her. Oh, thank God – she'd be able to apologise and explain. And it would be here, comfortably at home, that she'd find out who he was. A delicious thrill of excitement ran through her. She put Monty down and flew up the stairs four steps at a time.

Pushing open her door, it wasn't her mystery lover sitting on her bed but her mother, Elsa Peach, with her daughter's dog-eared and much-annotated copy of Elizabeth David's *French Provincial Cooking* in her hands.

'*Mum*,' Imogen said, dreadfully disappointed. 'What are you doing here?'

'Well, darling, I suppose I wanted to see where my daughter is staying. Is that so unreasonable? It was clever of me to find this place, wasn't it? Paul and I did it just by asking around – everyone here appears to know you and Monty. We met your friend Daphne, too.' Elsa looked around her with approval. 'And . . . this is not at all what I'd imagined. A room in a bookshop . . . really, darling, what a bohemian set-up! I rather like it.'

'Well, I'm glad. Where is Paul, by the way?'

'Having a drink with Gene in a place called the Siren, or something. He's being tactful – giving us some mother-and-daughter time, which is sweet of him, don't you think?'

It was tempting to say something Mitchlike such as 'Mother-and-daughter time, my ass,' but what would be the point of getting angry? Instead, Imogen sat down to pull off her muddy wellies.

'Have you been hiking, Imogen? In the rain?'

'Something like that, yes.'

'How *hearty* you are, darling,' Elsa said, unconsciously wrinkling her elegant nose. 'And I also wanted to have a look at that restaurant where you work. It seems to be closed, but Paul tells me it's terribly smart and famous – not a greasy spoon at all!'

'God, you are *such* a snob,' Imogen sighed wearily.

'All right, I admit it,' Elsa said, fixing her earnestly with her large pale eyes. 'But can you tell me why it's *so* wrong to want to see my children surrounded by Beauty—'

'Truth and Creativity, I know, I know . . .'

'You might scoff, darling,' Elsa said with a self-satisfied little smile, 'but it seems to me that you've been seeking all those things yourself – and that you've found them, here.'

Imogen stared at her mother in silence, then started to laugh. 'You're probably right,' she admitted, 'although . . .' *Although I'm still missing a pretty vital piece of the Truth*, she added silently to herself. *And all because I got cold feet at the last minute.*

While she sat at her desk to type her email apology, her mother chattered on. Imogen didn't pay very close attention – she was trying to find the right words to explain why she had, effectively, run away from *him*, the man she yearned for, who haunted her dreams, and who might well turn out to be the love of her life. She ended her message by suggesting another meeting at La Sirène on the following evening and then, just as she pressed Send Now, heard Elsa say something wholly unprecedented.

'I'm extremely proud of you, darling.'

Imogen looked up, round-eyed, to find her mother smiling at her.

'I won't deny that for years I wondered what on earth I should do with you,' Elsa went on airily, 'but now I'm here I'm frightfully impressed. You've actually made yourself into a successful chef at a gastronomic restaurant on the Riviera. Every family needs a maverick – and now we have one of our own. Well done, darling.'

'Thank you, Mum,' Imogen said, deeply touched. She went to sit next to Elsa, who opened her arms to her. Imogen pressed her forehead against her mother's shoulder and muttered, 'I'm really sorry I lied to you.'

'Ah, well . . .' Elsa said, patting her cheek. 'So you told a little lie. You needed to break away. I quite understand. I do remember what it's like to be young, you know, darling.' She smiled radiantly at her daughter. 'And you look so chic now – I barely recognise you. You're quite the Mediterranean *jeune fille*.'

They both laughed a little, then Imogen said, 'Mum, I'm going to have a quick bath. Why don't you get yourself some tea from the kitchen?'

'Thank you, darling,' Elsa said, without moving. 'Just milk. No sugar.'

56

That evening, sitting in bed reading about the nineteenth-century gastronome Antonin Carême, Imogen glanced regularly in the direction of her computer, expecting at any moment to hear a heavenly pinging sound announcing that an email had landed.

Carême had been the master of incredibly baroque set-piece cakes called *pièces montées*. Imogen examined the book's illustrations attentively: here were cakes in the shape of ornamental ruins, a golden harp, a Chinese pagoda, a cornucopia filled with fruit, a waterfall . . . Perhaps the cornucopia would be worth attempting for Daphne's wedding cake? But then again the harp was so pretty. Tomorrow morning she would call Di and ask her advice.

Imogen smiled to herself. Her mother had gone home in good spirits, and her beloved Di would be arriving in a couple of weeks to attend her sister's wedding. And there was something else to look forward to – her birthday.

Bunny had suggested celebrating it with a house party at her villa, hinting at a three-day extravaganza of food, drink and dancing in the company of Amaury, Mitch and Gene, and Enzo and Faustina. Nobody had ever made much of Imogen's birthday before. It was kind of Bunny to want to make such a fuss, and Imogen reflected happily that by now her American friend and the rest of the Saint-Jean gang felt like a second family. The icing on the cake was the extra guest Imogen intended to bring with her to Bunny's house. Because any minute now she would receive a message from *him* confirming their meeting tomorrow. And, this time, she would make sure to turn up.

It was now after midnight. She had been so absorbed in her book – perhaps she'd missed the signal. She got up to check her Inbox: still nothing from the-valentine's-kiss.

That was a little surprising. Surely he must have got her message by now? But Imogen wasn't worried – he must be busy – he would respond a little later. He wasn't, after all, away from their mysterious encounters or her daydreams about him, a mythical creature out of fairy tale – he must have a job, an ordinary life. For the first time, she found herself wondering about that – about what he did, day in day out. She sent him a wildly flirtatious message and went to sleep, secure in the knowledge that he would have replied by next morning.

But he hadn't.

Now Imogen began to feel uneasy. Taking Monty out for a walk, she noticed a dramatic change in the weather. It was as though all the Riviera light had suddenly been sucked out of the atmosphere. The summer rain came in earnest, with a droning kind of tenacity. The palm trees on the promenade looked bruised and exhausted against a leaden sky. The people of Saint-Jean-les-Cassis retreated indoors, with the exception of the town's devoted dog owners, who continued to parade their smartly mackintoshed and often booted charges, greeting each other cheerfully in spite of the dismal weather.

As Imogen and Monty walked past Chez Michel, she peered inside: new bistro furniture was being set out in the dining room under Daphne's supervision. Spotting her, the *pâtissière* waved, mouthing the words, 'See you later,' and Imogen waved back, doing her best to appear cheerful.

She sent further messages throughout the day, asking him where he was and why he wasn't responding, – without a single email sent to her in reply. Nevertheless she went to La Sirène that evening and waited for him in vain. She tried emailing again, with increasing anxiety, over the next day and night. Nothing. Deadly radio silence.

There was only one possible explanation, she thought, despairingly. He had not forgiven her. He would never forgive her. She had ruined everything by standing him up and had lost him for good.

By the end of a torturous week, the pain gnawing at her chest was searing, unbearable, and when tears came, it was with a violence she had never before experienced, streaming from her eyes like a solid curtain, which, when it occasionally dried up, left her face aching and swollen.

Mitch and Gene had been very kind, coming into her room at night to sit with her and hold her hand when they heard her sobbing in her sleep, and taking over the practicalities of moving the three of them, along with Monty, to Bunny's villa for Imogen's birthday celebrations. Informed of her young friend's situation, a stricken Daphne hugged Imogen and suggested that she might like a few days off, also offering to relieve her of all obligations to do with the wedding. But Imogen was determined to keep working and make the wedding cake, as promised, and after a while Daphne gave in.

'Hey, you know – about your actual birthday party?' Bunny said brightly, as Imogen sat on Mitch's sofa with her arm around Monty, managing to create the illusion that she was watching a particularly inane French variety show on television.

When her friend didn't reply, Bunny decided to plough on, 'I'd planned for us to stay in, but would you prefer to go out? We can go anywhere you like. Is there an amazing *restaurant gastronomique* you'd like to try? Or shall I book somewhere and keep it a surprise?'

'No, thanks – no surprises,' Imogen said with a tremendous effort. 'Don't bother, Bunny.' In reality, Imogen would have liked to cancel the house party altogether, but she didn't have the heart to disappoint her friend. 'I am looking forward to coming to your house,' she went on, resolutely and untruthfully. 'And I'll be happy to cook us all something. But I'm not in the mood for a big celebration.'

In the hope of jolting her friend out of her melancholy, the next afternoon Faustina tried a different tack. 'I did warn you about Prince Charming,' she said, as they walked their dogs together. 'Remember?'

'Yes, I remember,' Imogen admitted.

'I am sad for you,' Faustina said, stopping abruptly and

planting herself in Imogen's way. 'But somebody has to tell you the truth.'

'And what is the truth?'

'He amused himself with you for a while and now it's over.'

In silence, Imogen glared at her friend.

'This is *real life*, OK?' Faustina went on evenly. 'And *this* is how people behave in real life. I've done it too, exactly the same. Sometimes people just get bored.'

'He told me that he loved me,' Imogen said, looking out to sea.

'Oh, please! The oldest trick in the . . .'

'*No!* It wasn't like that!'

'So many men say it automatically, like hello and thank you. To be polite.'

'OK,' Imogen said, turning back to her friend. 'Thank you for . . . whatever that was. Shall we keep walking? It's cold.'

Life was moving forwards, Imogen felt, leaving her lagging behind. Bastien, for example, had not been available as a shoulder to cry on. He had recently come to his senses and, while they were temping together away from Boustifaille, taken a proper look at Larissa who had been in love with him since long before Imogen's arrival. The reason why she had been so hostile to *l'Anglaise* was now clear. Matters had progressed rapidly. They were currently busy looking for a flat together. And Larissa, now that she was happy and sure of Bastien's love, was being charming to Imogen – a welcome change after months of cold war.

As for Cheyenne, whose uncomplicated good humour and uplifting selection of tunes would now have been a welcome tonic, he had decamped temporarily to the Maldives with a new lady friend.

One thing did cheer her up a little: seeing Dimitri's name flashing on the screen of her ringing phone. Having relocated to Nice, he had absolutely no idea what she was going through, and when she spoke to him, Imogen found that she could get a bit of bounce into her voice instead of sounding as flat and miserable as she felt. In any case, such was Dimitri's swaggering confidence in his own attractiveness that he'd never shown much interest in any aspect of her private life that did not concern him directly.

'I'm going home to Brittany for a few days before the season really kicks in,' he said, 'but do you want to meet up before that? Come and see the restaurant. I'll cook you some lunch.'

'Will you?' Imogen said, feeling her face relax for the first time in ages. 'Like what? Sell it to me.'

'Scallop linguine with orange sauce?'

'OK. Next?'

'*Osso bucco?*'

'Yes. Pudding?'

He was silent for a moment, then said meditatively, 'You should have a taste of this amazing Parmesan one of the chefs brought back from Italy. Imogen?'

'I'm still here.'

'Maybe with *vin santo* and some of my rosemary biscuits. You know, for dipping.'

'Very good. Keep talking.'

'This is beginning to feel like phone sex. I should call you more often.'

'Idiot,' Imogen said, not without affection.

'So, are you coming?'

She would get to step outside of her painful obsession for a few hours, into a simpler, brighter reality where the topics of conversation would be Dimitri's job prospects and the subtleties of Italian cooking. Why not?

'Yes,' she said decisively. 'Can I come on Friday? It's my birthday.'

'Really, your birthday? In that case I will get you as drunk as possible, I'm warning you.'

57

As Imogen lay in her unfamiliar bedroom in Bunny's house with her arms around Monty, she gradually became aware of signs of effervescence outside her door. It sounded like Bunny and her other guests – Amaury, Faustina and Enzo, Mitch and Gene – were all wide awake. The phone kept ringing, for one thing, and people were running up and down the stairs and in and out of each other's rooms. What was going on? Sitting up, she rubbed her face and considered whether it might be an idea to wash her hair and generally make a bit more of an effort today. It *was* her birthday, after all. Besides, although she had no designs on Dimitri, she didn't particularly want to turn up in Nice looking like a drowned cat, which was the impression she had received last night when she'd taken a good look at herself in a mirror for the first time in days.

Later, as she came down to breakfast, she heard the sound of laughter coming from below and walked into the kitchen to find Bunny and Faustina bent double, clinging to each other in the throes of spectacular giggles. Imogen stared at them for a while, glad to see that the tension she had noticed a while ago between her friends appeared to have evaporated, but also very much wondering what was going on.

'*Imogen!*' Bunny managed to scream, after a desperate effort to get her breath.

'Yes, hi.'

'Oh . . . God . . . I'm . . . just . . . going . . . to . . . get . . . some . . . air,' Faustina gasped, wiping her eyes, before leaving the room in a hurry.

'Is everything OK?' Imogen said after a while.

Bunny sat at the table, head in hands and almost without making a sound, but with her shoulders still shaking. At last Imogen's American friend looked at her, swallowed a last bubble of laughter, then said, 'Everything's hunky-dory.'

'Right.'

Without warning, Bunny threw her arms around Imogen and hugged her fiercely. 'Oh, what a *glorious* day this is turning out to be!' She fell back into her chair, beaming. '*Whew.* And *what* a night!'

'Why?' Imogen said, pouring corn flakes into a bowl without any great enthusiasm. 'What happened last night?'

'Well, I ended up in bed with Faustina.'

'You did?' Imogen said, putting her spoon down. 'I'm a little surprised.'

'Not as surprised as I was, honey, I can tell you that.'

They looked at each other, and Bunny grinned.

'You're not joking, then,' Imogen said, narrowing her eyes. 'It really happened.'

'Yep. It did.'

'So . . .' Imogen said carefully, her corn flakes now entirely forgotten, 'which one of you made the first move?'

'Oh, *golly*, no!' Bunny giggled, with her hands flying up in every direction. 'Not like *that*.'

'No?'

'No. She thought I was somebody else, and I did too.'

'How do you mean?'

'Well, you see,' Bunny began coquettishly, 'I was on my way to meet a certain person in his room in the middle of the night . . .'

Imogen nodded, feeling that she was back on track. Amaury, of course.

'A *boy*, you know,' Bunny stressed patiently.

'Yes, Bunny, I know.'

'You mean you've guessed?'

'It wasn't that hard. I've seen the way you look at each other.'

'Really?' Bunny was puzzled. 'And I thought we'd been real discreet. It was meant to stay a big old secret for a bit longer.'

Something about this expression rang a distant bell in Imogen's memory, though she couldn't for the minute remember where she'd heard it before. 'Why?' she asked. 'Why did it have to stay a secret?'

'Aw, come on, Imogen – you can imagine why. With all that history.'

Imogen blinked. Perhaps she'd got the wrong end of the stick, but she'd understood from Bunny that she and her cousin were only distant relatives.

'It's just been one of those things that you *can't* fight.' Bunny was hugging herself. 'You see, he's just *so, so* manly.' She blushed and covered her face with her hands.

Imogen stared at her, astonished. *Manly*?

'The thing is that he's just *exactly* like Rhett Butler,'

Bunny went on with a dazzled kind of intensity, 'except he also speaks French.'

Imogen's eyebrows rose. She had never read or watched *Gone with the Wind*, but she did have an idea that Rhett Butler was not obviously like Amaury. It just went to show that you should never judge a book by its cover.

Bunny bit her lip, then said, 'It's like, oh, you know that scene in the movie where he's got stinking drunk because he's so crazy in love with her and she won't go to bed with him, and then she *defies* him and he just *picks her up* and carries her right up the stairs?'

'I get the idea.'

'Oh, it's *lovely*. It's my *favourite* scene in the whole movie,' Bunny said dreamily. 'Well, anyway, it's been sort of like that.' She stretched, catlike, and smiled. 'But he's real gentlemanly as well,' she went on, her face performing a comically rapid switch to wide-eyed primness. 'And we have lots and lots of other stuff in common.'

'Well, yes, of course,' Imogen said, feeling herself back on familiar ground. 'Like his interest in your art.'

'Yes! You know it's a whole new world to him – it's real sweet.'

'And all the stuff he knows about the eighteenth century. And the fact that he's such a wine buff, and his love of *haute cuisine*.'

'Gosh, I don't know about that, Imogen,' Bunny said, frowning. 'Mostly he's happy with a bowl of chestnut gruel. Kind of like Buddy with his grits, you know.'

'Chestnut gruel? Isn't that what they eat—'

'In Corsica, yes. He says it reminds him of home.'

'You're *not* talking about Amaury,' Imogen said after a brief pause, feeling rather foolish.

'Amaury! No! My gosh, I've *never* thought of him like that and anyway . . .' She paused, looking keenly at Imogen's face. '*Hey*. I thought you were following this story?'

'Actually, I wasn't,' Imogen admitted, 'but *now* I think I've got it. You were on your way to *Enzo*'s room in the middle of the night.'

'Yes.'

Casting her mind back to her conversation with Enzo about the party, Imogen suddenly realised that he'd been talking about Bunny. She, not Faustina, and not herself, of course, was 'his lady'. So that when he had spoken about playing a game . . .

'Bunny – at your party, did Enzo join in with the limbo dancing at all?'

'Oh, he sure did! That was when it all started. He was so good at it, and I just stood there staring at him, you know, at his physique . . . And then he emailed me the next day, and we started meeting in secret because we were so worried about Faustina's reaction.'

'I see. So what happened last night?'

'Well, meanwhile Faustina was on her way to meet—'

'Enzo too?' Imogen cried, sitting on the edge of her seat. So poor Faustina must have walked in on the pair!

'No, no, honey,' Bunny said, beaming at her. 'Not Enzo – Amaury.'

What? More madcap comedy of errors? Imogen was beginning to feel that she had accidentally wandered onto the set of *C'est compliqué la vie!* At the time she had dismissed the film as pure Gallic fantasy, but now it was beginning to seem like a masterpiece of realism. Amaury and Faustina? What, *really*? She frowned incredulously, and then remembered how a smitten-looking Amaury had babbled to her in the Wedding Room about the new world of colour, fire and music that was awaiting him. Then there had been the gradual change in Faustina's dress sense and her wistful words about the old-fashioned charms of chivalry, and, last but not least, in the bar at the Hôtel de la Plage, Amaury raising Faustina's hand to his lips without any of the stiffness he reserved for formal occasions because, Imogen now realised, they had by then become so close that reaching for her was for him an unconscious reflex action.

'Good morning, gentlemen,' Bunny said, as Gene and Mitch shuffled into the kitchen in their bathrobes. Imogen smiled at them and they both came over to give her shoulders a little squeeze.

'You see, Imogen, it all started because Faustina was following Amaury around, kind of like a detective,' Bunny resumed.

'Yes,' Imogen said. 'She was worried that he might not really be your cousin.'

'She explained. Anyway, after a while he clocked that she'd been shadowing him all over Montpellier, so he waited for her around a street corner and he caught her!'

'That must have been awkward,' Imogen observed.

'Not so much as all that. She confronted him with her suspicions and he thought she was just the sweetest thing and he couldn't stop laughing. So he took her to lunch, and one thing led to another. It turns out that Amaury can charm the birds out of the trees – but of course charm runs in our family,' she wound up, beaming disarmingly.

'Evidently,' Imogen said, also smiling. 'So . . . last night?'

'Ah, yes. Well, you see, what Faustina and I *didn't* know was that while we were upstairs Enzo and Amaury were down *here*, having this big man-to-man talk and straightening things out. Isn't that darling? Don't you just love men and their ways? So, anyway, at first I went into Enzo's room and she went into Amaury's, but they weren't there, so then, because she doesn't know the house all that well, she thought she'd got the wrong room, you see? So she crept into Enzo's room and of course there *I* was, lying in his bed, as quiet as a little mouse, waiting for him.'

'And then . . . ?'

'Then I flipped over and threw my arms around her all passionately and of course it was obvious that I'd got the wrong person. She's real small, for a start, so she got a bit *suffocated*. And, good golly, was I *shocked*! I wanted to scream the place down but I stopped myself just in time. Which is kind of ironic when you think about it because the person I was worried about waking up was Faustina. Anyway . . .'

Gene chuckled, looking over his shoulder at Imogen as he stood at the counter making coffee. 'Priceless, isn't it?'

'Babe,' Mitch said, eyeing her piercingly, 'you've spruced yourself up.'

'Yes,' Imogen said, smiling at him. 'I'm thinking of driving to Nice.'

'You're going to Nice?' Bunny said, looking unaccountably horrified. 'What, *now*? On your birthday?'

'But . . . what about Daphne's wedding?' Gene added.

'Well, it's not for a while yet.' Imogen was puzzled.

'Oh, but you must still have lots of prepping to do!' Bunny concurred. 'You should stay here. All day.'

'That's just it,' Imogen replied, noticing her friends' air of panic. 'I've done all the preparation I can at this stage. So I'm taking the day off. Thank God the cake is all worked out. I don't know what I was thinking, going for something this complicated.'

Imogen had done several trial runs for the wedding cake, and was now confident that she could put it together faultlessly on the eve of the ceremony. The design was an oversized *puits d'amour*, a deep puff pastry love well filled with layers of vanilla custard and crunchy nougatine. This sat atop an ornate neo-classical white plinth encased in meringue, against the side of which a gold-coloured spun-sugar ladder was propped up. At the top of this, a barrel-chested, pink-faced marzipan figure, easily identifiable by his chef's whites and hat, stood clutching a sugar lobster in one hand and a bunch of marzipan flowers in the other, while gazing romantically across the well, where a glamorous marzipan likeness of Daphne Blanding, wearing an exact replica of her own beach clothes – a large white floppy straw hat and a fabulously expensive and beautifully cut black swimsuit – was perched on the pastry edge, dipping one toe in the custard.

Imogen had found the designing of this kitsch masterpiece a welcome escape. For hours at a time the work had taken her mind off the painful subject of her desertion.

'It's been a lot of work,' Imogen stated firmly. 'I could do with a change of scene. So today, I'm going to Nice to have lunch with Dimitri.'

'Dimitri? Good idea,' Faustina said, sailing back into the room, her usual serene self. 'It'll make you feel better to have some sex.'

All at once, like characters in a play, Gene, Mitch and Bunny shot Faustina the oddest warning look, which Imogen was at a loss to interpret.

'*Of course* she's not going to have sex with him!' Bunny hissed. 'What a terrible idea!'

'Oh! *Oh!*' Faustina said, shaking her head pony-like, as though she'd suddenly remembered something. 'Don't listen to anything I say. I'm still half-asleep.'

'I have no intention of sleeping with him,' Imogen said, wondering what was the matter with everybody. 'We're just friends. He's going to make me some linguine – with scallops. I'm actually really looking forward to it. I love scallops.'

'Yeah, right,' Mitch snorted, twisting the lid off a jar of apricot jam. 'Like you're even going to get a *whiff* of that. He'll have you flat on your back before you've had a chance to sample the *amuse-bouche*.'

Imogen burst out laughing, then said, 'We'll be in a restaurant with plenty of other people. I think it's pretty safe.'

'Imogen, listen,' Faustina said seriously. 'Remember that you're still fragile and that men, well, they're a bit like sharks. They can smell blood.'

'It's just *not* a good day to go to Nice,' Gene chipped in, looking agitated. 'It's so crowded at this time of year.'

'You're all dead set against my going to Nice,' Imogen said slowly. 'Why?'

'*Hé, les filles!*' Amaury clamoured, bursting into the kitchen with Enzo in tow. 'Is she up yet? Are you going to warn her or . . .' Catching sight of Imogen, he stopped short, looked wildly about the room and then, recovering himself, said a courteous 'Good morning' and walked over to Faustina's side of the table.

'What *is* going on?' Imogen asked severely, getting up. 'Why are you all acting so weirdly?'

After a moment's silence Bunny said, with a perky smile, 'All right, you've rumbled us. We've been planning a surprise birthday party for you tonight. I know you said you didn't want one, but I give you my word that it'll be real simple and classy. We just *can't* let your birthday go without a little shindig – it wouldn't be proper.'

'Thank you,' Imogen said, hugging her. 'Don't worry, I'll be back in time for that. It's only a bite of lunch,' she added reassuringly, leaving out the part about Dimitri's plans for getting her drunk. There didn't seem any real point in bringing that up.

58

As Imogen's car screeched to a halt outside the railway station, she said crossly, 'Look at me, Monty – right back where I started, running other people's errands for them. Brilliant, isn't it? And on my birthday, too.'

She'd barely set off on her drive to Nice when her mobile had started to ring. She'd ignored it, only to hear it ring again, insistently, at two-minute intervals. She stopped the car as soon as she was able to and her phone gave voice yet again.

'Yes, Bunny,' she said irritably, picking up. 'What is it?'

'Imogen! My gosh, I'm *so* glad I caught you. Listen, I have a teeny-weeny favour to ask. Have you left town yet?'

'Yes, why?'

'Oh, you have? Well, are you quite far out?'

'Not really. Just outside Antibes.'

'Oh, that's perfect! Look, I know I'm being pesky, but the thing is, would you mind *very much* if I asked you to collect somebody from the station there, then turn tail and drop them back at the house? Just that – it'll be so quick that you'll hardly notice.'

Imogen sighed. 'Bunny, I'm on my way somewhere. Why can't you do it yourself?'

'I just *can't* and anyway, you know, it's not for me,' Bunny went on with unusual intensity. 'It's for *Gene*! He'd arranged to meet this person, and then he forgot! He's only just remembered about it. And the thing is that this person has *real important business* with Gene, and he's there now, waiting at the station, and none of us can go, you see, and anyway we wouldn't get there in time. But you're *almost* there, and it would only add half an hour to your journey. *Please*, Imogen!'

She had never heard Bunny make so little sense, Imogen thought, frowning. Her friend sounded close to tears. This thing must be pretty important.

'All right,' she said briskly. 'Calm down. I suppose I could call Dimitri and tell him to expect me an hour later.'

'Oh, *thank you*, honey. But *hurry*!'

'Does this man know I'm coming?'

'*Yes*,' Bunny said breathlessly.

'And what's he called?'

'Oh, it's—' Suddenly, the line went dead. Imogen shook her head. Bunny was always pressing the wrong buttons on things, wiping entire files on her computer and so on. No point in trying to ring back. That would just waste more of her time. The station at Antibes was small enough, and was unlikely to be thronged at this time in the morning. She could probably locate Gene's contact without help – or call Bunny from the station if necessary.

Before heading off, she quickly sent Dimitri an apologetic text message. He took ages to respond, and when he finally did, she was astonished to read, 'Another girlie drama. You're a lost cause. See you around. Happy Birthday! - ' What? But she hadn't meant to cancel! So in the end, she thought, drumming crossly on the driving wheel, Mitch's prediction had been entirely accurate: she wasn't even going to get a whiff of those delicious scallops. Well, that was great. Absolutely wonderful.

After pulling up outside the station, she leaned across Monty to have a look around. There were only a few people standing there: a group of backpackers, a woman with a young baby and an elderly couple.

Then she heard a man's voice saying her name and she turned to look out of her window. At first all she could see was a bit of white shirt and dark denim – his middle section – and then he bent down to look in.

'Hi, Imogen.' It was Everett's friend Archer. 'Thanks for picking me up.'

'Oh, hi.' Imogen frowned, puzzled. So *he* was Gene's contact? 'I didn't realise I was collecting *you*.'

She reached over to unlock the back door. 'Do you mind getting in the back?' she said. 'Monty likes to ride next to me.'

'No problem,' he replied, letting himself in.

Imogen started the car. As they headed for Saint-Jean, Archer leaned forward between the front seats to have a look at Monty.

'Hey, boy,' he said softly, reaching out a hand in the direction of the bristly muzzle.

Imogen glanced at the little dog as he licked her passenger's hand. 'He remembers you,' she said, accelerating. The traffic was picking up speed.

'We have met before.'

'Yes, of course,' Imogen said coolly, watching the road. 'The last time was in Saint-Paul-de-Vence for that amazing lunch.'

She could feel his eyes on her, and gradually she became more aware of his physical presence in her car, of his closeness. There was something oddly familiar about it.

'I remember that lunch.' He paused, then added, 'But we've met on other occasions.'

Imogen shook her head, digesting this statement. She looked at Monty. Instead of staring solemnly out of the window, as was his habit, the little dog was gazing at their passenger with benign interest. Puzzled by this uncharacteristic behaviour, she turned her attention back to the traffic.

Meanwhile, brightly coloured fragments began to fit together in her mind like a mosaic, forming a picture. Archer was Everett's closest friend, she remembered. He was the one who'd come with him to see Bunny's show at the Galerie Provençale and the one with whom the Doucet brothers had gone to stay for a while – in Menton, oddly enough, where that flamboyant Wedding Room was. And where he, Archer, worked in a museum. Which also meant that he was the one member of Bunny's American gang who'd been based here on the Riviera the entire time.

Glancing again in the rear-view mirror, she saw that he was now looking directly at her. Suddenly, everything inside the car became very bright, as in an accelerated version of the dawn. She found herself turning into a quiet road where she could pull over. She switched the engine off, and then turned around to look fully into her passenger's face, taking in the hazel eyes and quizzical eyebrows, the untidy hair and golden skin, the generous mouth, the broken nose.

Slowly, she gestured towards the latter. 'How . . . did it happen?' she asked.

'The first time, playing lacrosse,' he said, returning her stare with a seriousness to match her own. 'The second time, I ate a bad oyster and fainted in my plate. That's when it really broke.'

Imogen laughed. 'Not really?'

'Yes, really.'

'Does that mean that you can't abide oysters now?'

'I can abide them,' he paused, then added, 'I heard about the revamp of Boustifaille as a seafood place. It's a fine idea.'

Imogen stared for a moment at his hand – golden skin, long fingers, square nails – resting on his knee. Then she caught sight of her own hands, noticing how brown they had become, and that her bright red nail polish was beginning to chip. She could no longer hear any noise outside the car, only her own heart beating riotously. She looked up again. He smiled at her. She smiled back. *You*, she thought delightedly. *It's you, at last*.

'I know,' she said, her voice sounding quite unlike her own. 'I know exactly who you are.'

She turned away to unbuckle her seat belt, feeling as though, once released, she might actually float up in the air. She squeezed between the front seats to get to him. Within seconds, she felt his hands on her waist as he pulled her into his lap without a word. They looked at each other. Imogen noticed lovely flecks of green and grey in his eyes, and that his eyelashes were only dark at the very tips. He raised a hand to her face and his fingertips brushed her cheek, then caressed her hair. *Yes,* Imogen thought, trembling a little. *I remember this very well.* She recognised his touch with absolute certainty. All the same . . .

'I hope you don't mind,' she murmured, close to his mouth, 'but I really must check something.'

She braced herself for disappointment in case she had made another mistake. But there was no mistake: as his lips parted beneath hers she found herself instantly transported back to the trampled grass of Bunny's garden, standing in the circle of masked revellers, and in the darkened kitchen at Boustifaille, where, she suddenly remembered with blazing clarity, he, this man she barely knew, had pressed his mouth to her breasts and . . . Imogen pulled back, her face burning. It was impossible to meet his eye. She disengaged herself and went to sit as far away from him as she could manage – without actually leaving the back seat. Observing this, Monty climbed down between the front seats and came to put sympathetic paws in his mistress's lap.

'Imogen,' Archer called, reaching over to take her hand. She allowed this, glancing at him sidelong. 'I'm guessing,' he said, his mouth curling with amusement, 'that you're thinking about the stuff that happened in the blackout.'

She nodded and looked out of the window. Archer turned his attention to Monty, and after a moment's silence, during which she stole another glance at him, letting her gaze travel down his throat, his shoulders and chest, his hips, his long legs – the body her own body had already made friends with, he said softly, 'Is it OK that it was with me?'

Their eyes met and Imogen smiled. 'I think so,' she said. 'Sorry. I know that sounds a bit hesitant, but I'm trying to . . . adjust. It's easier for you; you've always known who I was.'

'I have.' He paused before adding, 'But I think I should tell you that my own behaviour came as something of a surprise to me too.' He raised an eyebrow and smiled at her.

Smiling back, she felt his caressing hand in the small of her back. He gathered her again into his arms, and she returned his embrace. It was all right, she thought, rubbing her face against his shoulder. In fact, it was better than all right – it was wonderful to be in his arms.

'Oh, my sweet girl, it's been so long,' he said, leaning in to kiss her again. 'I'm so sorry.'

At this, Imogen snapped out of her trance. She stiffened, her eyes filling with tears. 'Can you explain to me,' she said, wiping them off angrily, 'why you disappeared like that? Do you know how it made me feel? What sort of game were you playing?'

'It wasn't a game,' he said, taking her hands. 'It was the last thing I wanted to do.' He paused to draw in a long breath, then continued, 'After our missed rendezvous in the hills, I got lost in the rain and ended up staying out all night.'

'Really? It wasn't that far to walk back to the road,' Imogen countered.

'No, you're right, it wasn't. Still . . . this will sound ridiculous, maybe, but I was in a strange state, both physically and mentally. The waiting, I guess, the excitement. And then, when you didn't show up . . .'

'Archer,' Imogen said, realising as she said his name out loud that she was doing so for the first time, 'I'm really sorry. I tried to explain in my email. I don't know what came over me . . . I panicked . . .'

'Of course,' he said, placing his hands on her shoulders. 'When I read it, I understood perfectly. But back there, when I realised you weren't going to come, I just couldn't see straight. I don't think I even thought about finding the road or getting back to my car, not at all. I just kept on walking across those hills. And then, all that damn *rain*. Christ. Though at the time I didn't mind so much – I just kept walking. Then it got dark, suddenly, and I realised I had no idea where I was.

'The thing is, Imogen,' he said, smiling a little, 'I grew up in Manhattan, where we have a grid system and the streets are *straight*. So. I found myself in a difficult position. I didn't have a torch with me. I had no reception on my cell phone and couldn't call anyone. Also I'd left my coat in my car – not a clever move, as it turned out. Because the rain did stop eventually, but then it got very cold. I spent a horrible night, drifting in and out of consciousness, just cursing my own stupidity.

'At dawn I managed to get to a village and called a garage to pick up my car, which was miles away. I felt terrible, but it wasn't until I got back to Menton that it became clear just how bad it was. I collapsed on my bed in my clothes and it was lucky my landlord found me the next day. It was Saturday and my workplace is closed at weekends. I think he believed I was drunk and he just took my shoes off and then let me sleep it off without interfering too much.

'On Monday, he finally got in touch with my boss, and she took one look at me and got me to hospital. By then I was really quite delirious – with pneumonia. I kept asking for you. Apparently I was quite forceful about it and even punched a doctor because I thought he was refusing to help me, but of course nobody had any idea who you were. I'd got a pretty serious infection and it was showing signs of spreading to my lungs. No, don't worry,' he said, seeing the fear in her eyes, 'I'm OK now. Though maybe I'm not ready for another *Blair Witch Project* experience in the wilderness just yet.'

'If only I hadn't been such a coward,' Imogen blurted out helplessly, 'none of this would have happened. You would have come home with me instead of getting lost.'

Archer gave her a long look, and a smile that felt like the most intimate touch. He kissed her hands, and it was with some difficulty that Imogen resisted her desire to embrace him. She wanted to hear the whole story first. 'And what happened next?'

'In hospital, they doped me a lot because of the pain, and I really had no idea what was going on. My French is good but it had sort of deserted me, and because nobody there spoke any English, they mostly talked to my boss, not me.'

At this, Imogen remembered something Bunny had mentioned early on and said, 'Actually, you speak perfect French. Are you . . . ?'

'Yes, I'm half-French on my mother's side.'

'I knew that,' Imogen murmured, 'but I never put two

and two together. You spoke French in the blackout and also in your emails, and so I suppose I always assumed deep down that the person I was looking for was, in fact, French. I didn't think of you.'

Archer grinned at her. 'Ah yes, the French touch. I thought it would make it a more interesting chase for you. Nothing too obvious.'

'Go on,' she said, smiling a little.

'Well, it took me almost ten days to recover sufficiently to ask for my phone. At first my boss couldn't find it, and when she managed to locate the damn thing on the floor of my car and brought it to me, I found all these messages from Everett wanting to know where the hell I was.'

'Why didn't you ask him to contact me?'

'I had this pig-headed notion that I wanted to do it myself. I did respond to your email then, but you didn't reply.'

'When was this?'

'Three days ago.'

Imogen nodded. 'Yes. A few days ago Mitch took my computer away. I asked him to. I asked him to hide it somewhere because I couldn't bear to look at it any longer. I wanted to throw it into the sea. I thought you'd left me for good.'

'Imogen.'

She continued to look at him, breathing fast. He was silent for a moment and then said sombrely, 'I'm sorry I did this terrible thing to you.' He reached for her and she allowed her face to be kissed.

'I'm sorry too,' she said after a while. 'And you didn't think of calling Bunny?'

'If I'd been in a more practical frame of mind, I would have done. I was discharged yesterday and I'm afraid I only thought of her very late last night. So I called first thing this morning.'

'And you set this up together?'

'We did.'

Imogen looked up at him then, and a smile slowly spread on her face. 'I can't believe I fell for that ridiculous telephone call. Bunny is a terrible actress.'

'Is she?' Archer said, gratified to see her laugh. 'The original plan was for me to just turn up at her house this morning. I was supposed to be a surprise present for your birthday.'

'Oh?'

'So, happy birthday.'

'Thank you,' Imogen said after a lengthy kiss. She thought for a minute. 'Oh . . . but then, I left to go to Nice.'

'Yes. You created something of a panic for a moment there. But Bun kept her head and she managed to send you to me instead.'

Imogen nodded, silently thanking Bunny for everything, including the masterly way she had short-circuited her lunch plans with Dimitri. Bunny must have called him and told him the whole story – that explained the tone of his message.

'So. Now you know why I vanished for a while,' he whispered, pressing his forehead against hers. 'Shall I stay or get back on the train?'

'You can stay if you want.'

'Oh, I want. Can you forgive me?'

'Well, that's entirely up to you,' she said, throwing her arms around his neck.

59

Now she and Archer lay entwined upstairs at the empty bookshop – having reasoned that there would be time enough for celebrating with friends tonight and certain other things needed to be attended to immediately and in private. And what a wonderful release, Imogen thought drowsily, it had been to fall onto her bed together, giving in at last to the pent-up longing they had both stored up in the complicated course of their budding romance. There had been lengthy, hungry, insatiable kissing, soon followed by much gasping and laughing as their four hands all worked at once to undo his flies and Imogen wrapped her legs around his waist. When it finally came, the first impact – a deep, incandescent caress – made them both cry out. Again and again, holding on to him and biting his mouth as they made love, Imogen had thought, *It's you, at last. I remember you. I know you. I love you.*

Now she lay in his arms in a state of absolute peace and contentment, breathing in the intoxicating smell of his skin as her heartbeat slowly returned to normal. After a moment's silence Archer said, very low, 'Do you remember saying that you'd never been swept off your feet?'

'Did I say that?' Imogen was puzzled. 'To you?'

'Not to me. To Mitch. In the kitchen at Bunny's party.'

'You were there?' She raised herself onto her elbows.

'I'd gone back into the house. I happened to walk past the kitchen door and I stood there really just staring at you because you looked so pretty. And you'd seemed so disdainful before, when faced with all of us deadly Americans.'

'*Not* disdainful,' Imogen corrected, laughing. 'Bloody terrified. You were all unbelievably scary. You especially.'

'I hope you're no longer scared of me,' he said, kissing her shoulder.

'Well, maybe just a tiny little bit. Especially when you get very close like that.'

'Like that?'

'Yes. That's pretty scary.'

After a few minutes' silent wrestling, Archer said quietly, 'To be continued after this intermission. Anyway,' he went on, rolling over to lie next to her, 'when you said *that*, it made me want to do something for you, though at that point I didn't know quite what. I guess my plan, such as it was, was to talk to you, maybe invite you to dance and then ask you out on a date.'

'Which would have been lovely.'

'You're just saying that to be nice. Then when Mary-Kate came to fetch you, I decided to join in with the game of Blind Man's Buff, just as a way of staying close. I can't really explain what happened to me at that point – I just found myself walking into the circle and kissing you. It wasn't planned at all. Thinking back, I suppose wearing a mask must have helped – I didn't feel quite like myself, which allowed me to do something unusually daring. And then the kiss turned out to be much *bigger* than I'd expected.'

He shook his head, laughing. 'I was staggered by it, I guess, so I decided to walk away for a bit to compose myself. You know, before asking you out on that date.'

He paused to kiss her. Afterwards, she rubbed her cheek against his and declared, 'Just as good with my eyes open.'

'Thank you,' he said, grinning at her. 'So, anyway. While I was at the other end of the garden watching the limbo, I got to thinking of drawing things out just a bit longer. Valentine's Day was the perfect excuse not to reveal myself right away. It suited me, out of shyness, mostly, I guess. And because I felt out of practice. I don't know how much Bunny's told you about my divorce.'

'She did mention it,' Imogen admitted, kissing the tips of his fingers. 'She said you were through with love.'

'Right. That is exactly what I thought – Constance had left me feeling . . . cauterised. I was determined not to make myself vulnerable to anybody else again. But then you walked into the room in Bunny's house and I took one look at you, and then another, and you just changed my mind right there and then.'

Imogen cast her mind back to that day, and to her vision of a distant stranger, standing apart from the group in Bunny's sitting room and appearing to greet her only with the greatest reluctance, and marvelled at how very misleading first impressions could be.

'I think you made a strong impression on me too,' she said pensively. 'I just didn't register it consciously at the time. And then when I heard about what had happened to you, a kind of shutter came down in my head – I think I told myself that you weren't available.' She shook her head and laughed. 'And so I looked away from you, when actually I should have been paying a lot more attention.'

Archer smiled and brushed her lips with his, making her sigh. 'It was a shock to me at first,' he resumed, tightening his hold on her, 'to find myself feeling so strongly about someone when I really thought that part of me had closed down for good. Kissing you at the party felt like coming back to life after a long sleep.

'As for what followed, most of it came together by accident rather than design. For instance, that fuse box thing. I'd been to Boustifaille with Everett once and we'd accidentally walked into that courtyard where the kitchen is, cluelessly looking for the entrance to the restaurant. Some guy was doing something to the fuse box and he told us to walk all the way around to that other door. I remembered that later, one day when I hadn't been able to get you out of my mind. I drove to Saint-Jean, not really knowing what I was going to do. I went into the courtyard hoping to catch a glimpse of you in the kitchen, but there was nobody there.

'I played with your dog for a while, and then he began scratching at the kitchen door to be let in. So I let him in, but then he started to bark and I thought, "Uh-oh" and when you came into the kitchen on your own, I ducked down those stairs and found my eyes level with the fuse box and thought, "Hmmn, why not?" Then I let myself into the kitchen and there you were. That was pretty exciting, I thought,' he said, leaning over her.

'Yes, I thought so too. Do you remember kissing me . . . there?'

'You mean there?'

'Yes.'

'Like this?' he asked, demonstrating. 'Or like that?'

'Oh, like *that*, definitely, though I think you did it just a bit harder, like . . . *yes*!' She caught her breath and laughed, stroking his hair. 'That was it, exactly.'

'I'm not being strictly chronological,' he went on, moving further down the bed to slide both hands under her bottom and kiss her stomach, 'but I suppose a lot of it started when I realised, the day after the party, that thanks to Bun – ah, God bless her! – and her complete inability to blind-copy an email invitation, I had a way of reaching you directly and privately, in your own bedroom, and anonymously too, though again I can't say that I'd planned that exactly, and certainly not as a long-term thing. Because I was convinced,' he said, looking up at her, 'that we'd meet each other in the natural course of things with the Doucets . . .'

'And *then* you'd ask me out on that date.'

'Exactly,' he said, moving back up swiftly so that he could kiss her laughing mouth.

'You know what I think?' Imogen asked, teasingly. 'I think you're a natural Valentine's Day lover. Why go out on a boring old date when you can drive a girl wild with romantic mysteries?'

'Why indeed? Anyway, when Everett and Buddy went off travelling, I realised that I wasn't going to run into you again as soon as I thought. In a way, I was relieved, because . . . I suppose I was worried that you might be disappointed with the reality of me.'

Wordlessly, Imogen kissed his brows, his eyes, the bridge of his nose, and he smiled. 'Then at Bunny's show, when I finally got up the courage to talk to you, you jumped down my throat.'

'Oh, that!' Imogen said, wincing at the memory. 'I'm sorry. I misunderstood you completely. I thought you were being a patronising arse.'

'Oh,' he said, laughing, 'right. Well, no – just shy. And when we met for lunch in Saint-Paul-de-Vence, it sort of happened again. And then Bunny said someone had sent you flowers.'

'That was Cheyenne,' Imogen said, smiling. 'I always felt they couldn't have come from you.'

'Oh, I see. But then, I felt so tongue-tied around you anyway that I just let Everett do all the talking.'

'How long has Everett known?'

'When he and Buddy came to stay with me after Italy, I was acting kind of distracted. He knew instantly that something was up. When I explained, he thought it was quite funny, though I think he had his doubts about how long the whole thing could be sustained – for your sake as well as mine. He called me not so long ago to warn me that he'd just seen you and that you were getting upset.'

Imogen thought for a moment, then said, 'I think that might have been on the day when I briefly suspected Everett of being *you*.' She giggled at his expression. 'Oh, he soon put me right. But I remember he went off to make a mysterious call.'

'Was that when you found the postcards in the guide?'

'Yes.'

'Those were mine, of course. They were lying around at my place and I was using them as bookmarks for whatever I happened to be reading. In this case, Everett's guide to Rome, which he took away with him when he left. You really drove me crazy,' he went on, dreamily spreading her hair on the pillow, 'never being where I expected you to be. Like that time when I went to Boustifaille on my own, to be near you and leave that note. I couldn't believe my luck when I heard those Australians asking for a tour of the kitchen. I'm not sure *what* I meant to do if I came face to face with you in there – drop down on my knees, probably. But you weren't there. On the other hand, there was that amazing time when you suddenly materialised before my eyes in the *Salle des Mariages.*'

'The Wedding Room?' Imogen paused. 'You were there?'

'Yes, I work there – and at the Cocteau Museum.' He began to laugh. 'I opened a door and there you were. It was just like a dream. I was amazed, delighted. You seemed to be waiting for me.'

'In a way, I was,' Imogen said, pressing her lips against his chest.

'And then I saw you holding hands with that French guy,' Archer said, raising an eyebrow. 'Everett's cousin.'

'Amaury? Oh, *no*. I mean, he did take my hand briefly – actually, I think he was about to mention that you worked there – but we weren't . . .'

'I worked it out,' Archer said, amused, 'eventually. I saw him leave. And when you went away as well, I knew that it had only been a coincidence. But then so many other things had fallen into place by chance. The Doisneau photograph, for example – I've always liked it. Also I love Fragonard. There's something incredibly alluring to me about French eroticism of that period. Obviously, it made perfect sense to send you *The Stolen Kiss*. And when I lived in New York, I'd been to the Frick Collection hundreds of times to look at *The Games of Love*.'

'Ah, yes, the games of love,' Imogen repeated, reaching up and caressing his face – lovely, magnetic, still not entirely familiar.

'Yes,' Archer said seriously, looking into her eyes. 'That was it for me – the point of no return. I knew with absolute certainty that I was in love with you when I got the idea of sending you to Grasse to find your gift.' He kissed the hollow of her throat. 'I had the strongest desire to give you something that would make you think of me, but would also *touch* you. Really touch your body intimately,' he said, pushing her thighs open with both hands, 'like so.'

'Yes?' Imogen sighed, biting her lip and reaching backwards to grab hold of the bed frame.

'And hopefully get *inside* you,' he said, bringing his mouth firmly down on hers. 'Oh – Imogen.'

Epilogue

The summer season, during which Saint-Jean-les-Cassis's main strip, filled with crowds of sunburned tourists and ablaze with multicoloured neon signs, had pulsated in the warm air from dusk till dawn like a toy-town version of Las Vegas, had been and gone, including Daphne and Michel Boudin's small wedding party – a rather wonderful affair, which had woven together not only the happy couple's two destinies but also many of the differently coloured threads of Imogen's life on the Riviera.

While they all waited in the small town hall for Daphne to make her entrance, the mayor, wearing a tricolour scarf fringed with gold draped across his dark suit, stood chatting with Michel Boudin, who was attended by members of his own family – uniformly tall, hulking and dark-haired – and by the bride's sister, looking smart and sensible in a natty lavender suit and hat. As she sat holding hands with Archer, Imogen had looked over her shoulder. Among other smartly dressed denizens of Saint-Jean, she spotted Mitch and Gene, scrutinising and discussing the ornate nineteenth-century mouldings of the ceiling. Next to them sat Bunny and Enzo, looking like two lazy and very contented cats. Bunny had a show lined up at the Saatchi gallery in London – a professional breakthrough that, once it had been explained to them by Everett, had impressed her parents so favourably that they had even begun to come round to the idea of having an artist in the family. A little further back sat a blue-eyed Frenchman with his beautiful dark-haired girlfriend, who was laughing, her head thrown back, at something he'd just whispered in her ear – the newly engaged Amaury and Faustina.

The greatest treat had been to see Di turn up at the airport a few days before the ceremony, looking exactly the same, and – ever practical – only carrying a small ruck-sack, which later turned out to contain (vacuum-packed for ease of transport) not only her suit and hat for the ceremony but also a beautiful evening gown in midnight-blue lace, which she had changed into for the evening party.

'Well, dear,' Di had said that evening, as they stood together watching Daphne – a glorious sight in her short oyster-grey evening dress – and her husband perform a spirited quickstep in the newly renovated dining room of Chez Michel. 'Here we are. And have you enjoyed your adventure?'

'Yes, very much,' Imogen had said, throwing her arms around her friend. 'Di, I can never thank you enough for sending me here.'

'It *was* quite a good idea, even if I say so myself. Tell me, what are you planning to do? Stay here on the Riviera?'

'Yes. I'm looking for another job – somewhere a bit closer to Menton. Archer's been looking for a bigger place,' she added, smiling. 'Chef – I mean – Michel – gave me the most amazing reference. I've actually got a couple of interviews lined up in the next few weeks. Which is a bit scary, but brilliant. So there you are.'

'I am thrilled for you.'

'Well, we'll see,' Imogen said philosophically. 'It's not really about chasing Golden Spoons for me. I just want to spread my wings a bit and—'

'Find out what you're capable of,' Di concluded. 'Of course you do. Oh—' Di broke off, catching sight of Archer, who stood near the kitchen door holding Monty in his arms and smiling at Imogen. 'I *do* like your young man, dear.'

'I like him too.'

Di giggled, her eyes twinkling. 'He does appear to have . . . a certain something. Doesn't he?'

'Oh yes,' Imogen replied, laughing. 'He certainly does have that.'

In July Imogen and Archer had moved into a top-floor apartment in Menton's higgledy-piggledy old town. They had immediately fallen in love with the place. It was full of light and though, for the time being, a little short of furniture, contained everything they felt they really needed: a bed, a kitchen and a sofa which Monty approved of, and which, throughout the warm months of summer and autumn, had lived on the terrace where the three of them liked to sprawl together at night and look at the stars.

Meanwhile Imogen had started work as a chef at Paradis Pour Tous, a smart brasserie overlooking the sea in nearby Roquebrune-Cap-Martin. The owners were friendly and, after tasting their new recruit's dishes, had been only too happy to add her sea-urchin soup and *croustillant* of lamb to their menu.

At the end of a recent lunchtime service, the smiling waitress had asked Imogen if she'd mind putting in an appearance in the dining room – the people on table six really wanted to congratulate her. Then, stepping out of the kitchen, she had found a party consisting of Monsieur Boudin, Daphne, Bastien, Larissa and Dimitri, all cheering her on. It had been the most wonderful accolade.

Christmas had been spent at Bunny's house where Imogen, Archer and their friends had all hunkered down for a few days, playing cards, watching silly DVDs and getting ridiculously merry. Though Imogen hadn't minded being away from home at Christmas, she was nevertheless looking forward to visits from her mother and siblings, and also from her father, at the end of January. She wanted Archer to meet her family – it would be good to bring all the different parts of her life together.

Now the new year was unfurling under a pale winter sky, and it had been snowing – a fairly unusual occurrence on the Riviera – for the last few days. The weather couldn't have been more different from what it had been a year before at the time of Imogen's arrival, but it was just as beautiful. And today, to mark the Feast of the Epiphany in the French tradition, the Boudins had issued an invitation to eat *galette des rois* at Chez Michel.

Daphne and Imogen had made the *galette* together that very morning, sandwiching a layer of frangipane – almond paste scented with orange blossom – between discs of puff pastry. They had also given close consideration to selecting the small charm that would be buried in the frangipane.

'I put these bright little plastic charms in the *galettes* we sell in the shop,' Daphne had explained. 'They're very jolly. Every year, there's a different theme: Disney characters, vintage cars, jungle animals, Hollywood stars, anything you could possibly imagine. All French bakeries have them. *But*,' she had said, putting her head to one side in a way that was very reminiscent of Di, 'since this cake is *just* for our little circle, I think we should use a more traditional white-porcelain charm. Don't you think that would be nicer? They've been phased out – too expensive, I expect, to say nothing of people breaking the odd tooth on them. But I think we should be OK.'

She'd brought a shallow box out of a cupboard and opened it to show Imogen. 'You see, I have quite a collection. Why don't you pick the one you like the best?'

Imogen had sifted through a surreal assortment of horse-shoes, bells, doves, cockerels, round-faced men in the moon, stars, crowns, hearts and four-leaf clovers, and had settled on a small figure of a mermaid, which she'd held up for Daphne's approval.

'Lovely,' the *pâtissière* had said. 'Plonk it in, will you, dear? Good. Now pop the pastry lid on. *There* we are,' she smiled, deftly criss-crossing a pattern on the top. 'And into the oven.'

Lunch had been and gone, and it was time for the main business of the day – the *galette*. When Daphne had brought it out, Monsieur Boudin's gaze had alighted on Imogen while he said, 'Ah, she is the youngest person in the room, yes? So traditionally she must be the one who allocates the pieces of cake to everyone. That way it's really left to chance. You go hide under the table, Imogen, and at the same time you cover your eyes, OK? That way we know you can't see anything. And then you call out the name of each person who gets a piece of the *galette*. You understand?'

'Yes, Chef!' Imogen had said automatically, even though he was no longer her boss.

'And who's this one for?' Daphne's melodious voice sang out.

'For Bunny!' Imogen called back, covering her eyes. Monty, who sat next to her, barked in enthusiastic assent.

A delighted squeak rose from the American girl. 'Oh, I adore all these old European customs. Enzo, look at those pretty golden crowns. Aren't they darling?'

There was no answer, but Imogen thought she could hear the sound of two beautiful Corsican eyebrows being knitted together in the most aesthetically pleasing way.

'And this one?'

'For Amaury!'

'*Merci, chère Madame.*'

'Remember, everyone,' Imogen suddenly heard Michel Boudin's voice thunder, 'to be a little bit discreet if you discover the charm in your piece of cake. Don't advertise it, because otherwise it ruins the suspense *completely*. OK?'

'Calm down, darling,' Daphne said gaily. 'It's supposed to be fun.'

A soft growling sound, followed by, 'Yes, Daphne, I know, but it is *only* fun if we all play the game as it is supposed to be played. Or there is no point.'

'All right, everybody,' Daphne said, laughing indulgently. 'To please Michel, we're all going to make a special effort to do this properly. Try to conceal who's drawn the charm for as long as possible. Let's pretend we're playing poker.'

'Who's this piece for, Imogen?' Daphne asked again, in her role as mistress of ceremonies.

Imogen hesitated. She was beginning to lose track, sitting there in the dark. She resorted to counting on her fingers. She'd been trying to allocate the pieces of cake among the guests in the order in which she had first met them: Daphne, then Monsieur Boudin, Mitch, Faustina, Enzo, Bunny, Amaury and Gene. So that left . . . the person *she* was waiting for, and whose arrival had been delayed by the snowy roads.

'Well, of course we set one piece aside for the pauper who might knock at our door,' Michel Boudin proclaimed. 'It's the tradition. And we do not deviate from tradition in this establishment!'

'All right, Michel,' Daphne said, so entirely unruffled that Imogen wondered, not for the first time, if the *pâtissière* hadn't evolved (or even been born with) a sort of internal Michel Boudin dial that allowed her to turn her vociferous husband's volume down at will. It was probably genetic, because Di had demonstrated a similar ability on becoming acquainted with her new brother-in-law. 'Nobody's disputing that. But the thing is we also need one more piece for—'

As she opened her mouth to call out his name, Imogen heard the restaurant door open. A gust of clean, cold air rushed in, then a male voice said, 'Sorry I'm late, *Madame*,' sending a delicious crackle of electricity through Imogen's body.

'We got your message, Archer dear,' Daphne said warmly. 'It was sweet of you to say we shouldn't wait. We've had lunch, but you *are* in time for a piece of cake. Look: this one's got your name on it. Michel, *chéri*, please don't start on about the medieval pauper again. This young man is hungry – he'll do just as well.'

'Come in and get warm, dear boy!' Gene exclaimed. 'Is it still snowing outside?'

'A bit,' Archer said, before asking, 'Where's my girl?'

Imogen heard a chorus of suppressed giggles: they must all be pointing at her hiding place. Monty began to bark assertively. The tablecloth was lifted and Archer's face appeared, smiling when he spotted them both under the table. 'Come here,' he said, holding his hand out to her, and she came out into the light.

In the greenish underwater atmosphere of the restaurant, which at this hour of a winter's afternoon made the most of the shimmering marine tiles, his hazel eyes looked translucent and golden. She touched his face, marbled with cold, and smiled when she saw that snow had settled on his hair and even on the tips of his eyelashes.

'You look good,' Imogen said, brushing it off delicately, 'but not quite real. You need thawing.'

'Hey, snow prince,' Bunny said, waving lazily at Archer.

'Hey, Bun.'

'Archer dear,' Daphne said, 'give me your coat, sit down, and let me get you a glass of champagne.'

'Thank you very much.'

'And Imogen, this last piece is for you, obviously,' Daphne said, placing it on her plate.

'OK,' Michel Boudin said testily. 'Now the American boy is here, can we eat? I want my *galette*! I look forward to this moment all year!'

'Yes, Michel darling. And remember, everyone, to keep your poker face on for as long as possible.'

The *galette* was delicious and pretty soon all plates – their edges adorned with the words Chez Michel in dark blue script – were empty, but no charm had materialised. There was a tense silence during which they all looked at one another.

'OK then,' Monsieur Boudin said, in full Al Capone mode, '*where* is it?'

'I don't have it.'

'Nor me.'

'Nope.'

'Uh-uh.'

'Sorry, no.'

'Nobody's got it!'

'You're not *bluffing*, are you, Michel darling?' Daphne said cajolingly. 'Because I thought I saw a little something white peeping out of your frangipane . . .'

'No,' Monsieur Boudin said, his smile getting broader as Daphne tickled him under the chin. 'Ha, ha, ha, no, no, no, stop!' He wiped his eyes, then whimpered, 'I'm not bluffing.'

'You didn't forget to put a charm in the cake, Imogen?' Faustina asked.

Imogen shook her head and Daphne said, 'I saw her do it. No, it must be here somewhere, but where?'

'Look,' Amaury said, leaning back in his chair with one arm around Faustina's shoulders, 'the sun's coming out.'

Through the restaurant's glass front, the harbour presented a scene of radiant winter serenity. Snowy palm trees glittered against a pale backdrop in which the sea and the sky merged into one.

Archer turned away from the view to gaze at Imogen, at which point she smiled, released the mermaid charm she'd kept hidden under her tongue and, leaning over, passed it to him with a kiss. Laughing, he extracted it from his mouth and held it aloft.

'*Ah, mais non!*' Michel Boudin exclaimed, scandalised. 'That is not the traditional way to show that you have the charm!'

'Michel,' Daphne said firmly. 'Be quiet. They're in love.'

'Yes, Daphne, but you're supposed to drop it in the other person's glass. *That* is how you choose your king.'

'So long as she makes her choice clear,' Gene said, putting a hand on Michel Boudin's arm, 'does it really matter?'

Somewhat mollified, Boudin snorted, then began to gesticulate. 'We need the crowns at least! Where are they, the crowns?'

'For Christ's sake!' Mitch hissed, smoothing his pencil moustache with both hands in exasperated fashion. 'And I thought *I* was loud. All right, all right, give them to me already.' He stood up and marched around to the other side of the table. 'Babe,' he said tersely, attending to Imogen's coronation, before throwing the second crown up in the air. Imogen leaped to her feet and caught it in mid-flight.

'What's this?' Archer said, looking up at her with his

hands on her waist and just loud enough for her to hear. 'The lover crowned?'

'About time too,' she replied, smiling. 'You deserve it.' And she placed the crown on his head.

Acknowledgements

Many thanks to my wonderful agent, Teresa Chris,
for helping this inexperienced sailor steer through
the waters of the Mediterranean, and to my publisher,
Gillian Green, and her team at Ebury, for their
unfailing patience and support in getting
our ship safely into harbour.